LAST STOP BEFORE DAWN
by Michael J. Griffin

First published by Gargoyle Publications 06/30/12

For Pauline who inspired me with her love of books,
and without whom...

PART ONE:
FIRST LIGHT

1

This was a place that needed leaving. Rich Baker knew
that much,
even
if
he
knew
nothing else.
A party.
Smoke
hanging like storm clouds
over everyone.
Noise.
A cacophonic collision
of voices,
"Did you ..."
"She said..."
"He went..."
Yak yak yak yak
and music.
The Stones.
I saw her today at the reception.

Drunk, drunk, very, oh yes, drunk.

Vignettes melted down the walls of his mind like candle wax.

Crystal Tanner, whom he had once groped in a closet at a party just like this, going up her skirt like a mink and under the elastic ridge of her panties, one of the partner's wives, for chrissakes, slunk

over

to him,

falling out of her dress,

took the drink from his hand and, straddling his leg, jammed his Manhattan down in one gulp, painting the rim of the tumbler blood red with her lipstick.

"Hey,

Richie, Richie

you taste

good

baby,

let's get

outta

here."

It was Lundeen's penthouse all right. The windows were ablaze with the Chicago skyline. Lights vibrated against a field of black, little specs out there, out of control, jumping from place to place like fireflies, people behind each one.

Heat

Jesus,

it was

hot.

A terrain like Mars.

Choppers whopping and whopping, blowing sand.

Desert sweat. Blood?

2

Men in tunics.

Get

out.

Baker was leaning against the window. Someone knocked on it from the other side.

Tap

tap

tap

He turned around and looked out. The night had fled, just like that, turning blazing white, backlighting the shadow of a man.

"What

are

you

doing

here?

Are

You

okay?"

Baker jumped, startled, then put his hand on the glass and pushed away from the window and the shadowy man. Bodies blurred in his eyes. Faces stretched like reflections in fun house mirrors. Words bounced off him like confetti.

Across the undulating sea he saw her. She wasn't supposed to be here, but she was. Her hair was on fire, eyes like emeralds burning through him.

"Hey,

dickhead."

You can't always get what you want.

"Hello, Irish."

His words. Slow and slurred.

Candles on the mantelpiece, dancing flames, like church so many, many years ago. A prayer came to his mind. *Introibo ad altare Dei. Ad Deum qui laetificat, juventutem meam.* I will go to the altar of God. To God, the joy of my youth. Then Baker saw him.

Near the door,

Sean.

Oh, God,

great

joy.

My boy.

Sean. Not dead.

"No, pop,

still

dead."

Not dead.

Here.

"Sorry, pop."

But I

love you.

Jesus God

Jesus God,

please.

Baker began to cry; more of a howl, to be precise. Shuddering in his anguish, he held himself as no one could hold him anymore and sobbed. Who could understand this pain? Whoever did understand it? Only she. Maura. Go to her. Where is she? She was just here! He pushed through the crowd like walking through thick water.

Then he was in the elevator. Going to her.

The elevator was falling

falling
up.
Imagine that
falling
but upwards,
faster,
faster.

Rich Baker bolted upward, his eyes springing open and then snapping shut at the painful intrusion of bright light. He was neither here nor there, suspended between sleep and consciousness. His overwhelming desire was to glide back into darkness, but something, some instinct, pulled him out.

He opened his eyes again, more cautiously this time, and winced at the rapiers of white light that assaulted them. He was twisted tightly, that was certain. His legs ached. Electricity tingled through them to the sockets. His left arm was beneath him somehow, dead; his right one lay supine across his lap. An oppressive silence made his ears ring. His head thumped dully. Baker shook from his mind the last of the darkness and watched it spray away like water from the fur of a dog. He blinked one more time, and then, in an instant, everything jelled. He was behind the wheel of a car, but something was wrong, very wrong.

Blood. He was surrounded by blood. The passenger seat was sticky with it, as if it had been slathered on with a paint brush.

"What the...?" he said, recoiling, his legs stiffening, his shoulder banging against the door.

Blood. Clumpy and congealed, hanging in strings down the front of the seat, burrowing into the floor, assimilating the color and texture of the carpet. A smear arched diagonally across the window like a shooting star.

"What have I done?" Baker cried aloud, fumbling for the door handle, discovering suddenly that blood also covered his hands, welding his fingers together. Get away, get away from it, he thought. His hands ran the length of the armrest, fingers fumbling to unlock the door. Finally, it flew open and he tumbled out, slipping to one knee. His hand broke the fall, jamming into fine cinders that dug into his flesh. He righted himself and backed away from the car. He teetered, the connection from his mind to his legs still tenuous.

An accident? His blood? What had he done? Run the car off the road? Staggering backward, he frantically pored over his own body, looking for holes, seeking pain. He found none. He was twenty feet from the car now, but could see inside through the yawning door. Nothing else was disturbed. The air bags had not deployed. The windshield was not cracked. The engine was off, the gearshift in park. The keys hung motionlessly from the ignition; the windows were milky with steam. He plunged into the bits of memory scattered on the floor of his brain like so many puzzle pieces. Comprehension increased with each second, surging upward in his consciousness like the sun at dawn. Maura's car, the stark white Mercedes. Hers, not his. Why? How? Where was she, Maura? Like so many other things in his life, gone. The last vision of her was with the divorce lawyers. She was flinging epithets at him in sprays of spit. That was more than a month ago. Or was it? A vision crackled in his brain. The party. Faces, faces, a storm of faces. Was that her? There? Hair blazing? Coming to him?

And now this. Her car. Blood. Nothing else.

The cold, dirty November air tingled as he gathered it into his head and lungs, further awakening him. A repugnant odor, like boiled eggs and petroleum, made his stomach gurgle. His fingers clenched and relaxed, as they awkwardly tried to shake the sticky feeling from the blood that coated them. The stain ran like a map across his palms and up his sleeves and onto his suit coat. The world turned white behind his eyes for a second, and he responded by placing both hands on his knees, bending over and letting fly a meager but gut-wrenching stream of spittle and vomit. Hung over again. Shit, still kind of drunk. What a surprise.

Stretching to his full six feet four inches, Baker teetered, dizzy and out of control despite the invigorating intrusion of cold into his bloodstream, and he moved back toward the car, steadying himself hand over hand on the hood as he slid forward.

He needed a cigarette, and he fished the pack from his shirt pocket. He pulled one out, leaving on the white paper brownish red whorls from the residue on his hands. He patted his pockets, looking for a match, but could find none. Leaning into the car, he cursed to see the cigarette lighter socket occupied by the plug for the radar detector on the dashboard. Maura. Lead foot. How many speeding tickets had he fixed for her, even with the detector? His eyes scanned the interior of the Mercedes, abruptly coming to rest on a purse wedged beneath the passenger seat. He leaned in and extracted it. The leather clung to the sticky blood that had pooled around it. It was her purse, Maura's. Jesus Christ, he thought to himself as he opened it. Her recognizable stuff was all there, the perfume spritz she always carried, the dental floss, the tacky wallet she had bought at the Grand Canyon gift store, several sticks of

7

petrified gum with fossilized hair imprints, and a red plastic elephant—a toy of some sort? Baker hungrily parted all of this debris, finally landing on a box of matches with a funky art deco logo that read, "The Pachyderm."

He dislodged a wooden match from its moorings and struck it, shakily lighting the cigarette. He sucked hard, taking in as much smoke as he could hold. The rush of nicotine seemed to clear his head and give him balance. He dropped the box of matches into his coat pocket.

Where was he? He scanned the topography. He was in an empty lot, the remnant of what might have been a factory of some sort. To his right, a dirty red, rusted building was caving in on itself. Wind whistled through the broken glass. A pigeon suddenly fluttered out from between the remaining shards that clung to the frame. The noise, the movement made Baker jump.

At the front of the car, a field of muck and brown grass laid like a threadbare carpet between him and a distant horizon of huge white oil storage tanks. Black steel towers spewed flames into the blue winter air. The geography seemed to heave and roll with distant undulating thunder. To his left, a shimmering blue lake was framed in skinny cattails and skeletal trees. The far side of it was randomly dotted with fishermen sitting on folding chairs, virtually motionless. A street seemed to border the acreage behind him. A school bus hummed by, and gray water exploded from potholes beneath its tires. The bus brakes squealed from the wetness and its transmission whined through a downshift as the driver nudged it up the block. It stopped to pick up a Technicolor cluster of kids at the corner. It was normal. It was life, life going on in all its mundane repetitiveness. Except for one thing. All these activities existed on the periphery of his location, on the other side of a cyclone fence. As if he was some dead core in the middle of a vital world, like the eye of a hurricane. Then he wondered, was he, somehow, locked in?

Just finish the cigarette, just a second. She'll kill me if I smoke in her car.

He took a few deep, but quick, drags and that's when he noticed it. The window. While the rest of the car looked as though it had been shrouded in a sheet of frost, the driver's side window had a hole carved out of its center, a hole the size of two fists, framed in slashes.

Shit! He had been seen. Someone, curious about this fancy car in the middle of nowhere had come up to it and scraped the window clean and looked in and ... you couldn't miss the blood. A white hot blade tore through him and he stumbled, falling to one knee. He clenched his eyes. Last night. Or was it this morning? A man in the window.

"What   are you doing here? Are you   okay?" An old guy. Bundled up. His breath crystallizing in the cold.

Was that at the party? No, it was bright, so bright that Rich had to fight to keep his eyes open. Fear surged through him. Instinctual, musky, animal fear. The metallic taste of it in his mouth. The electricity of it jolting though his heart. Get out. Run.

He tossed away his cigarette and jumped back into the driver's seat, jamming his knee against the steering wheel. The fucking seat was up much too far for him. How the hell did he drive it this way, the way it scrunched his nuts? He reached below to adjust it, at the same time grabbing the keys. Would the damned thing even start? Or had he been there all night with the lights on, sucking the blood out of the battery? He turned the key, and the engine responded with a quiet purr as it engaged. Goddamned Mercedes. Man, they run. He reached down for the electric seat adjuster. Gently the seat glided back. Come on, come on. Finally it lurched to a stop. He pulled the shifter into gear, wrenched the wheel, and jammed the gas pedal to the floor. A cloud of pea gravel and dust erupted from beneath the tires as the Benz spun around and headed away from the bent and disintegrating building and across the sprawling lot.

In seconds the speedometer had reached fifty miles per hour, and he saw an open gate no more than a quarter mile ahead. It fed onto a thoroughfare, and he jammed the pedal to the floor as he raced toward it. Oh, god, I can make it.

Then, with only a few hundred yards to go, the emptiness was rapidly filled. The world squeezed around him like fingers. Coming at him was a police car, screaming in the morning light, flashers and sirens rattling the sky. On its rear bumper, snorting like a bull, was an unmarked cruiser, a blue light throbbing on its dash. Baker slammed on the brakes. The ABS system stuttered beneath his foot as the Benz rocked from side to side before thundering to a stop in a huge spew of road debris.

As he watched the smoke settle around him, the two cars screeched and squealed and surrounded him like the cavalry. Doors flew open and immediately closed, thump-thump, as two officers leapt from the first vehicle and jogged toward him. One had his hand on his gun. Baker cursed and shut off his engine. He pounded his head on the steering wheel. Through the settling dust they were like two huge clouds, featureless, silhouetted against the low hanging sun, becoming a miasma of shadows. Their breaths churned steam into the air like the smoke from a dozen bonfires. What now? Surely, they wouldn't shoot. He waited anyway.

"Come on out, sir, slowly now," a voice boomed.

Rich took a deep breath and opened the door. With one leg out of the car, he heard the voice again, "Hands up, keep your hands in the open, sir."

"Don't shoot. I'm not armed," Rich said, opening his bloodstained palms and pulling himself out of the car purely on the strength of his legs. In a second he was outside, hands raised. Instantly four uniformed policemen were on him, turning him around and forcing his hands to the top of the Mercedes. Where did these guys come from? Jesus, he needed a drink.

"It's okay," he said.

"Careful, we've got blood here," one of the officers said. The others backed off. "Are you injured, sir?"

"I don't... I can't... I don't think so."

"You're not sure?"

"Yes... I mean, I'm pretty sure I'm okay," Rich said. His head was drumming rhythmically and he leaned against the car once again to steady himself.

"Just stay there, and take it easy," the cop said. Then he turned and shouted over his shoulder. "Gloves, get me some gloves." Within a few moments he was slipping latex gloves over his fingers. "Hold still, sir," he said to Baker, frisking him, across his torso and down his pants. "Is this your wallet?"

"Yeah."

"Please remove it for me, and take out your driver's license."

Baker removed the wallet from the back pocket of his slacks and took the license out. He handed it to the policeman.

The officer pulled him away from the Mercedes. "Can you walk? Can you come with me?"

"I'll take it from here. Thanks, Perkins," a woman said. Baker traced the origin of the voice and saw someone slamming the door of the unmarked car. Wedging her way between two bumpers, she moved toward him. She was not uniformed, dressed instead in a long winter coat, light brown that matched the color of her skin. She stopped a few feet in front of him. "Good morning, sir," she said officially. "I am Detective Kane. Do you have any identification?"

"He took it," Rich replied, nodding toward the uniformed officer.

"Perkins?" she replied, looking at the cop. He moved toward her and handed her Baker's license.

Detective Kane was tall, five ten at least, with short hair the color and texture of a raven's wings and eyes of translucent amber. Nice, very nice, Baker thought, then, Jesus, what the hell is the matter with you? When he should have been mustering his instincts to protect himself from what was happening, he was, instead, peeling her out of her coat, gently removing her clothes, imagining her lying next to him, long and lithe and soft, touching her skin...

Suddenly a policeman lifted his head out of the passenger side of the Mercedes. "Detective, there's some major spillage in here."

Detective Kane walked over, leaned into the automobile and, without a single show of emotion, pulled herself upright. "Okay, folks, this is now a crime scene. Stand away from the car until we get the forensic people here. Touch nothing. Perkins, get Bones Jones on the horn and tell him what we have here. He might want to handle it himself." She pivoted back toward Baker. She looked at his license. "Richard Charles Baker of Chicago, Illinois," she said.

"Rich," he answered. "Most people call me Rich."

A voice called from behind them, "Detective, we've got a purse on the floor on the passenger side. Do you want it?"

Detective Kane turned her head away from Rich, but kept her eyes on him. "Mark it. Take a picture. Then leave it alone for now," she replied. Then she turned fully to Baker. "At the risk of being politically incorrect, may I presume that the purse is not yours?"

"It's not mine."

Kane tilted her head. "Then whose?"

"It is probably my wife's. Uh, my soon-to-be ex-wife's, actually."

"Is she here somewhere?" Detective Kane said, her eyes scanning the area.

"I , uh, don't... no, no, she's not here."

She eyed him. "Mr. Baker, might I ask you what's going on here?"

Damned if he knew, he thought, but understood before he could speak that saying so in those words would sound flip, sarcastic, detached. So, he mulled over several half-formed, nebulous answers. He did the best he could. "I don't even know where 'here' is right now."

"You're on the south side of Chicago. A bit out of your neighborhood," Detective Kane said, turning over his license and examining it again. "Are you hurt, sir?"

"Uh, no."

"You sure? You don't look too good."

"Yeah. I'm just... I just don't feel so good."

"Tough night?"

13

"Yeah, I guess."

Detective Kane was tapping his driver's license against the palm of her hand. "What brings you here?"

"I don't know."

"When did you get here?"

"I don't know."

"You don't remember driving here, maybe last night sometime?"

Rich shook his head. "I… I just can't remember anything."

"What do you remember?"

"I just woke up in the car," Baker replied. "Over there," he pointed in the direction from which he had come.

"Over where?" Detective Kane said, moving to see where he was pointing.

"About two, three hundred yards that way. Not too far from the water."

Kane glanced in the direction then turned to one of the cops. "Go over there and start looking around. Be careful. You see something, mark it, but leave it alone."

Suddenly there was a whopping sound from above. Rich staggered as he looked up. A helicopter, silhouetted in front of the sun, looking like a huge dragonfly, black and menacing, was hovering downward. For an instant he was somewhere else again. In the desert, in a maelstrom of horror. Jesus, please, please. What was going on? He grabbed his temples with his open palms and closed his eyes so tight that tears were squeezed from the edges.

Detective Kane glanced up. "Oh, boy," she said, "just what we need."

14

Rich stumbled dizzily in his own darkness and opened his eyes to regain his balance. He looked up again. "What is it? It's not yours?"

"Ours? No. I'd say a traffic 'copter for a local news station. They look down, see this, and turn on their cameras. You know the media," Detective Kane moved her eyes from the helicopter to Rich. "Mr. Baker, for all we know you're on live TV right now."

"Shit," he spat.

"Yeah, well, hey, it's America. It's the information age. What are you gonna do?" Detective Kane replied, shrugging her shoulders. "Before the day is over you will be streaming all over the world. Now, where were we? Oh yes, what the hell are you doing here, Mr. Baker?"

Rich felt like puking again, so he bent forward and put his hands on his knees to keep from falling. An acid-tasting gas moved through him, and he merely belched. He then shook his head vigorously before straightening up again. "I don't know," he whispered. "I just don't know."

"Well, Mr. Baker, why don't you try a little harder? You not remembering doesn't help much, now does it?" the detective replied. "What about the mess in the car and all over you? Nothing there rings a bell?"

Baker exhaled. She was getting impatient. He could see it. "Honest to God, ma'am, I have no idea what's going on here."

"You don't know," she said.

"That's right."

"You on drugs, Mr. Baker?"

"Drugs? No. I don't…"

"Been drinking?"

Rich cleared his throat. "Yeah, a little bit, I guess."

15

"You were in a helluva hurry to get out of here."

"Yeah, well, I was shocked to wake up... and find all this."

"Yeah, right," she replied after a second, exhaling slowly. "Am I correct in assuming this is your car?"

"Not exactly," Baker grunted.

"Go on."

"It's hers."

"Your wife's, or ex-wife, whatever she is?"

"Yeah, but it's only hers as part of our ongoing, uh, negotiations. In fact, it's paid for with my money."

"So, you're separated?"

"I guess that's the legal term for it. It's certainly the correct literal phraseology."

"Amicable?"

Rich hesitated. "Not particularly."

Detective Kane pursed her lips and Baker knew exactly what she was thinking. He thought it would be best to keep quiet.

"How can we get in touch with her?" Kane said.

Baker gave her an address and phone number, both in Lake Forest. "Good place to keep a Mercedes," Kane said offhandedly as she jotted the information down on a note pad and slid it back into her pocket. "We'll sort out everything soon enough. Mr. Baker, we're going to have to impound this car, just in case, you know what I mean? Just so we can check it out. We're going to take you down to the station so we can talk about things. Get you some coffee. Maybe an aspirin or something like that. Help you feel better, huh? Please come with me." She slid her hand into the crook of his arm, not in an intimate way at all, but one that firmly emphasized her control. Then, turning back to the Mercedes, she said to an officer,

"Stan, run a DMV report on that vehicle and check out this license." She handed the driver's license to him.

Detective Kane led Baker to a squad car where she opened a back door and motioned for him to slide in. Rich hesitated at the open door. He reached into his pocket and removed his pack of cigarettes, knowing he should ask if she minded if he smoked, but also realizing that by lighting up, he seized a modicum of control for an instant. Besides, he needed it, just needed it. "Am I under arrest?" he asked, taking a match from the box in his pocket, striking it, and shakily touching it to the tip of his cigarette.

As Baker inhaled, Detective Kane seemed to wince and hesitate, as if wanting to say something. He expunged the smoke and it fled like a ghost over his shoulder. She gently placed her hand on his head as he leaned beneath the car roof. "Watch your head," she said. He eased into the seat. She took the cigarette from between his fingers and dropped it on the ground, grinding it to death with her foot. "No smoking in city property, including police cars," she said. Then she slammed the door. Baker flinched and slumped in the seat. He immediately noticed the absence of handles inside the door, and for a brief, ferocious second he felt trapped. The front door to the squad car swung open, rushing sunlight through the screen that separated the seats. A grid of shadows was thrown over Baker. One of the uniformed cops slid into the driver's seat.

"Little wasted are you, buddy?" the cop cracked, chuckling.

Fuck you, asshole, Baker thought, but didn't say. He was drained, empty, squeezed in the vice of the circumstances. In a bitter brew of fear and exhaustion, he leaned his head on the back of his seat and closed his eyes. Immediately the darkness started to spin. He could hear Detective Kane giving orders in the background.

"Perkins, did you get hold of Bones? When's he coming? Okay, then, secure the scene until forensics gets here. I'll call for backup. When they get here start kicking the bushes looking for stuff. Get inside that building over there and catalogue anything you find."

Then from a distance behind the detective, Baker saw another commotion erupting. Two vehicles ripped into the abandoned field. One was a white van with a satellite dish on top, the other a white car. Both bore the familiar logos of Channel 7 Eyewitness News. "Goddamnit," he muttered.

"Oh boy," Detective Kane said. "Here comes the circus train." Then she turned back to the cop named Perkins, not missing a beat. "If a body pops up, call me at the station or page me. Head down to the edge of the lake. You know what we're looking for, tire tracks, whatever. There's a prize to whoever brings in a body." She then walked back to the car in which Richard Baker sat, slammed the palm of her hand on the front fender and said to the driver, "Read him his rights and get him out of here, stat."

The driver started the car and shifted it into gear. Baker leaned his head back and closed his eyes again. Immediately, the world went dark and Rich Baker was once more in the bliss of unconsciousness.

"Rich, stand up. Rich, come on, boy." He was back in the elevator. The walls were closing in. His legs collapsed beneath him. What? Where?

"Don't fuck with me. I mean it," he said. His words slowed, slurred, maybe not even in that order.

18

"Jesus heavy Christ this guy is. Hurry."

You can't always get what you want.

Faces came back. Crystal, her tongue hanging out, a breast falling from the distended neckline of her blood red dress. Baker's hand cupped the supple flesh gently. The candles blew out, the smoke hanging from the wicks like string.

Another bright room, now. Not Lundeen's apartment. Tubes. Plastic snakes curling. The hiss of machines. A face, nobody's face, turned blue and swollen and unresponsive, puffed up on the pillow. That's what a bullet does to a head, makes it blow up and turn colors.

The rhythmic clicking of the box in the corner. A doctor. He said, "There's nothing we can do."

"Nothing you can do? What kind of fucking doctor are you?"

"I am very sorry."

"Sorry? Sorry? No, not good enough."

Not good enough.

"I have to ask," the doctor said. "Are you interested in donating his, uh, any of his organs?"

Maura was weeping. She whispered. "Oh, baby, my baby."

But if you try sometimes, you just might find, you just might find, you might find, you get what you need.

Everyone at the party was laughing. Laughing. Laughing. Laughing. Then everything went away again.

2

The realization had begun to seep into Glory Kane's consciousness—like how an autumn mist slowly penetrates clothing and skin before settling into the bones—as she was returning to headquarters in her car. This could very well be her first murder case. Maybe. She had only made detective a few months ago and had been on the periphery of a few homicides and mysterious deaths, but this was the first that had come to her free and clear, and the implications thrust her heart into an entirely new rhythm. Be cool, she told herself. Don't rush things. Take your time.

Her desk sat butt-to-butt with other desks in a sprawling, messy bullpen shared by all the cops in the detective division. The walls had been painted once, probably during the Roosevelt administration—Teddy's that is. The putrid color had been yellowed by cigarette smoke and streaked with soot that had been rubbed off the clothes and expectorated from the lungs of the inhabitants and suspects passing through. The floor was dark linoleum, scarred from the wheels of desk chairs that rolled around on it like bumper cars at a carnival. The windows were gray with permanent grime. The entire floor clattered with the myriad sounds of people trying to keep order in a world that refused to cooperate. Phones purred. Computer keys clicked. Everything was laid against a backbeat of voices, a steady hum with expletives popping over the top of it like fireworks over a crowd.

Glory juked between rolling chairs, dodging waste baskets, and moved to her cluttered desk. She wiggled out of her coat, dropped her purse onto an uneven stack of papers, and hooked her chair with her foot to pull it backward. Then, in the same motion, she fell into the chair and slid into place at her desk. With one hand, she picked up the phone and dialed. At the same time, she typed her password into her computer. The screen bounced and flickered into action. With the receiver cradled between her chin and shoulder, and the edge of a paper coffee cup clenched between her teeth, she entered information into the computer to trace ownership of the Mercedes as the phone line pulsated with the gentle chime of a phone ringing. It rang once, twice. Come on, baby, pick up, she thought. A crowd had gathered around her. Murder did that. Drew a crowd. Wheels squealed as chairs pulled closer. Bodies began to stack up on the edges of her desk.

Glory smiled at them. They were pretty good guys, for the most part. Gave her shit for being the only female detective on the squad, but as far as shit went, it wasn't any more than they gave each other, just different. The phone rang once more and an answering machine clicked on. A recorded voice, light, lyrical, filled the receiver. "Damn," Glory whispered as the voice purred.

"Hello, you've reached Maura. I can't come to the phone, leave a message. Thanks."

21

Glory shook her head, left her name and number and hung up, and the room immediately percolated back to life.

First out of the chute was Chick Dybzinski. "Rock and roll, Glory Kane, you got a live one on the hook, yeah?"

Ned Bolton, whose desk abutted hers, slid his chair into the fray. "Gaff that mother and bring him into the boat. Way to go, Glorygirl!"

Glory felt herself blushing. "I guess you guys have heard the news."

"News travels fast in these parts," Bolton said.

"Especially bloody news," Dybzinski interjected.

"Rookie detective gets first murder one! Way to go, Citizen Kane!" Sim Carruthers said, slapping Glory a high five.

"So, Glory, you got enough to nail this bum, or what?" Roger Crewes asked.

Glory let this question settle into her mind. Her hands wrapped around the cup of tepid coffee as she sat there, momentarily lost in thought. What was with this guy Rich Baker? Well, for one thing, he was totally wasted. Hung over to beat the band. That could explain the memory lapse. But was he telling the truth? The computer screen revealed the story of the Mercedes. It was registered to a Maura Baker, so he was telling the truth about that. The first flux of thoughts was too, too obvious. The guy got drunk, picked up his wife, had a fight, killed her, dumped the body somewhere, then passed out at the wheel of her car. Too easy, she thought, although how many domestic disputes had she investigated where the obvious was the truth? Still, there was something about this that was gnawing at her. "I wouldn't jump to that conclusion, not yet, boys. We don't even know there was a murder, or a death of any kind. I've only just begun," she said.

22

The phone rang, almost shaking with urgency. Unlike most organizations that had changed to phones with softer trills, the system in the headquarters still used that good, old-fashioned, teeth rattling ringer that made the papers on the desk quiver. Glory picked up the receiver, "Area two, Detective Kane," she said, holding up an open palm to the crowd around her.

The voice on the other end of the line was instantly recognizable. "Detective, this is Mancuso from forensics. We were going through the car and found a roll of undeveloped film under the passenger seat. Just wondered if you wanted it right away or what?"

"Film? Who uses film anymore?" she mused. "You say it's undeveloped? Do we have connections with a photo lab to process quickly?"

"Yeah, Walgreen's. They can do it in an hour," he replied, chuckling.

"Get it done and bring it to me," Glory said and hung up. Then she turned back to the cops who surrounded her. "Like I said, guys, I'm not sure what's going on yet. We'll be talking to the suspect, uh, Mr. Baker in a little while, see what shakes."

"Anything you need, let me know, Glory," Ned Bolton said, patting her on the shoulder.

"Same here," Sim Carruthers interjected, and the other guys nodded.

"Anybody know cops up Lake Forest way?" Glory asked.

Sim Carruthers spoke immediately. "Yeah, I know several of the guys up there, what you need?"

"The car this guy was driving belonged to his wife. I just tried calling, got no answer. We need somebody to go to the house and check it out, see if she's there," Glory hastily scribbled the address onto a sheet of scrap paper and handed it to Carruthers.

"Yeah, can do," he said, taking the note.

Suddenly the cops parted like branches in the wind, and Lieutenant Frank Rodriguez, sleeves rolled up, tie loosened and split in a wedge on his shirt, moved forward. "Kane, gotta see you in my office." She picked up the manila folder containing her notes and followed him to the glass-enclosed cubicle at the corner of the room.

She walked in and closed the door. Immediately the outside sounds were muffled. She moved toward a side chair that was framed in stacks of paper and other debris that teetered on the desk, filing cabinets and window sills like piles of laundry.

Rodriguez moved a tall, uneven cube of papers aside and sat at the edge of his own desk. He was lithe, olive-skinned, with shining silver hair, and he moved and spoke with a sophistication and elegance that beckoned first and then mesmerized. He had been Glory's mentor, her inspiration as a young beat cop, and he always expected her to think first but think fast. "What you got?" he cut to the point.

"Found a guy in a Mercedes on the old steel property south. Blood all over the seat, all over him. Named Richard Baker from the north side. The Mercedes is registered to Maura Baker, his wife. Her address is up in Lake Forest. She's not in the car; did I mention that?"

"No, but that much of the story is already in the wind," Rodriguez answered. "Little out of their neighborhoods, huh?"

"In more ways than one," Glory said. It was seldom that people with addresses like Baker's wandered down to the seedy industrial realms of the south side.

"How'd you get this anyway?" Rodriguez asked.

24

Glory shrugged. "Luck. Anonymous phone call. I was in early this morning finishing up the section threes on the Watson case, and when the phone rang, I picked up. Guy on the phone says mysterious Mercedes is in the lot and the guy in it might be trouble."

"'Might be trouble?' or 'Might be in trouble?'"

"'Might be trouble,'" Glory replied. "I'm certain that's what he said. That's why I called for backup. But now that you mention it, it is an odd phrase, isn't it?"

"Yeah, it is. We'll worry about the grammar later. Did the caller identify himself?"

"Yeah, I asked him his name and he told me, Grant something or something Grant, the connection was not very good. Asked him again and lost the connection."

"Cell phone?"

"Sounded like one. You know, Wolf Lake is out there and a lot of the old refugees from the steel mill go fishing in the mornings. Maybe he's one of those guys."

"Odd that he would call the precinct directly, and your desk at that, instead of 911."

"Yeah, that is kinda strange, now that you mention it."

"To say the least," Rodriguez said, waving off the thought. "What about an ID on the call?"

"Nothing came up here, but I suppose we could run a trace."

Rodriguez pursed his lips and shook his head. "We might want to do that. We'll see. Go on."

"I wasn't sure what might be up, so, like I said, I called for backup. When I got there, here's this guy, covered in blood. I had him brought over here. Meanwhile, forensics and some of the blues are canvassing the property."

"Any apparent reason for the blood?"

"None. The boys are looking for a body. I told them to call me immediately if they find one." She pulled her phone out of her pocket and looked at it. Then shook her head. "So far, nothing. Bones Jones is on his way out, probably there by now. I thought he'd want this one for himself." Dr. Henry "Bones" Jones was the pathologist of choice. The cops believed he could identify a person from a cuticle.

"Well, it sounds like you did everything right," Rodriguez replied. "Where's Baker now?"

"Forensics is working him. Scraping him, getting prints, taking pictures. If something bad did happen, he's literally dripping with evidence."

"He get his rights?"

"Yeah, on the way here. And I'm betting he calls a lawyer as soon as he can."

"He paranoid, or what?"

"The guy bought his wife a home in Lake Forest and a Mercedes. My guess is he's got enough smarts, and enough cash, to let the pros handle this rather than taking it on himself."

"He say anything so far?"

"Not much. Says he can't remember anything about last night or this morning. Right now he's tight as a clam. 'Course, he's so hung over he can barely function. Maybe he'll talk when he sobers up."

"What's it look like?" Rodriguez asked.

"It doesn't look good. In addition to the blood, we found a purse in the car. Wallet full of money. Plenty of identification."

"Oh, yeah? The wife's?"

"Yep, Maura Baker. It's the wife, or should I say, the ex-wife, I mentioned."

26

"You find her yet?"

"Just called right now. No answer. Machine. Plus, as you heard, Sim is calling some pals up in Lake Forest to check out her place."

"I'm betting she's not there," Rodriguez said. "It's not likely she'd be leaving her car and her purse…"

"And a bucket of blood," Glory interrupted.

"… and still be alive," Rodriguez said. "Do we have enough to book him?"

Glory thought about it for a moment. She shook her head. "Right now the evidence is, at best, circumstantial, and we're not even sure a crime has been committed, other than, maybe, trespassing."

"Well, detective, congratulations on what might be your first homicide. You know that the pressure is really going to be on you to get an indictment and a conviction, for your own sake. Any doubts about handling it?"

"I understand the importance…"

Rodriguez didn't acknowledge her response, just plowed forward. "I've already got a call from Devalane," he said. Harold Devalane was the state's attorney.

"Devalane? What the hell does he want?" Glory asked.

"Oh, you know old Harold. He's a mighty ambitious one, and this might be the perfect high profile case to set him up for whatever he wants next," Rodriguez answered.

"I heard it's governor."

"Me too, and this is just the kind of thing that the media get hold of and it becomes national news," Rodriguez continued. "Wealthy woman, in the middle of a divorce, suddenly goes missing. Husband is prime suspect. It will be on all the national news shows and all over the blogs."

"Devalane's going to make sure nobody gets in front of him on this case, I'm sure," she said. "How the hell did he find out about it already? Is there something happening here that I don't know about? The whole world seems to know about this case and, what's more, believes that this guy Baker has killed his wife – or somebody – and I'm here, twenty-five minutes into the situation, the only person who has actually talked to the guy."

"I don't know how Devalane found out already, but it's not hard to get the radios cracking when you call for forensics and a backup team to scour an abandoned factory and half-frozen lake for a body. Word travels in these parts; that's all I'm saying."

"Well, it is what it is and I'll just have to deal with it," she whispered.

"I'm putting McKay on the case with you," Lieutenant Rodriguez continued.

This unexpected comment hammered her like a thunderbolt. She felt her throat constricting. The room receded. "Oh no," Glory said.

Rodriguez put up both his hands. "Now, simmer down, Glory," he said gently. "If this becomes what it looks like, it will be your first murder case. I want it to work. And you know we partner on murders. Jake is available. He's experienced."

"He's a dinosaur."

"Now, he's coming in here in a few minutes, and I expect you to handle yourself professionally."

"God, Frank, why McKay? Why not Sim or Ned?"

"They already have more on their plates than they can handle."

"But... McKay?"

"I know you don't like him."

Glory swallowed hard. She remembered the first time she'd met McKay. She introduced herself.

"Kane," she had said, sticking out her hand.

McKay grinned. "Would that be sugar cane or candy cane?"

"Hurricane," she had answered immediately. And the tone had been set.

"I don't have enough energy to dislike him—or like him for that matter. It's just that he's a cliché, stuck in the mud of 1955 when women did the laundry and stayed home," Glory said.

"He has an interesting perspective, that's for sure," Rodriguez chuckled. "He wasn't even born in 1955. And you know he's mostly just bullshit and bad gas. It's a big macho act."

"Yeah, sure," Glory pondered for a few seconds. "Okay, I can work with him, but will he work with me? So far, he has been able to pretty much avoid the possibility."

"I'll make sure he's okay with it, Glory, and despite his attitude, he's got instincts. You know that. And I don't give a damn about your ego or his. You're a good enough cop, but you've never been in this deep. This is one of those stories that can go viral, go big. That means big time pressure on you to get a solution. One tiny screw up on our parts—anything not one hundred percent kosher, can deep six the whole thing. You guys need to have each other's backs."

"Got it."

"So, I suggest that the first thing you do is find a body. The more time that goes by, the harder it gets."

As if on cue, the door swung open and the raspy voice of Jake McKay thundered into the room. "Body? Don't forget, a good cop can accumulate corpus delecti without actually collecting a corpse," he said.

So this is how it starts, Glory thought as she looked up to confront a prodigious frame obscuring the sunlight like a misplaced mountain. She exhaled. Jake McKay plowed into the room and took up a space next to Rodriguez's desk, casually draping his meaty arm over the top of a file cabinet. He fumbled in his shirt pocket with the leaking pen that was stuck there. He was sweating through his yellowing shirt that strained against his huge stomach. His tie, knotted haphazardly and then loosened at his neck, hung in two nearly equal tails that ended at the point of his sternum. His pants rose a full inch above his ankles. His eyes were pin dots of murky brown, his cheeks wobbly and white, and his face raced over his forehead in a swath of pink. "So, what's happening, kids?" he asked.

"And good morning to you, too, Jake," Glory said.

"Sure. Top of the morning to everyone," Jake answered, then turned to Rodriguez. "What's the skinny, Chief?"

"Not sure. Could be murder. Could be a hunting accident. Could be nothing, but probably not," Rodriguez answered.

McKay leaned forward and reached towards Glory for her files. "Let me see that," he said, his fingers grasping the corner of the manila folder in Glory's lap.

She pulled it away from him. "These are mine. What do you want to know? I'll tell you," she answered.

McKay backed off, his eyes wide. He opened the palms of both hands in supplication. "Well, excuse the hell out of me," he laughed.

Rodriguez stood up from his perch on the desk. "Now, listen, Jake. This is Glory's case, but I want you to help her."

Jake's eyes grew wide in disbelief. "You what?" his head snapped from Rodriguez to Glory and then back to the lieutenant. He caught his breath. Glory could see the veins on his temples emerging, pulsing. He stammered at the lieutenant, "Can I speak with you in, uh, private for a few minutes, Frank?"

Glory didn't let Rodriguez answer. "If you want to bitch to him in private about me being in charge of the case, and that I'm a woman, or a 'broad' as you prefer, and that I've never headed a murder investigation, and whatnot, let's not waste our time. Whatever you have to say to him, you can say in front of me."

McKay froze momentarily, staring at her. The veins in his temples were throbbing like two kinetic worms. He fumbled unconsciously with the pen in his pocket, obviously trying to regain some sense of composure. He stared her down for a few seconds. "Whatever," he muttered, then shrugged and turned back to Rodriguez. "Frank, what do you mean you're giving the case to her?"

"I didn't say I was giving her anything. She was here. She took the call. She responded to the scene. She caught the case. It's hers."

"But…" McKay stammered. "Shit, Frank, she's only been a detective for twenty minutes!"

Glory cringed at the raspy sound of a voice ravaged by forty years of smoke. She imagined his lungs as dried, brown autumn leaves, crinkled and flaking, ready to burn. She didn't even acknowledge his comment.

"You were only a detective for twenty minutes once, too, Jake. And look at you now. You're a legend, a modern Dick Tracy."

Glory thought, "Emphasis on Dick," but held it in.

Jake mumbled something unintelligible under his breath.

"That's the way it is. Take it or leave it," Rodriguez replied evenly.

McKay grunted and turned to Glory. "Tell me what you got so far," he said. "Please."

"That's so much better," she replied, then covered the basics in a few sentences.

McKay shrugged and muttered, "Scumbag offs wife. No time to clean up. Gets pinched. Two plus two equals four."

"Maybe he had a fight with somebody. Maybe the blood is his. Maybe his wife is alive and well and having a facial in some expensive salon right as we speak," Glory said. "Maybe we shouldn't jump to these conclusions until we've actually spent an hour or so examining the situation."

McKay argued, "My money says somebody is Casperized."

"Casperized?" Glory asked.

"Yeah, turned into a ghost," he said. "Like in hasta la vista, sayonara, bon voyage, dead, toast."

"I guess you'll be mighty surprised if we find her alive," Glory replied.

"Not really. It doesn't have to be the wife, though my money is on her. Maybe the guy eats broads—excuse me, women—for a living," Jake said. "Look, look at this prick. I saw him when he came in. The pattern of blood on his shirt. Not splatters, smeared, as if he handled, wrestled, struggled with a body. I say he got himself smashed, drove around blindly, maybe passed out, who the hell knows, woke up in a panic, and dumped the corpse in the first convenient hole. At the very least, something nefarious and painful went down, that's for sure."

"I agree with you there," Glory said.

32

"The car was found near Wolf Lake, right? Are you planning to drag the pond?" Rodriguez asked.

"Already arranged," Glory said.

"Good. That's a lot of water to cover. Could take some time," Rodriguez moved around his desk and sat in his own chair. He casually folded his hands in a pyramid on the sloppy desk pad. "You might want to see if there are any surveillance cameras in the area. Maybe one caught the Benz going in."

"Already on that. But the place is totally abandoned, so I'm not holding onto any great expectations," Glory replied.

"So, Glory, what's the next step?" Rodriguez asked.

"Like I said, I have already called Maura Baker's home and she doesn't seem to be there," Glory replied. "I've ordered a phone dump; I'm looking for a cell phone; and I'm checking all of her credit cards. I want to reassemble her life for the past few weeks. If she's dead, at least we'll know where she was before she died."

"Let's go gang up on old Richie for a little while," Jake replied. "In fact, I say we go down to the interrogation room and unscrew his head and empty out all the Pez. You know, a good cop, bad cop kind of thing." He made locomotive motions with his arms.

Glory shook her head. "The guy's still in forensics and, besides, he's in no shape to be interrogated yet. He needs to re-enter this atmosphere. He needs to cool off for a couple of hours, come down. I want to see if anything's happening at Maura Baker's home. We might have to head up there."

"Road trip! I love road trips!" McKay chortled.

Frank Rodriguez pulled himself straight, clapped his hands decisively and then opened them as if a consensus had been reached. "There, you see? Already it's working."

"You got it, Chief. Me and my partner are on the case," Jake replied.

Out of the corner of her eye, Glory could see Jake McKay smiling like a Cheshire cat.

"I'm sure everything will be just swell," she answered.

"Just follow me," McKay said.

"No, Jake, you follow me," Glory answered.

"Okay, boss."

"All right, you two, knock it off," Frank Rodriguez interjected, laughing a bit under his breath. "Just think of all the fun you'll have."

"We'll see," Jake replied.

"You bet," Glory said.

Rodriguez, still stifling a chuckle, added, "For cryin' out loud, try not to kill one another. Now, get on it."

They walked out of the room together.

McKay kept speaking as they walked. "Hey, you never know, detective. This could be some kind of mob scene gone sour. You know, big Benz, house in the ritzy suburbs. This guy could be connected. Could be dangerous, maybe some shooting. You might need me."

Glory slipped around an overflowing trash can and slapped the sheath of papers in her hand against Jake's stomach. "Thanks for the offer. If there's any shooting at all, you're the guy I'd want in front of me," she said, brushing past him and sitting down at her desk. "Get your stuff and let's go."

Immediately the phone rang. Glory picked it up. "Detective Kane here," she said. The voice on the other end was terse, clipped, but the words that came through the lines rushed into Glory's soul like ice. She listened, thanked the caller and hung up. Then she looked up at Jake McKay. "Shit! Just as I feared," she said.

"We going for a ride?"

"Yep," she replied, picking up her files. "And grab up the digital camera. We're going to need it."

"Ah, too bad. I wanted a crack at him while he was still punchy," McKay said, gesturing toward the pokey room with his thumb.

"We're just going to have to deal with him when we get back." Glory said, pulling on her coat.

"If his lawyer shows, he ain't going to be happy waiting for us."

Glory brushed past McKay and began to walk briskly to the door. "He won't mind. He's billing by the hour. And believe me, detective," she said, "this is something you're going to want to see."

3

They pulled into the circular driveway of Maura Baker's home, and the scene immediately made the hair on the back of Glory Kane's neck bristle. The premises had been cordoned off by yellow tape that slapped in the biting lake wind, and writhed against its tethers. The spacious yard was encircled by it, like a present wrapped in a bright, yet ominous, bow. The property was also encircled by squad cars whose radios crackled and hissed hoarsely in the silence of the biting cold afternoon and whose manically whirling lights threw strobes of blue and red against the ancient huge pine trees surrounding the sprawling brick home. Glory nosed her car between a sheriff's vehicle and an ambulance and turned to Jake McKay. He was huddled against the door, fast asleep, with the case files open on his lap.

"We're here. Let's go," she said, unbuckling her seatbelt.

"Yeah, yeah, ready," Jake McKay snapped to life, opening the door and his eyes simultaneously.

Glory ducked beneath the yellow restraining tape. They were no more than three steps into the yard when a uniformed Illinois state trooper stopped her.

"Sorry, folks, only authorized personnel beyond this point."

Glory flashed her badge at the man. "Detective Kane," she said. "Can you direct me to Captain Gearhardt?"

The trooper touched the brim of his hat. "My apologies, detective. Captain Gearhardt is inside," he said, nodding toward the front door. The sidewalk meandered between several large oak trees and manicured hedges that were spackled with ice that glittered in the afternoon sun. Glory's eyes swept across the landscape. The house was huge, sculpted in perfect pink brick. Its most imposing feature was the turret-like design of the entrance that extended two stories high and featured cut glass that displayed a winding staircase in the foyer. Glory wondered what it would be like coming home to a place like this every night. She had never seen anything so opulent, and here was an entire neighborhood of homes every bit as inspiring as this one. Just north of Chicago, on the banks of Lake Michigan, Lake Forest was dreamlike to Glory, and she wondered what people did to afford such luxury. The day was winter at its most brilliant, crackling with cold and color and a sky as deep blue as an endless ocean.

Her thoughts carried her to the front door that stood open in the bitter wind, as a forensic specialist dusted the knob for prints. She walked in, flashing her badge at the uniformed officer standing guard. McKay was several steps behind her, occupying most of the airspace in the doorway. "Captain Gearhardt?" Glory asked, and the cop pointed to a balding man standing at the foot of the stairs and talking with several people who were obviously part of a forensic team. He turned to her when he saw her approaching.

"Detective Kane, I presume?" he said, extending his hand.

"Nice to meet you," she said, taking his open palm. "This is Detective McKay." The two men shook hands.

"You got here quickly," Gearhardt said.

"Not as quickly as the third battalion, though," Glory answered bending her head toward the phalanx of town, city and state vehicles surrounding the place.

Captain Gearhardt almost smiled. "Everybody is looking for their little piece of the action," he said.

"Looks serious," Glory said, watching the buzz of activity that filled every room.

"Well, after you guys called and asked us to check to see if Mrs. Baker was in the home, we dispatched a patrol car. The officers came to the front door and knocked. Of course, there was no answer. Yesterday's and today's newspaper still on the porch, mail in the box. The front door was locked; so they came around to the back. Come on, follow me."

Gearhardt led them through a huge living room with a slate, walk-in fireplace and plush sofas. It was connected to a giant dining room with a crystal chandelier that glittered like a glacier over an ebony table with sixteen chairs.

"So, on the phone, you said you found Rich Baker in his car," Gearhardt said.

"Yes, that's right," Glory answered.

"What made you call us?"

"The entire front seat of the car was covered in blood and Baker was covered in it, too."

"That would do it," Gearhardt answered. "I think you're going to find this place interesting."

They entered a kitchen that was as large, it seemed, as Glory's entire home. At the far end was a mud room alcove with a door leading outside. The top half of the door was framed in six-inch glass panes. One of them had been shattered and pieces of it were lying like dust on the floor. Muddy boot or shoe prints snaked from the threshold, diminishing as they extended into the kitchen. A person in a trench coat dusted the door, and two others were measuring the soil outside the door.

Gearhardt stopped. "The officers found this door open. Not unlocked. Open. You can see the mud and the partial pattern of boots there. There's also a pretty good print in the mud next to the sidewalk outside. Fortunately, it's frozen, so it will be very easy to make a cast. A match to the boot type should be a cinch."

Glory looked at the threshold and then across the tiled kitchen floor. She could now see the faint marks of mud deteriorating as they moved closer to the foyer. "How far do the prints go?" she asked.

Gearhardt pursed his lips and began to walk. "That's where things really start getting interesting."

In a few moments they were up the stairs, standing in Maura Baker's bedroom. It was large, luxurious in soft blue hues, and looked as if a bomb had gone off. The floor was strewn with broken perfume bottles and make up containers, as if someone had swept clean the dressing table. A dresser had been overturned and its contents had been expunged onto the floor like the guts of a butchered animal. But all of this detail became foggy, peripheral, incidental to the screaming focal point that hit Glory between the eyes. A gnarl of bloody sheets cascaded from the bed, running towards the white dressing table where two bloody streaks slashed like whip wounds across the top and down over the drawers, until finally fading into the carpet. Two forensic specialists were quietly, methodically cataloging items from the scene.

"My God," Glory whispered.

McKay moved into the room, his eyes sweeping the scene, and Glory could hear the wheels of his mind grinding. "Jesus

Christ," he whispered, "Looks like our pal Rich had a fight on his hands." Jake walked over to the bed and squatted to glance at the torn and tangled bloody sheets.

"Yep," Gearhardt answered dryly, "looks like some damage was done on the bed and then she was pulled off the dressing table, as if she was hanging on."

"Can we pull any prints from the smudges?" Glory asked.

"Done. Problem is, there's no known record of Mrs. Baker's fingerprints. Best we can do is match them up with other miscellaneous prints from around the house."

"Any other residual?"

"The usual stuff. Some hair, minuscule particles of skin. By the way, did you pull any hair from the automobile?"

"As a matter of fact, we did," Glory answered, "and also blood, mud, tissue, Maura's purse, a veritable clue bonanza."

"That'll be helpful," Gearhardt said, but Glory barely heard him. She was in front of the blood-streaked dresser. The drawers beneath the dressing table were open. Loosey goosey paraphernalia were poking out. Glory pulled open one drawer, exposing a tangle of jewelry, gold chains, religious medals, cameos. Bright intruders in the bloody miasma of the room and in the cold gray mist of the weather outside beating at the window to get in. The detritus essentially ruled out robbery, she thought.

Glory trembled as she watched the forensics team scour the room, and a feeling of cold, empty, numbing despair came over her. Her mind flashed with scenes of colliding bodies. She heard the screams, saw the blood spraying the walls and floor. In reality, a deathly silence had taken up residence in the room. The only disturbance was the flash of the camera Jake McKay used to chronicle the scene.

The scene was heart wrenching, so empty, so forlorn, but at the same time, something from deep inside Glory tried to shout above the din of emotions that flooded her. Something was wrong here. The scenario was off balance, as if the house itself was part of surreal dream full of doors that led to entirely different places, different stories, different dreams.

A few moments later they were sitting at Maura Baker's kitchen table. Gearhardt poured coffee from a Thermos into Styrofoam cups for both detectives and into the lid for himself. Glory dropped her coat on the back of the chair and took the steaming brew. "So, what's your take on this, captain?"

Gearhardt shrugged. "Well, on the face of it, it looks like someone broke into the house from the back door, went upstairs, caused some sort of bloody mayhem and disappeared with the, uh, body or the wounded person, whatever."

"Did you know the Bakers, Captain Gearhardt?" Glory asked, wincing as she sipped.

"Everybody knows Rich and Maura. He's a big wheel around here. Connected like a plug into the political scene. Can't tell you how many times we dragged him out of the tank and drove him home to keep his name out of the papers."

Glory swallowed a dime-sized sip of coffee and let the heat burn through her. "Going to be kind of hard to keep this out of the papers, isn't it?"

Gearhardt nodded as he sipped from the lid of the Thermos. "Yeah, you might say that. I'm not jumping to any conclusions, but from what you guys found and what I see here, it doesn't look good for Rich."

"What kind of a man is Rich Baker?" Jake McKay asked.

41

"Sober, he's all right, a bit arrogant, but actually a pretty funny guy. Drunk, he can be a real asshole. Pardon my French."

"Is he the kind of guy who could kill someone?" Glory asked.

"Hell, anybody can kill someone if they have a good enough reason," Jake interjected.

Gearhardt looked up. "Hard to say, isn't it?"

"What about their relationship—Rich and Maura?" Glory asked.

"Let me tell you. There was once a time these two wouldn't keep their hands off each other, in a good way, I mean. Lots of touching. Made a lot of people uncomfortable. But then, it changed."

"What caused the change? Any ideas?" Glory asked.

"Well, you can pretty much trace it back to when their kid was killed."

"There's something we didn't hear about," Glory said, her eyebrows arching.

"No, they didn't talk about it too much," Gearhardt replied, blowing steam off the top of his coffee.

"What's the story on the kid?" Jake said.

"He was a college student, downstate. Nineteen years old. Walks into a liquor store. Not even old enough, fake ID. Punk comes in to stick up the place. Pulls out a gun, starts shooting at nobody in particular. Witnesses say he fired into the ceiling. Sean, that was the son's name, gets it in the head. Bullet wasn't even fired at him. Into the ceiling, bounces off something, probably a metal truss, who knows? Wrong place, wrong time. If he's in the john, or in the vodka aisle instead of at the beer cooler, nothing. Makes you wonder," Gearhardt paused, pursing his lips, shaking his head slightly. He took a breath and continued. "They take him to the hospital. For two days Rich and Maura stay with him, even though there's no hope. They finally shut down the life support."

"How devastating," Glory whispered.

Gearhardt nodded. "That was the beginning of the end for them. Too much to take, I guess. They say it happens."

"Did they somehow blame each other?" Glory said.

"Oh, hell, who knows? I imagine the turmoil is pretty hard to reconcile. All I know is that the wheels came off at that point. Rich went one way, Maura the other."

"Is he a violent man, Rich Baker?" Glory said.

Gearhardt set down his Thermos lid and spoke deliberately. "In literature, detective, you would call him passionate, and she was his equal in that respect, let me tell you. Their relationship, when it was good, it was, like I say, pretty good. But the flip side was just as intense. One thing led to another. Yeah, it sometimes led to physical confrontation. Rich started fooling around and was, shall we say, not very discreet when it came to his extramarital activities, and Maura wasn't about to put up with that kind of crap. She stabbed him once. With a pair of scissors. God, what a mess. That was, oh, about two years ago."

"Charges filed?" McKay asked.

"Nope. They both claimed he accidently did it to himself, but, you know, doesn't take a genius to read between those lines. It was pretty much the end of it for Rich. He moved out right afterwards."

McKay thought aloud, "So, adultery, another attribute to add to the growing list of Rich Baker's shortcomings."

"Rumor was it became a two-way street, eventually."

"I'm betting that wouldn't sit too well with Mr. Baker," Glory replied.

Gearhardt smiled cryptically. "Well, that's probably an understatement."

"And if it were true, it would be a motive for murder," McKay replied.

Gearhardt pressed his lips together again and pondered for a moment. "That's a tough one," he finally whispered. "They weren't even supposed to be within twenty feet of one another, or something like that, according to the restraining order."

Glory stopped mid-sip and her eyes widened. "She had a restraining order against him?" she asked incredulously.

"I didn't say that, detective," Gearhardt replied ironically. "He took out the restraining order on her."

4

Rich Baker watched the miasma of shapes through the mottled gray glass on the door, hearing sounds as muffled as the pictures. He was in a tight, tiny room with an ancient brown table and mismatched chairs. The walls were the color of baby shit, slicked and streaked with grease from the heads of punks leaning backward in the body language of defiance. One wall was lined with a blue-gray mirror, a two-way, he figured. Probably someone there right now, watching him. He extended his middle figure and jabbed it at the mirror.

The forensic cop had stripped him down, photographed him, dug blood from under his fingernails. Found a bruise on his thigh, big, the size of a half dollar and variegated purple like a bunch of grapes. Impounded all his clothes. Gave him a sweatshirt and sweat pants – probably straight out of someone's gym locker, or worse, yet, off some dead guy – reeking of body odor. Shit, he had to wear it home.

He took another hard swallow from a can of cold Coke. God, it helped, tingling as it went down, cooling his fever. "Coke tastes like your foot's asleep," Sean told him once, when the boy was just little, maybe three years old. He smiled at the

45

sound returning to his head. The boy came and went in his memory dozens of times a day, a different boy each time; sometimes little and in pajamas, sometimes in his university tee. At times, Baker wished he'd just go away completely, other times he rummaged through his mind looking for him, needing him.

Another uninvited companion in the room with him was fear. It hung silently in the air, but, again, Baker was not totally uncomfortable in its presence. He had met it the first time, in its raw, unbridled fury, when he was a soldier.

The big work had been done. The desert was potted with burning vehicles and singed bodies. Skeletal limbs stuck out of piles of ash. Plumes of smoke scribbled on the horizon. The air was sick with the stench of death and fire and explosives. Rich's squad was sent to clean up the stragglers, if they found any. It had not taken long, this war. But Rich had seen enough of it. He had wanted to be a soldier. Not anymore. Some of them really liked it. Planned to re-up after their current tour. Not him. Fuck this. Fuck these crazy bastards from Iraq. Fuck Kuwait and its fucking oil. He was going home and staying home as soon as he could.

In the meantime, these young men had to navigate the dangerous trails to get somewhere to do something to keep the peace, to move forward, to chase the bad guys home or kill them if they put up a fight. They trudged through the endless sands. The detail, seven soldiers, was en route to a tiny village in the valley. Desert sweat, a repugnant mixture of embedded sand and bodily fluids, ran from Rich's neck to his boots, like rodents chasing around in the walls of a house. The day burned silently. The jagged landscape was devoid of sound, seemingly devoid of life, no screeching birds or insect trills, no braying beasts, no wind. They approached the tiny outcropping of huts, but when they followed the path around a saw-toothed wall of stones, everything changed.

Two men, dressed against the raging heat in the familiar army tunics and baggy pants, had been huddled against the wall. They stood quickly, as startled to see the American troops as the Americans were to encounter them. Attack? Surrender? The thoughts flew on the wind from both sides of the encounter. Rich raised his hand in a sign of peace. Then he saw it. The rifle. Coming from across the man's back. It was now a matter of who could shoot fastest. The seven grunts opened fire before the two enemy soldiers could even get their rifles into firing position. Rocks exploded in front of them. One of the men immediately fell backward and lay motionless in the dirt. The other seemed to dangle in mid-air like a marionette, as the force of the bullets lifted him and cut him virtually in half. Fear had triggered the adrenal glands, and it wasn't yet satiated. So the seven grunts, all of them, kept firing as they walked to the two dead men, kept pouring bullets into the bodies, spraying the stones and skeletal vegetation surrounding the scene. Leaves exploded, and the two corpses virtually disintegrated. Then, as if on cue, the firing stopped and the trail went back to deathly silence.

One of the grunts started screaming. Baker wrapped his arm around the kid's neck and slapped his hand over the frantic, open mouth.

Back now; in the police station, Baker needed a cigarette. Badly needed one. He leaned his head against the wall to wait. Where the fuck is everybody? Why is this taking so goddamned long? He closed his eyes and tried to control the spinning in his head.

Sometime later—he really couldn't tell how long, he had dozed off—he heard noises, voices coming closer, and the sound startled him into consciousness. There was a smear of bodies against the glass and the door swung open. A little cop, someone he hadn't seen yet, ushered in a tall, gangly man who Rich only vaguely recognized. Rich stood up as soon as the lawyer passed the threshold. "Rich, hi, I'm Nathan Timmins, from the firm's criminal division. You doing okay?" Timmins offered his hand and Rich took it, shrugging and saying he was okay. Then he sat back down. Turning to the unknown detective, Timmins said, "I'd like a few minutes alone with my client, please."

"Oh, you've got time, pal, plenty of time," the cop said, smiling as he closed the door.

Timmins pulled up a chair next to Rich and spoke softly. "Okay, tell me what's happening."

Rich fidgeted in his chair. He didn't know this guy. "I called Malcolm," he said.

"And if you were being sued or needed counsel on a contract, Malcolm would be the guy you'd want in this room with you right now. But this is a little out of his area of expertise," Timmins answered. "He personally chose me to come down here and take you home. Now, let's get started."

Rich gave him a quick rundown. Timmins jotted the pertinent facts onto a legal pad. He perused them for several seconds and then looked up at Baker. "Let's start at last night. Take your time. I need to know everything."

"I know. But last night, it's all jumbled up."

"Where were you?"

"Lundeen's."

"Oh yeah, the big party. I couldn't make it. Kid was in a school play." He took a breath. "What about Maura? Was she there?"

Zipping images filled Rich's mind. The party. Her face. She seemed to be there, but somehow she wasn't. "I don't think so."

"You don't think so? That's not good enough."

"Okay, then she wasn't there. No, wait, she was." He put his face in his hands and moaned, "God, I don't know, I don't fucking know!"

"Okay. We'll deal with that later. Just say you don't know. Now here's what's going to happen," Timmins said. "They can't hold you unless they charge you. State law allows you to terminate the interrogation at any time if you have not been charged. So, no matter what they say or how strong they come on to you, they don't have a fraction of the evidence needed to bring charges."

"So, why don't we just get the hell out of here now?" Rich asked.

"We can, but I don't think it's a great strategy. First, we want to look like you have nothing to hide. You don't know, as you say, what's going on. Blame it on booze, blame it on pressure, whatever, but we're going to try to cooperate in any way we can. That's how I want it to look right now."

Baker sighed, slumped in his chair and locked his hands behind his head. "Yeah, I get it. Pain in the ass, though."

"Don't misunderstand, Rich," Timmins interjected. "We're not taking any shit in here. They get too aggressive, I'll come right back at them. It's just that we have nothing to hide and we're outraged at the way you've been treated, but we'll help, nonetheless, to get this over with. Capicé?"

"Yeah."

"Okay, one other thing. I'm going to sit right next to you. If I put my hand on your wrist and squeeze gently," he reached over and took Rich's arm, "like this, you stop talking. I don't care what you're saying or how eloquent you think you sound, shut up. Stop in the middle of the word. Don't think. Don't argue. Shut the fuck up. I'll take over from there. Okay?"

"Yeah," Baker said, unenthusiastically.

Timmins stood up and opened the door. He looked out for several seconds before closing it. Now if these assholes would just get here.

When she left Maura Baker's house, Glory Kane was fairly certain of two things. First, something heinous had happened to the woman, and, secondly, Richard Baker's lawyer was not going to be a happy camper, having to wait for more than three hours. She actually kind of relished that thought. Always distract the lawyer, make him—or her—angry about something totally unrelated to the case. The dozen or so photos that captured only a fraction of the carnage confirmed her first suspicion, and the greeting she and McKay received when they walked onto the headquarters floor confirmed the second.

As soon as they reached the top of the stairs, a voice erupted from the far corridor like thunder on a distant horizon and swelled to a huge bellow. A rail thin man with thick horn-rimmed glasses swept toward them. His suit coat swirled like the wings of a bird and his mouth spewed spit. "Are you the detectives in charge here?" he screamed. "And which of you is Detective Kane?"

"That's me," Glory said calmly.

The man swept forward, knocking over a waste basket and blowing papers off one desk like leaves in an autumn breeze. "Look, I don't know who the hell you people think you are down here, but I can't believe you'd take a man into custody and, for no reason, harass him all day long and not expect a lawsuit that will name you by names and send your butts back to directing traffic," he sputtered, screeching to a stop as Glory took off her coat and laid it on the back of her desk chair. The man leaned onto the desk with both palms so that his face was uncomfortably close to hers.

Glory didn't flinch and she didn't respond, either. Rather, she lifted a file folder and flipped through several pages in desultory fashion, letting the man's chest heave in silence. Finally she snapped shut the folder and serenely looked up at the guy. "Well," she paused, "and who might you be?"

The man's chest deflated, then inflated again, and the avalanche resumed. "My name is Nathan Timmins, attorney and friend of Rich Baker, and both my client and I have already put up with way more bullshit than anyone should have to." His open palm slammed on the desk.

"Well, now, Mr. Timmins, on behalf of the Chicago Police Department, I apologize for the delay," Glory said, sweeping up the file and moving past him. "It was necessary, as you will soon see. Let's go visit Mr. Baker." She didn't await a response, just moved past him and headed toward the interrogation room. When she opened the door, Rich Baker was sitting there, wringing his hands. Several empty cans of Coke lined up like soldiers.

"Sorry, Mr. Baker," she said, sitting down quickly. She pushed up a sleeve of her dress and rested her arm on the table,

51

opening the file folder with her other hand. "This is Detective McKay. He's working with me on this case," Glory said, nodding towards Jake, who took up residence in the corner, leaning casually against the wall. "Now, Mr. Baker, I have here a form signed by you acknowledging that you have been read your rights. Is this correct?"

Baker barely glanced at the paper. "Yeah. Can I get a cigarette?"

Glory pursed her lips and shook her head. "Sorry. No smoking here. Clean air and all that."

"Even the fucking cops are jumping on the pussy wagon," Rich growled. "We used to be a nation with balls. Used to be you could smoke anywhere except church. Now you can't even smoke in your own goddamned house because your kids will fucking die."

"Well, Mr. Baker, you seem to be coming back to life. That's good, because we're going to need you to be focused," Glory said, sliding the form to Timmins. "Okay, let's get to work here. Again, I apologize for the delay, and in the interests of time for everybody's sake, I'm going to cut to the chase."

"You can't even smoke at a goddamned baseball game anymore. No wonder the fucking Arabs aren't afraid of us. We're too weak to even smoke," Baker continued.

Glory ignored him and nodded to McKay, who moved slowly to the table and dropped printouts of photographs. "We've just been to your wife's home, Mr. Baker, and this is what we found. Why don't we cut through all the crap and you tell me, where is your wife, sir?"

Baker and Timmins spread out the photos and glanced at them rapidly. "Jesus," Baker whispered.

"Not a pretty sight, is it?" Glory commented.

"Looks a lot like the car we found you in," McKay interjected. "Same color scheme."

Baker put his face in his hands and rubbed his eyes. Timmins formed a neat stack of the photos and slid them back across the table. He put his hand on Baker's arm and squeezed. "Continue," he said to the detectives.

"Like I said, where's Maura Baker?" Glory said. "Tell us that and we can move forward."

Baker ground his fists against his temples and squeezed his eyes shut. "I honestly don't know."

"Were you with her last night?"

"I don't know... I mean, no."

"Which is it, Mr. Baker, no or I don't know?" Glory asked.

"No," he answered emphatically.

"How did you get her car?"

"I don't know."

"What are you doing with her car, then?"

He pulled back, hitting the seat with his back. He just shook his head. "Like I said, I don't know how I got there or what I was doing there, detective."

"You a gambler, Mr. Baker? Been, maybe, to the boats?" The gambling boats were moored across the state line in Indiana, a mile or so from where Baker was found.

"No. That stuff never interested me."

Detective Kane made some notes. Then she looked up. "Well, let's try to remember how or why you came to that abandoned factory. Take a guess. It would really help expedite things, maybe get you out of here faster."

"I don't know. Maybe somebody's trying to set me up."

"Set you up? What does that mean?" Detective Kane asked, looking into his eyes.

"I don't know."

"Well, then, who would want to set you up?"

"I don't know."

"Well, then, why would somebody want to set you up?"

"I don't know that either. I'm sorry. I haven't had much time to digest what's going on."

"Okay, let's try a different tack. What do you remember about last night?"

Rich looked out the window pensively. "Well, there was a party at the home of Miles Lundeen. Perhaps you've heard of him?"

Detective Kane shook her head. "Sorry, no."

"He and I work together. We're building what would be the tallest building in the world. Right downtown." He paused to wait for the detective's response.

Jake McKay cleared his throat. "So, you're in the, what, construction business?"

"I'm in real estate. Development, actually. I secure financing for buildings, malls, shopping centers, office complexes, things like that. I set up partnerships, build the buildings, sell them and pay everybody back."

"Lot of planning going on down here," Glory said. "You involved in that?"

Rich picked up one of the cans of Coke and tried to suck the last few drops out of it. "Here? No, no." He ran his free hand self-consciously through his hair, and he felt the sticky blood clinging there.

Detective Kane jotted a few more notes onto the yellow tablet. "Let's get back to the party. Got names of people who can corroborate your presence?"

"Yeah, Lundeen for sure. There were maybe a hundred people there. Our partners from China, lawyers, politicians. I can give you quite a few names," Baker said, "but, God, there were some pretty influential folks there. The mayor was there for a little while, for chrissakes."

The reference to the mayor didn't seem to impact the detective at all. "It would be very helpful if you could get me the names, uh, other than the mayor's. I have his." she said. "Was your wife there?" Kane wasn't looking at him.

Rich exhaled audibly and shook his head. An instantaneous storm of images raged through his mind.

She was across the room.

Her hair ablaze.

"Hello, dickhead."

Again, Baker grabbed his temples and squeezed his eyes. The pressure shot white electricity into his vision. He opened his eyes and refocused on the people in the room. "I don't think... no, I'm sure she wasn't there."

"No chance you went together," Glory asked.

Baker snorted. "Now, of that I am most certain. The only place you're likely to see her and me in the same room is in a court of law, unless you were to consider my funeral, where I'm sure she'd show up to spray paint graffiti on my corpse."

"So, not a pretty divorce, I take it."

"An understatement."

"You drove your wife's car to the party?"

"No."

"How did you get there?"

"Lundeen's apartment is only a few blocks from my own. I simply walked over."

"What time was that?"

"About eight o'clock."

"What time did you leave?"

Another explosion of images flashed in Rich's mind, an elevator, other people. That was all. "I don't remember leaving."

She didn't hesitate. "So, how do you explain the fact that you are now the driver of your wife's car?"

The image of the inside of Maura's Mercedes immediately overtook Rich's mind. Jesus God, the blood.

Detective Kane's face moved slightly in a gesture that made it look as though she'd been reading his mind. "What about the blood in your wife's car?"

"Maybe it's mine," he said, his words running over the top of hers.

"Yours? I don't think so," Glory said, leafing through the papers in front of her. "According to the forensics, you're pretty well unharmed. No open wounds. No blood in the gums or nasal cavity. Just a bruise on your thigh."

"Yeah, well…" Rich said.

"So, how do you think all that blood got into your wife's car?"

"I can't say."

"What about here?" Glory asked, tapping on the stack of photos.

Rich Baker shook his head. "I don't know! Jesus, can't you understand that?"

"Is it your wife's blood, Mr. Baker?"

"You tell me."

"I'm certain we'll be able to determine that," she answered, immediately shifting gears.

"So, let's not worry about the origins of the blood right now. Try, if you can, to remember how and when you left the party."

Rich took another long, pensive look out the window. "Like I said, I don't know. I can't remember," his words belied his exasperation. "Frankly, last night is, at this moment, kind of a blur." His hand trembled slightly as he reached for another can of Coke. The can teetered and then fell to its side, dribbling brown fizz across the table. Glory tore off a sheet of clean paper from her tablet and sopped up the liquid.

Baker whispered, "I'm sorry. I'm really very sorry. I'm trying to help…"

"Are you certain you did not see your wife last night?" Kane interrupted.

Again, a burst of crackling imagery zinged through Baker's brain in an instant. Maura across the room, but not really there, no, not really. Or was she? "No. I mean, yes, I am certain."

"Have you seen her lately?"

"What do you mean by 'lately'?"

"In the last, say, week or so."

"No. I haven't seen Maura for more than a month, and she was both alive and, I might say, quite lively at the time."

"Lively?"

"Yes. As lively as a cobra," Rich replied.

"So, you and she had a fight?"

"We merely resumed a war that has lasted several years."

"A war in which one of you might, for example, die, Mr. Baker?" McKay suddenly interjected.

"We all have to die, detective." Baker snapped back, and instantly Nathan Timmins placed his hand on Rich's wrist and squeezed.

"Quite true, Mr. Baker, quite true," Jake replied.

"Does she have a job?" Glory continued.

"Job? Shit. Yeah, spending my money," he growled.

Glory chose to ignore the tone and answer. "Any relatives with whom she might be visiting?"

Baker leaned back. "Her mother is in Michigan, New Buffalo. A sister in San Diego."

"Friends?"

Rich leaned forward forcefully. "Look, detective, she has friends, I have friends, you have friends."

"Any special friend?" McKay asked.

"What do you mean by 'special'?"

"Anybody schtupping her?" McKay asked.

"Detective, if your language and your tone don't improve immediately, I'll direct my client to answer no more questions," Timmins said, pointing a bony finger at McKay, then turning his eyes to Glory. "Perhaps you can reason with this Neanderthal?"

McKay made a face and exhaled, placing his hands behind his head and locking the fingers. "Might be a good defense, insanity. Jealous insanity. Just trying to give you a break."

"Let's cut through the bullshit, Detective Kane," Baker said suddenly. "Yeah, she's got a lover, or boyfriend, whatever. An old pal of mine, in fact. Guy who used to work with us. She had to do it that way, you know. Just had to."

Kane didn't even look up from her notepad. "His name?"

"Aaron Clayton."

"How would I contact him?"

"He's the managing partner of Clayton, Bedford and Walsh, an investment banking firm downtown." He recited the address and phone number.

"We'll be talking to him," Glory said, offhandedly, as she wrote down the information.

Baker's head was pounding. Oh, Christ. Everyone was going to know. Everyone was going to be dragged into this mess. Damn, damn, damn.

"Your wife's attorney?" Kane said.

Baker ground the heels of his hands into his eye sockets. Scratches of electricity crackled through his vision. "Yeah, her attorney. His name is Arsenault. Jim – James Arsenault."

"Got his number?"

"Not with me."

"Where's his office?"

"Uh, up on the north side. Belmont Avenue. Firm's name is Arsenault and Tomes."

"We'll find it."

Baker rubbed his eyes. "Why do you need all these people? What do they have to do with it?" Timmins again reached over and gently squeezed Rich's wrist.

Detective Kane finished a note and looked up. "They're important because I want to find your wife. If she's alive then…" she just shrugged, letting the words hang for him to obviously fill in the blank.

"So, Maura shows up buying cauliflower in a supermarket, I'm off the hook, yeah? Is that the deal, detective?"

Detective Kane raised an eyebrow. "I can't cut deals, Mr. Baker. That's the domain of the prosecutor. But if you think you need to make a deal, then I'll be happy to get someone here with that authority."

"No deals," Timmins said, raising his hands, palms up.

Glory Kane cleared her throat self-consciously. "Mr. Baker, I understand you don't remember much, or anything, really, about last night. Let's say you're completely hammered, you have some sort of confrontation with your wife? Things get out of hand?"

"I don't think so," he interrupted.

"Let me finish, please. I'm trying to help you here. If something occurred while you were in any way impaired, then, well, these circumstances can certainly be taken into consideration by the prosecutor."

Timmins shot out of his chair, "There's nothing here. You're grasping at straws. You've got nothing on my client. Nothing..." Timmins looked at his watch, "...except five more minutes. Charge him by then, or we're gone." He settled down and straightened his suit coat.

"Cool your jets, there, Ichabod," Jake McKay growled, freezing the attorney with an icy stare.

Timmins held his gaze for a few moments, then leaned back. He fidgeted with his cuffs. "You've got four and a half minutes left."

Glory stood up, screeching her chair against the wooden floor as she shoved it beneath the table. "Now, I've been a good cop so far, listening to you with your 'I don't remember this and I don't remember that,' and, frankly, it makes me want to puke." She walked away from the table. "I'm no attorney, but this 'I forgot' shit isn't going to hold up in court, because – let me tell you – I'm going to find Maura Baker if I have to put on hip waders and drag that lake with a garden rake. I'm going to find her."

"That's it. It's over!" Timmins cried, standing up and pushing away from the table. He grabbed Rich's arm. "Let's go."

Detective Kane wasn't finished. "And when you stand before that jury with 'I don't remember' as your defense, they're going to laugh you out of the court and right into Danville. So, I suggest you look deep..." she came back to the table and leaned on it, moving her head a few feet from Baker's, " ... deep into your soul, and you come to grips, Mr. Baker, with what you've done. And then, Mr. Baker, you come back in here and you tell us, and maybe, just maybe, if I'm not so goddamned mad at you that I can't help myself, maybe I'll give you a shot at something less than a lethal injection. Got it?"

"No capital punishment in the state of Illinois, detective," Timmins said.

"I know that, dickhead," Glory snapped. "But maybe we find Maura's body on the Indiana side of the lake and we get him tried there. Maybe we drag her goddamned body across the border. They have the death penalty there. Is it still the electric chair?"

"I think so," Jake interjected. "Put him on simmer."

Timmins stood up. "Nice try. Very funny. Let's go, Rich."

Rich Baker tried to rise, momentarily lost his balance and braced himself against the table. His breath had stopped. His heartbeat was gone. All that surrounded him had become a blur of emptiness. "Yeah, let's go," he whispered, standing straight up.

"We're done here, yes?" Timmins said, turning Rich away from the table.

Glory pulled turned and swept her hands toward the doorway. "Be my guest. And, really, have a nice fucking day."

As the door closed behind them, Jake McKay moved away from the table. He looked at Glory. "I thought I was going to be the bad cop."

"You missed your cue, buster," she replied.

"Good job, kid," Jake said somewhat begrudgingly.

And Glory actually believed he might have meant it.

5

The lady with the dog. Goddamn it, he hated that silver-haired old broad with the yapping fucking rat that she swathed in a red sweater each time she took it out to shit. And here she was waggling to the elevator with her fat ass up in the air before Rich could close the doors. The dog came first, a virtually hairless beige zygote with huge ears and black marble eyes that bulged as if someone was squeezing its throat – something that Rich would love to be doing at that moment. At the other end of the chain was smoky old Eleanor or Evelyn or Edie or whatever-the-fuck her name was, eyeing him up and down with lips as tight as a razor cut. Her gaze scurried over the tattered sweat suit and landed on the blood-stained hands, then ran back up again and down and up.

She didn't say a word. Never did. But Rich knew there was a mad kinetic energy forming and reforming ideas in her head that she was dying to articulate. Things like: "Where's the bimbo half your age? Where's your suit; lying on the gym floor with her cheerleading sweater? What's with the sweatshirt, all the better to hide your forty-five year-old gut from the teenagers?" Or, most frightening: "Did you finally kill her? Well, did you?"

She had been there one night, in this same elevator, when Rich and Maura had returned from some sort of bigwig reception. They had driven there, Maura had gotten them home and into the parking garage below the apartment. They had fought the whole way, and now it was continuing in the elevator. As usual, the drink and heady attention paid to him made Rich's mind swirl and his muscles twitch with aggression while rendering Maura into little more than flesh and bone jewelry on his arm. He didn't remember who started it; hell, no one ever started it. It was as if they were trained to perform on cue the moment they left the crowd, two of Pavlov's dogs conditioned to fight at the sound of silence. His fist was gnarled into her fur coat at her throat and he twisted. Her eyes burned furiously from the pressure around her neck and from her own anger. She pounded him on the chest. They didn't even notice the elevator stopping on the first floor.

When the doors opened the old lady got in, and Rich and Maura froze, shaking, sweating, still tied up in one another's clothes, fury in their eyes. Rich instinctively loosened his grip. Without a word, Maura released her gloved hand from his chest and swung at him, a huge roundhouse windmill swing that connected with a sickening crack against his ear. He grabbed her and pinned her against the wall. The old lady stood stiff and white in the corner. Rich turned to her. "What are you looking at, you dried up old cunt?" he snarled.

And now, here she was again. The elevator doors hissed shut. Rich made her reach across him with her bony, blue-veined hand rattle-trapped in cheap jewelry and punch in her own floor number. Fuck her. She smelled like cold cream and sweat. It made him want to puke. So did the lurching and swaying of the elevator. Jesus, the hangover was tenacious. It

64

beat and screamed through him, mixed with adrenaline in the blender of the day's events that still seemed terrifyingly real, yet unreal at the same time. He was reasonably sure he was dying, that the storm of booze and bad habits that raged through him had at last knocked his soul off its foundation. An uncontrollable spasm shuddered through him. If he had a drink. Maybe just a drink.

The elevator slowed with a gut bouncing motion and stopped. The doors swung open. The dog was out in a yip. Then the old lady exited and Rich followed. He swore he heard her make a farting noise with her pursed lips when she stopped at her door, as if she were spitting the horrible sight of him onto the floor.

Rich Baker's anemic, stuttering hand unlocked his door and he walked inside his home. The fifty-seventh floor apartment was both a testament to his success and a triumph of architectural design. The wondrous and ever-changing skyline of Chicago poured in through two huge walls of floor-to-ceiling windows for an effect the architect had called "kinetic artwork." No curtains or blinds of any kind were employed to keep the awesome vista out or lock anyone's privacy in. The living, dining and kitchen areas were a sprawl of contiguous open space that was tenuously segmented by well-placed sculptures and furniture. The couches and matching chairs were auburn leather, a dining room table and chairs were green-tarnished copper twisted into funky curlicues. Koa wood, with its distinctive whorls and high gloss, dominated the walls that were accented in chrome. It was a man's place, a man-looking place. Rich had planned every inch of it with the architect because it was his downtown place, a second home, which he used when he stayed in the Loop. The family home was a brick mansion

up in Lake Forest, some thirty miles north of the city. Maura
had decorated that one.

He fluidly moved toward the liquor cabinet without even
turning on a lamp. The crystal clear cold of the night allowed
all the ambient lights from the surrounding buildings to run into
the apartment, illuminating it mysteriously, unevenly in a
dazzling imbalance of colors and white. Just enough to make
getting through easy.

He slid open the mirrored and chrome door of the cabinet
and removed a bottle; he didn't even look, anything would do,
anything with a snarl under the cap. He poured the liquid three
fingers deep into a crystal tumbler and brought it shakily to his
lips. But something stopped him, inches away. His hands, the
blood, caked and flaking and now umber because of age and
lighting. He moved to the nearest light, the soft blue glow
emanating from an aquarium to his left. He held both hands in
the light, watched it weave through his fingers. The filth of the
day, the filth of the actions, made him nauseous. Her blood.
Maura's blood. Jesus, what had it come to?

The glass of booze shook. A face glared back at him
through the cloudy water, the face of an old, red-eyed man with
skin that sagged beneath its own weight and puckered up in
black-rimmed bags under the eyes. Once when he was a child
his father bought him a Halloween costume, a decaying skeleton
man, something like that. The horrible rubber mask of a twisted
and mutilated face full of pustules and dripping eyes so
frightened him that he could not bear to let it cross even the
minutest slit of his vision. Even wearing it, hiding behind it,
frightened him; the rubbery smell, the feeling that it was
crushing his face, the fear of not being able to breathe through
the tiny nostril holes.

Now this was the face staring at him through the reflection in the aquarium. And these were the gnarled and bloodied hands of the monster, offering him a cup of poison. But he could not rip off the mask and go running into his daddy's arms where it was safe and warm.

He shook himself loose of the vision and pulled away. He could hear Maura's voice deep in his memory. He walked across the great room, not feeling his legs or his heart. On the mantel over the marble fireplace was a photograph of the two of them at Jackson Hole, Wyoming. They were both young. No boils or melting skin on his face there. He was strong and invincible, ruggedly handsome with a wide open smile that had long since disappeared. She was luminous and beautiful, with cascading red hair and eyes as green as dew soaked ferns. Their lives had not yet been polluted by the acid rain of distrust and betrayal and, ultimately, hatred that had fallen into it, soaking everything to the bones until they shuddered painfully.

They had always called this trip their coming out party. Rich had been a struggling junior-level assistant in a venture capital company, a glorified go-for whose most compelling responsibility was riding with clients in the limo to and from the airport. It was during one of these situations that he saved a huge deal for the company by persuading a reluctant investor not to back out. For that bit of resourcefulness, his bosses had rewarded him with a bonus, a promotion and a trip to the company condo where he and Maura spent idyllic days skiing on flaking snow beneath crystalline azure skies and nights between silk sheets, their first taste of the good life. To Rich, it was like blood in the jaws of a wolf. His days, his nights, the myopic focus of his existence were committed to the hunt, the tracking, the instinct to bury himself in the camouflage of his emotions. He drove himself through the topography of a changing economy to seek, stalk and kill for the blood taste of money. Within five years the junior executive had bought out the original partners, but the cost was more than dollars. He wouldn't know it until it was too late, but every deal pulled him further and further from Maura, perhaps only a few inches at a time, like a fabric being dangerously stretched until the threads begin to break. Theirs had been an enormous love. There was primitive fury in their passion, a heat that singed the fibers of their souls. They knew it, were frightened by and inexorably drawn to it. It was a cocoon in which they could hide from their own fears until there was no other world outside. And now it was not just gone, it was dead.

It was also on this trip, the one captured in this photograph, that Sean was conceived. At least that's the way they figured it. His photo was on the shelf, too. A youngster in a baseball uniform. A product, perhaps a victim, as it turned out, of their love.

A pain as acute and real as a blade tore through him, and he heard himself howl, the broken wolf alone on a mountain. He threw the glass of booze across the room. It shattered against a chrome sconce on the wall, popping the light bulb inside it and making a spider pattern on the Koa wood. He tore at his clothes, ripping off the strange pants and shirt. His fingers unconsciously probed the white splatter of scar tissue on his abdomen where Maura had once deposited a scissors blade. In a few seconds he was trembling beneath the needle heat of the water cascading from a shower head and watching his wife's blood swirl off his body and disappear down the drain.

6

Darkness forgave the house its many sins; the way it leaned slightly to the north; the constant fatigue of the front porch that sagged beneath the entrance like a frown; the chips and scabs in the hideous dirt gray asphalt shingle siding. Night covered all these ugly things, making the amber glow that emanated from the windows a vision of pure beauty and joy for Glory Kane, as she dragged herself up the front steps toward the beckoning light and the warmth it promised.

The chilly night air was seasoned with the sounds of its occupants. A tomcat howled needlelike in the alley. A siren answered in the distance. The refinery huffed and puffed far away. It was past midnight, not much, but enough to coalesce with the cold and pump shoots of weary aching through the detective's body. She fumbled with the keys and desperately clung to the folders of paperwork that fanned beneath her arm as she kicked open the screen door. A few more seconds of rattling the key in the slot, and she was greeted by the familiar aroma of her home.

The inside of the old two-story belied its exterior. Here was a cheerful environment of forest green and tan with an eclectic array of furniture, a burgundy overstuffed sofa, mismatched coffee tables that she had painstakingly stripped and repainted to integrate into the decor, four purposely mismatched wooden chairs around an ancient butcher block table. The old roll top desk that occupied one corner of the living room was home to a virtual skyline of files and folders.

There was no man here. But did she really need one? Certainly there had been some in her life, but not one – not a single one – who could accept her choice of profession with its endless hours and its constant danger. Her last serious relationship was more than eighteen months ago, and there were no prospects on the horizon. So, the hell with it. The hell with them, with men.

But sometimes, like tonight, wouldn't it be great to have someone here, waiting? Someone who could just...

She shook out of her coat while dropping the stack of files on the desk and glided quickly into the kitchen. She opened the refrigerator. The hint of food awakened Glory's appetite that had gone into hiding shortly after she had returned to the office. She had eaten a donut with the texture of a hockey puck sometime early evening, and now her stomach growled as she removed a plastic bowl of spaghetti with noodles dried and crusted on the ends and a cyclone of sauce in the center.

What she wanted was a drink. She was a raw nerve, stripped of skin and muscle, tendrils pointing straight up to receive, painfully, even the slightest gust of wind. Wine, just a glass, was what she needed to dull the sensation. So, she nestled the cold plastic bowl beneath her arm and rummaged past old lettuce, brown and disfigured, a carton of milk and some eggs, finally locating the bottle at the back of the shelf. Just a couple of sips would, perhaps, dissolve her anxiety to a mere frenzy. God, if she could just rewire herself, she thought. But she had always been too proud, too driven, too manic to dwell in any other skin.

She had worked her way through college, three jobs, five years. Thought criminology was a huge opportunity for a woman. Got her degree. Then went to the academy, where she discovered she could shoot, believe it or not, better than anyone in her class, even though she had never fired a gun before. She came out top of the class, became a patrol cop. Then six months ago, a detective. On her own. It was a good gig, although she couldn't get used to the devastation that crime deposits in its wake - druggies twisted into room corners, dead before they could extract the needles from their arms, hysterical babies with cigarette burns on their backs, c-store clerks with their chests blown open for sixty bucks, a case of beer and potato chips. Many nights she brought their faces, their agony, home with her, but somehow she couldn't see herself any other way.

She plopped the bowl of spaghetti into the microwave and programmed the buttons. It whirred to life. While the spaghetti popped and sizzled, she poured her wine into the crystal glass on the kitchen counter. If anything, she knew how to drink it right, even if it had gone a little sour in the fridge. She brought it to her nose, took in the bouquet, swirled it in her glass. Took a sip through her teeth and swished it in her mouth. Then she took another slow sip for real. It snaked through her warmly, tingling her arms and fingers. Just what she wanted.

The images of the day melted and ran down the edges of Glory Kane's memory. She had worked on Rich Baker as best she knew how, cajoling, manipulating, listening, going easy, going hard, knowing that everything still had not entirely jelled.

She knew all too well her own chameleon colors, coming on concerned and almost sympathetic, then snarling and snapping with the nastiest of dogs. Rich Baker was a car wreck with more damaged brain cells than he could count. But beneath the wobbling, frantic shroud of his hangover, she could see a tough nut, a guy who was no dummy. Most notably, there was something in his eyes, a distant dark sorrow, perhaps. It lurked in his background somewhere, like a child hiding behind a bush, only peeking out curiously, refusing to reveal itself. He was a lost soul, she thought, or worse, he had lost his soul somewhere along the way, discarded it like a torn shirt. What wasn't there, what she couldn't see even in those angry moments when he spoke of his wife, was any trace of hatred. No, the words came out in an almost invisible sadness, a resignation, as if he had given up. Then again, maybe he was a good actor. That's why she wouldn't let up, and by the time Glory was done with him, his face was even more pallid and pasty and his eyes had become glassy and unfocused. Did she get all she could have gotten from him? Well, probably not, but it was too late to worry about that.

She turned her attention to the other events of the day. The search team at the abandoned steel mill had found virtually nothing. No body, no other blood. A stamped out cigarette where Baker said the car had originally been. But no sign of Maura Baker, dead or alive.

Glory had phoned Jim Arsenault, Maura's attorney, immediately after the interrogation, desperate to not leave the office before speaking to someone, anyone, who may know the whereabouts of the woman.

"Well, I haven't seen nor heard from Maura in, perhaps, two weeks or so," Arsenault's soothing, gentle voice came through the phone lines. "Why? Is something wrong?"

Glory explained the situation. Arsenault's response was not unexpected, "My God. I can only pray she is alive," he whispered, genuinely upset. He then cleared his throat and regained his composure. "So, you think Richard has done this to her, perhaps killed her?"

"It's a little too early for that speculation," Glory said. "Right now we just want to find her."

"Dead or alive," Arsenault finished the thought. "My God. My holy, holy God."

"You are handling, uh, representing Maura in this divorce, is that correct?"

"Yes."

"How is it going?"

"Well, it's a very simple process, really, or should be, as far as I'm concerned. The couple had no property, no possessions, no home, a beat up Volkswagen beetle, when they married. All assets were acquired after their union, and the state is very clear on distribution of undisputed joint property in divorce situations."

"Fifty-fifty," Glory said.

"Precisely."

"What did that mean in ballpark dollars and cents for Maura?"

"Oh, if she keeps the home in Lake Forest and with the distribution of other assets, three, four million dollars."

"A lot of money."

"Indeed."

"Has Richard been resistant to the concept of paying out this much?"

"You can say that. Nothing about the divorce is pretty, although nothing about any divorce is pretty. But this one is very rancorous, lots of shouting, name calling..."

"Bitterness?"

"Yes. Very much so."

"Hypothetically, Mr. Arsenault, could something in Rich Baker have snapped, maybe set him off, out of control, to the point of..." she paused to find the right words.

Arsenault found them for her, "Murder? Hypothetically? Nothing is out of the question. Richard Baker is a very, shall we say, passionate man, very driven, very used to getting, having his own way. He doesn't like being disappointed."

"I see," Glory said.

"On the other hand, the murder of his wife, particularly in the rather dubious scenario that you outlined, doesn't seem like Rich at all."

"In what way?"

"Rich is a strategist, a planner. His ideas always have beginnings, middles, and conclusions. It doesn't make sense that he would leave so many loose ends; I mean, passing out or falling asleep in the car, blood all over the place. Too sloppy for him, much too sloppy."

"What if he was incapacitated in some way? Drunk?"

Arsenault's voice had a shrug in it. "In cases of impairment, anything can happen, I suppose."

"Mr. Arsenault, thank you for your help. Please call me if you hear anything from or about Maura." She gave him the phone number.

"Certainly, if there is any way I can help, any way at all."

74

The bell rang as the microwave stopped and she removed the bowl, refilling her glass with her other hand. Sitting down, she began to eat with one hand as she spread out the Rich Baker file and the photos of him, his clothes, the scene in Maura's home and the contents of her purse. Then she suddenly remembered something else. She set down her fork and pushed away from the table. Going to her coat, she rifled through the pockets until she found what she was looking for. As she had left headquarters, Mancuso from forensics had bolted up the stairs and handed it to her. Glory had simply stuck it in her coat pocket. An envelope, bright yellow and red, Kodak, its flap hanging loose like the tongue of a dog. She opened the envelope, as she walked back to her kitchen table, and removed a stack of photographs. Color pictures. Pages of red heat. As she sat back down and picked up her fork again, she spread the photos on the table next to her plate. A soft amber light spilled over the images from the plastic Tiffany rip-off that hung over her table, but she could make out the images very clearly. Immediately she knew she had found a face to put with the soft voice on Maura Baker's answering machine. The glorious, beaming redhead in the center of virtually each shot had to be her, had to be Maura.

Maura, hair afire against a neon backdrop of elephants and palm trees, was seated at a table strewn with the detritus of dinner. She was intimately leaning toward a man, her lips inches away from his ear as if some secret had been caught, but not heard. And the man wasn't Rich Baker. Glory leafed through the shots to find more of the same, obviously taken the same night, a strikingly handsome couple enjoying one another and the night. An intimate dinner? No, Glory thought, as she brought food to her mouth with one hand and shuffled through

75

the photos with the other. Some kind of party. There were several group shots, a dozen people, seated at the same table. Empty bottles of wine formed a miniature city skyline in the center of everything. In the background were waiters in turbans. It was simply a stack of photographs. Maura Baker occupied the thin confining spaces of the snapshots, alive, and seeming to enjoy the camera's presence. The photos were time-stamped two nights before Baker had been discovered in his wife's car.

The plate of lukewarm spaghetti had disappeared, tasteless and unsatisfying, and Glory stared into a bowl streaked in red swirls like a finger painting gone mad. The sight of it evoked images of the car swathed in dried blood. Deep in her heart she imagined the screams. Ice rippled through her. For an instant she became Maura Baker. She could almost sense what it was like to watch life pour out of her own body and spill onto the ground.

Her brain was on nuclear meltdown, so she gathered the photos and papers together and stacked them neatly. Maybe they would make more sense in the morning, she thought. Yes, in the morning. The morning. Then she stopped. The minuscule part of her mind that was still functioning had frozen her hand in mid motion. Glory Kane brought the photograph closer to the light above the table and looked closely. "Well, well, well," she whispered, "this is too damned easy."

Jake McKay slurped the last piece of mostaccioli through his lips and chewed it with as much vigor as he had mustered to masticate the first bite. He slugged the wad of pasta into his gullet with a noisy swallow of beer and fought to suppress the garlic-laced belch that, nonetheless, escaped from his pursed mouth.

A pulsating puddle of crimson spilled across the checkered tablecloth from the humming, flashing beer sign that hung outside the window. McKay loosened his tie even more, opening it almost to the middle of his chest. He leaned back in his chair and picked at his teeth with a matchbook cover. Damn, a cigarette would taste good now, he thought to himself. Just one. That's all. But he had quit smoking nearly nine months ago and he knew what one, just one, would do to him. Who the hell wanted to live forever, anyway? That's what he used to tell himself. Until he did the math one day and figured out that he had smoked close to 15,000 cigarettes a year for nearly 30 years. That was damned near a half million cancer sticks. The thought that something could have that much control over him was scarier than cancer would ever be.

A waiter came and cleared the plates. Jake didn't have to say a word to him. The guy knew that a piece of cheesecake was automatic. It was the same ritual every time McKay came in. Within half a minute a huge piece of Eli's world famous Chicago cheesecake was sitting in front of him, this one swirled with blueberries. Jake went into it like a man possessed. Yeah, he had given up smoking. He could live with that decision. But food? No way, baby.

As he chewed, he thought about what had transpired that day. He knew what Rodriguez was doing, putting Kane on the case. She had taken the first call; departmental protocol automatically made her lead detective. Plus, she was a woman. God only knew what havoc she might have wreaked if she had been taken off. What if she had sued? Women were doing that every time a guy asked them out, for chrissakes, or because their boobs were too small and when the doc fixed them with silicone and a few got sick, they all went after the surgeons for millions. What the hell for, he didn't understand. If they didn't want guys hitting on them, then why the hell did they go and get bigger boobs? What the hell did they think guys would do?

Anyway, with the political climate what it was, the department didn't need the publicity. Problem was, Kane wasn't ready for the case and she was already making noise like there was more to the story than met the eye. Bullshit, McKay thought, jamming a huge piece of confectionary into his maw. The sooner we wrap up this prick, guilty or not, the better off we'll be. And this detective wasn't going to let some namby-pamby broad with a conscience prevent him from doing it.

He belched again, mingling the garlic from his mostaccioli with the syrup from the blueberries.

7

Rich Baker had slept like a corpse, unbreathing, it seemed. Exhaustion had lain upon him more like a rock than a blanket. But when he opened his eyes he could feel it. The hangover was gone. His head, clear. He could stand and walk without pain or hesitation. He had slept perhaps only four hours. Morning was just stirring. A smear of pink meandered between the buildings outside the huge panoramic windows. Yet, somehow, those precious few hours of sleep had eradicated his queasiness. Power sleep. He could do it when he was younger, almost at will. Take a cat nap and get up charged and ready to rock. That was how he felt now. Cured. At least in this one sense it was going to be a better day. At least he could confront its challenges with a clearer head. He stood up. He had work to do. He moved quickly through the living room and into the bath. Fifteen minutes later he emerged and greeted the new day that rushed in through his windows.

It was the way the sun rose every morning, its angle, the way its light bounced and reflected off the steel and glass of the buildings that turned this wall of glass in Rich Baker's apartment into a huge mirror. He stood before it, seeing himself, a ghost floating in the ethereal mist of dawn. His white shirt was perfectly starched. He liked it that way. Straight. Blindingly white. Coming back at him through the glass. The sun ricocheted off his gold cufflinks, firing blazing stars back into the room. He adjusted his necktie then reached for his suit coat. Yes, okay. This was good. But the day that erupted in the sky before him was permeated with the anxiety of what was happening in his life, and its reality colored the world differently, gave it a different texture, a new, uncomfortable shape, a bitter taste. Oh, Jesus, he had seen the world change like this one other time.

Sean.

And it took so long, so long to right itself. Perhaps it hadn't actually sprung back to its original shape, this world. Maybe he only thought it had, and it was the booze that put just enough haze on the reality to create this illusion. And now, the claws and teeth of his true life had begun to tear away the haze. Maura. Unbelievable. Was it true? Dead? No, not possible. There is a mistake. Yeah, but shit, he'd heard those voices inside before. They cried to him when Sean was killed. He fixed them. Fixed them good.

He slid into his suit coat, tugging at the shirt cuffs to expose just enough of the white edge. Paramount in his plan today was appearing calm, controlled, and perfect for Miles Lundeen. How was this, this fucking mess, going to fly with Lundeen? Christ, it could screw up everything, blow the plans sky high, wipe him—wipe them both—out. Innocent. Baker had to be innocent. He double-checked his tie, running his index finger into the crease beneath the knot, making a perfect dimple. He thought. What, me? You've got to be shitting me if you think that I'd, even for a second, be remotely connected with something this terrible. My God, Miles, it's ridiculous, absurd.

Look at me. Just look at me. It was all a play, this confidence, this bravado. He had perfected it over the years. Rich Baker had, in fact, built his fortune on this game, from the first time he walked into Union Station with a briefcase packed solid with a quarter of a million dollars.

He was there to meet a man he'd seen only in newspaper photographs, some second-tier politician, but a guy who could deliver the variances Baker's company needed. As he waited for the guy in a narrow corridor near a row of metal lockers, his eyes tingled with anxiety as they scanned the crowd. His breath was quick, uncontrolled. There was always a chance that the whole thing was a set up; that this alderman would be a stooge for the cops, and the minute the transaction took place, they'd swoop down like the cavalry. So, Baker learned early, even that first time that what and who he was looking for wasn't necessarily who he was waiting for. So, when the guy finally showed, the game plan changed. Baker took control and led him through the crowd, cutting back and forth, knifing between anonymous people shuffling in and out, watching for the same person to appear twice. That was all it took. Seeing the same guy or guys two times meant he was being followed. Baker would take as long as it took to feel confident he had dodged them, or assured that he was not being followed. Finally, he ducked into an alcove as the exasperated alderman followed like a puppy. One more check to ensure they were alone, and the exchange took place. It was like that the first time, and every time thereafter.

Rich Baker lifted an overcoat from the back of a chair, slipped into it, turned and walked across his living room and into the hallway to the elevator. The doors dinged and opened. Mercifully, it was empty. He would ride alone, he hoped, all the way down. As the elevator lurched downward, his stomach growled. He still hadn't eaten. Food was so far from his mind. Coffee tingled through his veins, giving him a little jolt, scrubbing out the booze. His head was, remarkably, getting clearer. Once again, he had defeated a hangover. Quiet. God, the quiet of the ride as the light jumped from number to number.

The elevator dinged as the light on the lobby key extinguished. Thank God. Get outside into the cold air. Walk four blocks to the office. It was going perfectly, so far. Then the doors parted and the serenity and isolation of the morning were shattered.

First warning, a stroke of white light. He reflexively turned from it. Flash bulb. Sun guns from the video cameras. He could see, wincing against the sudden, sharp lights, heads converging on him. Dozens. Through the glass, television vans, video dishes atop. They came and came, these people, sweeping him up and into a tide. Microphones came out of the forest of bodies.

"Mr. Baker, where is your wife?"

"Did you murder your wife?"

"What will this do to the project?"

"Is it true you've hidden the body?"

Baker took a deep breath. What to do? Flee, get away from them. No, wait. Stay calm. That's the plan. Remember the plan?

He stopped and held up both hands. "My only comment to you is that I categorically and unequivocally deny being involved in any way with my wife's disappearance. Now, please, let me get on with the task of clearing my name."

The reporters squeezed tighter and the questions erupted again. Baker, again, held up his hands and pushed forward. As calmly as possible he tried to make his way through, finally resorting to flailing at the mass of arms and equipment, forcing himself through like cutting through a jungle of thick growth.

He broke through the lobby, out the glass doors, but they followed him, jogging to keep up. The cold air grabbed him. Ordinarily, he'd walk the four blocks to the office, but not now. With the reporters in pursuit, he jogged across the lawn, stepping gingerly over a low wrought iron trim fence, and burst out into the street, flagging a cab that had just turned the corner. The yellow car slowed, but before it could stop, he opened the door and folded himself inside. The voices followed.

"Mr. Baker, where is your wife?"

"Who could have killed her?"

"When was the last time you saw her?"

"If not you, then who?"

"Is it possible she's alive?"

Thump. The door closed. Muting the sound. Baker gave the address to the cabbie, who turned and looked over the seat. "Four blocks? You want me to drive you four blocks?" he growled, words coming in a thick accent. Fucking camel jockey, Baker thought. The cab smelled of putrid air freshener. The guy was wearing a fucking turban, for chrissakes. Baker reached into his pocket and pulled out a neat stack of bills held tight by a money clip. He pulled off a fifty and tossed it to the driver. "Take the long way," Baker said. "I need to go in the back entrance."

"Now I understand," the cabbie said, knifing with a jolt into the flow of traffic.

"Did you see what's out front?" Miles Lundeen cried, the veins suddenly visible through the knife blade silver hair on his temples. He stood up from behind the triangular marble desk, eerily empty of accoutrements, as Rich Baker entered the office.

"What, no 'how're you doing, pal? You okay?' Nothing like that?" Baker said, navigating his way towards one of the huge leather wing backed chairs in front of Lundeen's desk. "Jesus, Miles, I went through a fucking blender yesterday."

"You! I had to run a gauntlet of press to get into my own office!" Lundeen said.

"They were at my apartment, too," Rich said, He dropped into the chair and reached into a humidor and withdrew a cigar. Be cool, he thought. He's a little more excited than you anticipated. Stay calm. Rich clipped the end of the cigar and lit it. "Don't sweat it. They'll be gone tomorrow. You know the type. It's one day's news."

Lundeen flapped his arms. "Jesus Christ, this is a major debacle! They think you're fucking O.J."

"Now wait, just cool it, Miles," Baker said from the chrome and suede chair, trying to remain calm by attempting to draw life from the cigar. "You know I'm not involved, for chrissakes. You've known me for fifteen years."

"Jesus, Rich," Lundeen said, gnawing a thumbnail and pacing the office that undulated on no less than four strategically placed levels, each a swirl of carefully choreographed marble. The office was huge, round, with one semi-circle side punctuated by a wall of Greco-Roman columns that framed a fireplace and a huge glass bar. The other half of

84

the room was bordered by curved windows that broke out to the muscular skyline of Chicago. The expanse of brilliant reflective white gave the room the look and feel of a tundra, and, right now, Miles Lundeen was like a polar bear on the prowl. "I knew, just knew, that your booze-sucking habits would explode in your face sooner or later, and it looks like they have."

"They have nothing, nada, zilch on me," Baker said, lying, but effectively quelling the rampant undertow in his guts with a plume of blue smoke that churned from the cigar.

"Nothing?" Lundeen asked. "That's not what Nate Timmins tells me." Lundeen suddenly stopped cold. He paused for a beat. "Tell me everything."

So much for lawyer/client privilege, he mused. "You talked to Timmins?"

"Of course, Rich. He works for our attorneys, and he's saying that we're—you're—in more trouble than you obviously think you are."

"He's a fucking lawyer. He has to say that. Christ, Miles, you've worked with enough of them. They tell you you're going to lose to cover their asses."

Lundeen turned and caught Rich with a sharp glare. "Rich, you're on the threshold of a murder indictment. That's serious. I don't care how you look at it. I think it's serious."

"They haven't even found her body."

"Will they?"

"I don't know."

"Or will they get enough on you from other places? You know they'll be here to see me. What am I going to say, Rich? I was with you last night." Lundeen, turned to the window and steeled himself with a few deep breaths. "Am I going to say you're a gentle, genteel man incapable of murder?"

"You could say that," Rich said, a bit of irony in his voice.

"Am I going to say you left my place in full possession of your faculties? Sober as a judge?"

Now Baker stood up. His knees threatened to buckle beneath his weight, but he stopped them through sheer force of will. "I expect you to say whatever needs to be said to get your business associate and your friend off the hook."

"All right! All right!" Lundeen said, raising his hand. "Look, just tell me what happened."

Baker then recounted the story as best he could, finishing it with a declaration. "It's no big deal."

"Rich, it is a big deal. The mayor has already called."

"Shit."

"Yeah, and he's wondering if that's it, if everything's falling apart."

"Okay, I can fix it with him. I'll call him today."

"He won't take your fucking call," Lundeen screamed, pounding a fist on his desk. "He's going to practically deny he ever heard of you. He's running away from this as fast as he can."

Baker sat motionless for several seconds. Finally, he spoke. "Just give me a few days to figure this out. I can figure it out."

"I got a call from Huang at four o'clock this morning," Lundeen said.

Huang was the CEO of the Chinese corporation that was largely funding the project that would result in the next tallest building in the world being built, once again, in Chicago.

"Huang? Is he in the states?"

"No, he called from Singapore."

"He knew about it already?"

"Obviously."

"How the hell did he know?"

"I don't know, man, I don't fucking know! What difference does it make?"

Baker exhaled a huge cloud of blue cigar smoke. His legs began to shake as if they were freezing. "What'd he say?"

"Rich, this is a major problem with them. You know how they are, for chrissakes. All that Shogun bullshit, honor, integrity—all that crap."

Baker interrupted. "Shogun is Japanese, not Chinese."

"Well, whatever-the-fuck it's called, my God, you dishonor or disgrace your company by wearing the wrong fucking colored suit or not bowing low or long enough, and they bury you in a tiny office where your total responsibilities are to sit at your desk and shut the fuck up all day until you fucking die. Murder? You think they're going to stand for murder?"

"I didn't murder anybody, goddamnit," Rich shouted, throwing the cigar into a large ash tray and standing up.

"Well, I'm not sure that matters."

"What are you trying to say to me, partner?" He dropped the last word like a stone.

"I'm saying, Rich, that Huang wants me to fire you."

Rich gasped audibly, then tried to cover it with a laugh. "You can't fucking fire me; we're partners."

Lundeen moved slowly to the edge of the window and looked out. The Gothic filigree of the top of a building—green copper smudged and streaked by decades of weather—sat in the center of one bank of windows as if it were framed. He paused. Rich could only hear the shallow spurts of his breath going in and out. Finally, Lundeen said, "Come over here, Rich."

87

Baker obediently moved to him. Lundeen put his hand on Rich's shoulder and gazed out the window. Pillows of clouds wrapped themselves around the jutting tops of the skyscrapers beyond the glass. "Look out there," Lundeen said, pointing. "Right there between those two buildings you see clouds and sky. Know what I see? The world's tallest building. Nova Center. A hundred and twelve stories looking down, down on the Sears Tower. I named it Nova Center because it's going to explode on the skyline like a star."

"I know why it was named that," Rich said quickly. "It was my idea." He had been involved virtually since the beginning, had helped ride the concept over the dangerous terrain of investors and politicians.

Lundeen continued. "Now, the average person walking down the street thinks you build the world's greatest skyscraper with steel and glass and concrete, and that by piling more of that stuff until the pile is higher than the next guy's, voila', you've got the world's tallest building. But you and I know, Rich, that materials don't make a building any more than blood and bones and ligaments make a man. It's the soul, the guts, the fortitude, the vision, the will that separate men. And to build—to fill that empty space with a vision—requires a wicked brew of politics and influential friends and well-placed cash; of making sure that so-and-so is happy, 'cause if he's happy, the mayor will be happy, and if the mayor is happy, then the bond underwriters are secure, and the investors are confident, and the publicity is positive, the media rap is good, and the taxpayers aren't squawking. And all of that political and social infrastructure must be in place before the footers are poured."

Baker turned away from the window and faced his partner. "Seriously? Really? You're lecturing me on what it takes to do a deal like this? Like I'm some kind of intern?" Rich snarled. "Give me a fucking break. I'm not your goddamned lackey. I'm the guy who made this happen!"

"I'm not taking any of that credit away from you Rich. Can't you understand the untenable position your activities have created for me? The largest investors in this deal are Chinese, and they have very strict ways of looking at things like this. Disgrace is a bad thing, bad. I love you like a brother, Richo, but word got into the chattering gums of the newscasters that Miles Lundeen's business partner on the world's tallest building is about to be indicted for murder of his own wife, for chrissakes, and now I've got unhappiness running down the line like piss down the pant leg of a two-year old. For the love of God, they've even named this case, 'The Socialite Murder.' It's the perfect, goddamned media story, a beautiful socialite possibly killed by her husband. It will dominate the media. And if Woo and Huang back out, the world's tallest building falls to the ground and breaks like glass, before it's even built." He stopped, turned and walked back to his desk. "And you may not be able to see it, but I can. I can see it as clearly as I can see it standing there, tall and regal and proud. I can hear it groan, hear the explosion of it as it shatters." He took a deep breath and wiped his open palm against his forehead. Not looking at Rich he almost whispered, "And I can't live with that. Can you?"

Rich was temporarily frozen by Lundeen's icy stare. He coughed subconsciously. "What do you want me to do?" Rich moved back to the chair and fell into it, picking up the discarded cigar and relighting it in a storm of blue smoke.

Lundeen eased himself into his throne-like chair and puffed out his cheeks as he carefully chose his words. "You have to get out, Rich, out of the deal."

"Fuck!" Rich cackled, spitting more smoke into the air. "You snap your fucking fingers and I'm out? It's that easy? I don't think so, pal. I don't think so."

"Rich, listen, we're friends, been friends for a lot of years. You know I'm not just going to cut you loose. It's only temporary. I'll write you a check, today, two million just for you to back off and wait. Plus we're willing to cover the defense costs. That gives you more than enough walking-around money until this thing blows over. Then we pull you back in when the smoke clears."

"I don't want any goddamned money, Miles. That isn't the point! You sashay in front of the windows talking about your dream, your vision. But it's not just yours, it's ours! Who got you the fucking money? Who brought Woo and Huang into the picture? The Columbine family? Who spent three weeks living on stewed cat in a horse shit Moscow hotel getting that Russkie syndicate involved? Who made the deal, for chrissakes?"

Lundeen leaned back in his chair. "Rich, I'm the last guy who would underestimate your contributions," he paused, drifting into thought. "Okay, I'll make it five million, but you gotta promise to just back off, get as far away from this as you can. Stay out of the office. Be gone. Until it's over. Then we talk again."

Rich Baker uncoiled from his chair, all six foot four, jamming the cigar once again into the ash tray as he stood. "Hey, Miles, fuck you," he said turning.

Lundeen leaned on his elbows and massaged his temples. Then he slammed his palms on the desk and lurched forward. "Cut me some fucking rope here, will you, Rich? In a couple of months I'll be launching this project at a major press conference. The television stations will be there. The mayor will be there. For chrissakes, the fucking president is sending us a congratulatory message over the tweet or twit or whatever it is. Do I need the fucking TV cameras swinging toward you on the dais? Yeah, yeah, that would be real fucking sweet. I can see the headlines now. 'Man Indicted for Murder Announces Building Plans'." By now, Lundeen was fully standing. He caught his breath and dropped back into his chair. His voice crept back to a whisper. "Rich, Rich, Jesus, I can't do it. And I swear to you, you'll not fuck this up for me."

There was a frightening calm to Lundeen's demeanor, and Rich Baker, again, tasted the bitter bile that fear boils in the stomach. From the instant he had awakened in his wife's car in that strange, putrid-smelling place, he had been sparring with fear, a dark adversary unlike any he had ever encountered. Sometimes the recoil was so great he could feel his life force draining through his feet. Sometimes it was an annoyance, an itch, a healing cut, a sore muscle that only hurt when he moved a certain way. But no singular moment, not the interrogation by the cops, the cruel dreams that ran through him like bad fuel, nor the blurred, bleak prospects of the future, chilled him as desperately as the sudden malevolent tranquility that descended upon Miles Lundeen. God, yes, he knew what had instantly transpired somewhere in the whirling gears and pulleys of Lundeen's psyche; a decision had been made. And he raced through the huge spectrum of possibilities, knowing the potential ultimate one. Because, when it came down to business, no strategy, no tactic, regardless of legality, morality, or integrity was outside the reach of Miles Lundeen. People could become friends via their utility to his needs, but if they became problems, or obstacles to success, nothing was more important than mitigating them. Baker understood this because Lundeen was simply the other side of the ink smear that was his own life. Lundeen's veneer was thin as tissue and transparent as glass, because he and Rich shared the same soul, and few crevices or corners were unknown to the other. So, looking at Miles Lundeen now, seated at his desk, not speaking, the sprawling marble sanctum surrounding him, a gaping emptiness temporarily shrouded only in clouds through the windows, Baker realized the grim truth, realized what he would do if he were Lundeen. He gave no thought to how he would do it, what method or madness he would employ. But he knew that somehow, some way, he would make the problem disappear. Permanently.

Fifteen minutes after Miles Lundeen was certain Rich Baker had departed, and after he had allowed himself to shake uncontrollably until finally quelling the tremors with two stiff shots of Jameson's, he picked up his telephone and pushed a speed dial number. The rhythmic tune of the trilling was connecting him to another world. He heard a single ring and immediately a voice.

"Yes."

"Mr. Huang?" Lundeen said.

"Have you taken care of things?" Huang's perfect English was seasoned slightly with the short-clipped cadence of a Chinese accent.

"Yes, sir, I have."

"You are certain there is no potential for interference?"

"Well, sir, you know Richard Baker as well as I..."

"If you are not certain of his absolute disassociation with us and the impossibility of his reappearance, then you have not taken care of things as we discussed."

Lundeen gasped silently and began to shake again. Thank God he was thousands of miles away; although, for all he knew, Huang could see right through the phone.

"Mr. Lundeen, are you still there?" Huang said.

"Yes, sir." He caught his breath. "Sir, I will personally ensure that Mr. Baker is now and forever disassociated from this project. He will not interfere in our progress."

"Yes," was the curt reply. "Then we are finished."

8

The photographs hit Jake McKay's lap with an emphatic thump, leaping out of the envelope in a symmetrical fan. "What's this?" he asked, looking up at Glory Kane, who was maneuvering the car out of the parking lot and onto the street.

"Forensics found an undeveloped roll of film under the passenger seat in Maura Baker's car. I had them develop these," Glory replied.

McKay pulled the shots out and glanced at them as if studying a pinochle hand. "This must be our Mrs. Baker, I assume?"

"That would be my guess."

"Yowie, zowie, she's a babe-o-matic."

"Yeah, I suppose," Glory replied tersely.

He pointed at one of the shots. "And this guy here, I'm guessing is what's-his-name, the guy she's doing?"

"Yeah, Aaron Clayton, Baker's old business partner."

"You're going to find out for sure?"

"That's our first stop, big boy. We're going to the office of Mr. Clayton, and then to the place where these pictures were taken."

"You know where they were taken? How'd you figure that out in your sleep?"

Sleep, indeed. Glory hadn't gotten more than two hours, in fits and starts. "Simple. Baker, Richard, had a matchbox in his pocket with a logo on it that said 'The Pachyderm.' Same as the ones on the table right there, as you can see. I used an extraordinarily exotic new technique to track down the address. The phone book."

"Your genius beguiles me," McKay said.

"Don't get your hopes up."

McKay grunted. "Nice party, it looks like to me." He continued thumbing through the pictures.

"Private party is my guess."

"Yeah, why do you say that?"

"The rest of the place is empty," Glory said, reaching down and pointing at a photo, her eyes still on the road. "Nobody at any of the other tables in the background."

"Maybe it was a slow night," McKay grunted.

"Check out the right hand corner of the picture."

He pulled a shot from the stack and held it closer. His eyes squinted. "Well, I'll be damned," he said.

"Saturday night," Glory said, reaching over and tapping the imprinted date on the corner of the photo. "Unless this is one lousy restaurant, it should be much more crowded on Saturday night."

"You're probably right about the private party aspect."

"It's two nights before we found Baker."

McKay placed the photos back in the envelope and set them on the seat next to Glory. "Okay, what do you think it means?"

"Well, first it means Maura Baker, if that is her, was alive three days ago."

"And that means..." he let the words hang.

"A whole bunch of people saw her that night."

"And we're going to find out who."

"Bingo," Glory said. "You catch on fast."

Within a half hour, elevator doors were opening and they were emerging into the opulent lobby of Clayton, Bedford and Walsh, International where a huge marble wall with a brushed gold logo was lit by a crystal chandelier.

"You better make sure you got all the cow shit off your shoes," Jake McKay whispered, as they made their way to the impeccably dressed and coiffed receptionist.

Glory approached, pulled out her badge and flipped it open. "Good morning, I am Detective Kane and this is my, uh, partner, Detective McKay. We need to see Aaron Clayton," Glory said.

"Oh," the receptionist said, a bit stunned. "Was he expecting you?"

"Doubtful," Jake said.

The receptionist started to push buttons on the switchboard console, but then stopped, removed her headset and moved away from her desk. "One moment. Uh, please have a seat, I'll be right back," she said, before disappearing around a partition.

Glory dropped into a huge leather couch and felt suddenly out of place. The decor seemed to stare at them as if sizing them up to see if they actually belonged here among the stunning antique furniture and vases, the undecipherable modern art mosaic that hung on the wall behind the receptionist's desk, and the huge displays of original art that lined the corridor off the lobby. Not to mention the people. People dressed in impeccable suits, men and women. Stiff, formal, very, very clean. Glory noticed them noticing her—animated, busy, whispering people—and she stirred as each flight of them swept into the lobby. She flinched apprehensively at each furtive glance. Oh no, this wasn't her; wasn't her blood and breath. She felt like a solitary cloud in a pristine sky with her same everyday coat with the loose threads and her chopped off flats that were built for getting away, not for getting laid.

A minute later the receptionist mercifully returned to her position. Sitting down, she said, "Ms. Diedre Matthews will be with you very shortly. Can I get you some coffee?"

Who was Diedre Matthews, Glory wondered. And what was "very shortly?" "No thanks," she replied.

Jake paced the expensive, plush carpet, gnawing a fingernail. As they waited, he occasionally made his way back to Glory and dropped a piquant comment like: "It's easier getting into freakin' Fort Knox than this place. Of course, Knox ain't got quite this much money."

"Investment banking pays well, I guess," Glory said.

"This don't look like no bank to me," Jake answered. "Where's the teller lines, the vault, that machine that gives you money?"

"The ATM?" Glory chuckled.

"Yeah, where is it?"

"I don't think it's that kind of bank."

"I didn't know there was more than one kind of bank. I mean, a bank is a bank, I thought."

"I guess we'll find out in a few minutes."

They waited for ten, fifteen minutes as the receptionist lolled through phone calls and a paperback novel. Jake was wearing a path in the carpet. Glory looked again at her watch. She didn't have time for this bullshit. She caught Jake's eye and sensed that he'd come to the same conclusion. The big detective shook himself into a standing position, smoothed his coat and took to the reception desk in three huge strides. He waited impatiently as the young woman repeated the name of the organization after several gentle rings, and then routed phone calls with the flick of her fingers.

Finally, Jake leaned over the desk partition and dropped his badge on the desk where it landed with an emphatic thump.

"Look, mizz receptionist, let me go through this one more time only slower so that you understand. I'm a cop and I don't have all day to sit in some fancy-assed lobby. I want to see Aaron Clayton or this Diedre Matthews now or I'm going to walk through this joint with my gun drawn and scare them out of their hiding places."

The color poured out of the receptionist's face like sand through an hour glass. "Yes, of course," she stammered, bolting out of her chair and disappearing again behind the partition.

Jake chuckled and folded his arms. He spoke to Glory. "You just gotta know how to talk to 'em, that's all."

Almost as quickly as she had disappeared, the receptionist returned, leading another woman into the lobby. "Hello, my name is Diedre Matthews, executive vice president of the company," she said, extending a hand first to Glory and then to Jake. "Mr. Clayton is not in town at the present time, but perhaps I can be of some assistance. Please follow me." Without awaiting a response from the two detectives, Diedre Matthews was leading Jake and Glory through a maze of offices into a conference room with a glass-topped table as large as an aircraft carrier. Diedre Matthews, it was a name that just seemed to fit in this world of slashing colors and artwork, Glory thought, as they entered the room. She was forty plus and hard around the eyes, like someone who had been in a tough business for a long time. Her hair was somewhere between blonde and old.

"Have I seen you before?" Diedre asked, motioning toward a chair. Glory sat down. Jake prowled.

"I can't imagine where," Glory answered.

"Have you ever done any modeling?" Diedre asked, sitting next to Glory.

"No," Glory answered.

"Hey, how about that time you dressed up like a hooker to bust a ring of pros?" Jake said. "Who said we don't need chick cops?" He pulled out a chair and fell into it.

Diedre glared at him for a second then turned back to Glory. "Well, that's not exactly what I meant. It's just that you're stunning. Your facial features, your cheekbones—you really ought to consider it. I bet it's a lot safer than police work."

"I'm sure it is," Glory answered to be polite before changing the tone of the conversation. "You say that Aaron Clayton is out of town. Any idea where he may be?"

Diedre shook her head. "He took a vacation, Wyoming to be exact. He's a hunter. Heads out to the woods without any forewarning, usually right after we've closed a big deal. To unwind, you know?" She stood abruptly, moving fluidly to a credenza upon which sat silver tea and coffee pots and an array of fancy china. "My goodness, where are my manners? Coffee, tea? Or I could get you a soft drink."

Glory nodded. "I'll have tea, no sugar, please."

"Black," was all Jake said.

The drinks were quickly poured and served and Diedre sat down again. "When he goes like this, he really goes off the grid.

He usually backpacks into the wilderness. At least, that's what we assume."

"Is he reachable?" Glory asked.

"Generally not."

"No cell phone? No internet access? Seems funny in today's day and age to be so isolated."

"Mr. Clayton, as president of the corporation, pretty much comes and goes as he wishes. It's one of the perks of the job, I guess," Diedre replied calmly, lifting her cup of coffee to her lips and gently blowing away the steam.

"When did he leave?"

"Sunday."

"A week ago or day before yesterday?"

"Day before yesterday. Might I ask what this is all about?"

"We need to question Mr. Clayton about his relationship with Maura Baker," Glory said. "Do you know her?"

Diedre hesitated, obviously pondering how to answer. "Well, as a matter of fact, yes."

The instinctive reaction of Diedre Matthews—a slight jump, as if she'd been pinched—caused Glory to reach into her canvas carrying case and extract the envelope of photographs. She pulled out a shot and dropped it on the table. "Is the man in this picture Aaron Clayton?"

Diedre inhaled deeply as if steeling herself. She paused. Then, in a soft whisper said, "Yes."

"And the woman is Maura Baker?"

"Yes."

"Sure as hell looks to me like she liked this guy," Jake said. "Or do you think she's talking business with him, what with the way she's practically sticking her tongue in his ear?" The intimacy of the couple in the photographs was palpable.

100

"Whatever Mr. Clayton and Ms. Baker's relationship is, it's their business," Diedre said.

"Well, we have reason to believe that Maura is, well, let's just say that she's missing right now, missing under suspicious circumstances."

"My goodness," Diedre replied in a breathy, somewhat frightened voice. Then she seemed to stiffen and await another word from Glory.

"You don't read the papers or watch TV or do the internet?" Jake inquired.

"No, no, I actually was in here quite, quite early," Diedre replied. Then her eyes widened. "What news are you talking about?"

"We believe, I mean it's possible, that she could have met with some violence," Glory answered.

Jake interjected, "It's all over the place. 'The Socialite Murder' they're calling it."

Deidre's hand came to her mouth. "Oh, my God. Maura's been murdered?" Her hands began to shake and she set the coffee cup down.

"We don't know that yet. For now, she is classified as missing," Glory said.

"Have you seen her in the last few days or so?" Jake asked.

"No, not for a few weeks, I guess."

"Any chance she went with Clayton out to Wyoming or wherever?" Jake said, pushing his coffee away.

Diedre stifled a nervous chuckle. "Uh, no. I don't think Maura was the type to, shall we say, appreciate the rustic charm of sleeping in a tent in the woods."

"You said you saw her a few weeks ago. Where was that?" Glory said.

"It was at a company function, a celebration party we had. We'd taken a company public, very successfully, I might add, that same day. It would have been, let's see, two weeks ago Friday."

"And that's the last time you saw her?"

"Yes."

"I wonder if Rich was there?" Glory asked, jotting a note and turning to McKay.

"Maura's Rich? Oh, heavens no. I can't imagine that," Diedre said dismissing the concept with a wave of her hand. Then she rested it on the table and her mood changed. "Her husband? What? Does he have something to do with this?" The "he" was uttered with such vituperative inflection that Glory winced.

"Do you know him?"

Diedre nodded. "Yes."

Glory continued, "You see, Diedre, we picked up Maura's husband, Rich Baker, yesterday morning. We have reason to believe he was involved in, perhaps, her disappearance or even death."

"My God, I just can't believe it," Diedre replied.

"At Mrs. Baker's home and we saw signs of a terrible struggle," Glory said.

"Oh, no. This is very hard to..." Diedre Matthews was stuttering, finding it hard to string together the words she was thinking; so she just stopped.

Jake McKay leaned forward and made a church with his puffy hands. "I understand Mr. Clayton and Mr. Baker knew one another."

"Yes, yes they did. Mr. Clayton once worked with Mr. Baker over at Nova Corporation. He, Aaron, left there, oh, about five years ago to form this corporation. I worked there at the time, also. I came with Aaron when he started this."

"And these two companies, they don't see eye to eye?" Jake asked.

"Well, we really don't overlap too much. Nova is a development corporation. Building buildings, malls, shopping centers, like that. We're an investment banking corporation."

Glory stirred in her seat. "What does that exactly mean?"

"We're involved, specifically, in helping corporations raise capital through IPOs— that's initial public offerings—where a company goes public. We also help companies raise capital through private venture firms, orchestrate mergers of companies, help corporations with investments offshore for purposes of tax savings. We're really quite diverse."

"Sounds like it," Jake said, "and I didn't understand any of it. Don't sound like a bank at all to me."

Diedre laughed. "Well, it's not really a bank, detective. It's mostly lawyers and accountant types, if that helps clarify."

"Sounds like a fun group," Jake replied, rolling his eyes.

"Work hard, play hard," Diedre said, staring at Jake . "You'd be surprised."

Glory interjected. "Back to Mr. Clayton. Can you describe his and Mr. Baker's relationship?"

"As far as I know, there really wasn't one. I mean, Aaron never talked about, or to, him, as far as I know. Once upon a time, they were pretty good friends. Used to go on these hunting trips together, in fact."

"What happened?" Glory asked.

Diedre shrugged her shoulders. "I don't think anything actually 'happened,' as you say. They simply drifted apart."

Jake made two fists and pounded them together. "No so-called friendly competition, two old warriors, nothing like that?"

Diedre shook her head. "Not that I know of."

"But this, this relationship between Clayton and Maura Baker, now there's a situation that could be some trouble, no?" McKay asked.

"I would suspect that's possible."

"Maura Baker. Were you close to her? Was she a friend?" Glory asked.

"Well, I don't really think of myself as her friend. Maura is very closed, private, keeps to herself," Diedre replied, "I mean it's not that we're not friendly, just not, uh, friends. You understand?" She touched Glory's arm gently to emphasize her point.

"A little earlier you seemed to react, shall we say, negatively at the mention of Rich Baker," Glory said. "Why was that? Did Maura ever talk to you about him?"

Diedre sighed. "This is kind of uncomfortable for me, you have to understand. I knew Rich and Maura back at Nova, and now here with Aaron, it's a whole different time, you know? Things changed between them, Rich and Maura. He drank too much, ran around. I didn't admire him, let's just put it that way. I think Maura's relationship with Aaron was as much to get back at Rich as it was to fill any space in her life." She stopped suddenly and wrung her hands, shaking her head. "No, no. Strike that. It's total speculation on my part, and I have no right to speculate."

"It's quite all right, Diedre. Your opinions help us form a picture of the folks involved," Glory replied, patting the woman's hands.

McKay broke in. "But the two of them, Clayton and Mrs. Baker, this whole relationship thing with them—it could be a problem for Rich, yeah?"

"I suspect it would make him angry at the very least."

"Angry enough to…" Jake McKay let the words hang.

"I don't know, detective," Diedre whispered.

"Had the affair between Clayton and Mrs. Baker been going on for some time?" Glory asked.

Diedre paused. "Maybe six months, maybe a little more."

"When did Rich Baker find out about it?" Jake asked.

Diedre shrugged and subconsciously played with her hair, curling and recurling it. "I really can't say." Her fingers held a twist. "I don't know."

"For a smart and intelligent corporate executive, you don't seem to pay attention to your co-workers very well," McKay said curtly, shaking his head.

"I find it both smart and intelligent—whatever the distinction between the two—to stay out of the personal lives of associates, Detective," she replied. "I have enough shit to clean up without stepping into other people's personal piles."

Glory eyed him angrily. Then she showed several more photos to Diedre. "There are other people in these photos. Do you know any of them?"

Diedre picked up the photos, one by one, and studied them for several seconds. Her eyebrows furrowed and she shook her head. "Funny, no I don't know anyone else in the photos," she said, gently handing them back to Glory. "These folks are total strangers to me. I have no idea who they could be."

"Not clients or anything like that?" McKay ventured.

"Nope. Unless they're new or prospective clients," she said, picking up one of the photos again. She studied it for several seconds, then shook her head. "No idea."

Glory took the photos and placed them back in the envelope. "You say there's no way to contact Aaron Clayton?" she asked.

Diedre paused, thinking. "It's not easy. He likes being alone, alone, alone. Strict orders not to bother him. Unless there's an emergency." She was tense now, veins bulged on her hands as she nervously entwined them.

"Well, Ms. Matthews, this would certainly fit into that category, wouldn't you say? Can you try to contact him?" Glory asked.

Diedre pushed herself away from the table. "Give me a minute." Then she left the room.

Jake was up and roaming the conference room, examining the framed prints that lined the walls in perfect symmetry. "Bet you a buck she can't get hold of Aaron Clayton," he said.

"What makes you think that?"

He turned from the artwork and moved back toward the table. "Just the way things sound and look. I wouldn't be surprised if he's as dead as Maura right now."

"Now, there's a leap that I'm not ready to make. You keep forgetting, detective, we don't know that Maura is dead," Glory interjected.

"Oh, she's dead. I've seen enough blood to convince me of that," Jake said, rubbing his hands together like an excited child. "Puzzle pieces coming together. She's having an affair with the ex pal of her husband. Old Richie/Dick, he can dig the other babes, but his wife better not get into a horizontal hold with no man. We're getting closer to motive."

106

"My instincts tell me it's not as simple as that."

"Instincts, schminstincts. Use logic. Evidence, facts, are all that matter."

"Well, I find quite frequently that it pays to go with your gut."

"That's the difference between men and women. Men think. Women react."

"Are you insinuating that women don't—or can't—think?"

Jake flinched. "You're just different; that's all I'm saying. Men are rational, women emotional. Facts versus instincts."

"You know, you're not a totally incompetent cop, but you've got a piece of undigested meat in your gut that has turned you into a nasty sonofabitch."

"What are you talking about?"

"Your whole demeanor. The way you talk to me. The way you talked to Diedre Matthews. I mean, 'For a smart and intelligent executive...', give me a break."

Jake glanced out a window at the skyscrapers. Finally he responded. "I talk to everyone the same way."

Glory shook her head. "Not really. With men your tone is jovial, sarcastic, like it's all in good fun. It's a whole different tone when you're talking to women."

"I talk to her like I'd talk to a man. That's the way it sounds to me. It's not my fault you don't hear it that way."

"Well, you better listen more closely. Seems like you're almost afraid of women like that—Diedre—and me for that matter. Composed, in control, and, in her case, making more money in a year than you—or I—make in ten. The fact that she has a title and the power to go with it."

"Don't care. She's just a source of information to me, and when we're done with her, I won't even remember her face," McKay replied. "That's all she is to me, one way or the other."

"You know, Jake, one of these days I'm going to figure you out," Glory replied. "I'm going to crack through that veneer and find out what makes you tick. Because I don't think you are what you pretend to be. Hell, I don't even think you are what you think you are."

At that moment, the door to the conference room swung open. Diedre Matthews returned and, from the look on her face, it was obvious that the news wasn't good. "I called the lodge where he usually goes; they haven't seen him or heard from him."

"Do you have any other ideas where he might be?"

"Uh, that's not all," she said visibly shaken.

"Yeah, go on," Jake prompted.

"He never even got on the plane."

9

This was the place, all right, an explosion of colors and noise. Bright crimson palm trees sprouted from planters scattered throughout the tables, giving the impression that the dining was to be done outdoors in a jungle. The centerpiece was a huge plastic elephant, complete with ornate saddle and decorative headdress. Sitar music, subtle, but pervasive, wafted through the room. Waiters in turbans and glistening white suits moved from customer to customer, carrying trays of food that cast wondrous aromas into the air. The tables were rapidly filling up. Glory looked at her watch. It was almost noon already. The day was being devoured quickly by the task at hand.

"Smells pretty good," Jake McKay said. "What is it?"

"Chutney, I think," Glory said, shrugging.

"Looks like a pretty high-end place. Big fancy hotel with a big fancy restaurant. What do you figure a room costs here a night?"

"More than either of us would ever spend."

They moved to the front of the line at the reservation desk. A dark-skinned woman, exotic and elegant in a tight white outfit, smiled at them.

"Do you have a reservation?" she asked.

"No, we don't. We'd like to speak to the manager, please," Glory said, flipping open her badge.

The girl's eyes widened and she said nothing more as she disappeared into the gaudy foliage. Moments later, Jake and Glory were being led around the counter and into a small office in the back. There, at a desk, sat a stern faced man, his lips pursed so tightly that the skin on his face seemed to converge at the point of their junction. "Do not the police at least have the common courtesy to establish an appropriate appointment prior to barging in on the threshold of one's busy lunch rush?" he asked tersely, not bothering to stand, nor offer a hand nor introduce himself.

"Sorry about that," Jake said. "But crime waits for no man and neither does the investigation of the same."

Glory shook her head. What did that mean? Jake struggled into a seat in front of the man's impeccably clean and empty desk. Glory sat down in the chair next to Jake's. "You are the manager of the restaurant?" she asked.

"I manage the entire property," he replied, barely moving his lips.

"You mean, like, the whole hotel?" McKay asked.

The man nodded almost imperceptibly.

"Just a few quick questions," she said, removing the photos from her purse. She handed them to the man. "Were these photos taken here last Saturday night?"

The man perused them for several minutes, discarding some, stacking others to the side. Finally, he looked up. "Yes," he snipped. "Am I quite finished now?"

"Look, hotel manager man, you want to do this here or in our offices at the station? You know that can be arranged,"

Jake said, flipping the man's name tag with his finger. "I've got a hole the size of my fist going clean through the lining of my stomach and the pain medication is wearing thin. When that happens, I get testy, real testy. So, I recommend for both of our sakes that you..." he reached across the desk and fingered the man's name tag, "...Roland from Spokane, lose the fucking attitude and start talking."

The man blanched and cleared his throat. He picked up one of the photos. It was a shot of Aaron Clayton and Maura Baker at a table. "I have seen these people, of course. These photos were taken at a private party this past weekend."

"Are you certain?" Glory asked.

"Quite. It is hard to forget someone so stunning. The woman. But the dress, not sure I would wear that dress with hair her color. Too, too much, too much red."

"Do you recognize anyone else in these photos," Glory queried, pushing the stack closer to him.

"Well, of course, I suppose I saw them all here Saturday night, but I know none of them by name, if that's what you mean."

"Any of them ever been here before?" Glory asked.

He winced slightly, furrowing his brow as he pondered the question. Then he pushed the photos back across the desk. Shaking his head he replied, "I see so many—there are so many people in and out of here—they could be anyone. I don't know."

"You said this was a private party on a Saturday night. Doesn't that kind of put a crimp in the biggest night of the week?" Jake asked.

Roland cleared his throat. "Well, they pay for the whole place, a premium, more than we would clear on even a big night. Plus, this time of year, the hotel is not so booked up. And, it's also a lot easier."

"In what way?" Glory asked.

"They bring in the whole show themselves, the food, the waiters, the whole nine yards. We supply the drinks and the cooks. That's all."

"What was this, some sort of wedding reception or something, what with all the private food and whatnot?" Jake asked.

"Well, I didn't see a bride or anyone like that, if that's what you mean," Roland replied, subconsciously rearranging papers on his desk around a leather reservation book and diverting his eyes from those of the two detectives.

"How many were here?" Glory continued.

"A dozen or so."

"Who threw the shindig?" McKay asked.

"Threw it?" Roland replied blandly.

"Yeah, the bash," McKay tapped on the leather reservation book. "Why don't you just look up their name in this fancy book here?"

He did not blink. "Vincennes," he replied.

"Vincennes. What does that mean?" Glory said, writing down the name.

"It is the name of the company that utilized the restaurant for their private dinner last Saturday night."

"You sure? You don't have to look it up or nothing?" Jake said.

"I am quite sure. This company—Vincennes—owns the property."

"The hotel and restaurant?" Glory asked.

Again, Roland nodded very delicately.

"So, some of the corporate big wigs were in the group?" McKay said.

"I would suppose so."

"You don't know?"

"Frankly, no. We're not told who is who or who owns what."

"Some kinda secret society, this Vincennes?" McKay asked.

Roland shrugged. "I merely manage this property. The regional manager to whom I report was not at this event. That's all I can say about who was here, or not."

Glory continued. "Any sign of trouble at the gathering? An argument? Anything like that?"

Roland shook his head. "No, everyone was quite civilized, if not a bit mellow from the wine and drinks."

Glory pulled a photo from her pocket and handed it to Roland. The murky image staring back was Richard Baker, a shot taken at the station the previous day. "Did you happen to see this guy at any time that night? At the gathering, trying to get in, lurking around outside?"

Roland fingered the print for several seconds, studying it. "Eeeewwwww! He is a bit ruffled, isn't he? Quite disheveled, in fact." He handed back the photo. "I don't believe I saw him at all that night, but, of course, no one at the party looked like that."

"Yeah, well, this was taken sometime later, after all the fun," McKay replied. "He's a big guy, six-four or so. Hard to miss."

"Well, if he was here, I missed him," Roland replied. "As for whether or not he was lurking around, I just don't know."

"How long did the whole thing last?" Glory asked.

"The dinner was over at about ten or so. As for the party itself, well, I can't say."

"They didn't stay here?" Glory surmised.

"Correct," came the terse reply.

For a few seconds, silence lingered in the air. Then Jake broke it. "Well, you gonna continue the story or are we gonna keep playing twenty questions till my patience runs out and I stuff your scrawny carcass up that plastic elephant's ass?"

Roland smirked at the crudeness of the cop. "I assume they went upstairs to the penthouse suite to continue the festivities."

"The penthouse suite?"

"Yes."

"Where's that?" Jake asked.

Roland let out an exasperated sigh. "It's on the top floor. Hence the name, penthouse."

The two cops asked a few more questions and Glory thanked Roland for his dubious cooperation, made a mental note to look up Vincennes, closed her notebook and made her way toward the hotel lobby with Jake in tow. Instead of heading toward the revolving doors that led to the street, she turned and walked to the elevators.

"Hey, this way," Jake said.

"Let's go upstairs," Glory replied, turning her head slightly and striding across the lobby toward the sliding doors. Jake gathered himself and fell into step.

When they entered the elevator, they pushed the button for the penthouse, but nothing happened. "You need a key," Glory spat, leaning out the sliding doors. She spotted a bellman and called to him. He walked perkily to the elevator, a smile on his face. Glory grabbed him firmly, but not angrily, by the arm and coaxed him inside, flashing her badge. The smile immediately vanished as the blood drained from the bellman's countenance.

Glory asked, "You have a key to the penthouse?"

114

"Uh, no, only the head guy has one."

Glory pushed the kid out the door. "Go get him and make sure he has the key. Make sure he has the key and doesn't say anything to anyone. You've got thirty seconds."

The bellman stumbled out the door and McKay turned to his partner. "What's the urgency to go up there," he asked, his eyes rolling upwards.

"I have no idea. I just want to see what's up there. See how Maura Baker spent one of the last nights of her life."

"We're screwed on procedure if she's laying up there on the rug. No search warrant."

"We'll get around that," she said. "Reasonable cause."

Jake shrugged. "You're the boss."

Less than half a minute later a middle-aged man in uniform approached the elevator. "My name is Clyde and I am the supervisor of the bell desk. Can I help you?"

A foursome of guests attempted to enter, and Glory shooed them away with a flash of her badge. Then she took Clyde by the sleeve and pulled him in. "Get us to the penthouse, please," she said.

Clyde stammered as he fumbled with the keys on his belt. "Uh, that is private quarters for use by the owners. I'm not supposed to allow unauthorized…"

Glory pushed her badge closer to Clyde's nose. "Is this authorization enough?"

The bellman swallowed hard and inserted the key that unlocked button access to the suite. A few minutes later, the doors opened and Glory and Jake moved not into a hallway, but directly into a frenzy of activity. A plush living room of dark mahogany and leather was in a state of complete renovation. Furniture was pushed and stacked in corners and covered in drop cloths as a team of workers in white jump suits rolled up the carpeting. The sweet smell of fresh paint permeated the atmosphere. Light poured in through the windows, illuminating a cloud of dust that hung in the air.

One of the workers nudged a large buffet away from a wall that didn't match the newly painted ones and stopped when he saw the two strangers standing in front of the elevator doors. He walked toward them, wiping his hands on a towel that hung from his waist. "Can I, uh, help you?" he stammered.

Glory held up her badge. "What's going on here?"

"Renovation," the man answered.

"Problem with the old decor? Fire? Flood? Something like that?" she said.

The worker shrugged. "Nope. Just changing things. Happens all the time in these places. Perfectly good room gets torn apart 'cause the owners want some new hot color or whatever," he chuckled. "Thank God. Keeps my kids in college, it does."

"You work for Vincennes?"

"Vincennes?" the man replied.

"Company that owns this place."

"Well, if they own the place, I guess I work for them, but this is my company, these guys here," he motioned toward the crew with his hands.

"Nothing weird here about the decor? Holes in the wall, blood on the carpet, nothing like that?"

The man shook his head. "Routine, like I said."

"Mind if I look around?" Glory asked, not waiting for an answer and moving slowly through the rooms.

A half hour later Glory and Jake were back on the street going to their car. "Clue me in on why I just spent an hour literally watching paint dry," McKay growled.

Glory knew what was eating him. She understood that the single thing that separated mediocre cops from the best was the ability to distinguish what was important and what was not in any investigation. The instinct to discard useless information was a priceless God-given talent that cut through bullshit, compressed time and yielded more convictions. But these basic instincts also had logic to them, reasons for judgment. What was going through her mind was pure ether, formless, without basis. So she understood why McKay would be angry about squandering the time they had spent at the Pachyderm and the penthouse in what appeared to be an obvious dead end.

Jake reiterated his question. "An hour watching paint dry."

She didn't know how to answer him. "You won't understand this, Jake, because it's not a fact, just a hunch," she said softly. "I smelled death in that room."

10

Rich Baker awakened early the next morning when dawn was still a soft breath not yet exhaled. Sleep had not been easy, but it had come over him at last, and he soon knew that he would pay any amount to be able to crawl back into that protective oblivion. In that first instant of consciousness it was like awakening any other day. But almost immediately reality battered down the doors of his perception and rushed in to fill him with the electric anxiety that reverberated through him to the ends of the hairs on his arms. He lay in bed for several minutes, the voice and face of Miles Lundeen rattling through his mind, knowing that no matter how much he wanted or how hard he tried, he would not sleep again for a long time.

So he got up, neither tired nor awake, lodged somewhere in a murky in-between. He shuffled into his living room in the sweat pants he had worn to bed. He wrapped an afghan around his bare shoulders and automatically turned on the television set. Its vacant drone filled the room with what would have to do for company. He shuffled to the kitchen.

Rich stood at the kitchen counter and poured a cup of coffee. He ran his fingers through his hair and yawned. His consciousness flickered, as if his life plug were hanging loosely from the socket. The coffee helped with its stinging heat and bitter taste. He leaned on the counter and sipped slowly, feeling the warmth light up his nerves. He took his cup and moved toward the couch. On the television the driving music of a news broadcast paced a tumbling, pulsating logo as it assembled itself on the screen. An announcer droned an introduction that Rich mimicked aloud. Flopping into his leather chair, he watched and listened, drifting away and back, away and back. Then a certain sound rumbled through him like a thunder clap. Too familiar. Not supposed to be coming from this box and this time of the morning. His name.

He fumbled for the remote control and raised the volume on the set. The announcer, too perfectly coiffed and alert for the hour, feigned a concerned, dour expression as he spoke. "In other local news, police are looking for the estranged wife of a well-known Chicago real estate developer. Maura Baker, seen here in a recent photo..."

Rich leaned forward. It was Maura, all right. Some sort of office group. He'd never seen the shot before. How the hell did they get a picture of her so goddamn fast?

"... Rich Baker, from whom the missing woman is separated, was picked up by detectives near an abandoned steel mill..."

Rich was two feet from the screen now, staring at the picture. Maura was centered, obviously surrounded by other people. Must have been at some sort of conference or something, Rich thought.

"... in Mrs. Baker's late model Mercedes. Sources close to Channel 7 News state that the automobile interior was covered in blood."

There were two partial faces in the photograph flanking Maura. One was unidentifiable. The other, cut almost exactly half way through the bridge of the nose was someone Rich recognized.

"...Detective Glory Kane, who is leading the investigation into the apparent disappearance of Mrs. Baker, refused to comment on the condition of the Mercedes..."

The photograph was suddenly replaced with a video clip of the lovely Detective Kane as she avoided the thrust of a microphone. Rich recognized the topography. It was the abandoned lot where he had awakened.

"Police are asking for the public's help in trying to locate Mrs. Baker..."

The photograph came back to the screen. Baker looked not at his smiling, obviously happy, and alive, wife, but at the cheekbone and glimmering eye at the edge of the picture. It was that asshole Aaron Clayton, he thought, and he could barely discern that below the cut line of the photograph where Maura's legs were submerged was Clayton's grabby, grubby hand, resting gently on Maura's knee. Rich Baker raised his forefinger, making a gun of his flesh and bone, and pointed it at the image of the man on the screen. "Bang!" he said, dropping his thumb like a hammer.

The same television imagery and mottled voices fluttered into the sudden consciousness of Tucker Hines, who sprawled on the couch on which he had slept. He groggily reached for the pack of cigarettes on the cluttered coffee table in front of him and shakily lit one. He peered through the haze of smoke that gently floated in the air like so many strings of clouds. He struggled to pull himself upright, having to literally throw himself into a sitting position because his back was encumbered by a huge hump, a malformation that turned his overall shape into that of a legged seahorse. He made a grunting sound and lurched upward, wobbling unsteadily as he sat up. He coughed a cloud of smoke from the shaking cigarette clenched in his teeth. Ashes tumbled down the front of his sleeveless t-shirt and onto the boxer shorts he was wearing. Then he leaned forward and squinted at the images on the television.

"Hey, I seen that broad," he grunted, removing the cigarette from his mouth. He was, as always, talking to himself. No one was there to hear him. No one was ever there in Tuck's filthy apartment. Who would come here? A woman? Forget about it. What woman would be the lover of a hunchback? Maura Baker's face blazed back at him in blurred, bleeding colors. The image startled him, made him lean forward, closer to the set. "I seen that broad before, ain't I?" he said. But who was she? And where had he seen her? Yeah, she was a babe, looking almost like a movie star, but that wasn't it. She didn't remind him of someone, she was someone with whom he had an encounter of some sort, if only a fleeting one. He racked his brain. Then, bingo, like that, it all came together. He thought—no, he suddenly knew—where he'd seen the face, and he began to cough, spitting out clouds of smoke, choking.

He struggled to his feet and shuffled lazily into the bathroom where he stood over the toilet, pulled his penis sideways out of the leg of his boxer shorts, and let fly a stream of piss. When he finished, he spit his nearly smoked cigarette into the toilet bowl where it died with an emphatic hiss. A lot going through his mind. Mostly it was about money and how he could convert his tenuous connection to Maura Baker into some of it. As he shuffled back to his living room, scratching his genitals and yawning, his mind was reeling. She was missing, the newscaster had said.

"Ain't that a fuckin' shame," he groused. "Good lookin' broad like that here one minute, kaput the next."

The gentle trilling of his telephone suddenly disrupted Rich's idyll. Eyes ahead, he picked up the receiver.

"Rich, sorry to call so early." Nate Timmins' voice came reed thin through the lines.

"Yeah, no problem. What's up?" Rich backed up the tape again, pausing it.

"They're coming over now with a search warrant, those two cops, the woman and the Neanderthal, and a forensics team."

A rush of adrenaline lifted Rich from his chair and he impulsively shut off the television and watched Maura's image get sucked into a tiny pin dot.

"Rich, did you hear me?" Timmins repeated.

"Yeah. How did you come upon this information?"

"I have my ways," he replied impatiently.

"What am I supposed to do?" Rich's heart was ricocheting around his chest.

"Wait for me. I'll be there in, oh, thirty minutes or less."

"Do I... is there anything I should, like, get out of the house?"

"You got any drugs?"

"No. No drugs."

"You got a woman there?"

"No."

"Unregistered weapons?"

"I don't have weapons," he said, exasperated.

"Any incriminating evidence? Anything to connect you to the other day?"

"Everything's kosher."

"Okay, then just sit tight. I'll be right over."

11

Detectives Kane and McKay and a forensic team of three moved in unison silently through the yawning elevator doors. "It's this way," Glory said, pausing in the hallway and gathering her bearings. "Numbers are going up."

As they passed one door, it suddenly opened a few inches, throwing a soft blade of light onto the hall carpet. Glory stopped. She could see the form of a person, short, with one eye staring through the crack. A dog, small, started barking frantically. A voice came from behind the door. "Are you the cops? The cops?" a woman's voice croaked.

Glory turned to face the door. "Yes, we are."

"Coming to arrest that murderer are you? You better be. It's about time. The murderer."

"Do you know him?" Glory said, moving closer to the door. The dog was hysterical now, yipping at a painful decibel level.

"You got a badge? Let me see your badge, lady," the old woman said.

Glory reached in her pocket and pulled out her badge, holding it up to the door. "Do you know Mr. Baker?" she asked.

The lady leaned forward, her cheeks pressed against the threshold. "Is that real? Is that a real badge?"

"Yes, ma'am, it is," Glory said, trying to sound patient. "Do you know Mr. Baker?"

"He's one of them heathens, that's what he is. Fornicating and drinking himself blind. Oh, I know him. He's a mean one, he is. Bound for everlasting torment," she said, opening the door a little farther until it pulled the restraining chain tight. Glory looked down and saw the dog at the lady's feet, trying to charge forward, and the lady pushed it backward with her foot.

Glory flipped her badge closed and dropped it back into her pocket. She leaned over and whispered to McKay, "Jake, why don't you take a few minutes with this lady, find out what she knows."

Jake let out an exasperated sigh. "Oh, for chrissakes..."

"We have to canvass the tenants, anyway, at some point in time. Five minutes, that's all you need."

"Yeah, five minutes," he grumbled, moving toward the lady's door. "Ma'am, you mind if we chat for five minutes?"

The door closed and the chain rattled. Then it opened and Jake walked in. The dog barked frantically as the big man entered the apartment. Then its yipping was muted by the closing of the door.

Timmins had beaten the detectives and the forensics team to the apartment. "How long will this take?" he asked Glory, ushering them in.

She saw Baker, sitting on a leather couch, pensively smoking a cigarette. He looked much better than the last time she'd laid eyes on him. "Several hours, at least four," she replied, handing the folded warrant to the attorney. "We're going to be digging pretty deep."

"I expect a complete inventory of everything removed from the premises, today, before you leave," Timmins said.

"Sure," Glory answered.

He examined the search warrant slowly and handed it back without further comment. "Come on, Rich, let's go get some breakfast," he said.

As the door closed behind the two men, Glory breathed deeply and swept the room with her eyes. It was a man's place, no doubt about it. Lots of dark wood, and brass, metal furniture. "Let's go to work, boys," she said. "I assume the bedrooms are back there, down that hall. Why don't you start there?"

Glory moved slowly through the living room, pausing to examine the photographs on the mantel. She picked up one, Maura and Rich in younger days. Next to it was a snapshot, framed in a cheap wooden frame. Maura and Rich were playfully swinging a young boy between them. The child's feet flew akimbo off the ground as he virtually bubbled with delight. She could feel the unbridled, innocent joy captured in that precious moment. Sean. The boy who died.

She set down the photo, then walked into the kitchen. Gleaming appliances that looked as though they'd never been used were framed in cabinetry of dark teak wood. She ran her hands over the umber slate counter. She had never seen anything like it. Rich Baker had done well for himself, that much was evident. Still . . .

She moved down a hallway, examining the original artwork on the walls—morose, gray and black abstract anger flooded one canvas. Another featured a face, melting against a storming background. What was in the soul of this man that would attract him to such art? She came to a break in the wall, an

126

open space created by wide open double doors. His office. Here's the place to start. She went to the desk and sat down.

"You think there's a God? There is no God," Jake McKay bellowed from the distance. "'Cause if there was a God, he'd be just a tiny little bit more fair about spreading the wealth around down here."

"I'm in here, Jake, down the hall on the left," Glory called.

McKay was there in an instant. "You see this place? Holy mother of mercy!" He froze as he entered the room. "My God, that desk cost more than my house."

Glory agreed. The desk *was* worth more than his house. The thing was a wondrous work of art as much as a desk, a hand-carved wood tableau of angels and archangels battling for the supremacy of heaven. The center front featured a raging St. Michael with a flaming sword dispatching Lucifer to the netherworld. "Seeing all this wealth is turning you into an atheist, is it?" she queried.

"You think this turd works any harder than you or me? Did he ever have to lift a ten-year-old kid out of a puddle of his own blood and give him mouth-to-mouth while life just continued to pour out of the bullet hole in his back? What in God's name is that worth, for Christ sakes? Not enough to buy one of this guy's friggin' suits!"

"What did you learn from the old lady?" Glory said, looking up.

Jake hesitated. "Uh, nothing," he said, pointing an index finger at his temple and rolling it in circles. "Wacky. She said her radio gets alien broadcasts. Made me listen to it."

"Well? Does she get alien radio stations?" Glory said.

"I think so," Jake replied.

"Well, too bad we're not on the alien investigation team," Glory said, going back to her work. "Why not check out that file cabinet?"

Glory opened a side drawer and immediately saw a large envelope with a single word written on it: "Maura." She removed it and could feel that it contained papers and a DVD. She opened the unsealed clasp and dumped the contents on the desk. Several insurance binders of varying shapes and sizes slid gently out as did the DVD.

In the corner Jake McKay sat on the floor and plopped a stack of files onto his lap. "The bastard ever sit out in a car staking out a crack house in the middle of the night with the wind howling through the edges of the car window a hundred miles an hour and fifteen below zero while cigarettes piled up three inches higher than the ash tray?" He stood and replaced the sheath of files. He slammed the drawer shut. "Hell no, he didn't. Sonofabitch has never been cold in his life, the nickel dick."

Glory browsed through the insurance binders. Adding quickly she estimated over a million and a half dollars' worth of benefits, and Rich Baker was beneficiary on every policy except one. That was earmarked for Lisette Darby, Maura's mother. How odd that these policies would be arranged like this, Glory thought. And what was the significance of the video? The label on it was entitled "Christmas," and Glory stood up and walked over to the television in the elaborate case at the opposite end of the room. A sculpture of three hollow wire-frame people on a metal bench was placed very precisely in front of the television, but low enough to not obscure the view from the semi-circular leather couch behind the sculpture. Glory popped in the DVD and turned on the monitor. In a few seconds she got picture. She walked back and sat on the couch.

Jake was slamming another drawer shut. "You think that weasel ever sucked himself into the wall in a dark hallway, praying that the guy behind the door wasn't so fried on drugs that he'd come out shooting, and if he did that the bullets wouldn't find you? Yeah, right." The cabinet shook as the drawer thundered into its cavity. "Well, nothing here, think I'll check the bedroom," Jake said, in a suddenly calm, matter-of-fact tone.

The picture was dark, dominated by the color orange and slightly out of focus. Gradually, it sharpened and Glory could see the lights of a Christmas tree flickering and leaving snakelike flares as the camera rode past it. The only sound was a steady, rhythmic breathing as the living room struggled into focus. The camera passed a darkened chandelier that Glory immediately recognized as the one in Maura Baker's home, then moved across a mantelpiece festooned with garland and hung with cards, past a softly dancing fire in the hearth.

The camera finally swooped back to the Christmas tree, pulling back to widen the shot. It was then Glory could see her. At first she was an ill-defined jittering mass of white, backlit by the lights and candles of the tree. The camera adjusted automatically and immediately. Her red hair was as blazingly beautiful as the amber scene itself, framed in light surrealistically white, like a halo created by the fire of the lights. Shadows lay across her face, but not enough to obscure the soft, dreaming expression dwelling there. Maura Baker was lost, wandering a time and place known only to her, completely oblivious that she was being recorded.

A voice broke the silence. "Santa will never come if you don't go to bed."

Maura, obviously startled, jumped, and a tiny squeak escaped from her mouth. But she quickly composed herself. She smoothed her white housecoat and turned to the camera. The robe was only partially closed. The skin of her neck and chest peaked through, dissolving into a shadowy "V" bordered on both sides by the shape of her breasts. Even Glory found herself mesmerized by this uncommon beauty and a provocative sensuality that was simple and unstaged. "Oh," Maura almost whispered, "there's no hurry for Santa. This is the best part, the anticipation. That's the most fun."

"You were a long way from here," Rich Baker's voice came softly from behind the slightly swaying camera.

Maura tossed her hair. It caused streaks of exploding light to fly out from behind it like insects. "I was. Indeed I was."

"Where were you?"

She made a face. "Why should I tell you?"

"Because I am your great love and you tell me everything."

Maura pondered the comment. "That is very true, but can I have no secrets?"

"Secrets are either happy or sad. If they're happy, then I am deprived of a chance to share that happiness. If they're sad, then I am deprived of a chance of helping them go away."

This was Rich Baker, Glory wondered? The voice was unmistakably his, but the tone and timbre didn't fit the image she had constructed of him in her mind.

Maura paused and turned to the tree. Again, the lights erupted around her head like an honor guard of celestial angels. She didn't look as she spoke. "I was a little girl again. If only for a second. All I knew was joy. Everything else stayed away."

"So, that is a happy memory. That's good."

"Yes, very."

"But you're not a little girl anymore?"

"No," Maura said turning back to look at the camera, and as she did the bathrobe opened even more.

"That's good," Rich replied, "because what I have for you isn't for little girls."

Maura stared at him provocatively for several seconds and then tossed her head back and laughed, a musical, lilting, lyrical laugh. "I'll bet it isn't," she said.

The screen exploded into a gray miasma of static and noise. Glory sank into the leather upholstery of the couch as the television hissed incessantly. She was ashamed and saddened, confused and exhausted for entering this scene, this world, this private moment between two people, and for a brief flashing instant everything she was about burned in her mind. She started to tremble, not knowing whether the involuntary tremors in her chest were rage or pity. How could Rich Baker have savagely ended the life of this beautiful woman? What madness drove him? And what were the reasons this video was so carefully placed in the envelope with a stack of insurance papers?

She ejected the DVD from the machine and slowly walked back to Baker's desk. She replaced the disc in the envelope and tugged at the desk drawer. It opened an inch or two and stopped, jammed against something. Glory rattled it, and what was jamming it shook loose as it opened. Glory removed a ring of keys. She quickly counted seven keys on a small ring that was topped off by a plastic circle with the name of a car dealer on it. Each key was identified with a small piece of tape bearing carefully hand-written letters. One caught Glory's eye. The

131

tape read "big house." Was the "big house" the home in Lake Forest, Maura's home? It made sense. She reached to the floor and lifted her portfolio. From it she extracted a manila envelope, marked it "keys—Baker's apartment," and dropped the keys into it. She was going to see if any of them could get her into Maura's house. And if one of them could, then why would Rich Baker break out a window pane on the back door to get in?

Suddenly, her colliding thoughts were interrupted by a huge bellow from somewhere beyond her immediate consciousness. She jumped and was quickly standing. Jake McKay was holding a pair of boots. "Look what the boys found in the closet. Old numb nuts didn't even bother to clean them up!"

Glory came to him in a few long strides. "Boots. Muddy boots. So what?"

"Seems to me we've got a plaster cast of a print made outside Maura Baker's back door." He held the boots high as a member of the forensic team opened a plastic bag and strategically placed it beneath them. Jake dropped them, saying, "Preheat the oven, kids, we're about to cook a turkey."

Four hours later, after wrapping up all the paperwork for the day and bringing Lieutenant Rodriguez up to speed, Jake McKay was home, ambling up the sidewalk of the brick bungalow in which he had lived his entire life. He was in a good mood for a change, singing an old Nancy Sinatra song. "These boots are made for walking," he crooned, "That's just what they'll do. One of these days these boots are gonna walk all over you."

They were going to get this guy, Rich Baker. They had the boots. And tomorrow the divers were going into Wolf Lake near the spot where Baker was found in his car, and McKay was sure they'd pull out Maura Baker's body and that would be that. He gingerly ascended the concrete steps of his home, a bungalow of beige brick, identical to the home next to it, and all the rest on the block. That's the way they did it in those days. The neighborhoods were built, bang, bang, bang, one house after another, by the owners of the factories nearby. Probably used the same plan because it was faster and cheaper and they had mills and foundries that needed people. The idea was to get the immigrants in and to work as fast as possible. Don't give them too much to think about, choosing this style or that. Keep things the same.

McKay fumbled in his pocket for his keys and paused to gaze at the stone flower vases that his mother, years ago, had placed on each pillar that flanked the steps. There wasn't anything in them anymore. Dry dirt and bent twigs, bird poop, candy wrappers the kids tossed in there on Halloween. After she left, the flowers went—well—to pot. Dad didn't have the time to change the dirt and water them, and he probably didn't care anyway.

McKay shook his head. This was her home, and then, one day, she was gone—off to find "herself." And every afternoon Jake would come home from school, and he would sit in her chair, with the knitted blanket tucked in its crevices, and wait for the old man to come up this very same porch, his feet shuffling on the concrete, just the way Jake's were at this moment. How many times? Thousands. And sometimes the old bastard would show up three, four hours late, staggering and spitting and puking as he bounced off the pillars, and he

133

would bust through the door screaming at her, even though she wasn't there anymore, or as if, maybe, she had finally come home. Jake would get the old man's dinner out of the oven where he'd put it to keep it warm, and serve it to him. Not until Jake had become a man himself did he even begin to understand the emptiness that ran like a river through his father's soul.

Jake wiggled the key in the lock until it finally caught, and he entered his home. The first thing he did was reach to the left and flip on the living room light. And then, as always, setting right there on the table next to the front door, a pre-poured glass of bourbon that he grabbed and slowly brought to his lips. The first taste always hit him like a fist, and he savored the sheer power of the alcohol to do that. He stood and let it run into him, smacking his tongue and lips to loosen the leftover taste. Then he took a second slow sip. This one was cooler, more benevolent. He luxuriated in its magnitude. He swirled the remaining liquid in the glass and then brought it to his mouth. As he took in the nectar, he let it set on his tongue for several seconds before swallowing.

One drink. One a day—not counting the beer at dinner. That was it. He wasn't going to become his old man.

Then, as his arrival ritual continued, he emptied his pockets into the ash tray. His keys, loose change, and this piece of paper. With the now empty tumbler still in one hand he used the index finger and thumb of his free hand to unfold the note—the note he had received from Baker's neighbor, the whacky old lady. Two lines, scrawled in the old lady's handwriting. He smiled and contemplated the note for a few seconds. He had decided to keep it to himself; not show it to Glory. He would look into it himself. No sense in mucking up the works. Then he let the paper fall and spilled a handful of coins over the top of it.

"These boots are made for walking. That's just what they'll do," he sang. "One of these days these boots are gonna walk all over you."

12

Tucker Hines was outside Clancy's Liquor Emporium with a fifth of cheap whiskey in his pocket, hopping from foot to foot with his arms flailing against his chest as if he were a baby bird trying to learn how to fly. It was cold, as cold as it gets here in Chicago. Snow whistled in the air and swiped at his face like the claws of a cat. Where was the little bastard, he muttered aloud, jumping a bit at every car that turned a corner, looking for the beat-to-shit old Chevy with the dragging tailpipe. The little prick who would be driving it had finally answered his phone calls and Tucker had told him to be here, at this time. Right now he needed not only a drink, but also a buddy to drink it with.

Guys like Tucker Hines—deformed, shunned by normal society, despicable, not only in looks, but also in personal habits and presentation—understandably had few friends. In fact, the great curse of his mountainous hump was not the hideous cruelty it pervaded on his body, but the heartbreaking loneliness that resulted from its existence. He had learned to live with the physical pain, but he couldn't tolerate the prospects of being alone. So, the friends he had, he held onto with a fierce loyalty and love. If friendship meant standing on a street corner freezing his ass off waiting for a hillbilly, then that's just the way it was, baby.

He hadn't seen nor heard from his best pal, Taters Poteet for several days. Poteet had been excreted directly from the hills of Kentucky onto the streets of Chicago. He was a brainless idiot, too stupid to recognize danger if it bit him in the 'nads. He was a go-fer, drugs mostly, taking his pay out of inventory and delivering little packets of joy through the distribution maze that kept the junkies of Chicago on their asses and happy. No big deal, a little bit here, a little there. Small time stuff. So far removed from the main man that he didn't know shit; so small time that he wasn't worth busting. A week before, Poteet had called Tuck for help in making another kind of delivery to a very important person. And while it wasn't what Tuck normally engaged in, it was legitimate, totally clean, not dangerous, and an easy three hundred bucks.

The two of them had met a private plane at a private airstrip out in the boondocks. They had driven Poteet's rickety Chevy onto the tarmac for a quick move of cargo from the plane to the pre-heated car. The booty was lobsters, seven heavy boxes of them, specially flown in for a big party.

After loading the car, Poteet drove downtown to the back of a restaurant where he and Tucker carried in the boxes. A huge kitchen, gleaming with stainless steel, was in a state of choreographed frenzy as chefs in pristine white frocks and hats stirred and poured and drizzled and arranged plates of food too beautiful to describe. The aroma was overwhelming, as garlic and butter and unknown spices coalesced. A large stove, festooned with glimmering pots, seemed afire as each vessel expunged a hurricane of steam into the room. Tuck and Poteet followed the brisk, frantic commands of the head chef as they humped the noisy boxes into the fray. The lobsters had begun to stir and were scratching at the cardboard walls that engulfed them. Several other chefs ran over and ripped the crates open to reveal the lobsters that writhed in a mass of gray-brown energy.

As the crustaceans were tossed unceremoniously into the boiling water, a line of turbaned waiters entered the kitchen and lifted trays piled with the artistic wares of the chefs. The head chef reached into a cabinet above the counter and removed a stack of white linen. He unfolded one and tossed it to Poteet. It was immediately followed by another turban.

"Here, you put these on. Help. Snap, snap," he said gesturing at a tray. Then he started to toss one to Tucker, stopped and shook his head. Without another word he turned and began barking orders to the wait staff.

This was a world into which Tucker Hines had no entree. Even Taters Poteet with his bad hillbilly teeth and unwashed hair was more presentable than the wretched hunchback. So, Tuck merely stood near the swinging door and watched the crowd in the private dining area glimmer and shine as they received their plates.

It was then that Hines caught the first glimpse of the hot red hair. It erupted out of the crowd like a volcano, and he couldn't take his eyes off the woman who bore it. She was seated in the center of the room, actively engaged in conversation. The two men on each side of her, one a gray-haired, middle-aged man, and the other younger, maybe thirty or so, were obviously hypnotized by her presence. The thirty-year-old in particular couldn't stop his eyes from drifting to the two perfect breasts that rested not-so-discreetly in the loose scoop of her plunging neckline. Tuck stared at her for several minutes, between the ebb and flow of the marching waiters who obscured his view, and then gave it back to him.

Then he was grabbed by the shoulder and spun around. The head chef was pulling him away from the door. "You done. You done here now. Go home. Go, go!"

The memory of this scene actually warmed him on the street corner in front of Clancy's as he awaited Poteet again. He was certain that the blazing red hair he had seen that night was the same that electrified the front page of the newspaper he had, at this moment, tucked into his pocket. But Poteet had been there all night, and he would know for certain. Tucker Hines fended off the cold with his flapping arms one more time, then extracted the whiskey bottle from his pocket, keeping it tightly wound in its paper bag, twisted the cap to break the seal, and took a long, hard, hot swig. He put the cap back on and slid it back into its resting place.

Suddenly there was a rumble followed by the telltale scrape and bounce of the busted muffler, and Poteet's car rattled into view. It pulled to the curb and Tuck lumbered over and slid into the passenger side of the front seat.

The inside was dead blue from cigarette smoke and exhaust that wafted through the holes in the floor. Hines juggled himself into a more comfortable position.

"Hey Tucker, what y'all up to?" Poteet said steering away from the curb and into the traffic. He sniffed at the air. "What's that I smell?"

Tuck removed the bottle of whiskey from his pocket and handed it over. "Heat in a bottle. Want some?"

"Open it for me, will ya? Whatcha think, I can steer with my dick?"

Tuck twisted the top and handed the bottle over again. Poteet took a swig, swirled it around in his mouth, swallowed and coughed. "Goddamn. That's good!" He took another hard swallow, leaned back and gargled with it, and handed the bottle to the hunchback. "That's 'nuff for now. Thanks partner."

"Where the hell you been?" Tuck asked. "I been trying to find you for three fucking days."

"Had to head down to kay-why."

"What's kay-why?"

"Ken-tuck. Back home. My cousin got married. My old daddy sent me plane fare, God bless him. He's as ornery as…"

"Yeah, that's really interesting. Ornery. But I ain't got time to bullshit right now," Tuck said. He reached into his coat pocket and removed the newspaper. He unfolded it and handed it to Poteet. "Take a look at this, will ya?"

Taters grabbed the paper and held it in front of his face, alternately glancing at it and looking out the streaked windshield at the same time. "What you want me to freakin' read while I'm driving?"

"You don't gotta read shit. Look at that picture there on the front of the paper."

The steering wheel turned slightly, quickly, and the car swayed as Poteet tried to take a good look at the photo. "What about it?" he said after a few seconds or so.

"You ever seen that woman before?"

"Shit, how the hell do I know? Is it a movie star or something?"

"No."

"Then what's she doing on the front page?"

"That don't matter," Tuck said. "Just tell me if that's the same broad that was at the big shindig last week up at that hotel where we delivered the lobsters."

"The Lakeside? You mean The Pachyderm? Let me see," he fumbled with the paper that had folded away from him. "Gimme a second, there's a red light up here." He stopped the car and took the paper with both hands.

"I don't rightly remember people usually at these shindigs. It's safer that way, if you get my drift," Poteet said, "but you gotta be dead from the neck down to forget this fox. Mama, mama, mama, she is one hot piece of prime."

"Yeah, prime," Tuck groused, shaking his head. "So, you're sure that's her?"

"Hell, look at the friggin' picture closer, you fucking moron," Poteet said, tossing the paper back to him and stepping on the accelerator. "She's got a stirrer in her hand with the elephant on it, and you can see the waiters in the background with those goofy fucking turbans on their heads. The friggin' photo was taken that night! So what?"

"So nothing. I just thought it was kinda strange, I mean you and me seeing her that night and now she's on the front of the paper gone missing."

"Hey, folks go missing all the time in that crowd. You oughta know that, you fuckin' dipshit. You think this was a meeting of the college of fucking cardinals or something?" Poteet laughed through rotted teeth and took another swig of whiskey.

Tucker laughed at the remark as well, shaking frantically as he fumbled through his layers of clothing for a pack of cigarettes. "College of cardinals! Ain't that the fucking truth."

A few seconds passed as the laughter died down. "So, where to?" Poteet said.

"Let's finish this bottle, get something to eat. Maybe out at the Stewart Tap."

"Sounds good to me."

By the time Taters Poteet arrived at his own apartment several hours later, the booze had begun its dirty work on his insides. He was ricocheting off the banister and into the side wall as he pushed himself upstairs. He put the neck of yet-another bottle in his mouth and held it with his teeth as he rummaged through his filthy clothing for his keys. It took several more seconds to actually select the right one and nuzzle it toward the lock. But the instant he put any pressure on the door at all, it magically swung open.

"Sumbitch, what the fuck is this?" he said, swaying as he passed through the threshold. Immediately he saw two men sitting on his couch.

"Hello, Taters," the big one said.

"Hey, boys, what the fuck you doing here?" he replied, standing in the middle of the room and waving the bottle as he circled around to the front of the couches. "Want a drink?"

"Not now," the big guy replied.

"Oh. Okay," Poteet said, ambling toward the counter and setting the bottle down with a distinct clank. "What you doin' here at my place?"

"Working, Taters."

"Working?" What the hell did they mean by that? He knew what kind of work they did and... "Working? Here? I don't get it." Suddenly animal instincts took over, and he sensed, felt, smelled the menace that had engulfed the room. "Oh, goddamn..."

The second man stood up and reached into his coat. "Jesus, Taters, I hate to have to do this," he said, extracting a large silver pistol with a shining silencer at the end of the barrel.

Poteet's eyes bulged. His heart seemed to explode in his chest. He felt the heat of uncontrolled piss running down his pant leg. "Oh, oh, Jesus, sweet Jesus," he cried. "What did I do? Moxie, tell me! I didn't do nothing. I swear to God, boys. I didn't!"

"Your name's on the list, Po. That's all I can say. It's orders from the high court. Strictly business. I'm really sorry," the man said, lifting the gun. "I'm gonna make sure you don't feel nothing."

Taters Poteet collapsed to his knees, sliding forward in the putrid puddle that had formed on the wooden floor. He put his hands together as if in prayer. "Please, boys. Please, please, please don't kill me! I'll go away. I'll get the hell out right now. I'll stay away."

The man walked toward him, grunting resignedly, breathing hard. He walked to Poteet's back. "Just put your head down, Po. Don't look back."

"Please, Christ, God. What did I do? I didn't do nothing."

"Po, you gotta know I am really sorry about this," the man said and silently raised the gun and held the barrel a few inches from the back of Poteet's head. "Stop shaking, Po. I don't want to miss." Finally, he grabbed Poteet by the hair and pulled his head back.

"Oh God, oh God, oh God, oh God," Taters cried.

There was a sound, something between a whoosh and a pop. And a glob of Tater's brains splattered onto the floor like a bug hitting a windshield.

13

"Jesus Horatio Goddamn Christ," Jake whispered as he and Glory entered the palatial office of Miles Lundeen. "Just when you think you've seen it all, it gets even better." The secretary had led them to the chairs in front of Lundeen's desk. "The friggin' desk is bigger than a Buick. What is that anyway, marble?"

"I think so," Glory answered.

Before sitting down, Jake gazed out the window. "Look at that view."

"Incredible."

"Now I know why the architects put all that frou-frou and gingerbread on the tops of the buildings. It's so the rich bastards in the top offices can see it. This way they don't need paintings and shit."

"Well now, detective, you posit an interesting theory, but one with which I would have to disagree," a voice, reed thin and nasally came from behind. Miles Lundeen floated to his desk like smoke between the furniture and up the multiple steps. "My observation is that every building is a tribute to the man who dreamed of it, and the amount of decor placed thereon is a reflection of his own image, placed for his own amusement and gratification and for the wonderment of all others. Hello, I'm Miles Lundeen," he said extending a cadaverously bony arm with skin as tight as paint.

Glory took the proffered hand first. "Detective Glory Kane," she said. The grip of Lundeen belied his slight frame. It was firm, certain, assertive.

"My goodness," he said breathily, "they don't make detectives like they used to." His eyes wandered over Glory for several seconds. He held her hand longer than conventionally accepted.

Glory spoke. "This is Detective McKay." Lundeen's hand slipped somewhat reluctantly from hers. The two men shook hands. Lundeen gestured for them to be seated, and he took a seat on a side chair on the opposite side of the coffee table. Glory was slightly surprised at the implied intimacy, the obvious congeniality of this arrangement. She had fully expected Lundeen to sit on the throne-like chair behind the huge marble desk like a god. For some reason, he had chosen to descend and sit with the mortals.

The administrative assistant reentered the room carrying a tray with an antique china coffee set, a silver teapot and embroidered napkins held by silk ribbons. Miles Lundeen rose immediately, and in a very mannerly, fashion took the tray and placed it on the table in front of his guests. "We have fine gourmet coffee or tea, or, if you prefer, I can get a soft drink or mineral water?"

"Coffee is just fine," Glory said.

Lundeen deferentially poured for her, then proffered to pour for Jake, who declined with a slight wave of his bulbous hands.

"Mr. Lundeen, as you know, we're here to talk about Rich Baker in regards to the disappearance of his wife."

146

"Of course. This is a regretful tragedy," Lundeen said. "It makes no sense to me whatsoever."

"Well, we haven't determined whether or not 'tragedy' is the correct word for it," Glory replied. "We're still not sure Maura Baker is even dead."

Lundeen notched an eyebrow. "I see. How encouraging."

"You were with Rich Baker the night before?" Jake asked, cutting in.

"Yes, I was. Me and approximately a hundred other people."

"A real big shindig, huh?" Jake said.

Lundeen smiled. "Shindig. Indeed."

Glory said, "Tell us about it."

"We were having a celebration. At my apartment. I daresay that a bomb in the room would have wiped out two-thirds of the wealth and power in this city. The mayor was there, you know, and the Cardinal."

"Well, I don't know about you, but I'm impressed," Jake said. Glory wrinkled her brow. "Must have been quite an occasion."

Miles Lundeen wiggled into a new, somewhat conspiratorial posture, leaning forward, placing his elbows on his knees. In a near whisper he said, "Next month we're staging a press conference to introduce our plans for building the tallest building in the world, right here in Chicago. We invited the investors, the government officials, the power elite, so to speak, in kind of a sneak preview."

"Would it be possible to get a list of the people who attended?" Glory asked.

Lundeen's eyes flared instantaneously then settled. He shook his head. "My goodness, I wouldn't want to intrude on the privacy of their lives. Is that really necessary?"

Jake sat back and crossed his legs. "We could subpoena the list, Mr. Lundeen."

"We're simply trying to find out if anyone saw Rich Baker in the company of his ex-wife, saw him leave, heard him say he was meeting her, and so on," Glory said, softening the tone of the dialogue.

Lundeen stared for several seconds, first at McKay then back to Glory. He then set his coffee cup and saucer down and walked to his desk where he picked up the phone and spoke in a soft whisper. He hung up the phone and was back in his seat, sipping coffee.

"For the record, Rich Baker," Glory said, "he was at the party?"

"Of course. He's a partner in the project, has been integral to the process."

"He was here the entire evening?" Glory asked.

"As far as I know, yes. As I said there were a hundred or so people here. I wasn't there to babysit Rich Baker."

"So, he needed babysitting, did he?" Jake queried.

Lundeen was mid-sip. He swallowed, wincing at the hot coffee. "Please, detective," he answered sarcastically.

"Was Baker inebriated?" Glory asked.

"Of course, this is Rich Baker we're talking about here."

"Pretty shit-faced, huh?" Jake said.

Lundeen set his coffee cup down on the table and exhaled a soft chuckle. "Not the exact words I'd use, but accurate in a crude, inarticulate sense." He held Jake sternly in his gaze for a second, and Glory saw a flash of fury in the millionaire's eyes that erupted and dissipated in an instant.

"What time did the party break up?" Glory said.

"Approximately two, two-thirty."

"Did Rich stay the whole time?"

Lundeen pursed his lips, thinking. "I think so. He wasn't necessarily the last to leave, but he was here until at least one a.m. Why? Does this have some bearing on his guilt or innocence?"

Glory shook her head. It would mean something if they had a body. With no body it was just a way to keep the facts coming. "All facts are relevant, some just more so than others." She shifted her position again. "Did you see who he left with?"

"No."

"Was Maura at the party?"

"Again, no, no, she wasn't."

"You knew both Rich and Maura?"

"Indeed, for, oh, fifteen years."

"Describe to me their relationship."

Lundeen pondered for a few seconds. "Well, that would take a whole book and a person much more articulate than me. You might say that Rich's relationship with Maura was in a continual state of flux. Sometimes it was fine; sometimes it was distant; and sometimes it bordered on the obsessive."

"Go on, tell us more," Jake said.

Lundeen picked up the coffee pot and tilted it towards Glory's cup that had been barely touched. He hesitated there, then refilled his own that he had hardly set down since the questioning began. In the same motion he returned the pot to the tray and took a brief sip. "Rich Baker was—is—an ambitious, driven, yes, you might even say ruthless man.

Anything, anything he wanted he got, but having it was never, ever enough. Possessing it, covering it, smothering it, clutching it cutting off its breath..." he made a fist with his thread-thin hands and squeezed until the veins on his wrist bulged, "...were what Rich Baker had to do with anything he defined as 'his'." Lundeen relaxed the balled fingers and set the free hand back down in his lap. His color changed. Calm seemed to flood his face. He took another sip of coffee. "To assume, even for a moment, that Maura would escape such scrutiny is, of course, absurd."

Glory inhaled softly. "And if he felt a possession slipping away from him?"

"He would, of course, react within the context of his personality."

"Does that mean he was capable of murder?" Glory asked.

Lundeen dismissed the comment with a wave of his hand and snorted. "My God, detective, we are all capable of murder. You in your profession should know that better than any of us. This disgusting propensity is the most pitiful flaw in our species. It exists to some degree or another in every human, I believe. No one is immune."

"No one?" Glory said.

"Not a single soul, I venture to guess, on the face of the earth. One merely needs a good enough reason—rage, jealousy, anger, fear, malice, a need to mete out justice—the list can go on."

Jake McKay kneaded his chin. "Money," he added.

"Perhaps," Lundeen answered flatly.

"I see it all the time," Jake answered.

"Ah, I'm sure you do detective. But is money really the reason? Is it frequently necessary to actually murder to get what you want? Or is there another reason? For example, I could not conceive of murdering a man to steal fifty dollars; yet, I could conceive of murdering one who stole fifty dollars from me—not because of the fifty dollars, but because of my innate need to punish someone who would violate the sanctity of my, my, uh, space. So, you see, the reasons are extraordinarily complex, and when they are roused in our psyches," Lundeen made a gun with his forefinger and thumb and pointed it at McKay, "bang. Anything is possible. Wouldn't you agree?"

Something inside Glory cringed at the veracity of his comment. Certainly, she had witnessed enough human destruction, from gang hits to domestic violence to realize the somber truth in the statement.

A noise from behind made her shuffle in her seat. Lundeen's administrative assistant entered the room and handed him a single sheet of paper. He glanced at it for a few seconds, then handed it to Glory. "I beg you, detectives, to use the utmost discretion here. These are some of the most important people in the city; or, should I say, in the world."

Glory could immediately see that it contained the names of the people who attended the party, but the addresses and phone numbers of each person had been obviously obscured before the photocopy was made. Lundeen was making it tough, putting the onus on them. She didn't like it, but could live with it. She folded the paper and placed it in her briefcase. Then she continued. "Baker. How did he get home?"

"Well, I don't know, but I assume he walked. His apartment is only a few blocks from mine. No sense in driving."

"Then how did he end up in his wife's car?" Jake asked.

"I couldn't tell you, detective. I was unaware he even had his wife's car."

151

Jake was suddenly pushing. "Is it likely he would have his wife's car without his wife?"

Lundeen shrugged, draining the last of his coffee. "Again, detective, I don't know. I can only speculate that your implication is logical. At the current state of their relationship, I doubt Maura would be lending her car to Rich."

"So, if he had the car, he had the woman?"

"Conjecture," Lundeen huffed.

Glory sat forward. "Did you have a chance to speak with Rich at all that evening?"

"Yes, several times, in passing, small talk mostly. It's noisy. It's crowded. Almost everyone is drinking too much. Not easy to carry on a conversation of any substance."

"Any indication that he had any recent contact or conflict with his wife prior to the meeting? Or any mention of him seeing her later? Meeting her somewhere?"

"Nothing, nothing like that."

"Did he even mention her?"

Lundeen paused, gazing out the window for several seconds. Then he turned his attention back to the two detectives. "He did mention her." He looked away once more. "I was in the hallway, waiting for the restroom to open. Rich came out."

"What did he say?" Glory asked when Lundeen paused again.

"He said, 'You know she's sleeping with anything with a cock.' Just like that. I knew he meant Maura, I mean, who else would it be?" Again, he hesitated.

"Go on," Glory said.

"He said that she was 'punching'—his word—Aaron Clayton, just to get back at him."

"You know Clayton?"

"Of course, he once worked here."

"Then he bragged that he knew of people who could fix—again his word—who could fix Clayton once and for all."

"Bragged?" Glory said incredulously.

"Sorry, wrong word. Commented might be more accurate. You must understand, by that time of night, he was pretty much in the bag."

"Anything else?"

Lundeen lifted the nearly empty coffee cup to his lips and tilted his head back to suck out the last few drops. When he straightened, he set the cup down. He looked directly into Glory's eyes. "Then he said, 'Maybe I should just kill the cunt, too, and get it over with'."

14

The flippers easily broke through the thin icy fuzz on the black water of the lake, and the divers, in their bright blue wet suits, were quickly diminished by the liquid gravity until their heads were like six blue balls bobbing on the surface, then disappearing, one by one. The old fishermen ringed the lip of water that meandered through the cattails that were frozen like spoiled Popsicles. The lights, the cars, the crackling of police radios, the mute twirling of ambulance flashers, the inflated yellow rafts that dotted the lake's perimeter, and these men in rubber suits had beckoned the fishermen from their silent and private fishing corners. They were the old-timers, the grizzled retirees from the oil refineries, with skin as wrinkled as old clothes and flecked with silver ice. They leaned on their poles and with a desultory rhythm emerging from their toes, tapped the buckets setting on the ground by their feet.

"Whatcha' lookin' for in dere now?" one of them said to a uniformed policeman, who walked by without answering, causing the old man to lean to the fisherman next to him and say, "What're they lookin' for in dere now, you s'pose?"

"Prolly a dead guy," somebody answered.

Jake McKay hugged himself against the cold. Another uniformed cop nudged next to him. "I thought Kane was on this case."

"Yeah, she is, but it don't take two of us to watch a bunch of frogmen go swimming. She's up in Michigan talkin' to the mother," his words came out in puffs from his nose and mouth. He watched the bleak water, motionless, like blacktop, its surface seemingly oblivious to the activity underneath. "Let me ask you a question," he said to the cop.

"Yeah?"

He blew into his gloved hands. "Would you eat a fish out of this lake?"

"Probably have," the guy said.

The lake had been created at the turn of the century through a series of dams and divergences that allowed the oil barons of the day to plow flat the sand dunes and erect the fire-breathing skeletons and huge tanks that comprise the oil refineries. The lake was dissected by a freeway. Long fingers of gravel and weeds jutted out into it several hundred yards apart. It was here that the old fishermen parked their cars and fished. And even though federal legislation had been enacted to prevent the dumping of wastes into the water, the damages caused by ninety years of using the lake as a toilet had not been mitigated.

"Me, too," McKay said. "Probably ingested enough PCBs to blow out two stomachs. Funny thing is, I always thought a bullet would get me before the fish did."

"It's not too late," the cop said, chuckling.

Time snuck between them, silently, gradually changing the landscape. Where once a pink sky settled over the horizon, now a sheet of dismal gray hung. Every now and again a head would bob to the surface, a sudden azure buoy popping through the still glassy barrier, and all the shore watchers—cops and EMTs and fishermen—would stir instantly, only to audibly expel a unified breath when the diver would simply change positions and then re-submerge.

"This is like watching paint dry," McKay said.

"It's one big mother of a lake," the cop said. "We'll be lucky they find anything today."

Even the fishermen became bored, at first smoking and murmuring and conjecturing about what might be found at the bottom of the mysterious lake, but eventually pulling apart like the seams of an old shirt, wanting to abandon this stifling silence for their personal fishing corners.

Jake McKay moved among them. "You guys all fish here every day?"

"Pert near every day there's most of us here, but it changes," said a fisherman with a shocking white beard over a deep ebony face.

"Any of you guys see anything suspicious here last Tuesday?"

"What they lookin' for in dere?" another guy said.

"Well, now, we're looking for a body," Jake replied, "and if any of you guys saw something suspicious the other morning, it would be a big help."

The bearded man leaned slightly forward as if speaking for the group. "Didn't see nuttin'." The others chimed in with shaking heads and looks of consternation.

"Nope."

"Can't say I saw nothing suspicious."

"Not me."

McKay exhaled an exasperated breath that came out of his nostrils like a ghost. "None of you guys, huh? A dark blue Mercedes?"

A voice came from the back of the group. "I seen that car, I think," and a wispy, slightly bent man came forward. His bundle of winter clothes added several pounds to his frame, but couldn't hide how spindly and small he was beneath them.

"What's your name mister?" McKay asked..

"Name's Roy Jula," he said.

"Hula? Like in the dance?"

"Yeah, only with a J."

"And you saw—what?"

"Well, that fancy car. I can see all the ways to here from my kitchen window right over yonder," he pointed with a bent finger to a house across the water. "That car was out here, oh, real early, still kinda dark, actually, but I think I seen there was two people, or maybe three..."

And then, suddenly, an explosion of activity pulled everyone away from the conversation. Two heads broke the surface, and one of the men gestured. There was a crackling of radio noise like the sudden eruption of a flock of birds from a field. The people began to run the shore parallel with the position of the diver. The back of a truck opened up and men in matching gray parkas began to remove nets and ropes and hooks. The rubber rafts seemed to turn in perfect synchronization and head to the area.

"Roy, gimme your address and phone number," McKay said, pulling his glove off with his teeth and scribbling on a small pad as Roy Jula provided details. "Now, Roy, are you home most afternoons?"

"Yeah."

157

"Okay, I'm going to stop by your place." He looked at his note pad, "Can't do it tomorrow. How about the day after? Is that okay? About, let's say, two o'clock," Jake was writing as he spoke.

"Should be."

"All right, that's Saturday, two p.m. Thanks," McKay said through clenched teeth and gloved fingers. He flipped the notepad shut and dropped it into his parka pocket and moved towards the crowd.

Within a few minutes, something was being brought to the surface. From the shore it looked like a net full of bluish clay and rags, but the shape soon defined itself. An arm hung akimbo through a rip in the net.

"Can you see, can you see?" Jake excitedly said, running, slipping against the soft ooze of the shoreline.

"They got something," the cop answered.

"Now we'll get that bastard," Jake cheered.

January bellows its cruelest off the flat, frozen tundra that surrounds Lake Michigan, and the moment Glory emerged from her car, a thousand needles of wet, icy air stung her face. The day had turned, seemingly instantly, as winter days in the Midwest do, and the crisp blue skies had morphed into sheets of dismal gray.

Glory was already too tired, too cold and too frustrated to be assaulted in this way by the weather. She had trouble finding the house in this dunes community that was crisscrossed with wandering roads and bad angles, laid out over the desultory tracks of roaming wildlife. Three times she followed a different street that dead-ended into a dune like an arrow in a target.

Finally, she arrived at what she believed to be the home of Maura Baker's mother. She could barely see the roof of the house peeking out over the snowy sands of a dune that partially hid it from the road. Dune grass, frozen like crystal, wafted in the wind, cutting at her legs as she climbed an obscure path of intermittent fieldstone to the crest of a dune. The house was behind it, and she had to descend a rickety wooden stairway down the backside of the dune to get to the front door. The still frozen lake yawned in front of her, silent and foreboding, as if it were hibernating. The atmosphere was so gray that the place where the lake and the sky collided was all but invisible.

The home was unusual in its angles, like the bow of a ship built into the hill. Icicles hung from the gables over the front door that had an ancient face of flecked burgundy paint. Glory didn't have to knock. The door was swinging open as she approached.

"Detective Kane, yes?" a woman dressed in a bulky handmade sweater said, ushering Glory in with a gentle gesture. "I'm Lisette Darby. I hope you didn't have too much trouble finding this place."

"None at all," Glory answered reflexively, knowing instantly it was a lie.

Lisette Darby led Glory to a small table for two, set against a stunning backdrop of frosty glass that afforded a sweeping vista of the lake. She was slight, almost quiet in her appearance, but still stunning for her age. Her hair was the color of embers, ever-so-gently flecked with gray. Her eyes were pale, translucent, somewhere between blue and green, depending on how the light hit them. Glory could see Maura in this mother's countenance.

159

A huge bouquet of ruby red roses erupted from a china vase in the center of the table. As Glory sat down she couldn't resist leaning into the wondrous aroma emanating from the flowers. Lisette must have noticed. "Aren't they wonderful!" she exclaimed. "I grew them myself. Would you believe such beautiful roses could be grown in January?"

"They are very lovely, and, no, I would never have known anyone could do this in the middle of winter."

Lisette arranged the roses moving petals and stems minuscule distances. "It took me years, centuries actually," she laughed. "Would you like some herbal tea, or coffee perhaps?"

Glory shook her head. "No thank you, Mrs. Darby."

"Please, call me Lisette. And what's your name, dear?"

"Glory."

"Glory? Not Gloria? How unique. Very lovely."

Glory liked Lisette Darby immensely already. "My father was a preacher. All his children had what he called 'inspired' names. My sister's name is Angel; another's is Faith; and my brother is called Obedience, if you believe it. We call him Obie."

"That is just precious," she answered, again fidgeting with the roses.

Glory cleared her throat and silence came between them. "Lisette, as I mentioned on the phone, I've come to talk about Maura."

The woman's hands stopped fidgeting. She gazed out the window pensively for a few minutes. "You can't tell on a day like this, but watching the sun set over the lake is magnificent," she whispered. "And on those perfect nights, the skyline of Chicago, tiny from here, can be seen." Then she turned her attention back to Glory. "Are you sure you wouldn't like something to drink?"

Glory smiled. "No, thank you."

Lisette steeled herself with a deep breath. "Have you heard anything new, detective?"

Glory decided not to mention the discovery in Maura's bedroom. "We're still accumulating clues, but in the meantime, your daughter is merely missing."

Lisette exhaled and again turned to the window. "How can I help?"

"Tell me about Rich and Maura."

The woman paused silently, and Glory imagined that millions of images and bits of information were flooding Lisette's memory, and she was waiting to fish one out, the right one. Finally, she spoke, slowly, with a gentle twinkle in her eye. "Richie, that's what I called him, Richie—no one else could get away calling him that—was our hero. He was tall and handsome and charming. His veneer was as thin as tissue— now there's a mixed metaphor, I should be ashamed of myself—ha ha. He was always so, so gregarious on the outside. But you knew he was a shy little boy inside. In fact, he was quite different internally, you know what I mean, the gas and spirit that churns in the soul? Different from Maura. Maura was the one who was always cocksure and aggressive, not Richie, not at first, anyway."

Glory couldn't imagine a shy bone in Rich Baker's body. "That's quite a different picture than you get meeting him now," she commented.

"Of course. You're only seeing a few inches of this man, what's left over after all the wear and tear of the years," she replied softly. She stared out the window and thought for several moments. "People change. Like these dunes. You know, they're constantly being moved by the wind, eroded by the waters. They're never the same. I'll go out this spring and where once a tree stood for twenty, thirty years, there will now be a new mound of sand burying it to its chin. Where once there was a path, there will be rolling, undulating waves of new grass. Just that quickly, it seems, but you know, we don't really realize that time and the elements have been working on these changes for centuries. We never saw them coming. Time is in the wind and the snow and the tides, moving inexorably through our lives, killing us as it goes."

Glory felt a dull ache in her own heart. "Lisette, when was the last time you saw or talked to Maura?"

The lady turned from the window. "Oh, maybe a week or so ago. She called me at least once a week."

"Any sign that things were coming to a head? Hints of a problem?"

Lisette paused in thought, then answered matter-of-factly. "No, but then Maura and I had a difficult time sometimes talking about things that I could, for example, talk to you about without any problem. I mean, you know about Sean. Maura couldn't, wouldn't talk to me about him. Never mentioned his name in my presence after..." Lisette pulled out a chair and sat down at the table next to Glory.

"I know," Glory said, gently reaching across and caressing the woman's white hands for a second.

Lisette continued, "I didn't even know when she and Rich, Richie, were having problems until well after it was too late. Though I suppose it's not surprising, not surprising."

"Why do you think that was? That Maura didn't talk to you about these things?"

"Oh, it's mother-daughter stuff, baggage from the past, I suppose. I was always maybe too hard on Maura, pushing her. You see, Glory, I always believed that for women to deal in a men's world, they had to keep their emotions in check lest, their feelings emerge and betray them. Psycho-babble, I know, and totally wrong for someone as feisty and fiery as Maura. Let's just say we are constantly working out the dynamics of our relationship. But we love each other, God, we do."

"So, you were surprised when things started going bad in Rich and Maura's marriage?" Glory said.

"Well, in a way, no, but deep down inside, yes," Lisette answered. "I mean, these were two people who, I'm telling you, literally couldn't keep their hands off one another. Used to drive my husband crazy because they couldn't sit together without wrapping their arms and legs around each other. God, it was so romantic. And they were always, you know, giving one another little pats and pecks whenever they passed."

"Sounds perfect. You would think they could have drawn on that."

"Oh, goodness, who knows? Rich started drinking. Then he started thinking with what my husband euphemistically called 'the other little head,'" she leaned forward and smiled wickedly at this reference. "Then, you know, like they say, shit started to happen."

Glory jumped inside, surprised to hear that word come out of the mouth of such a genteel woman. "Did he ever threaten her? Hit her?"

Lisette stopped cold again and burrowed into the silence, finally emerging. "I have a hard time thinking of him as a violent man," she replied slowly, "but I guess you never know."

Then after another pause she froze Glory with a look of abject fear. "Do you think she's dead, Glory?"

Glory reached across the table, through the bushy overhang of the glorious roses, and took the woman's hands in hers. "I don't know, Lisette, but we should be prepared for the worst."

Lisette looked imploringly at the detective. "So the premise you're working on is that Rich killed her?"

"Do you think that's possible?"

Lisette gazed out the window again, obviously in deep thought. "I don't think so," she finally said. "Not Richie. Not him." She collected her thoughts, turning away from Glory for a few seconds. Then she came back. "Let me tell you a story. Sean learned it at, I think, Boy Scouts or something. It was a campfire story. He laughed and laughed when he told me," Lisette's eyes sparkled at the memory. "Anyway, it seems someone lost his knife in the weeds and the boys were looking for it, but it was getting dark. One of the boys moved closer to the fire and looked there. The other kids said, 'Hey, he dropped it over here. Why are you looking over there by the fire?' And the kid answered, 'Because it's not as dark over here, I can see better.'" Lisette laughed. "I don't know why I thought of this story right now. But I guess it's appropriate."

Yes, Glory thought.

"In other words, dear, don't look in the wrong places just because it's brighter there. Hunt down your own lie," Lisette replied in a voice of eerie calm and total control.

"What does that mean, 'Hunt down your own lie'?" Glory asked.

"Take what you believe and seek not to prove it true, but to disprove it."

Glory looked across the table at the frightened woman. It was almost as though she were trying to hold onto something, a piece of the past; as if losing both Maura and Rich would be too much to bear. "It's an interesting perspective."

"Otherwise, you begin your race from the finish line rather than the starting line—there I go again with the metaphors! You feel as though you must now prove that conclusion. In the midst of your zeal, you risk overlooking many, many facts. You will shoo them away as if they were flies. Yet they can lead you to their feast."

Glory smiled at Lisette's way of making her point so visually, yet she had to listen. "Go on," she encouraged, turning to face the woman more squarely.

"It's like growing roses in January," Lisette replied, again fussing with the arrangement. "Year after year I wanted roses to bring some spring into the cold gray days of winter, and year after year the facts told me I couldn't grow them, so I never did. Then I decided to take what I believed to be the truth and prove it a lie. Voila! You now see roses where once there were only thorns."

This was a truly remarkable woman, Glory thought. "I've never thought of things that way," she replied.

"Remember, your goal is not to discover what you already believe, but to discover the truth. Be skeptical of the obvious. It is a devil's trick." Then Lisette stood up abruptly and walked toward the kitchen. "How about a drink now? Some whiskey, perhaps? I'm going to have a stiff one."

Jake McKay bulled his way through the crowd that had rapidly converged on the frogmen who were pulling the rubber dinghy onto a gravel-strewn fragment of shore. The old

165

fishermen and the other cops and searchers formed a tight ring around the craft, and all eyes were fixed on the crumpled body that lay on the deck.

"What the hell they got there?" one of the old-timers said.

"Dead as a mackerel," another intoned, and the air was filled with a cacophony of dueling voices.

"Good Lord God Almighty."

"Ain't never seen nothing like that before."

"How the hell you suppose it got in there?"

McKay moved in and leaned over the boat. Immediately, disappointment flooded him. For lying in the bottom of the craft was a melting mass of humanity, and even though it was certainly enough to hold the interest of the crowd, McKay was done with it instantly. Not only was it not the remains of Maura Baker, but it was an old man. The flesh was the color of concrete, virtually dripping off the bones. His clothes—a sleeveless t-shirt and a pair of polyester checkered pants—were almost fused to the carcass. McKay's experience immediately told him that this poor sap had been in the water a long time, at least since summer, if only judging by the clothes. Who he was and how he got there didn't mean shit to the detective. He pulled himself away from the corpse and split two observers with his hands, cursing as he thundered across the swampy shore toward his car.

15

The water rolled black, a cauldron of boiling ink, and flying from it were demons and beasts composed of ethereal vapor, elongating as they broke free from the torrent and becoming raging clouds. A swirling vortex of jiggling lines erupted upward as if some subterranean drain was expectorating its contents. And then, from the center, a fissure appeared, a minuscule speck of white flame, swirling closer, larger, screaming as it came, assuming a shape, round and fleshy. The slippery ebony ooze ran in rivulets through the crevices and bends, and the alabaster mound defined itself. A hand. Unfolding, flexing as it ripped through the dark liquid membrane. The fingers unfurled, stretching frantically upward as the water fell away. Then came the arm, thrusting, reaching for release from the darkness.

He reached for it, the desperate hand, and found himself immobilized, frozen, his own appendages pinned helplessly in vague, shapeless mud. Jesus, could he get it? A fraction of an inch at a time he strained, and, then, finally, he clasped it, felt its fingers warm and firm entwined in his own. He pulled, and the whirlpool thinned, swirling backward into the vortex to reveal a

167

body, sleek, perfectly shaped, familiar, and a face, buried in cascading hair the color of fire, a gentle face, smiling at him.

Maura. Coming out of the darkness back to him. He could bring her back if he could just find in his sinew and bones the strength to free her from death's grasp. Closer, closer, until her face was inches from his and he could feel the warmth, the scent of her breath.

And then it froze, white hot, the hand in his. The warmth fled as if being cast out. The face turned stark, frightened. The eyes bulged; the lips, the smile turned to a grim, horrified cackle of sublime evil. He squeezed, pulled, cried her name, but no sound came out.

His fingers, erupting in sweat now, clenched around their possession harder, and suddenly the hand shattered, like thin ice, falling in a billion tiny stars across the universe of swirling darkness, and Maura was swept back into the abyss.

"No! No!" he cried, as the vortex burned out like the white light of an old picture tube. Rich Baker found himself sitting upright in bed, sweat burrowing through his chest hairs.

A dream, only a dream. It was all just a dream. Wasn't this Maura lying next to him in the dark, wrapped in sheets and flowing hair? This warm, milky body breathing gently? He leaned over her, his eyes knocking against the night shadows as if they were some huge wooden door keeping him out. The body took shape, sloping mountainous curves, a valley formed by two perfectly round breasts, a secret, hidden place still under the sheets. He pulled them back.

Gently, he touched her shoulder with his fingers, then leaned onto it with his forehead and began kissing it. "Oh, Maura, thank God," he whispered.

She stirred, moaned and turned to him, moving into a cool stripe of blue light that had intruded into the room from somewhere outside. "Who?" she replied, her breath smelling of sleep, her body stained with the aroma of sweat and sex.

And then he saw her face. "Maura, no!" he cried.

"Who the fuck is Maura?" the woman snarled.

The dream came and went, day after day, alone or with someone. Several days—several dreams—later Rich Baker sat in the wordless, withering darkness, dawn leaking through the variegated skyscraper landscape of the city in the window behind him. In one hand he held an unlit cigarette, in the other a remote control. Across the room Maura beckoned to him seductively. He held her with his eyes, not hearing her words, but letting the essence of her voice fall over him like a blanket. He merely wanted to envelope himself in her presence, letting his mind imagine her perfume, the natural aroma of her hair, the feel of her warm breath. With a gentle touch he would move her. Her image jiggled, split for a moment into fragments; white jagged lines creased her face that moved jerkily, quickly. Then he would touch the button on the remote again so that the video resumed normalcy. Back and forth, over and over. The volume low. Her voice so far from her image. He watched her with an aching so subtle it was hard to grasp. If only life could be rewound like the tape. If only chosen scenes could be erased and new ones spliced in. Wouldn't it be so much better, to be forgiven simply with the flip of a switch?

He turned off the DVD and dropped the remote on the table. He had work to do.

Over the years, Rich Baker had designed and produced a life that was structured to his own version of perfection. It had become a virtual file cabinet, with drawers for its various fragments, each numbered and alphabetized. His business life occupied the top drawer, amassing the greatest amount of space, and he had fractionalized it so precisely that it was virtually at his fingertips. His downtown apartment was only a few blocks from his office. His office was across the street from his lawyer's office. His accountant, doctor, even a mistress, were all within a few blocks. And this precisely designed square of his world had become so familiar to him that it seemed wrapped in a benign aura in which he felt totally and continually safe. His world transcended his vision to permanently nestle into his subconscious so that he could navigate through it like, he imagined, a blind man becomes familiar with the placement of furniture in his home. So, dizzy from drink, or exhausted from work, until the world spun him like a merry-go-round, he could stagger along the sidewalks, knowing exactly where to place his hands to steady himself, where to lean to rest.

But in recent days, with everything that had suddenly collapsed around him, he realized that he no more owned nor controlled this environment than he could change the wind, that this perfect cocoon that he had spun around himself was full of cracks and leaks through which predators could slip.

He was outside now, walking his familiar territory toward his appointment with his attorney. He was still early, so he stopped at the coffee shop on the way to Nathan Timmins' office. It was a thin place, long, wedged between two skyscrapers like a child's book between two encyclopedia volumes. It was a private place almost, abuzz with regular clientele. They knew him there. The waitress knew him, knew what he wanted, brought him a cup of coffee and the newspaper almost as soon as he sat down. The counter people knew him. Some of the other patrons greeted him, although he didn't necessarily know their names, nor they his, but the faces were the same ones they'd been dragging in to this place for years. It was where the neighborhood folks came to eat huge bagels and drink coffee and read the Tribune, which was exactly what Rich had done to kill an hour as the pedestrian traffic shuffled past his window like a herd of steam engines, each puffing out its own trail of smoke.

Although it was, of course, different now. Certainly they acknowledged him, but the air in the place virtually trembled from their unspoken words. Their silent thoughts rumbled like distant thunder. Rich Baker was a different person now, wasn't he? Maybe a killer. Maybe not. The truth would come out. But in the meantime...

By the time he had exited the shop, morning had completely overtaken the night. It was a typical morning for Chicago at this time of year, lost between frozen and thawed. The piles of snow against the curbs were ragged, brown and dripping. The air was thick and wet and cold.

Rich came out of the coffee shop. He pulled up the collar of his coat and pulled a stocking cap out of his pocket. He pulled it down over his eyebrows—better for hiding more of his face. He put his hands in his pockets and hunched his shoulders as he stepped onto the sidewalk. The morning rush was over. The sidewalks were only dotted with people. Rich walked briskly alone. He didn't see—had no reason to notice— the car that pulled slowly away from the curb and systematically kept pace with his footsteps. He jogged against a yellow light at one intersection where a one-way street ran into the main avenue.

But the next stoplight was a different story. Rich arrived there virtually alone just as the light turned green. With only a cursory glance to his left, he jutted into the intersection. Halfway across he heard a sudden screech of tires that snapped his head back to his left. A black sedan seemed to be up on two wheels, snorting smoke and wailing, bearing down on him like a bullet. The few other walkers on the curbs and sidewalk fragmented like pieces of a glass plate dropped on the pavement. But Rich Baker froze for an instant and everything became slow, methodical, and surreal. The sedan seemed to regain its balance and shoot forward toward him, and it became instantly apparent to Baker that this was no car out of control. Quite the contrary, it was a car on a mission.

And he was the target.

For a millisecond he was rigid, as if his confused brain was searching frantically for a lost command to tell his body what to do. The car was raging toward him, a split second away. Suddenly, everything went upside down. He felt himself leave his feet, as he flew through the air. Instinctively, he thrust out both of his arms, transforming the free fall into a dive, like a baseball player stealing a base with a headfirst slide. The pavement rushed up to greet him. His hand slammed into the cold, wet, fragmented bits of cinders and salt, followed by his cheek. The car was no longer in his sight lines, but he could still feel it near him, like a raging bull.

The slick, wet, half-melted pavement seemed to carry him forward. He seemed to float across it quickly, so quickly that everything blurred as it rushed by. There was a sudden jolt as his shoulder crashed into the front bumper of a parked automobile. His head disappeared into the darkness beneath it. One hand was wedged beneath a tire. An enormous weight pinned him to the ground. He tried to turn over, to throw off the burden, and, then, it was gone. Someone—who?—someone had tackled him, had knocked him out of the way, had saved his life. He laid there for a second, then turned, unfolding to a semi-crouch. His eyes scanned the bleak, horrified faces of the other people. He pulled himself upright but was instantly jerked in the opposite direction by a sound that was either a scream from the crowd, a screech of tires, the bleat of a car horn, or an instinctual premonition from deep in his bowels. And as he turned, he saw himself, once again, a few feet, a second away from the murderous automobile that had, again, reared back and charged.

Rich twisted away from it and, placing his hand on the hood of the car under which he had momentarily lain, vaulted himself over it. The world spun; the tops of buildings appeared, then vanished. He bounced off the hood and into a clutter of newspaper boxes, snow and curb. He heard a bone shaking crash and an explosion of glass. The parked car lurched forward, then stopped. There was another squeal of tires as the assault car peeled itself away and tore down the street. Then everything went black.

He stayed in the darkness, but had no way of judging how long. He could hear bits of conversation around him. Someone was helping him up. He was standing. A man in a dark coat was supporting him, talking, but Rich couldn't understand the words.

Then things clarified.

"Are you all right?" the man was saying.

Rich brushed cinders and bits of glass from his hands. He nodded.

"... no accident," someone was saying.

"... went right for him..."

"...call the police..."

"... didn't get the license number..."

"... happened so fast..."

"... the police..."

"... my God, that man saved his..."

"... call the police..."

"... we should get the police..."

"... hey, I know this guy..."

Rich Baker suddenly regained total focus. His pants leg was crusted with cinders. Bright pink flesh peered out from a greasy slit that ran from his knee nearly to the cuff. The windshield of the parked car threw back into Rich's face the image of a ghost, pallid, with huge eyes cracked red like desert clay and hair that seemed to explode from the scalp, frozen in frantic disarray. The images of what had just happened to him flew through his mind in random fashion. He struggled to put them in order, pacing them to the Uzi-like burps of breath that he inhaled and expelled.

His instincts took over. No police, he thought. No more questions. He shook himself free of the man who'd helped him up and began to run as rapidly as he could away from the crowd. He could hear their voices fading as he limped down the street.

16

Roy Jula felt old in the bones. That's what happened whenever he stayed out too long at the lake. Too long and winter was able to gnaw through his layers of clothes and burrow into his joints, making the walk home across the tundra more difficult and slower. But this day it seemed a small price to pay for the four perfect-sized lake perch that lay in his bag. He warmed himself by imagining the butter sizzling in the pan. But it only worked in temporary spurts to take his mind off his toes that had begun curling into themselves to keep warm.

Goddamn it, he thought, his knees throbbing, this is slow. Ice crunched beneath his feet, occasionally breaking and dropping his foot into shallow puddles, causing him to stumble forward, almost losing his balance. Losing his balance; he hated losing his balance. He hated elbows that ached each time he shifted his bag and his pole from one arm to the other. He hated being old. As a kid he could navigate this field like a deer, in minutes. He could ramble across the gravel and into the weedy part and then, Christ, fly over the fence like a bird. But old age sat on his shoulders like a sack of coal, and there was no way he could haul his ass over that fence now, so the distance became four, five times farther because he had to go around the fence and through the alley and then back up onto the street.

The problem was, this was going to make him late, and he wanted time to take a bath to chase the chill from his bones before the big burly cop showed up to question him about what he had seen.

Jula came finally to the alley. A cat with a broken ear and a pus-swollen eye rattled out from behind a garbage can and began following him, its good eye and sensitive nose affixed on the basket of fish. He half-heartedly tried to shoo the hungry beast away, but the cat wasn't buying it. It followed him out of the alley and onto the sidewalk. Jula passed in front of the window of the coffee shop and automatically turned into the doorway. His toes were digging through the bottom of his shoes, and he wasn't sure he'd make it the four blocks home without warming up for a second.

"Well now, once again the fisherman returns from the sea," the red-faced, undulating mound of man in a white apron behind the counter, called out as Roy entered. "How's the catch today, captain? And who's your mangy friend?" he said, pointing at the cat that was up on it hind legs and scratching at the glass on the door.

Roy just made a shooing motion towards the cat and then patted the basket. "A good day, a real good day," he replied, nodding to the others in the small room. Three of the neighborhood guys were dropping cards onto a table and pulling tricks. This was a good place, a warm place, a place where Roy was comfortable. Here the guys could talk politics or sports over a single pot of decaf and nobody was chasing them out or expecting much more from them. It was as close as any place came to being a second home to Roy Jula and the other old-timers of the neighborhood.

The cook poured Roy a cup of coffee and set it before him as the fisherman took a stool. "Out a lot longer than usual today, weren't you?" the cook said.

Jula took the cup and blew away the steam, drawing the radiant heat from the edges through his hands and into his aching joints. "Too damned long," he said, "liked to frostbite my liver. Next time you see me gone for so long, send the cavalry, yeah?"

From behind he heard an expletive being uttered as a card snapped against the table top. "Hey, Roy, wanna do some euchre with us?" the man said, writing his points down on a small pad.

Roy turned on the swivel stool. "No can do, guys. Got an appointment."

"What, you having the old prostate checked again or what?" the guy said.

"You like that doctor an awful lot, don't you?" one of the other players added, wiggling a finger toward Jula.

Roy chuckled. "Well, now, even though it ain't the business of none of you rum heads, I gotta meet that big hairy cop who was down at the lake the other day, when they found that body."

The cook leaned on two flour-stained arms. "I thought that body wasn't who they was looking for."

"Wasn't," Roy said, sipping slowly from the coffee. "They want to know what I saw."

"What did you see down there?" the card player said, shuffling the deck.

"That's a damn good question. I was sitting in my kitchen actually. It was dark. Couldn't sleep. Must have been about four o'clock in the morning. You don't see car lights that often out that away, so when they come in, I sat at my kitchen table and watched 'em."

The cook was bent over the counter, listening carefully. "Yeah, so what did you see?"

Roy pursed his lips. "Car lights. Shadows moving behind them. I don't really know. All I can tell you is that car didn't stay there all night. I swear it got there, there was a lot of commotion for a few minutes, then the lights left. I was surprised to see it out there when the sun come up."

"You seen a whole bunch of nothin'," the card player said, "and if I was you, which I'm glad I ain't, I would stay the hell out of it."

The feeling was coming back to Roy's toes, and he was drinking the coffee faster now. He glanced at the clock on the wall and started to slide off the stool. "Why you say that?"

The player was dealing cards now. He didn't look up. "'Cause you don't really know nothing and all talking to the cops is gonna do is pull you into a situation you don't want nothin' to do with. I'm telling you, they'll hound your butt for weeks. All I'm saying is who needs that crap?"

Roy was shuffling towards the door. "Yeah, you're probably right. Damn! Me and my big mouth."

"Have a good one, Roy," the chef said.

Roy was back out in the cold afternoon air, and his bones reacted quickly, stiffening again, despite the temporary relief provided by his respite at the coffee shop. His mind was now reeling with colliding images. What was he going to say? Hell, he wasn't even sure what he saw. The car, that's for sure. It

178

was dark. The lights came in suddenly out of nowhere and then were turned off. A few minutes later they were back on and moving out. So why was it there in the morning? Another car? Could have been. Maybe not even the same car from the dark time. Maybe some kids drinking beer. Should he speculate to the cop about this? What if he was wrong? Wasn't that like perjury or something? Could he get into trouble for saying something wrong that he wasn't totally sure of? Shit, he thought, he shouldn't have opened his big mouth.

Somehow, the diseased feline was back purring at his footsteps. He wanted to kick it into a snow bank, do it a favor, put it out of its misery, but he didn't.

Ten minutes later he turned the corner of his block. His home was at last within striking distance, and he felt like there was a chance he would make it, despite the ache in his feet and knees. Then the scene hit him. A black sedan was sitting in front of the brick bungalow, exhaling blue clouds from its exhaust. Jula's hand trembled from the cold as he raised it enough to shake down his sleeve to see his wristwatch. He swore the burly cop said two o'clock, and it was only quarter to one. Shit, this meant no bath.

The cat followed as Jula approached the black car, hesitating to see if its occupants were indeed waiting for him. He then turned and moved up his sidewalk. Behind him, he heard a car door open. Then another. A voice called to him. "Excuse me, are you Mr. Jula?"

Roy turned, stopping on a thin patch of ice that had puddled up from the crack in his sidewalk. He turned, expecting to see the burly cop. But there were two men there. Men in long gray coats. Neither of them was the cop. "Yeah, that's me," he answered.

179

"Mr. Jula," one of them said, closing the door and coming forward, "we have to talk." With three long strides, both men were beside him. One placed a gloved hand on Roy's shoulder and steered him toward the house at a much more gingerly pace, looking around suspiciously as they ascended the porch.

17

That little motherfucking prick was all Tucker Hines could think of as he struggled up the first flight of stairs to Taters Poteet's apartment. First, because the turd was four floors up and he ought to try to carry a hump like this up a winding staircase, and secondly, but most importantly, because the weasel dick was supposed to meet him for breakfast and a small job Tuck had arranged for him, and now the defective sperm wasn't even returning his phone calls. Tuck stopped at the landing and leaned on the rail, catching his breath. What the hell was the matter with Poteet, anyway? He disappears for nearly a week without telling anyone, then comes back and now this. The hunchback collected himself, took a deep breath and continued up the wooden steps that whined and creaked under his feet.

Finally he made it to the fourth floor, and as he moved toward Poteet's door he shouted, "You better be there, you little fuck, 'cause I ain't coming up the side of Mount fucking Everest to find you not at home." He dragged his hand across the wall to steady himself and flecks of paint and plaster snowed onto the floor. "Open up, shit face," he cried, pounding on the door with his fist. All the way up, he could smell the place. It

181

always took a few minutes to adjust to the sour, rotten egg, urine, and feces brew that hovered in the air, but today it was worse. Something different. Something lurking in the walls.

He knocked on the door again. Silence.

Tucker Hines wheezed and raised his fist again, thundering the door so hard that the single light bulb that hung from a chain on the ceiling flickered as it swayed. Pissed now, spit collecting at the sides of his mouth, he grabbed the door handle and pushed. There was no resistance as the door swung open, and the instant it did, he was assaulted by a wave of unbearable stench. Recoiling from it, he pulled his arm across his face to staunch the hideous odor. Of course, he knew what it was he smelled, even though he had never encountered it in real life. Death. Death, pure and evil.

He took short, quick breaths, half through his mouth, rancid air filtered through the cloth of his winter coat. A choir of flies droned rhythmically in the dim light. *Flies, my lord, in the middle of winter.* Death did that, brought them right out of their hibernation.

His eyes struggled in the darkness to pull together the scene. It took a few seconds to coalesce and, the instant it did, Tucker Hines, fell to his knees, buried his face in his hands and sobbed. "Oh, my friend," he cried. "Look what they did to my friend."

18

Emptiness has its own sound, and it can be as cacophonous as an explosion. Like any good cop, Glory Kane could feel absence or presence in a room, feel it with a stunning sense of accuracy. And the starkness, the silence, the temperature of the ambience of Roy Jula's home rolled over her like a wave as she followed Jake McKay across the threshold. She could see the same recognition on her partner's face, a sense of foreboding and confusion that he expressed with a slightly stifled exhalation of air. Glory and he had been here twice before, first at the appointed time and again the next morning, to speak with the craggy fisherman who claimed to have seen something in the early morning hours at the lake near the refinery. Both times they pounded on the door to no avail and wedged themselves between frozen hedges and the sides of the house to peer in the windows. Finally, they went next door where a thin haired little lady by the name of Mrs. Petrovich gave them the name of Jula's daughter.

It was Maria Jula Taylor's trembling hands that opened the door for the detectives. She then moved aside to let them enter, clutching her blouse around her throat and waiting in the foyer. "Good afternoon, I'm Detective McKay, this is Detective

Kane," Jake said, driving in like a bull, his head swiveling hard enough to squeak, his meaty hand flashing his badge. "Can we come in?"

"I'm Maria Jula, uh, Taylor," she said.

"Nice to meet you, Mrs. Taylor," Glory said, extending a hand as Jake stomped by and disappeared into a dark hallway. "When was the last time you spoke with your father?"

"Umm, Sunday afternoon. I always call him on Sunday. I live out in the western suburbs, so I check on him at least once a week."

"Did he seem agitated, despondent, confused, sick?"

Maria Taylor emphatically shook her head. "No, no, not at all. He was just fine."

Glory nodded and moved into the living room. Although the warm air was fetid and stale, as furnace heat becomes in the winter, it did not carry the instantly recognizable and repugnant stench of death, a fact that Glory could instantly discern. It took several seconds for her eyes to adjust to the darkness, but as the room took shape, Glory sensed that the door had not only separated them from the outside, but also was a passageway to another time. From the large rose bouquet patterns on the wallpaper yellowed from decades of cigarette smoke and oil heat, to the brown curved sofa that dominated the living room, Roy Jula's bungalow was a fossilized look at his life in the mid 1960s, an intact mastodon frozen in ice. On the wall behind the swivel rocker of pea-green Naugahyde was a painting of John and Robert Kennedy, and Pope John Paul II smiled and blessed the room from a cracked frame above the television. The blonde veneer end tables were ring stained and chipped, and the buffet was littered with fishing paraphernalia, rubber Day-glo worms, kinetic-colored lures, shining hooks.

But even these items, when examined closely, were laid out neatly, in rows. In fact, the entire living room was extraordinarily neat and clean.

Glory carefully swept the scene with her eyes that stopped on a newspaper that had been reassembled, sports page first, on a coffee table. She picked it up. It was two days old. "Mrs. Taylor," she called to Jula's daughter, who was still standing, frozen in anticipation, by the door, "did your father get the newspaper delivered every day, or did he buy one somewhere?"

Maria cautiously came a few more steps into the room. "No, uh, he always bought it just down the street at the coffee shop, just right down at the end of the block."

"Is there any place he may have gone? Relatives he might be visiting?"

Maria sat down on the edge of the couch, kneading her hands. "No. I mean he wouldn't without letting me know."

"So, it wasn't like him to just leave?"

"Not at all. Not at all like him. In fact, I couldn't imagine him sleeping in a bed that wasn't his own. His whole world was this block, and the lake out there where he went fishing every day."

Glory moved slowly to a wall where a history of family photos stared back at her. She recognized Maria in several of them, the same angular face that had accompanied her to adulthood. She gently reached out and straightened a picture of an attractive woman and man, one of those hand-tinted portraits. "Is this your mother and father?"

Maria smiled and nodded.

"How was your father's health?" Glory asked, moving away from the collage of photographs.

"Excellent. My brother and I always laughed that he was too mean to live and too strong to die," she replied, a slight crack in her voice.

Glory sat down next to her on the couch. "What do you think might have happened to him? Where he might have gone?"

Maria's voice quivered, and she shook her head. "I don't know," she whispered. "He – I can't help but think that something awful, just awful, has happened to him. But I don't know what it could be. I mean, he knew the lake so well, it's almost impossible to conceive he'd fall in or anything. All I know is, I'm scared, very, very scared."

Glory took her hands and squeezed them gently. She then stood up and moved across the burnt orange shag carpeting towards the kitchen. The kitchen was bright and as clean as the living room. No dishes in the sink. No crumbs on the counter. A sheet of white daylight angled in between the checkered curtains on the window behind the sink, seemingly bouncing off the white Formica table top. Glory glanced out the window and stopped. She could see quite clearly across a scraggly, mushy field, the mountains of storage tanks that pock marked the horizon and, in front of them, the strip of gravel side road where Rich Baker had been found that morning in his wife's car.

She sat down at the kitchen table to check the view from there. Although the window above the sink was too high, the array of glass panels on the back door provided an equally lucid panorama. It would have been possible for Roy Jula to sit here eating a piece of toast and watch the entire episode unfold.

Her thoughts were shaken by the booming sound of McKay's voice beckoning her to the bedroom. She stood up and went toward the sound.

She was quickly through the hallway and into the bedroom, and she was, once again, struck by the neatness of it all. The bed was made, covered in a multi-colored homemade quilt. The dresser top, like the buffet, was arrayed in fishing stuff, but otherwise immaculate.

"What's wrong with this picture?" Jake said, his hands on his hips.

"Nobody lives here, that's what's wrong," Glory replied.

"At least not today."

"I found a newspaper in the living room. Two days old."

McKay pursed his lips and shook his head. "Old Roy is gone."

"Looks that way."

"Seems to be a trend in this case, people disappearing in puffs of smoke."

Glory agreed. "It is a bit puzzling, isn't it?"

"Let's go door-to-door, talk to the neighbors."

"I'll go down to the coffee shop at the end of the block, talk to the proprietor. Mrs. Taylor says her dad bought a newspaper there every morning."

Jake made a grunting sound. "A dime will get you ten that no one has seen old' Roy in at least two days."

Glory nodded. "That's a bet I'm not willing to make." Then she walked back to the living room to talk to Jula's daughter.

187

19

It looked as though a bomb had gone off on Glory Kane's kitchen table. Papers and photographs, open manila folders and note cards were strewn from end to end and spilled onto the floor. It was a huge puzzle, but the pieces had no edges; the image it was to create had no focus, no shape nor form. She was certain of only one thing: this was not as simple as it appeared. People were disappearing, clues were showing up in the oddest places. Richard Baker was either totally incapable of murdering his wife, or destined to do it, depending on who you talked to. Rodriguez was breathing down her neck. Harold Devalane, the state's attorney, was breathing down his. Oh, but he was loving it, too. The reporters. The microphones. Glory could see the gears meshing in Devalane's head. Everyone was learning his name. This was going to be perfect.

Problem was, in the mountain of clues that cascaded across her kitchen, there wasn't one, not a single image or idea that put Baker and Maura together that night. Despite what Jake McKay or Frank Rodriguez or the media or the public thought, a defense attorney with the savvy and experience of Nathan Timmins would shred the tissue thin evidence that the state did have. Then all hell would break loose.

Glory couldn't—wasn't going to—let that happen. She needed one piece, that was all. She felt it in her bones. There was something out there, a tiny hunk of connective tissue that could bring this all together. She just didn't know what it was or where to look next.

She stood up and ran her fingers through her hair. Sleep? Oh yeah, that's where she should have been. But forget about that. She couldn't get there and she knew it, wouldn't be able to all night. Her reverie was suddenly shattered by the sound of her telephone. She moved away from the table, tossed the sheath of papers she was holding back into the debris from which it sprang, and picked up the receiver. "Yeah," she muttered into it.

"Detective Kane, this is Dr. Jones. I have something, er, someone here you will want to see."

Lying on the sterile white table was yet another reason Dr. Henry Jones had earned the nickname "Bones." For, even though the middle-aged man on the slab had only been dead a day or so, he was not much more than that—bones wound tightly in skin as thin as tissue paper that was blue and whorled with veins like marble. The corpse's lips were pulled back in a hideous hyena-like grin. One eye was nearly closed, but the other was wide open, reflecting back the harsh pink light that hovered overhead.

Bones Jones jumped at every flash of car lights that bent around the corner and jabbed through the windows of the basement laboratory. He got jumpy like that at night, jumpy like that after nineteen straight hours of work. He was a doc, he knew exactly what was going on in his body, but he couldn't help it. There wasn't time to sleep, and he hated the thought of the wasted opportunity, anyway. He supposed that this weakness stemmed from his inability to delegate. He had to check on every corpse or bag of bones or bucket of sludge that came into his forensic pathology lab. Nobody else, at least not at first. He was first, always first.

He was sixty-two years old and not about to change. But he was feeling a surge of energy. What fortuitous luck that Detective Kane, too, was a denizen of the night, that he hadn't angered her by calling so late. But he knew she was under pressure and what he had under this sheet would be important to her, although he wasn't certain how.

He puttered around in the harsh light, picking up scraps from the floor, pacing the room. He thought for a second that most people would be anxious in the same situation. Hell, most people would be anxious just being alone in a room with a corpse that looked woefully lost, as if wandering somewhere between life and death, lost until he could be buried or burned. It was not a sight fit for the world, this dead thing on the slab. It was neither human nor non-human. Forty years in the business had waxed Dr. Bones Jones with a veneer through which no sentiment, no connection, no feeling for the specimens on his table could penetrate. Even friends of his whom he had autopsied—whose brains and hearts he had held in his hands—were merely bones and tissues and organs, a random coalescence of protoplasm that just happened to have formed itself at one time into the shape of a human being. To him they were, indeed, specimens, science projects, mysteries.

And as Bones Jones gazed upon the mottled purple body wrapped in swaddling clothes and bathed in fluorescent lights, he wondered what secrets it held. Perhaps Detective Kane could fill in the blanks.

He pulled the sheet over the corpse's head, sat down, lit a cigarette and waited. Holding the smoke between his fingers, he mocked himself. How many packs a day? How many charcoal lungs had he pulled, dripping and disintegrating in his hands, out of corpses? He knew exactly how his own must look as he placed the cigarette again to his lips and watched the embers on the tip glow orange and comforting as he inhaled.

Another wedge of yellow light threw a pattern on the wall. This time, however, it didn't continue rolling past. This time it stopped, and Dr. Bones Jones took a last drag and stubbed out the cigarette in an ash tray. He moved quickly to the door in anticipation of the guest. Seconds later he was opening the door, and Glory Kane entered, dragging some darkness in with her.

"Well, well, Detective Kane. Welcome to my humble abode."

"Hi, Bonesy," Glory said. "You have something for me?"

He gently closed the door behind her. "Well, of that I am not quite sure." He shuffled Glory toward a chair. "Here, sit down, sit down. It's late, you must be dead on your feet."

Glory glanced at the chair but instead circled the corpse under the sheet on the table. "Is this why I'm here?"

"Uh, yes, more or less." Jones moved to the corpse and took a corner of the white linen. He pulled it back.

"Who is it?"

"A John Doe. Pulled from behind a dumpster out on Kedzie. Here, take a look," he said, gently turning the head of the corpse enough to reveal a bullet hole at the base of the skull."

"Classic gangland hit, looks like to me," Glory said.

"I'd say so, too. Do you recognize the guy? "

191

Glory leaned over and examined the face more closely. "Looks almost happy to be dead doesn't he? No, I don't know him. Should I?" She wiggled out of her coat and laid it across a nearby chair. Jones walked to the other side of the room and picked up a plastic bag that had been setting on the counter, pulled another chair closer and nimbly occupied it, facing her.

"Well, remember you told me to contact you if anything came up, no matter how insignificant it may seem?" he was fumbling in the plastic bag. He extracted what he was searching for. "I thought you might find this of interest." He handed her several boxes of matches, all bearing the now familiar logo of The Pachyderm.

Glory took it in her hands and flipped it over and over. "These were—where?—in his pocket?"

"Yes, ma'am."

"What's he, a match collector or something?"

"Well, judging from his clothes and general condition, his teeth and so forth, the crude haircut, I'd say he was, well, indigent or really poor. Maybe some kind of street punk. You know what I mean. Not quite homeless, but living from day to day."

"Doing odd jobs for gang bangers, druggies, etcetera?" Glory finished his sentence.

"You know the kind better than I do."

"He was found on Kedzie, you say?"

"Yes."

"That's the other side of town."

"Not far from this place The Pachyderm."

Glory looked at the match boxes for several more seconds. "What the hell is going on here, Bonesy?" she said softly. "Is it just coincidence? Another bloody mess, somehow, if even peripherally, attached to the restaurant where Maura Baker was, to our best knowledge, last seen." She handed back the evidence and rubbed her eyes. "Any theories, Bones?"

Bones Jones shrugged. "Not particularly, but I thought maybe there was some connection."

"Your thought was good, Jonesy," she replied. "Do you think you'll be able to ID this guy at some time or another?"

Bones Jones' eyes twinkled mischievously. "Oh, heavens to Betsy, yes," he laughed. My guess is his finger prints are in AFIS, or maybe some DNA in the database. We'll put his face back together and circulate some renderings. Unless this guy never lived, we should be able to put a name to him."

Glory fidgeted in her chair, repositioning the coat across her lap. "Of course I knew that. It's just that..."

"It's just that it's your first murder case and you are anxious and you can't sleep, and so you're wandering the dangerous streets to visit a decrepit old man who shares your insomnia," Jones said, laughing.

"Something like that," Glory answered sheepishly.

"Well, let me reassure you that I have identified hundreds, maybe thousands of corpses, many with much less evidence than we have already accumulated here."

Glory sighed. It was obvious to Dr. Jones that she was growing weary. He set down the plastic bag at the head of the corpse, stood up and shuffled to a built-in wall of drawers. "Let me show you what I mean," he said. "My prized possessions. Souvenirs, mementos that put me on the board, so to speak." He pulled opened a drawer and was squinting to read the tabs on the meandering line of manila folders. "Ah, yes. Here, here we go," he said. He removed a file from the drawer. From it he extracted a small white envelope, the contents of which he shook into his hand.

"There we go. Take a look at this," he said, coming back toward Glory. He proffered an open palm to her. She leaned in and examined an array of tiny objects in Bones Jones' hand.

"What are they?" she asked. "So small. That one looks like a fingernail."

"Small in stature or weight, perhaps, but monumentally huge in the truths they revealed." Jones plucked one of the objects out of his hand with his thumb and forefinger. He held it up to the light. "This is a tiny piece of a sesamoid bone from a foot. We found it, and the three other fragments, rattling around in, of all places, a washing machine."

"A washing machine?"

"You bet. Must have been fifteen years ago. A guy reported his gay roommate missing," Dr. Jones dropped the fragment back into his hand and began gently sorting through the other debris with his index finger. "Well, the police found body parts half buried in a forest preserve, just bits and pieces. The guy had been hacked up pretty bad. So, the cops' first instinct was the roommate, but they couldn't find anything connecting him. They scoured the car, picked the house apart. Nothing." He stopped and then lifted another piece, again holding it out to her. "Then we found these tiny pieces in the crevices of the washing machine agitator in the guy's apartment. This one here," he handed it to her, "was especially meaningful. It contains the tiniest smudge of paint."

Glory took the fragment and examined it carefully. She shrugged her shoulders. "I don't see it."

"Oh, it's there, and it matched perfectly with factory paint used in the manufacture of a specific brand of ax. And the

194

hacked up body had the same paint on it. Just so happens, the roomie had purchased a brand new, spanking clean ax from a local hardware store right around the time of the other guy's disappearance."

Glory's eyes widened in sudden revelation. "I get it. The roomie chopped him up, spread him around, but these tiny pieces fell—I don't know, like in his pockets—and when he did the wash, they came out."

"Like they say, it all comes out in the wash," Bones chuckled, taking the piece from Glory and funneling them all back into the envelope. "We matched these samples with the parts found in the forest preserve, were even able to identify the weapon. It was as easy as that."

Glory smiled. "That's why you're the best."

"Indeed it is, and, indeed, I am," Jones chuckled, shuffling back to the cabinet. In a few seconds he was back and had lifted the plastic bag from the table of the corpse. "Oh, by the way, I thought that you might want some photographs of this John Doe to show around, you know. So I snapped some earlier." He walked to a printer on a counter and extracted three photos from the tray. "Don't know, maybe they will help both of us. Perhaps you show them to someone who knows the guy, save the state some money," he said, handing them over. "I hope I didn't disrupt your evening."

"Jonesy, you're the king, you know that," Glory said.

"Yes, I am," he replied.

PART TWO:
ASHES TO ASHES

20

He slipped easily into his invisibility and wore it as if it were a smock. He could become smoke or fog if the situation demanded it; could morph into a puddle on the pavement. He was bricks and mortar, wallpaper, a potted plant. He confidently felt that he had never been seen when tailing someone. Perhaps it was his eyes and their uncanny ability to see clearly through distance and darkness that allowed him to hang so far back, beyond the boundaries of most people's peripheral vision. He was also virtually immune to the elements. Cold, perhaps, came to his skin, but bounced away as if dismissed by some impenetrable shield. He could stand for hours wrapped in a winter's night without so much as a shiver. This night he had dissolved into the ethereal miasma of street noise and mist as he followed Rich Baker.

Baker was easy. Baker was a walker. There was no luck involved here; no need to hail a cab while another was still in sight. The stalker could just hang back and watch the lanky rich man move like a cat in his own jungle, so used to preying on people, unaware that he was being preyed upon.

The stalker had picked up Baker the instant he had emerged from his apartment complex and followed him to the lobby of the hotel where he connected with a beautiful red-haired woman. Hooker was the stalker's first thought. But younger than Baker by a long shot. High class, nonetheless. Very high class. A grand a night, he thought, not counting dinner. And probably worth it to a guy like Baker, to whom a thousand dollars was piss away money, and to whom getting his rocks off in a different place every night was like therapy.

They had eaten dinner, Baker and this beautiful woman, in the swank hotel restaurant. There was much nuzzling and laughter. At one point, she had reached below the table and allowed her hand to climb Baker's leg like a spider, coming to rest finally in his crotch. Baker had tried to act nonchalant as she rubbed him there, but his eyes had stuttered briefly as he became aroused. It was funny the way they, too, felt invisible, unaware that their every move was being watched.

Moments later they slid out of their chairs. Baker cleverly kept a coat folded over one arm and strategically placed it to hide his crotch. They went upstairs. The stalker merely watched the numbers on the elevator to see on which floor they'd stopped. Then he followed. He found their room easily enough. The sounds of serious passion leaked through the crack in the door, groans, cries, pounding. The stalker could see the fluttering of shadows through the crack, and he laughed as he imagined Baker's white ass bobbing atop the redhead right there on the floor next to the door.

He walked over to the house phone by the elevator bank and rang the room. He could hear the phone ringing across the hall, a fraction of a second sooner than the gentle trill that came through the receiver. It rang seven, eight times and he stopped counting. He wasn't about to hang up. There was a click and an out of breath voice, "Yeah?"

198

The stalker simply smiled and hung up.

Rich Baker, tie askew and shirt unbuttoned, sweat on his brow, hung up the phone. It rattled from his trembling hand as it nestled into the cradle. A ring, shattering the silence and the darkness of the room. Followed by some kind of mechanical noise for a nanosecond, then a click, and silence. Strange. Eerie in its implication. Who? A wrong number? Logical, but Rich no longer believed in logic or coincidence, and the unexpected intrusion now caused him to stop the slight tremor in his fingers by purposely slowing his breath. Since that cold morning, Rich Baker felt the world differently than he had ever felt it before. It was both instinctual and tactile. He could be walking down the street, for example, and see a couple speaking to one another a block away, and he would find himself thrust into that distant conversation, his mind focused on what they were saying while the rest of the world blurred. He could also feel his environment in the tips of his fingers. Everything, every sound, every rustle of leaves, the splash of tires in a mud puddle, the rhythmic drip-drip-drip of rain against a window, the wind turning a corner of a skyscraper and heading for him—he sensed them all in crackling electrical messages absorbed by his very being. He felt the tingle now as the receiver stopped its tiny trembling.

The girl, Jessica—was that her name? Yes—was on the bed now, her hair cascading across the pillow, her knee bent upwards in an inverted V as she removed her silk stockings.

"Who was that on the phone?" she asked.

Rich stared for a second at the instrument, as if it might ring again. "Uh, wrong number. I guess. Nobody."

She bounced upright on the bed and began unbuttoning her silk blouse. Then she paused. "You want to help me with any of this?"

Rich slowly took his eyes away from the phone. "Uh, no thanks."

"Okay," she bubbled, pulling the loosened blouse over her head. First, two perfect—too perfect—breasts lolled out, then her hair, exploding.

"Wait," Rich said, putting up a hand. He moved toward the mini bar. "Let's talk. Is that okay?"

She tossed the blouse aside and ran her fingers through her hair. "Sure," she said, shaking her curls.

"Something from here?" he said, opening the mini bar door.

"Oh, beer, I guess."

Rich took out two Heinekens and walked over and sat on the edge of the bed. He handed her a bottle. "Are you old enough?" he heard himself say, and the pathetic humor of the situation sickened him, the truth in it, as it left his throat.

"Duh. Of course," she said, taking the beer and opening it. Foam came to the top immediately and she slurped it off.

"How old are you?"

She took a sip. "Me? How old are you?"

"I'm forty-eight."

"Well, I'm twenty-eight." The light from the nightstand cast an amber glow onto her breasts, turning the nipples dark, almost black.

"Really?" Rich said. "Twenty-eight, you say?"

"Did I say twenty-eight? I meant, uh, twenty-two, no three."

Sean would have been twenty-three. "How long have you been, you know..."

"An escort? Two years." She sipped again from the green bottle. Rich watched the delicate muscles of her neck and throat constrict as the liquid was absorbed.

"Do you enjoy the work?"

"Yeah, mostly. It's not too hard, and, hey, I couldn't make this much money any other way.

"So, you do it strictly for the money."

"It's a job, you know. That's all. Nobody usually wants to make it any more than that. Guys like you. You're a businessman, so I try to keep it businesslike, in a friendly way. I deliver, you pay. It's ancient. Commerce at its best. And I get to go to a lot of nice places."

"You've met a lot of men."

"Yeah. A few hundred, maybe."

"They all pretty nice?"

"Mostly. A few creeps here and there."

"Were you ever frightened? I mean, did you ever think you might be hurt by someone?"

She had brought the bottle to her mouth, but stopped it a fraction of an inch from her lips. Her dark brown eyes peered demurely at him. "You're not going to hurt me, are you?"

"Of course not. I was just wondering if you've ever been scared. There are a lot of real jerks out there."

She shook her head. Her hair caught the light and bent it through its waves. "No. I mean, I charge so much I guess I mostly get high class guys," she paused, "like you. Once there was a guy who made me call him Elvis and made me sing while he, he did his business. I didn't know all the words, I think it was 'Is She Lonesome Tonight?'"

"'Are you?'" Baker interrupted.

"Am I what?"

201

"No, the name of the song is 'Are You Lonesome Tonight?'"

"Yeah, that was it. But, hell, how was I supposed to know all the words? I mean, Elvis! Give me a break. Like, a thousand years ago!"

"So, you didn't know the words. What did he do?"

"He hit me, but I don't think he meant it. I don't think." The last three words were whispered.

"How about friends in the business? Any of them ever get hurt?"

"Sure. One girl, not really a friend of mine or nothing, but I know her, got beat up pretty bad, just last week."

"Doesn't it make you, well, nervous?"

She shrugged. Her ample breasts barely moved. "No, not really. One of the hazards of the job, like working construction on a tall building or something. You just gotta keep your balance and wear a hard hat. Ha-ha."

"Do you have a family?" Rich hadn't moved from the edge of the bed, hadn't opened his beer.

"Yeah."

"Are they from around here?"

"No, they're from downstate."

"Do they know what you do for a living?"

She giggled, "Of course not, they'd kill me. They think I'm a salesperson. Industrial paint products. I made it up. Actually, I was out with a guy who did that. It sounded good to me, so that's what I told my mom."

"Is it worth it? Hiding the truth from your parents?"

She bounced forward on the bed and handed him the now empty beer bottle. "Hey, you're running out of time, buddy boy." She wrapped her naked torso around his and ran her fingers into his open shirt. "I'm on the clock."

"Do you know who I am, Jessica?"

"I don't think so."

"You don't watch TV? The news or anything?"

"The news is too depressing."

"Yes, it is. It really is." Rich gently pushed her away and stood up. "Put your clothes back on, Jessica," he said, walking toward the dresser.

"Why? Is something wrong?" she said, concerned.

"No. Nothing's—I've changed my mind."

She grabbed her silk blouse and rolled it around in front of herself, looking for the right holes. "You've already paid me, mister, I hope you're not looking for a refund. I've spent quite a bit of valuable time tonight with you. I expect to..."

Rich reached into his pocket and pulled out his clip of money. He removed five one hundred dollar bills. "Yeah, keep what I already gave you and take this." He tossed the bills onto the bed; they fluttered and scattered.

"What's that for?" Her eyes were wide with excitement.

"It's a tip."

"Cool," she said, pulling the blouse over her head and again shaking her hair. She then reached for her skirt and slid into it effortlessly.

"And here's another one. This world is a lot colder and crueler than you think. A girl like you—your folks can't afford to lose you. Believe me, I know. Go home to your family."

By now, young Jessica was standing, fully dressed, hopping on one leg as she put on her last shoe. She finished, bent down and scooped up the bills on the bedspread. "Sure, mister, anything you say. Go home. That's what I'll do."

But Rich knew she wouldn't.

21

Once again Glory Kane couldn't sleep, wouldn't sleep, didn't sleep, but it wasn't just the overwhelming pressure of the case. She had never been much of a sleeper. Not even as a little girl. Drove her daddy crazy, her getting up before dawn and watching television, MTV and stuff like that. To her, sleep was a monumental intrusion on the important things of life, so she applied only the minimal effort to the ritual, three or four hours each night.

So, like most mornings, she was at headquarters when the grimy windows were still smudged by night. The few cops and aides who were there were from the vampire squad that performed overnight surveillance, or the blues who hauled in the South Side hookers. There were, in fact, a half dozen of them only a few feet from her desk, lined up in wooden chairs at the railing. They reeked of cheap perfume and said nothing as they examined their nail polish with their legs crossed and their feet bobbing.

Detective Kane was at her desk transcribing pages of scribbled information onto sticky notes that she arranged and rearranged in a spiral notebook. Like the pieces of a puzzle, they were fit together, but a clear picture was still a ways away.

Her phone rang and she pounced on it instinctively like a cat on a mouse. She was answering before the receiver even got to her mouth. "Area Two. Kane."

"You're working on that case, the woman who nobody knows where she is?" the gravelly voice asked.

"Maura Baker. Do you know something about it?"

"Something's going on. We have to talk."

"And who are you?"

"I seen that broad that night. At The Pachyderm."

Glory's heart sped up. Now he had her attention. "Go on."

"And some weird shit has gone down since then."

"Like what?"

"Can we meet?"

"Where?" Glory flipped a page over in her notebook and wrote down the address he gave her in the margin of one sheet. "Okay, how will I know you?"

When he told her, she didn't know if he was kidding or not.

Glory Kane recognized him through the grimy windows of the diner, even from across the street. She was here, in a wet, muted early morning storm, standing at a noisy intersection that hissed with every car that passed. The sky was as gray as a corpse. Sleet descended like spit. Still, she paused at the corner and contemplated the little diner that was squeezed beneath an abandoned brick building like a cigarette pack under a boot. The weather was thrown back into the shimmering street from the glass of the window. But it wasn't enough to obscure the twisted shape of Tucker Hines. The uncontrolled and incessant jutting of his head like a chicken picking feed would have given away his identity, even if he didn't have a hump perched catawampus on his back, forcing his head slightly askew.

206

She had waited for McKay to show up, but when the time had elapsed, she left without him, leaving a sticky note on his desk. She wondered what she was getting into now with this hunchbacked guy, if her zeal to get to the bottom of the case was totally obscuring her judgment. But she had come this far, so what the hell, let's at least see what he has to offer. She jitterbugged between two cars and splashed against the light to the other side of the street.

The diner leapt upon her like a cheetah the moment she opened the door: the smells, hot and smoky and sticky with grease, and the sounds, a rhythmic swirl of voices and clinking, clattering dishes. Private conversations. Plots thickening. Business being conducted. Affairs being terminated or commenced. Bombs being planted. Drugs going down. And Glory Kane was quickly absorbed into the silky gray ether to talk with a pathetic hunchback in furtive whispers and shrouded language about murder.

Tucker Hines was a puddle of street grease sopped up in a cheap suit. Glory said a silent prayer and moved towards him. "You Hines?" she said.

"Well, well, well, I wasn't so sure you was even gonna show up," Tucker Hines said, smiling slightly through a rotted picket fence of brown teeth and gaps. "I already done went and ate, but you can go ahead." He stood up, leaning and twisted as an oak tree, and extended a hand. Glory took it as she approached. The grip was soft, cold, dead.

She slid into the booth and looked at her watch. She was a few minutes late, but from the empty plate in the center of the table with a thin swoop of ketchup spiraling towards its center, she surmised that Tucker had been here for quite some time. The table cloth was also dribbled and dabbed with yoke stains, although, Glory figured, those could have been there for days. "Well, I'm here," she said, sliding into the creaking chair. "What do you have for me?"

Hines was folding a napkin over some pieces of bacon. Glory watched as the hunchback folded, unfolded and then carefully folded the paper again, making a perfect envelope of tissue through which the grease from the bacon was already emerging.

He looked at her and stopped his careful wrapping. "Something wrong?"

She shrugged and shook her head. "No, not at all."

"Yeah, I'm taking this bacon with me. Why not? I paid for it."

"You got a dog or something?"

"No dog. Died a couple months ago. Good fuckin' dog. What's it to you?"

Glory felt uncomfortable with everything, the setting, the food, the person sitting across from her. "Nothing, just asking."

"I paid for it, I'll wear it on my head if I want."

"No problem," Glory whispered. She folded her hands on the table and took him in. He wasn't ugly in a monstrous sense. Only his hump and his general hygiene made him repulsive. His small eyes were dark and buried in a massive brow. His hair was an explosion of untamed fury, thick, tangled, uncombed and sprinkled with gray. But he exuded an atmosphere that made Glory uncomfortable. His incessant head bobbing caused her to lean back and away from him.

"They serve breakfast here all day?" Glory said.

"Yep. Pretty good, too," Tucker replied. "Then again, hard to screw up eggs, yeah?" He began laughing which quickly turned into a cough. His eyes reddened and filled with water as he tamped down his emotions.

Just then a waitress approached and stood wordlessly in front of them. With her hip cocked and a vacuous look on her face, she glared at Glory purposely diverting her eyes from the hunchback. Glory looked at the waitress. "Just coffee," she answered and the waitress immediately turned and began to walk away. Glory called out to her, "Yeah, and a donut or a sweet roll, something like that." The woman didn't turn around, and the detective wondered if she'd even heard her.

Glory looked at Tucker. "So, you got something for me?"

"Well, like I said on the phone, maybe I can be of some service to you," he answered, leaning back, putting an unlit cigarette in his mouth.

Glory wondered if he was going to light it. "Okay, I'm listening," she replied.

"In regards to the case you're working on."

"Yeah, go on."

Tuck eyed her knowingly. There was no doubt in Glory's mind that he was calculating exactly what he needed to say to get things started. The hunchback leaned forward. The cigarette in his mouth made his eyes squint. So did the smile that gently creased his face. "Yeah, well, it's really quite simple" he said, nodding. "I know that woman on television."

"You're talking about Maura Baker?"

"Yeah. Maura Baker, that's her."

"How do you know her?"

Tuck smiled sheepishly. "Well, I don't really know her, but I seen her around, you know?"

Glory opened her mouth to speak just as the waitress arrived again and set down a sweating glass of cola and some sort of sandwich leaking a mushy mayonnaise concoction. "Diet Coke, chick salad," the woman said.

Glory reflexively responded, "No, I said coffee."

"I wish people could make up their minds," the waitress snapped, picking up the plate.

"Forget about it, this is fine," Glory replied. The waitress dropped the plate back on the table and then turned and walked away. When she was out of earshot, Glory turned back to the hunchback. "Okay, tell me how you know or have seen Maura Baker."

"Well, I occasionally pick up some odd jobs from some folks who you and your kind might consider unsavory characters."

"Criminals? My gosh, I'm shocked to hear this," she said, barely concealing the mocking tone in her voice.

Tuck shrugged. "And I recently had the opportunity to have seen her at a function for what the team of workers was put together by a guy who you might put on the list of unsavories."

"List of unsavories, huh? What was the occasion?"

Tuck shook his head. "Don't really know. A buddy of mine just asked me to help him hump some boxes of lobsters from an airplane to the party. Hump? Get it? Who better to get to hump something than me?"

It was a joke, but Glory wasn't comfortable laughing. "Go on."

"This pal of mine, he works directly for a guy named Pompa Louie, that's his nickname, but I don't know his real name. Anyway, he pulled together the crew to handle this party at The Pachyderm."

"You were there?"

"Yeah."

"So, this buddy of yours, he works for this Pompa Louie character, and he recruited you to work this gig. Do I have that right?"

"You're doing good."

She took out a pad and jotted the name down. "Looks like I need to talk to him, too—your pal. What's his name?"

A cloud seemed to descend upon the hunchback. He seemed to be choking out the next words. "No, that ain't gonna be possible. And that's another reason we gotta talk." He looked away from her and stared out the window for several seconds. Then he cleared his throat and said, "Uh, this friend of mine, he was popped in his apartment a few days ago." Tuck reached back and touched the base of his own skull. "Right here, like an execution."

"Where did he live?"

"Out on the west side."

The conversation with Bones Jones and the corpse on the table flashed through Glory's memory. *Guy gets capped execution style. Same guy?* She'd bet a paycheck on it. "I think I heard about it. What was his name?"

The hunchback's eyes had turned bright red and were welling up with tears. "Poteet. We called him Taters. Prolly not his real first name. It don't matter."

Taters Poteet. "And you saw Maura Baker at this party?"

"Yeah. She was with this real slick dude. Guy in a suit. Silver hair. Good lookin' enough. Seemed to have a broomstick up his ass, though," he coughed out the last part in a spasm of laughter. When he regained control he continued. "Anyway, she's a great looking broad, so you remember things like that, you know?"

Glory thought about what he was saying. Slick dude in a suit. Silver hair. Aaron Clayton. "And you're here why? You think your friend's death and Maura Baker are somehow connected?"

The hunchback shrugged. "You tell me."

Glory immediately answered, "I don't know."

"Well, then maybe I can help you find out."

"In what way?"

"I ain't too sure, but I know that this buddy of mine who called me in to help load up the lobsters etcetera was a punk go-fer for some pretty bad dudes." He leaned closer until Glory could smell his rotting breath. "Some dudes of the highest badness."

Glory had to admit, she was curious. "Give me names. Adjectives won't do."

Tuck paused, leaned back and inhaled aggressively. "Adjectives is free. Names require scratch." He rubbed his thumb and fingers together in the age old gesture for money.

Glory suspected this was coming, unfortunately she had neglected to even mention this meeting to her boss, Frank Rodriguez. So, she had nothing with which to negotiate. She took a deep breath. "What do you want, and, most importantly, what are you going to give me?"

Tucker pulled the cigarette from his pursed lips and shook some invisible ashes in the general direction of a saucer on the table. He used the cigarette like a pointer and shook it from side to side in front of her. "It's really quite simple. I can get into places and talk to people that wouldn't give you the time of day, no offense. Now, for a small fee, I might be able to provide you with enough info maybe make your case a little easier." He took a slow, pensive drag on the unlit cigarette, exhaled some invisible smoke, and then leaned back in his chair and folded his arms.

"What kind of info?"

The hunchback shrugged. "How the hell am I supposed to know till I get it? All I know is you're going to sooner or later find out about her hanging with these cats, and you're going to need someone who can get in and find out what was really going on. I'm the guy and I'm here now."

Glory still wasn't sure what to believe. The guy seemed genuine, but she needed to convince herself once and for all. She reached beneath the coat she had laid on the seat next to her and removed one of the photographs Bones Jones had given her. "Here's another guy, died. Is this your buddy?"

Tuck placed the cigarette in his pursed lips and squinted at the shot for a second. Recognition filled his eyes. "No, that ain't him, but I know him. Jesus, they got him too, huh? Popped in the skull just like Taters. Boom!"

"That's not Poteet?" Glory asked.

"No, not Taters. That there guy is name of Benny the Razor. He was working with us that night, too," the hunchback replied.

"Benny the Razor? Got any more info than that? Like a last name?

"Sounded something like Razor, maybe like Razovich…yeah, I think that's right."

"Benny Razovich," Glory muttered as she wrote down the name.

"Looks like a lot of people who worked that party is getting taken out, huh?" Tuck interjected. "Him, Taters, the broad. Now, it's getting interesting, don't you think? You might wanna make a deal with me before they take me out," he laughed. Then the smile immediately disappeared.

"Fair enough. What's your price?"

The hunchback's eyes popped open and he grinned through his putrid, infected teeth. His hand subconsciously ran over the table like a large spider. The cigarette bobbed in his mouth. "Simple. I need three things. First, twenty five hundred bucks, a grand up front to defray my out-of-pocket costs. Second, a first class airplane ticket, one way, to Australia. One way. That's cheaper. See, I'm saving you money already. Three, a passport. Oh, and one more thing, if there's any kind of reward or something..."

Glory swallowed hard. What did a first class ticket to Australia cost? Probably at least two grand—so, they were looking at a total of plus or minus five grand. She couldn't imagine the department springing for that kind of cash. "You're out of your mind," she said.

Tuck pulled the cigarette out of his mouth and pointed it at her. "Have it your way, lady. Nothing ventured, nothing gained, I guess."

"I guess."

"So, I guess we're done here, then," Tuck said, pushing away from the table. "I'm gonna go outside and finally light this cigarette before my nerves to haywire."

"Looks like it," Glory said, trying to bluff. She wanted the information desperately, but she knew if she took these kinds of demands back to Rodriguez, she'd be thrown out of his office in an instant.

The hunchback wobbled as he stood up and pulled his coat off the back of the chair. He clumsily, yet quickly, wrestled his way into it. Please say something, Glory thought. Give me something to bite on. To cops like Glory Kane the world was full of tumors—dark, seamy, dangerous infections—and Tucker Hines was a knife. If anybody could cut through the skin and bone and go directly to the diseased organ, it was guys like him. He would get fifty pounds of bullshit and two pounds of truth, but that was all she needed. Don't leave, she cried inside.

He stood unsteadily for several seconds, staring at her. Finally, a second before she was going to ask him to sit back down, he spoke. "Look, I'm not an unreasonable guy. I know I can get you information that, if it don't make your case, it at least can save you one hell of a lot of time, a hell of a lot more than a couple of grand worth, I'll tell you that."

"Sit down," Glory said, exhaling as slowly as she could.

He dropped back into his chair. "I knew you was a reasonable type," he said, suddenly breaking into a brief coughing fit.

"Two grand in cash?" she said emphatically. "I never heard of a snitch–an informant, excuse me–getting that much."

"No offense taken. I know exactly what I am. And it was twenty five hundred with a grand up front, plus the ticket and etcetera. Like I said, it's very dangerous information you want. I mean, look at that picture if you don't think so. It's dangerous information, and that makes it very valuable and very expensive. I mean, I don't know all the answers, and getting them from guys I do know can cost. Guys don't just talk. I'll be lucky to keep half what you pay me."

Glory nodded. "Yeah, yeah, I get it, but we're not used to paying that kind of money for information. Especially up front. You ought to know that."

Hines stared out the window for several seconds. "Look. I'm willing to negotiate. Get me the passport, the upfront

215

money, and when I'm done give me another grand." Before Glory could answer him, he put up one finger. "But wait. If this info proves out to be enough to nail her husband's ass or whoever, then you send me another other grand. Is it a deal?"

"Well, I can't promise anything."

The hunchback's eyebrows notched. "But you'll try?"

"I don't get this one way ticket to Australia," Glory said.

"Simple. Figure it out. Oughta be easy. Lots of bodies with bullet holes in them turning up around town, yeah? I don't wanna be one of them."

"What about the passport?"

"Ah, that should be the easy part for you. I got a few, shall we say, blemishes on my record, things that I gotta stick around for."

"Court dates."

He looked up at her, "Yeah. I can't leave, can't even get a passport until those are cleared up. I need you to do the cleaning up. Now there ain't no murders or nothing like that hanging out there. Petty shit. Little bit of larceny here and there. Shouldn't be hard to erase." He fiddled with the debris on the table, crumbs of toast, coffee stains.

"Yeah, that we might be able to arrange, especially if it's not too big a deal."

Tuck suddenly began to convulse in a coughing fit. He wracked so hard, food particles and spittle from deep inside sprayed out. Finally, he got hold of himself. "Fucking things will be the death of me," he said, taking the unlit cigarette from his mouth.

Jake McKay was surprised and delighted with his good fortune. He had gotten to the office more than an hour late, and Kane wasn't in yet. That meant he didn't have to put up with her icy bullshit. But, at the same time, it wasn't like her, he thought. She freaking lives here. But at least he wouldn't have to lie about why he was so late.

He had stopped at Area Six headquarters. He was greeted with familiarity and even a certain conviviality by the cops there. From Sarge at the front desk, who let him pass with a wave and a nod, to the guys he knew at their desks and in the hallway, he met no resistance, only occasional curiosity, guys wondering, "What's he working on now?"

His contact, Jimmy Keeley, saw him from across the bullpen and motioned him forward. "Come on, not here," Keeley said, moving through a swinging door and disappearing. Nobody thought anything of it. It wasn't unusual.

Jake followed Keeley through the door and into the fetid, wet locker room to which it led. A shower hummed in the background, throwing steam into the locker area. The faint smell of urine emanated from the stalls on the opposite wall. Jimmy was at a locker, twirling a combination lock.

"It's about time," McKay said, coming forward. It had taken more than two weeks for Keeley to get what Jake had ordered.

Keeley looked up from the lock. "You know, you pompous fuck, it ain't like I can walk down and just for no fucking reason run the tags on two cars. We got regulations. You gotta sign in, give reason. I had to go in the back door for this information."

"You got it, what, in there?"

"Yeah," Keeley said, removing the lock and clanking open the door.

Jake's heart was beating excitedly. The little bit of information he had gotten from that crazy woman in Baker's apartment building was proving to be tantalizingly potent. "What? It's a freakin' state secret you gotta keep it locked in there?"

Keeley stared woodenly at him. "You just might be surprised. It ain't something you leave laying on your desk." He removed two sheets of paper and began to hand them to McKay, but then pulled them back. "You got something for me?"

Just then, the shower shut off, echoing silence back into the room. "Come on," Keeley said, pulling Jake by the arm to the far corner of the room. "You got mine?"

"Right here," the detective said, removing four Chicago Bulls tickets from his pocket. "Center court, Friday's game. You're about ten rows up."

"Oh, that's beautiful," he said. The exchange took place and Jimmy looked at McKay while fanning out the tickets. "I'm gonna tell you once and once only. We ain't never talked about this. You got no idea where this came from. They ask, you found this stuck on your shoe or it must'a blew off someone's desk. But it wasn't me."

"You know me better than that, Jimmy."

"No, I mean this time you got a tiger by the tail, and I ain't nowhere in the jungle. You understand? That info from whoever that broad was, is lethal. You better be careful."

Jake McKay separated the pages as he spoke. "What the hell's in here, anyway?"

Jimmy Keeley put the tickets in his pocket. "Like I said, it's your tit in the wringer."

218

McKay eagerly glanced at the information. "Holy shit," he whispered, a rush of excitement pulsing through his fingers.

22

Rich Baker had somehow found his way back. Precisely how, he did not know. He was certainly familiar with the overall contours of his city, its most visible landmarks, and the primary thoroughfares that stitched it together. But when it came to the nooks and crannies, his knowledge was limited to the geography he primarily inhabited. Which street led to which alley, which was one-way, which ones dead-ended, these were all matters of trial and error for him whenever he ventured beyond his own boundaries. Yet, somehow, using the large anchors of the skyline of Chicago, he had wended his way back here, to the place he had awakened some six weeks before. He had ventured, this time, in his own car, also a Mercedes, fitfully traversing seedy and dangerous neighborhoods where most retail shops were boarded up and the few that were open sported steel bars on the windows. But there was no question in his mind that he had rediscovered the site of his ignominy. The rancid boiled egg odors, the dead brown cattails rimming the lake, the silent rusted building lying like a huge dead behemoth in a barren vacant lot were so firmly imbedded in his memory that there was no mistaking them the instant he pulled off one of the main streets and snaked onto the premises.

Why had he come back? He asked himself that question. What was it the cops on TV always said, "The criminal returns to the scene of the crime?" Was that it? A return to where he (maybe) committed an act so heinous that it had completely fried those particular memory molecules of his brain? He wasn't entirely sure. He only knew that something had compelled him here and he pulled his Benz to a stop on the pea gravel in what he could best determine was the exact spot where he had awakened.

He shut off the purring engine and sat for several seconds, soaking the silence into every fiber of his being. Silence. What a nuisance it had become during this ordeal. It clung onto him as if it were the only friend he had, and, indeed, that was not too far from the truth. With the exception of Nate Timmins, he had fallen out of favor with virtually every inhabitant of his past life. No friends called. No colleagues came by to offer help or condolences, or even to ask him what might have happened on that last stop before dawn. His only refuge was hookers and strangers, and the brief instances of intimacy that they provided soon became unsatisfying, meaningless. Oh, the media were there with their thrusting microphones and endless repetition of the same question. But even when encircled by their fury, he was still alone. So, on this sunny afternoon, he had begun his exploration, not only of this desolate spot, but also of his desolate soul.

He opened his car door and stepped out. Again, he was assaulted by the choking smells. God almighty, how did people live in this air? His shoes crunched on the frozen gravel as he sauntered in desultory patterns. In a few minutes he found himself just steps away from the rusting old building. A piece of the steel wall had been folded down alongside one of its beams like a piece of wallpaper, creating an entrance into the cavernous structure. He ducked carefully into the crease,

221

sucking in his stomach to ensure that his parka did not catch on the ragged edge of the steel, and literally climbed inside.

It took a minute or so for his eyes to adjust. The building meandered in both directions as far as he could see. It must have been two or three football fields long, he figured. Amazing that men with their limited physicality, their one hundred seventy-five pounds of meat and bones and gristle, could nonetheless wrench from their imaginations structures of such immense proportions, and then, somehow, get them to move with the magic of steam and fuel and electricity until they bent and shaped products that would be used to build even bigger things. But this, now, was a dead place. High above in the rafters some birds fluttered in groups from here to there, agitating the utter silence with the beating of their wings. And Rich Baker knew that there were other creatures lurking in the nooks and crannies, huddled and frightened. This was, nonetheless, dead to the rest of the world, this old steel mill. Concrete footings where huge rolling machines had once pulsated were now poking serendipitously through the ground, and steel reinforcing rods jutted from them through clusters of weeds and grass. The remnants of a gargantuan overhead crane stretched the entire width of the structure. It had been stripped of its essential components, leaving only the skeletal remains of wheels and pulleys and chains.

The complex mechanism reminded him of the steel rails and chains that coaxed a roller coaster train to the top of its first hill, where the cars would seem to stop for an instant as the chain released them before plunging to a terrifying fall that pulled your stomach up to your head, where it pushed the air and a scream out of your mouth.

Once he had taken Maura and Sean to the Great America theme park in Gurnee. Sean was, maybe, seven or eight, and he had cajoled Rich into letting him ride one of the angry coasters that looped and twisted and turned them upside down. Maura, never one for wild, uncontrolled motion, stood below and waved as they clicked up the first incline.

"You're not scared, are you, buddy?" Rich asked his son.

Sean was gripping the bar so tightly his knuckles nearly broke through the skin on his hands. "Can they stop it, daddy? I don't want to go." he whispered.

"I'm afraid it's too late now, partner," Rich answered, just as the car ascended the last few feet, stopped for that blood curdling instant and then hurtled downward. Sean began screaming at that exact instant and didn't stop until the ride ground to a halt.

Tears poured down the little guy's cheeks and Rich had to pry his frozen fingers from the bar. "Come on, son, let's go."

"I, I can't."

Rich pulled his son's last hand free and lifted him from the car. The boy threw his arms around Rich's neck and clung to his father tightly. "Come on, boy, walk for yourself," Baker said, attempting to put his son's feet on the ground. Sean was having none of it. "Come on, quit being such a baby, Sean. The ride's over." Then, for a reason he would never understand, he began to laugh.

They made their way down the ramp and, seeing his mother, Sean finally broke loose and ran to her, burying his face in her blouse. Rich followed a few steps behind, laughing uncontrollably, tears ringing his own eyes.

"Don't laugh at him!" Maura mouthed.

"Oh, for chrissakes, Maura. It was only a roller coaster ride. He begged to go on it. Quit babying him."

Maura glanced at Richard with fury in her eyes as she gently stroked her son's hair. "He's only a little boy."

Baker stopped chortling and grew serious. "Well, he's acting like a little girl."

"And what the hell is that supposed to mean?" she screamed, stopping passersby in their tracks.

Baker instinctively, immediately realized his mistake. "Nothing, it means nothing. I just want the kid to be strong. It's not an easy world, Maura, and you have to know how to overcome your fears. The earlier the better."

Maura pulled the boy closer to her and kissed him on the top of his head. "Go to hell, you prick," she said between gritted teeth.

The scene at the roller coaster and the sounds of the midway, the flashing lights, the clowns, the colors, the screams of excited riders that provide the backbeat to the music of the environment, all receded in Baker's mind. Prick? Oh, yeah, he could certainly be a prick, he thought, as he turned and started to walk out of the building. But he only got a few steps when he knew, just knew, that something was wrong.

There was someone in the parking lot. Another car. He could hear it rumbling as it scrunched on the semi-frozen pavement. Shit. If they find him here...

He cautiously moved to the peeled away hole in the wall. Standing back in the shadows, he peered out. His instincts had been correct. A car, black, huge had entered the vacant lot from the open gateway at the far end and was moving slowly toward his Mercedes. Who? Had he been followed? It wasn't

224

a cop car, unless it was undercover. Punks. Yeah, maybe punks. This was, after all, a bad neighborhood. Baker cursed. Why the hell had he come here? What value did it have? And now...

Then the car sped up as if its driver had just now noticed his Benz. Gravel clouds churned beneath its grinding wheels as it got closer. What the hell were these guys doing? *Damn, they're going to ram my car!* His instincts pulled him forward through the opening in the wall. But he stopped almost as quickly. What the hell was he going to do? Get in front of the car? Oh, shit, this was a disaster. If these punks wrecked his car and he couldn't drive away, how would he explain it? Or, if they stole his car . . .

They were a few hundred yards away now and gaining speed when Rich saw something out of the corner of his eye. From between two smaller outbuildings another vehicle emerged like a bullet and almost instantly was alongside the first car. The second car was newer, clean, forest green, a Ford or something, Baker thought, and its front bumper was literally inches from the fender of the black sedan. The two vehicles were enveloped in a swirling fury of dust, hurtling at what had to now be fifty or sixty miles an hour toward his Mercedes, when suddenly the green Ford made its move. Its dolphin-like nose leaned quickly to the left, digging into the side of the other car, sending it into a momentary uncontrolled swerve. Instead of letting the driver regain control, the green car attacked again, this time even more violently. The explosion of metal and plastic shook the silent afternoon, and Baker watched as the black car, now totally out of control, spun several times, sliding, sliding, sliding into a forest of cattails at the edge of the swamp. It sputtered several times, creaking in protest. Its horn began to bleat, rattling the

225

air, and it finally settled sideways in the mud, slowly slipping deeper and deeper.

The green car had sped ahead, pirouetted a perfect 180 degrees and tore through the parking lot back toward the main road. Baker saw his opportunity and sprinted for his car as fast as his long legs could carry him.

23

"Okay, okay, he'll be here in a few minutes," Lieutenant Frank Rodriguez muttered to the two people in his office. Glory Kane sat, her legs crossed and her elbow resting on the worn out armrest of the chair in front of the cluttered desk, and Jake McKay leaned, pot belly protruding, against a file cabinet. Rodriguez, who didn't sit well anyway, was pacing in the tight, debris-strewn area behind his desk. He motioned to a stack of files on the surface. "This is it? This is all we got?"

"The whole shooting match," McKay answered tersely.

Rodriguez shook his head. "I just don't think it's enough. It ain't enough. And Devalane is going to be in here in…" he looked at his watch, "…any second now."

Harold Devalane was desperate for a case that would elevate his profile and enhance his political ambitions; and this was it. Glory knew that he had been riding Rodriguez like a horse since the discovery of Richard Baker. Now he insisted on a meeting to go over the evidence, and she had to agree with Rodriguez; there wasn't enough to get and indictment.

"We just need more time," Glory replied calmly.

"Time? My God, what's it going to take?"

"Gosh, Chief, we're on it twenty hours a day," Glory said.

Rodriguez wiped his face, squeezing his own cheeks with his huge hand. Then he answered, "Yeah, yeah, I know. Look, I'm sorry. I know it's not... I know you're doing everything you can. It's just that my goddamn telephone rings every five minutes and it's the prosecutor or the press or the mayor, and none of them can believe we still haven't arrested this guy."

It had been almost six weeks now since the beginning of the case, and Glory and Jake had met with Rodriguez every other day or so to discuss the pertinent developments. This meeting, however, deviated from the routine, what with the imminent arrival of the prosecutor, and Glory was extremely uncomfortable. Fact was, the case was a mess. Nothing added up, no matter how she arranged it. They had no body. Key witnesses were missing. Nothing was as it appeared. In short, they had, at least temporarily, reached a dead end.

"We're not too far from it," Jake said.

"How far?" Rodriguez asked.

"We just need one break," Glory answered, even though she wasn't totally convinced.

Rodriguez squeezed his temples with one hand and flopped into his chair. He let out a huge ball of air. "What kind of break? What would break the case wide open?"

"It sure would be a lot easier if we could establish that Maura Baker is, indeed, dead," Glory replied grimly, "and a body sure would be helpful."

"Then we should drag the lake some more?" Rodriguez queried.

"Well, I know we've been through it once, but it is the most logical dumpsite, based on the condition of Baker when we found him. I suppose it's possible he left her somewhere else, but, I mean, he was a mess. I just don't see him dropping the

228

body in one place then driving all the way to the south side to take a nap. Doesn't make sense," Glory replied.

Jake pulled away from the file cabinet and swung his hand as if swatting a fly. "Body, schmody. Maybe there isn't one. I think we have to be prepared to live with that fact. Baker might have ground her up into hamburger, or burned her to soot, or put her someplace God can't even get to. I think we've got enough stuff for probable cause, enough bits and pieces to make a pretty impressive string of the evidence that ties right on that turd's big toe."

"Glory?" Rodriguez said arching an eyebrow.

"Well, I do have something new. A possibility," she replied, leaning over the stack of folders on the desk.

The door swung open and Harold Devalane swept into the room. He was a large man, over six feet tall and weighing at least 230 pounds. His very presence made the space shrink. "Sorry about this folks, running late," he said.

"Good morning, Harold," Rodriguez said.

"How's everybody?" he replied, pulling up the chair that awaited him.

"You're right on time. The detectives here were just beginning to present their case," Rodriguez said. He leaned back, chewing on a pencil. "Talk to us."

Glory opened a file and spoke as she leafed through it. "Well, I just got these reports from Bones Jones. There is some interesting data here. The blood on the car seat had been there for approximately six to nine hours. We found Baker at seven a.m. That puts the time of, uh, death, I guess, at about midnight, give or take, which is about the time Baker left the party at Miles Lundeen's." Her fingers turned pages, finally stopping and extracting one. "Toxicology reports on Baker's blood show high levels of alcohol."

"Nail his ass on drunk driving; that'll get us started," Jake interrupted.

Glory cleared her throat and continued. "Here's something else." Her finger traveled down the report form and stopped on a box. "He was also whacked out on Thorazine."

"What's that?" Rodriguez said.

"It's a tranquilizer, nuclear powered, used in the late fifties, maybe early sixties. Bones Jones says it was one of the breakthrough drugs used to treat mental illness. Not used so much anymore. Kept the person in a slow motion stupor, and enough of it would knock you out for days. And Rich Baker had enough residue to suggest he'd taken a dose that would bring a buffalo to its knees."

"Ouch," Rodriguez flinched, "No wonder he doesn't remember anything."

Glory continued. "What's not surprising is that the blood and some of the hair samples taken from Maura's bedroom match the samples taken from the car. Presumably the blood and some of the hair are hers. We know for a fact that some of the hair is Richard's"

Devalane leaned forward, his chair squeaking. "I like what I'm hearing. Fact is, that might be enough to indict."

"Maybe, but as I see it, the problem is, there's no trace of blood from Rich Baker anywhere. Not in the car, not in the bedroom, nowhere." Glory closed the file and dropped it onto her lap, still holding it with a finger placed between several pages.

McKay came off the file cabinet. "Who says he has to bleed? He could have jumped her from behind. No, no," he gestured with his hands in a knifing motion, "he snuck into her bedroom while she was asleep and boom, nailed her."

Glory raised an eyebrow. "There were undeniable signs of a struggle, hand prints on the dresser, as if she were clinging to it to be kept from being pulled off. The sheets were tangled all over the floor, full of blood. Furniture was knocked over. I can't imagine he got through that unscathed. I mean, even O.J. had a cut on his finger."

Jake waved her away. "I still say he didn't have to bleed. Shit, he's six foot four, whatever, and she's a woman."

Glory inhaled deeply and exhaled immediately. "Because she's a woman she couldn't fight back? Is that your point, detective?"

Jake leaned toward her, his face reddening. "My point, detective, is that he was bigger, stronger and caught her by surprise. You can take that any way you want."

Rodriguez stood up and raised both hands. "All right, you two. Simmer down."

"What about the hairs? Don't they put Baker in both locations?" Devalane interjected.

Glory nodded. "Indeed, they do. But we already know he was in the car, so it's no help there. As for the bedroom, well, he did live there until recently. No matter how well someone cleans, it's impossible to get every hair. They may have been there for months."

Devalane interrupted. "So, you're saying that the only connection between Richard and Maura on that night is the fact that he was found in her car?" He didn't wait for an answer. "Well, that's not all bad. That is still a pretty powerful connection."

Glory answered immediately, waving the folder at McKay. "What bothers me is that there's no other physical evidence placing Rich Baker in Maura's bedroom that night. Not a smudge of blood, not a single fingerprint anywhere near the action."

"Hmmm, now that's a problem," Devalane replied.

"What about the boots?" Jake interjected.

Glory nodded tentatively. "All right, the boots match the prints in the mud outside Maura Baker's house."

"Bingo!" Jake said, clapping his hands together in a singular reverberation.

"That might be all we need," Devalane said, brightening.

"Yes, yes, it puts him in both places," Rodriguez exclaimed, standing up.

Glory pondered her next words for several seconds. She felt as though she was being sucked into the muck of a swamp with no boundaries, so thick and tangled with trees and branches that the sun was blocked out and even a nebulous sense of direction was obscured. She was the rookie on the case, and, while she chided Jake for his obvious obsession with Rich Baker, she found no irony in her own obsession with Maura. "Well, now," she exhaled, "the problem with the boots and prints is that, well, they don't make sense."

Jake McKay winced and waved her away. "What the hell are you talking about?"

"Logic, Jake, logic. Things aren't kosher here."

McKay dismissed her with a wave. "Baloney," he said.

"Shut up, McKay, and let her talk," Rodriguez said, freezing the big cop with a stare. Then he turned to Glory, "Go ahead, kid."

"Yeah, go ahead," Devalane echoed.

Glory raised her hands and paused, gathering her thoughts. "Let's reconstruct the night as we know it, and add some speculation to connect the scenes. Okay. First of all, Baker is at a party. He gets blitzed, has some sort of jealous epiphany and heads to his wife's house. But first he has to stop by his home and get his boots, because he sure as hell isn't wearing these clodhoppers to a formal dinner party with his suit."

"They were in the trunk of his car," Jake interjected, his voice putting closure on the statement as if he'd just blown her theory out of the sky like a clay pigeon.

Glory looked at him. He wasn't thinking it through, hadn't thought it through like she had, hadn't stayed awake at night staring at the ceiling running scenarios through his head. "What car?" she said. "His car? Since when does his car figure into the equation? And if it does, the whole thing gets confusing. Because if he drove his car to her place, then how did he end up in her car? And how did his car get back to wherever it was?"

Frank Rodriguez chewed on the end of the pencil. "You thinking he had an accomplice?"

"Perhaps," Glory said, "But that really gets complicated."

Jake hissed out a cloud of air. "Okay, he took a cab to her place after picking up his boots. Simple as that."

"Not so simple," Glory answered. "He's running around like a hamster in a cage. He goes from the party to his apartment, where he gets the boots; gets some kind of ride to Maura's house, kills her there, drags her body to the car, drives blind drunk to the south side, dumps her in the lake and..." she raised a finger to emphasize her point, "... and somewhere along the line drops his muddy boots back at his apartment because, when we found him, he was wearing his dress shoes." She brought her hands back together and dropped them in her lap.

The color had drained from Devalane's face. "Shit," he spat.

"One more thing," Glory said, leafing through papers in the manila folder, "I don't know how he could have made a footprint in the mud outside Maura's back door. The temperature fluctuated from nineteen to twenty-two degrees overnight. The ground would have been frozen." She closed the file and shrugged. "The footprints had to have been made at some other time. Plus, he had a key."

"A key?" Devalane asked.

"Yes. A key to Maura's house. We found it in his desk. It fit her doors, front and back. He didn't need to break in. He merely had to unlock the door."

"Damn," Rodriguez said, "What do we do?"

"Lose the boots," Devalane replied. "Keep them out of the mix until we have a better explanation. All they do is screw things up."

McKay ran his huge hand down his face from his forehead to his chin, pursing his lips as he emerged from behind his fingers. "It's the only thing worth a damn we got from Baker's apartment."

Devalane had lost the brief wind that had blown into his sails from the discovery of the boots and fell back into the chair. "This case, in the event you haven't seen or heard, has become the cause célèbre, or however you say it, of the Midwest. The media are obsessed with it. Every battered woman's group has made Maura Baker its poster girl, and we can't even prove she's dead! I mean, if we could just prove that much, it would be a start." He exhaled and leaned forward, resting his elbows on his knees. Silence filled the room for several seconds. Then Devalane continued. "Maybe we're looking at this the wrong way. Maybe everything didn't happen that night. Maybe this took place a few days before, and Baker was trying to ditch the car or something."

"Interesting," Rodriguez sighed.

"I definitely think it's an angle we should explore," Glory answered. "It would answer a lot of those questions, but still doesn't get us any closer to proving that Baker is involved."

"Maybe this boyfriend of Maura's is tied in with Baker," McKay replied. "What's his name again?"

"Aaron Clayton," Rodriguez interjected.

"Yeah. Any sign of him yet?" Devalane asked.

Glory shook her head. "Afraid not. We know he was supposed to go hunting in Wyoming and he left for the airport in his BMW and never got on the plane. We've spoken with his closest relatives, his co-workers, his attorney and no one, no one has seen him or heard from him. There has also been no trace of his car anywhere."

"How the hell do you lose a car?" Devalane asked.

"We have an all points bulletin out. Every cop in America should be looking for that silver Beemer. Every now and again we get a pick up, but it never matches," Glory said.

"Gotta believe this Clayton guy is dead, too," Devalane said offhandedly.

"No doubt about it," McKay answered. "The sentiments are unanimous: this guy doesn't disappear like this without telling somebody."

"Be nice if we could, somehow, connect these two stories," Devalane said. "That way, if we can't get Baker on one, we maybe can nail him on the other."

Glory cleared her throat. "There's something else. I started to tell you about it when Mr. Devalane came in." The three men looked up. "I met up with a guy this morning. He was at the party where those pictures were taken, the ones of Maura and Clayton."

"Keep going," Rodriguez said.

"And he identified two other guys who worked that night who have since been found dead—murdered, to be exact," she replied.

"You're shitting me," Devalane said, his eyes brightening.

"Holy smokes, Glory," Rodriguez replied.

McKay sprang away from the filing cabinet on which he had been leaning. "What the hell...where did this information come from?" he bellowed. "And why don't I know about it?"

"Well, Jake, I just got the lead this morning. I waited for you..." she didn't finish. She knew she could fry him right now with his propensity to amble into work late every morning, but she had more important priorities.

The color had returned to Frank Rodriguez's face. "Go on, Glory, give us the skinny."

"I don't know a lot more than that. I got a phone call from a guy named Tucker Hines, a hunchback who lives on the west side."

"A hunchback, you mean, like...a hump on his back?" Rodriguez said.

"Exactly," Glory replied. "Not a pretty sight."

"Oh, my lord, now we've got Quasimodo in the scene," McKay said.

Glory glared at her partner. "He thinks he can help."

Rodriguez dropped the pencil on his desk and gestured with his hands. "What's all this leading up to? I mean, what's the connection?"

"That's what's so puzzling," Glory said, taking a deep breath. "I don't know what any of this means, this appearance of Maura at this party. Maybe nothing. Maybe a lot. Maybe Rich Baker is somehow connected with these creeps. I mean we know enough about what he does, or did, for a living. Building tall buildings costs hundreds of millions of dollars. Big time investors can come from all walks of life. You know and I know that these drug studs are investing in all kinds of legit businesses. Who knows? All we know for sure is that we have two missing bodies, Maura's and Aaron Clayton's. Plus, we have two other bodies coming indirectly out of that party at The Pachyderm. Guy named Taters Poteet, and a petty hoodlum named Benjamin Razovitch. Both these guys showed up with a bullet in the back of their skulls sometime after the party. Poteet was Tucker Hines' best friend, and he's pretty upset about it— the death." She raised her hands and then dropped them back in her lap.

"And now he wants revenge," Rodriguez surmised.

"And money," Glory replied.

"My goodness," Devalane said. "This could be bigger than we thought."

"Well, I don't know about that," Glory replied. "And we won't know unless Tucker Hines can get into it for us."

"And his info has a price," Rodriguez said.

"Indeed it does," Glory replied. "Indeed it does." She laid out the terms of Tuck's proposal. When she was finished, Devalane whistled.

"Freak's out of his mind," McKay chortled.

Rodriguez looked at Devalane, who was obviously contemplating the situation. "What do you think, Harold? Can your office spring for the dough?"

"Mother of mercy, that's gotta be, what, close to five grand?" he answered. "What happened to the days when a few twenties could get you what you wanted?"

"Gone like the dodo bird," Rodriguez answered.

Devalane continued, "On the other hand, if it means nailing a murderer..." he let the words hang.

"Blood money is all it is," McKay interjected.

Glory knew how desperately Devalane wanted this case to move forward. So, she was not at all surprised when Devalane stood up again and clapped his hands. In fact, she expected the reply.

"Let's do it! But you tell that Hines guy that he better not lead us on a wild goose chase, or I'll have his ass, too."

Glory exhaled audibly. "I guess that's good. I suppose we'll find out."

The room grew quiet for several seconds. Glory could hear the three men breathing in the ether of renewed optimism, could hear her own heart thumping in her chest. Frank Rodriguez broke the silence. "What else?"

"Sure would be nice to find Maura," Glory whispered.

"Right. I'm going to rustle up the frogman posse and keep them swimming until they pull something out of that water that looks like Maura Baker. We'll put the hunchback on the payroll and see what he comes up with. In the meantime, you guys are still on the job, too. Now shuffle off to Buffalo and get me an eyewitness or a weapon or a bloody fingerprint, something that sticks Rich Baker to his wife's death like Super Glue. Now, does that seem like too much to ask?"

"Not at all, Chief," Glory chuckled.

238

Jake McKay left the meeting and disappeared into the locker room at the end of the hall. To his great satisfaction the place was empty. He stripped and walked into the shower. The faucet groaned and pipes clattered as he turned on the water, and he jumped out of the stream that shot at him like ice before instantly frothing into a storm of heat. He slowly melted into the stream, letting the hot, hot water gush over his skin. The showers were built in the old days when water was free and bountiful, and the ancient pipes delivered their goods with hurricane force that kneaded the muscles as it washed them. The cumulative effects of the heat and pressure made his bones sag. They weren't what they used to be. They echoed with weariness and a dull, thumping pain. This was the cure. But there was more symbolism to the shower than Jake wanted to admit. He was also washing away the utter disgust he had for himself.

Of course she had been right, Glory Kane. He knew it. And the information he had received from Jimmy Keeley confirmed the fact. In reality, Kane wasn't a bad cop at all, and everything she'd brought up during the conversation with Rodriguez and Devalane was well thought out, properly conceived and rationally presented. Christ, he should have done it. He was the senior cop. It was his job to lay it out, to present the facts, to tie things together. But his own—what?—hatred for scum like Rich Baker was blinding him, and he knew it. Frankly, he didn't give a shit if Baker was guilty or not. He just wanted to nail somebody. It was the law of averages; for every hundred scum balls that walked, maybe one innocent guy got nailed. So what? How many scum bags are walking the streets that are guilty as hell, but they got off because the law let them off? The truth didn't matter to them, and it won't matter to Rich Baker

239

when his high falutin' attorney gets a hold of the case. It'll go on for years, so long that what's true will become false and what's false will become true, until nobody can tell the difference anymore. That's why he wanted to nail this prick now and make him feel hunted, boil his guts inside him, make him scared every time he inhaled.

But that wasn't the way Glory Kane saw it at all. She was after the truth. So, what did he do? He tried to intimidate, embarrass, belittle his partner, and, Jesus, she hadn't tried to show him up. She was just doing her job.

It was as if there were two Jake McKays inhabiting his body. One he could control; one he couldn't. He heard the bad one talking, heard him laying shit after shit on Kane. He wanted to stop the bad one, but the words came flying out like someone had opened a jar. And he hated that bastard.

Jake McKay's life was an open wound. In a quarter century on the force he'd been scathed by too many visions, splattered with too much blood, and every day the storm winds of his profession burrowed into his scars, digging them deeper. He'd seen too many people die, from partners to kids to scumballs who deserved it. And he'd seen too many pricks walk out, smirking at him, going back to their fancy cars that drug money or pimping had bought them while he drove home in his beat-to-shit Plymouth with rust spots on the doors that looked like a map of the moon.

Kane. She hadn't been there yet. There were still ideas and ideals that meant something to her. And that was what pissed him off; not that she cared, but that he didn't.

He tried to imagine when her change would come. He knew when it hit him, when it barreled into him like a runaway truck. His second year on the force. The call had crackled over the radio. Shots fired. Dark alley. He was less than two blocks away. He was there in thirty seconds, his car bouncing through pot holes and sending splays of brown water into the air as he ripped down the cinder alley. His headlights swept the scene and for several seconds he saw only the usual decor of the environment, garbage erupting from dumpsters, piles of tires, the pin dot eyes of varmints scurrying away from his headlight beams. Then he saw the guy, looking at first like a black plastic bag leaning between two fifty gallon trash barrels. But this dark pile was writhing, feet scissoring in the wet cinders. McKay instinctively radioed for backup and medical assistance.

He pulled the car to a lurching stop and jumped out. In three strides he was hovering over the man, rolling him on his back. The sickly yellow glow of his car headlights made the rapidly expanding pool of blood in which the man was festering look purple.

"I'm dead, I'm dead," the man cried, holding his midsection.

"Just hold on pal, you're going to be all right," Jake said, pulling the man's suit coat back and probing the huge jagged continent of blood and sticky ooze that covered his white shirt.

It was obvious to Jake that this was no pimp or pusher or street rodent. This was a well-dressed, small-boned businessman. "What happened?" Jake said. He had to lean close to hear the man's words.

"I'm dead, I'm dead," he gasped.

"You're not dead, buddy," Jake shouted, reaching behind the body and feeling the blood thump out through the exit wound. He knew what was happening here, could imagine the heart frantically pushing blood out, waiting for it to come back to complete the natural cycle, wondering where it was going. "What's your name? Do you know your name?"

241

"Ben – Ben – Benchley. Tom Benchley."

"What happened here, Tom?" Christ! Where was the backup? Where was the ambulance?

"P–punks. Wanted money. I gave it. They sh – shot anyway."

"Goddamnit!" Jake growled, holding the man's head on his lap, wanting to go back to his car where the radio cackled in desultory bursts of static and words.

"I'm dead, I'm dead. My – my kids," the man's voice had been screwed down to a whisper.

Jake couldn't wait any longer. He lifted the man up like a sack of potatoes and loped to his car, gently setting him in the back seat. The hospital was six blocks away. Jake knew the guy wouldn't make it.

"I'm dead. I'm dead," he gasped.

By the time they got to the hospital, he was right.

It took weeks to get the stench out of his upholstery. But the man's voice never totally disappeared.

24

The move from the bright afternoon sun, through the semi permeable membrane of smoke and bodies in the dark, blinded Tucker Hines for several moments, and the music gutted his consciousness. It was as if someone had thrown a dark, noisy bag over his head and cinched it at the neck, so helpless and victimized did he feel by this oppressive environment. He stood inside the doorway waiting for his equilibrium to catch up, struggling to give form and definition to the whirlwind of activity. Strobes ripped the darkness like slashing knives, throwing blood red swaths on the wall. Neon pulsated through blue tubes, and the light seemed to strip away clarity rather than give it, until the bodies of the naked girls that were wrapped around the poles were rendered only as silhouettes. High up across the back of the bar, neon lights were wrought into the shape of the words, "The Australian Bush."

The longer Tuck stood there in the smoky, blazing darkness, the more lucid the scene became, and he could finally and clearly see the muted shapes of men sitting around small tables and dark, fleshy girls writhing on the stage and over the thighs of generous patrons in bleak corner booths. The hunchback seemed to draw no attention as his eyes scanned the atmosphere in search of a familiar face. There was a heady rush of adrenaline as he observed the room. Danger hovered over Tucker Hines' occupation like mist over a swamp. Dealing in the nebulous commodity of information was sometimes even fatal, and it was often hard to know if you went too far until you had already crossed the line. Like walking on rice paper, the approach was the first delicate step in the process. Most people kept knowledge tucked in secret pockets and were immediately suspicious when someone reached in, attempting to extract it. The wrong word, an unconscious gesture, a runaway inflection could lead to disaster.

He subconsciously patted the bottle of rum he had slid into his pocket specifically for this situation. It was the currency of choice for the information he was seeking. Every encounter had its own rules, its own plan, and this one had to adhere to a crucial tenet: give nothing away. Make the extraction of information as invisible as possible. Disguise it as simple conversation, matter-of-fact. That's what the rum was for.

Frankly, he was surprised Detective Kane had gotten back to him so fast, and even more startled that she had agreed to all his terms. Yeah, he only took two-fifty down, but he could live with that for now. Hell, he would have settled for half across the board. What he needed most was the passport, and that, as the saying goes, was in the mail.

The song screeched and collided to its conclusion, and Tuck embraced the microsecond of silence that peeked between it and the next number that exploded in its own nuclear palpitations. But somehow that instant of silence reoriented Tuck, and he spotted his target. The corpulent Pompa Louie lounged in one of the booths, the one directly below a smoky blue strobe light. A young woman in a g-string with a spaghetti strap that disappeared up the crack of her ass was humping over Pompa Louie's groin, her head thrown back and her tongue lolling in feigned ecstasy. Tuck nimbly slid between a crowd of men who surrounded a girl riding a pole like a vertical horse and slid into the booth next to his friend.

Pompa Louie acted as if this girl and her activities inches away from the noticeable bulge in his pants weren't even there. He laid his hand out in the space that separated him and Tucker, and the hunchback took the hand and their fingers rolled and gripped in a ritual handshake. "Tucker! My man," Pompa Louie said, then turned his attention back to the woman, who was obviously moments away from the orgasmic conclusion of her fantasy lap dance. "Give me a few minutes, yeah, and I'll be right with ya."

She looked so young to Tucker, and he wondered what possessed girls to do this, even though he knew. Her breasts were small, the nipples like two drops of blood. The g-string was tapered only slightly wider than the straps holding it. Her thumb had disappeared behind it and she was gasping. Suddenly Pompa Louie reached out and took her wrist. She stopped immediately, the emotion draining from her face. Then he deftly slipped a hundred dollar bill beneath her g-string, lingering there for a second, no more. She pulled away from him and removed the bill with her forefinger and middle finger. Pompa Louie blew her a kiss as she walked away.

"Good lord, you gave her a hundred bucks for that!" Tucker shouted over the din. "My tits are bigger than hers!"

"Yeah, but yours is on your back," Pompa Louie said.

"Hey, if women had tits on their backs, think of how much more fun slow dancing would be."

Pompa Louie laughed and stood up. "Let's move where we can talk," he said, unfolding himself. He was a mountain of a man, with raven black hair that was tied back in a pony tail. His arms seemed to stretch to the ground. He reached and picked up his drink and stumbled into the aisle. This was good. He had obviously been drinking for awhile. I'm halfway home, Tuck thought, as he stood up and followed.

They slid sideways between tables and around a corner and up several steps to a platform reasonably protected from the incessant explosive sound. There they found a table and sat down. Tuck wiggled out of his coat and set the bottle of rum on the table with an emphatic flourish.

"To what do I owe this?" Louie asked.

"You owe nothing, my friend," Tuck replied, twisting the top and refilling Louie's glass. "I am merely seeking out my old comrades to have with me a celebratory drink. They don't mind we bring our own in, do they?"

"I'm the king of this castle," Louie said, raising the glass to his lips. Then he paused and toasted Tuck. "You're ugly as dinosaur shit, but you're okay with me," he said, taking a sip. Then he savored the taste and set down his glass. "What are we celebrating, anyways?"

"Big changes in the life of yours truly."

"Whozat? You?"

"Yessir, my friend," Tuck answered, then suddenly stood up and waved at a waitress. "Can I get a fucking glass of ice here, please?"

"Changes like what?" Louie asked.

"I'm blowing this pop stand for good. Going far, far away!"

"What, like a whole 'nother country or something?"

246

Tuck smiled sheepishly. "Can't say where, pal. But it ain't here, that's for sure. Get the fuck outta here," he reached over and slapped Louie genially on the knee. "So, I'm seeking out my old friends and having a drink with them." The waitress brought a glass of ice and Tuck filled his, refilled Louie's and they clinked glasses.

"Somebody after your ass, Tuck? Maybe I can help you out."

"Nope, nothing like that. Been planning this and saving up for years."

Pompa Louie raised his glass in toast again. "In that case, here's to far away!"

Tuck brought his glass to his lips in an exaggerated flourish, but only took a small sip. So far, so good. Now, be careful. "So, what is the word around the campfire, my compadré?" he asked.

"You hear about Jerry the Clap?" Pompa Louie said.

"Yeah, died of the clap. Can't believe he didn't see it coming."

"Ha! That's a good one. Don'cha know it? The faggots got everybody thinking that the only thing you can get that kills ya is AIDS, and our good friend, the big "G," is getting tired of AIDS getting all the good pub," Pompa Louie said, leaning forward and punctuating his words with the cigarette he held between his thumb and forefinger. "Now, this is what you ain't heard."

Tucker moved closer, curiously, his head doing the nerve stomp. Suddenly a shadow was thrown between them. The hunchback looked up. A waitress was standing there, one of the dancers, a stretch of flesh accented by two sparkling pasties. "You want more ice?" She bounced, her hip jutting out and in.

247

Tuck cricked his neck to get her in his sights. "Yeah, fine." He waved her away. The waitress left and Tuck re-screwed himself towards his friend. "So, what don't I know about Jerry the Clap?"

Pompa Louie continued to direct the cadence of his words with his cigarette. "Well, I know this guy whose brother is dating a nurse who is real close with the nurse who was on the floor the night Jerry the Clap croaked." He slid closer. "This is what she said; she said that the germs from the gonorrhea got so agitated that the infection swelled him up till his head was like a pumpkin."

Tucker bobbed uncontrollably. "Damn, you mean there ain't no antibiotics or nothin' to stop that from happening?"

"Problem was, Jerry had the damn stuff for so long, by the time he went to the doctor, it was too fuckin' late."

"What an ignorant fuck."

Pompa Louie wiggled as though the secret was scurrying through him, looking for a place to escape. "Shit, that ain't nothin'. Listen to this if you wanna fuckin' puke. This nurse, she said her friend the nurse said that the infection just kept blowing up Jerry's head, fucking bigger and bigger, and she was in there giving him a shot or taking his temperature through his ass or something, and while she was there his head exploded!"

Tucker's mouth dropped and the cigarette that had been stuck there fell onto the table. "Get the fuck outta here!" he exclaimed.

"And there was juice and brains on the wall and bits of his eyeballs on the pillow case, and the nurse, she ain't been able to go back to work, she's so fucked up."

Tucker couldn't contain himself, and he started laughing, as he nimbly picked the cigarette up and out of the tiny hole it had burned in the tablecloth. He began to cough, sucking in air. Tears rolled through his eyes. Pompa Louie caught the same fever and began laughing equally as hard, until the table between them seemed to hop with their vibrations. When he regained a bit of composure, he said, "That's the craziest fuckin' thing I ever heard, Pompa Louie, and you've told me some happy shit in my time."

Pompa Louie spread his arms. An affected hurt look raided his face. "Hey, I'm not shitting you, partner. You ask anyone who went to the Clap's fuckin' funeral and they'll tell you the coffin was closed because the corpse inside didn't have a motherfucking head!"

Tucker grabbed his aching stomach and rolled back into the chair. "Like a pumpkin?"

Pompa Louie made a sphere in the air with two hands. "This big."

This wrenched the hunchback into more convulsive laughter that didn't subside until the waitress had returned with two glasses of ice, and a tiny pool of water began to form in the bottom of them.

Tucker threw back a swig from the glass and began to noisily chew a cube. "This big! Like a pumpkin! Unbe-fucking-lievable. Jerry the Clap."

This kind of talk went on for nearly two hours, as the rum evaporated into the bloodstream of Pompa Louie until his lips were banging together like two cymbals. Just what Tuck had planned. Louie was outta control, but still lucid enough to know what he was saying.

"Well, Pompa Louie, you turd, I gotta hit the road," Tuck reached behind himself and began to untwist his coat.

"No, man, not yet. There's still some rum left!" Louie exclaimed, shaking the bottle.

Tuck deflated back into the seat. "Yeah, the hell with it. One more for the road." As he emptied the bottle into his buddy's glass and feigned refilling his own, he carefully chose his next words. Raising his glass and taking a sip, Tucker slid his chair closer again. "How about what's going down about that party at The Pachyderm?" He spit the ice cube back into the glass and patted his coat, fumbling through pockets looking for another pack of smokes. "You did up the crew for that, didn't you?"

"Hey, you wanna get something to eat? They got hot dogs and shit here, I think," Pompa Louie said.

The hunchback raised a hand and shook his head. "Nothing for me. But if you're hungry, go ahead."

"Yeah, maybe, if the waitress gets here before her tits drop to her knees. Come on, Sylvia, I'm dying over here!" A waitress finally sauntered trance-like to the table and he asked her for a menu. "The only thing on the menu here, cowboy, is pussy," she replied. So he ordered another drink.

Tucker pursed his lips and snorted through his nostrils. What now? He had broached the subject and Pompa Louie didn't answer. Should he bring it up again?

Louie drained the glass and slammed it down on the table. "Yeah, I did the crew for that and then something happened upstairs afterwards and now my boys are getting waxed left and right by that miserable prick."

Louie's brain had been so addled by drugs, booze, genetic sludge, throbbing music, and goofy fucking speculation by somebody who knew his cousin's next door neighbor's ex-wife's gynecologist, that almost anything he said was so caked in bullshit that it would take a magnifying glass and a pair of tweezers to dig out the truth. The hunchback slurped at his melting ice, sliding another cube between his teeth and gnawing it gently until the cold shot through his tooth nerves and made him jump. "What miserable prick is that?" he finally asked.

Pompa Louie took a noisy drag on his cigarette and held the smoke deep. "No, no, don't go there. That's dark and dangerous territory from which nobody returns. The bastard's fucking up my business big time but my heart's still beating and my lips better stop if I want to keep it that way."

"You know Poteet was my best pal," Hines said. "Tell me a name and let me worry about it."

"What you gonna do with a name, man? Go fight the dude like some big shot?" He balled up his fists and made like a prize fighter. "Tell you where that will get you, in a box right next to your pal Poteet."

"I guess that will be my problem."

Pompa Louie, pimp, smuggler, pusher, small time racketeer, eyed the hunchback curiously, his bemusement showing in his face. It was almost as though he would like to tell Tuck just to watch what might happen. He exhaled, leaned back and extended his arm, laying it on the back of the booth. "Bedrosian. Nicholai the big prick motherfucker king of the world asshole Bedrosian. There, now go kill yourself."

Tucker tried to place the name. "I'm not sure I know..."

"Well, Nicholai Bedrosian is the biggest cheese in an Armenian syndicate, managing everything from hookers to heroin. The fucker is also numero uno with the fucking F.B.I., and he's on the loose somewhere and ain't nobody knows where, 'cause he scooped out of an attempted bust in Jersey a few months ago, where there was enough coke and smack to finish his fuckin' career with a nigger roommate and an asshole stretched wide as a garage door."

"Yeah, keep going," Tucker said, his heart pounding. If there was even a grain of truth to the story, this could be more than he ever expected.

Another drink was set before Pompa Louie. Without looking up he handed the waitress a bill and waved her away. "The story is very, very weird. Now, you'd think they would be on this guy like stink on shit whenever he came to America, but they never could nail him. He's like a fuckin' Houdini or whatever. Seems Bedrosian and his boys rented out the whole restaurant at the Lakeside Hotel, that elephant room, and the king himself was there partying with the common folk like some kinda Mother Theresa or something."

"And this is the night..."

"Yeah, the night you and your pal Poteet picked up the lobsters and delivered them. I guess you should consider yourself lucky nobody has popped your ass yet, come to think of it. Probably 'cause you weren't upstairs. "

"What's upstairs?"

"Well, Bedrosian and his cronies keep a penthouse suite. Right next to it is another suite, and it's connected into one big party room. Bedrosian keeps one side for his whores, so's the guys can, like, visit the smorgasbord and take their pick and then head off next door for a little hide the sausage," he pumped his index finger through a circle he made with the finger and thumb of his other hand. "Well, while everybody is having the good time, something happens. "

"What?" Tuck asked.

"That I just don't know. But anyone who might have seen it seems to be disappearing."

"You weren't up there?"

"Nah, nah. I was at the dinner for a short time, more or less keeping my eye on the girls. I supply him with some of the professional snatch that his boys love so much, as you well know. But I ain't up the chain far enough to get the big invite upstairs. You either gotta be a slave or a big roller. You're either working up there or playing."

"Anybody you know still around who was up there?"

Louie looked up at him and started chuckling. "You know, you're one ballsy freak. What, are you working for the cops now or something?"

Tucker Hines froze, fighting to not give away anything. Louie was stoned out of his mind and a crazy sonofabitch, but he wasn't dumb. "Ah, shit, forget about it," Tuck said, waving through the cigarette smoke. "I was just fuckin' curious, that's all."

"Yeah, well, curiosity killed the cat."

"I ain't no cat, pal, tell you that." The two men started laughing.

"Ain't no cat," Pompa Louie roared, swallowing the last few drops of his drink and slamming the glass down. Then he turned to Tuck. "Rojas."

"Paco Rojas?" The hunchback knew him. Rojas was another dim-witted go-fer who often ran errands for mob types.

"Yeah. He was there that night," Louie replied.

"Where is he? I ain't seen nor heard from him for some time."

"Yeah, well, he got busted the next day in front of a school where he was trying to do some commerce, so they put him in the County. Probably the only reason he's still alive. He gets out in, like, six months."

Tucker knew the county jail about as well as anyone. He also knew Paco Rojas would love to have a guest. The hunchback gently squeezed Louie's arm, released his grip and stood up. This two hour ordeal had cost him a bottle of booze and left him with a splitting headache. "Louie, you been a real help."

"Let me ask you something, if it ain't too much trouble," Louie said. "What's all this to you?"

Tuck spoke exhaling the words. "Motherfucker killed my best pal."

"Yeah, well, I'd watch my Ps and Qs if I was you. It's a good thing you got plans to go somewhere. I got a feeling you're gonna need to get out of here when this is all done."

25

Rich Baker was listening to the wind, watching it rattle the steel louvers that stretched across the concrete pillars of the parking garage. The shadows of late afternoon turned everything charcoal gray. He hugged himself and sat on a concrete abutment waiting for the usual occupant of parking space number one to return. He glanced at his watch. Any minute now. He knew Miles Lundeen's routine, knew that he was obsessed with time, schedules, appointments. Thus, he knew that Lundeen would come here, home, to the expensive condominium, to change clothes before going out to dinner. Lundeen didn't wear the same clothes to two consecutive events. One suit for work. One suit for dinner. He was like Nixon, for chrissakes, Baker thought. Wore a suit on the beach.

Baker heard a car accelerating up the ramp and saw the headlights sweep the walls of the parking garage, and he stood up from the abutment and tucked himself behind a pillar. The element of surprise. Get Lundeen far enough away from his car that he couldn't easily jump back in and drive away; so he couldn't hide himself from what he deserved.

Sweet purr, the sound of the engine as the big Lexus glided to a halt, almost couldn't tell the difference between running and off. Miles Lundeen opened the door and stepped out. He locked the doors with his remote control. He was wearing his long black cashmere coat. He was carrying a briefcase. His strides were long, spindly chicken legs carrying him to the elevator bank. Around the corner, away from the car now, before Lundeen could push the elevator button, Baker called his name.

"What? Who? Who is that?" Lundeen was squinting, his emaciated head jerking, trying to find the direction of the voice.

"It's me, Miles," Baker said, coming from behind the pillar, out of the shadows, into the soft yellow light. "You remember me surely, don't you, Miles?"

Baker had certainly caught him off guard. Already pale and gaunt, Lundeen's color seemed to seep away like air from a leaking balloon. "Rich? Is that you?" He took a step forward and raised his shaking hand waist high. "How are you?" he asked tentatively.

"Oh, Miles, peachy, just peachy," Rich responded, looking at the trembling hand that had been proffered to him. Thinking twice, he took it and shook. Lundeen was already obviously unnerved enough. No sense in increasing or prolonging the agony.

Lundeen pulled back his hand and thrust it into his pocket. "What, uh, what brings you here, Rich?"

"Well, Miles, we have some uncompleted business now, don't we?"

Lundeen bristled visibly. Rich swore he could see the hairs stand up on the back of his partner's neck. "No, no, Rich, we don't have any unfinished business. I thought we took care of everything."

"Not everything."

"I had the money directly deposited to your bank account. Didn't you get it? If there was a mistake, I'm truly sorry, but I can get it fixed."

"The money was there."

"Okay, well, good." Lundeen cleared his throat subconsciously and turned toward the elevator. "I guess that's it, then."

Baker reached out, grabbed Lundeen's arm and turned him around. "No, not yet."

Lundeen tried to shake out of the hold, but Baker held on. "Rich, damn it, let me go. What the hell's the matter with you? Are you drunk again?"

"Sober as a nun, partner. I want to get this right." Rich let go of Lundeen's arm.

"Yeah, what?"

"Simple. I've played your game. I've laid low. You haven't seen me. I haven't come back to the office, haven't confronted you in public. Look, even here, in the garage, private, nobody around."

"Yeah. What's the point?"

"I've played the game by your rules."

Lundeen shook a bony finger at him, "We had a deal."

"Yeah, well, did it include killing me?"

Lundeen was turning red now. "What the fuck are you talking about?"

"You know what I'm talking about. I'm being followed. In the last month I was almost nailed twice."

"Bullshit!" Lundeen shouted, his voice echoing in the concrete vault. "You're a goddamn paranoid drunk. Now get the fuck out of my way."

"I just want to know why, Miles, why me? What the fuck did I do to deserve this? You want to know what I think? I think you and Huang killed my wife and pinned it on me just to get rid of me."

"You're out of your fucking mind," Lundeen sneered, turning away.

"What I can't figure out is why. Why you needed me out," Baker had attempted to grab Lundeen's arm, but the man shook free of his grasp.

"You better get some help, pal."

"So, here's the new rules. I'm back in for a full cut."

"What the hell are you talking about?"

"I'll stay out of it as long as you want, but I'm getting my percentage of this deal come hell or high water. I don't care how you want to do it."

Lundeen swallowed, obviously trying to compose himself. Then he shook a bony finger at Rich, "We had a deal."

"You had a deal, Miles. And you crammed it down my throat. Now it's my turn."

Lundeen was turning red now. "Forget about it."

"I'm like an elephant, Miles, I never forget anything, you yourself used to say that to me."

"Well, you can forget this cockamamie idea."

"No, you're going to do it for me, partner." The last word was said with venom. "You owe me, you cocksucker." Lundeen had turned and begun to walk away, and Baker grabbed him, this time harder, digging his fingers into the cadaverous arm.

Lundeen yanked his arm, but couldn't free it. "Get your fucking hands off me, you psycho!"

"One more thing, Miles. I've made arrangements."

Lundeen's eyes widened fearfully. "What do you mean 'arrangements'?"

"If I get killed, no, if I get hurt, a fucking scratch shaving myself, a massive heart attack, if I choke on a chicken bone by myself in my own kitchen..." He stared menacingly at his ex-partner. "...if anything—anything—happens to me, you're next."

Lundeen was getting his second wind. Rich could see it in his eyes. Sunken and distant as they were, they nonetheless housed an evil beyond estimation. "Then what? Then what, Rich? What are you going to do to me? Have me killed?" His voice was calm now, sinisterly matter-of-fact. "Kill me like you did her? Like you killed your wife for chrissakes?"

"You know I..." Rage pulsed through Rich Baker. He shoved Lundeen and the skeletal man pitched forward, then down to the concrete, instinctively breaking his fall with his elbow. His briefcase burst open on impact, spilling papers onto the floor. The wind immediately picked some up and began playing with them.

"You're a goddamn fucking looney toon, you bastard!" Lundeen cried, as he pulled himself to his feet and began to chase the flying papers.

26

Icy slivers of rain were chewing up the windshield of Glory Kane's car. The rhythmic swoops of the wipers just seemed to smear the stuff in taffeta patterns on the glass. She and Jake McKay were finished for the day, a day that had started at six in the morning, some fourteen hours before. They were heading home from the Loop, driving beneath the huge Chicago Skyway toll bridge that soared above the neighborhoods of South Chicago and Northwest Indiana. The metal grid work loomed large between the streaks.

"Three bucks plus to go over a freaking bridge," Jake McKay groused from his slumped position on the passenger side.

"I suppose it's worth it if you're in a hurry," Glory answered flatly.

"If we were in a goddamned hurry, we wouldn't have wasted so much time interviewing all those society twits with their rattling jewels and Rolex-la-di-da watches."

"You never know what's a waste of time in this business until you do it," Glory said, but not totally disagreeing with her partner. Glory and Jake had spoken to more than a dozen people who'd come into contact with Rich Baker at Miles Lundeen's party. And the most they got out of it was that, by the end of the night, Baker was, indeed, drunk and bouncing off the walls. In fact, the interviews had become so tedious, that Glory was mentally assembling the people in chronological order, based on their descriptions of Rich's condition. The first people to speak with him, a Mr. and Mrs. Bennington, had described him as somewhat quiet, very reserved, very formal. And the last person, an attractive divorcee named Sherry Arnell, had been accosted by a very wobbly Baker in the hallway. By then, his inhibitions had been frayed enough to allow him to grab her ass as she looked at a painting on the wall.

Bottom line, they'd gotten nothing of particular interest out of the individuals. Ms. Arnell had literally dragged Baker back to the living room and watched from the hallway as the crowd swallowed him up. No one admitted seeing him leave.

"By the end of the day, the room smelled like a whorehouse," Jake was saying as Glory snapped back to the present.

"Lot of perfume, that's for sure. Not much else."

"Those women. They not only have to look and sound rich, they gotta smell rich, too. Made me want to puke."

Glory shook her head. "You have any trouble with the men?"

"Assholes, for the most part, but at least they didn't smell like two-legged funeral homes."

"You don't much like women, do you?"

Jake recoiled. "There you go again with that shit. What makes you say that?"

Glory decided not to answer the question. She just pressed on, "I just wonder why."

"Why what?"

"Why you don't like women."

"I like women, all right."

"Home, cooking, barefoot—like that?" Glory mused.

Jake turned toward her, scrunching his huge shoulders against the door. "You know, you act like that stuff is criminal activity."

"It's not 'criminal', as you say. What's almost 'criminal' are men like you who think that's the only place women should be."

"You ever think maybe that's the best place for them?"

"Sometimes it is, sometimes it isn't. I just think they should have options. I mean, just because your mom stayed at home..."

"Who said anything about that?"

"I just assumed..."

"You don't know a damned thing about me. You're as judgmental as I am."

"Well, you're right. I apologize. I shouldn't assume anything."

Jake sat in silence for several moments. Then he spoke softly. "Yeah, well, she stayed home until I was eight. Then she was gone."

"She died?"

"Might as well have."

Glory inhaled deeply. "I'm sorry."

"Not your problem," Jake grunted, "not mine either."

"I'm just saying, I'm sorry I made an assumption. I know better than that," Glory replied. "If you ever want to talk about it..."

Jake interrupted, "Yeah. Don't hold your breath."

"Did she every come back into your life?

"Okay, in that case, hold your breath."

The cellular phone in Jake's pocket trilled, breaking the silence. He fumbled beneath the seat shoulder strap and extracted it, flipping it open.

"McKay," he said, then muttered and grunted as the voice on the other end continued. He ended with, "Shit," as he flipped it shut.

"What's up?"

"Turn it around," he said wiping his face with his flabby open palm. "They found Aaron Clayton."

"Where?"

"Wisconsin. Just over the line."

"Wisconsin?" Glory answered incredulously.

"Yeah. Think we need our passports?"

She didn't react. "Dead or alive?" she asked.

"Humph, what do you think?"

Wisconsin seemed to explode over the horizon, creating a rolling vista of sugar colored hills laid out against a violet sky. Snow rimmed the otherwise crystal clean highway in jutting drifts six, seven feet high. The recent thaw in the Chicago area had a much more formidable task here, a hundred or so miles north, having to chew down a full winter's worth of snow.

"Well, at last I've been to the edge of the earth," Jake grumbled, as he looked out the car window. "Who would have thunk it was in friggin' Wisconsin?"

"Bet you didn't even know the night sky was that dark," Glory said, sweeping the horizon with her eyes.

"Yeah, what are all those twinkly things, anyway? Looks like somebody shot it with a twelve gauge." Jake said. "And I thought snow was gray."

263

Glory chuckled and glanced from side to side as she drove. "Should be here somewhere, up here on the left."

"Yeah, there, there's lights up there," Jake said, pointing. Glory could see the red and blue flashers splattering the night sky. She pulled up next to the car.

"Follow me," the cop said, from his already lowered window.

They were led onto a dark, empty side road. Detectives Kane and McKay could see where new snow had fallen over plowed indentations like the self-healing tissue of a keloid scar. Ten minutes later they pulled through the open gates of what was obviously a junkyard. The cop pulled over and they followed. He stepped out of his car.

"Name is Sheriff Red Taggert," he said. Glory and Jake introduced themselves as they stepped out of their car. "We're gonna walk from here. Don't mind walking do you, eh?"

Sheriff Taggert, perfectly pear-shaped despite his bulky brown parka, waddled past them. "You folks seem to be going to a whole lot of trouble there, coming up like this so late at night. Could have waited till tomorrow, fer sure."

"Well, I don't think so," Glory answered.

"Now, that's more like it, the smell of oil and grease," Jake McKay said, a thump of delight in his voice as his rubber boots squished in the mud of the junkyard.

Mountains of rusted, leaking, deceased automobiles ringed the perimeter like mountains lost in the mist. The air was vaguely pungent with the odor of oxidation and drippage, and while they slithered through the maze like sewer rats, the big detective pointed out the festering hulks of cars he remembered from his childhood.

"Right there, that red one on the bottom, at least it looks like it was red, that there is a 1959 Chevy. You can tell by the horizontal dorsal fins. And over there is a '62 SS, and, goddamn, look at that, a '64 GTO!"

The snow on the paths between the cars had been eroded by the ins and outs of wrecker trucks and the plodding feet of dogs and men until literal rivers of mud wound through the wreckage like veins. Effluent seemed to crawl up Glory's legs, and she wondered what critters and creatures ran free in the darkness, sniffing at her skin. She began to think twice about whether the idea of coming tonight was wise.

"You know, the problem with cars today is that they all look alike. You can thank the Japs for that. Shit, they all look alike, so they make their cars all look alike, and then we follow suit," Jake continued. "Look, look at that! A '57 Caddy! You could damn near stand up in the back seat, not to mention screwing like a sailor without a single cramp."

"You know, Jake," Glory replied, "as each day goes by, I'm more amazed at your enlightenment."

"Thanks," Jake said, obviously not getting the dig.

"Right up this away," Red Taggert said, pointing. A cloud of expelled breath circled his head. "They're right around this corner."

Glory could see a halo of light beaming up from behind a range of stacked and smashed cars. They followed a widened spot in the road that dissected the globs of wreckage and came to the lighted spot. To Glory it seemed, at first, like a campfire in the middle of nowhere, but the illumination came not from a fire, but from a large wrecker with its headlights and a spotlight trained on a late model BMW, that looked almost new save for the fact that it had no tires, its hood was gone, its windows removed, and it was lying upside down like a dead bug.

A kid, early twenties, stringy greasy hair, wearing a denim jacket over a lumberjack shirt and blue jeans with exploded knees hopped down from the truck. He tossed a cigarette that fizzed in a puddle when it landed. Taggert said, "This here is Chuckie Luntgarten. He runs the junkyard here. This here, Chuckie, is detectives, uh, I forgot your two's names."

Glory and Jake introduced themselves. "What's going on here, Chuckie?" Jake asked.

"Well now, I was just working here, ya know, lifting these here cars up to take over to the smasher over dere," he pointed to what gradually revealed itself to be a building some fifty yards away. "We do that, don't ya know, when they've pretty much been mined for the good parts, and this here is the pile we take them from. So, I seen this here Beemer and it was underneath a Hondo on top of it, and I didn't remember it ever coming into the place, plus it looked pretty new to me, ya know?"

"So you were suspicious about the car? Then what did you do?" Glory asked.

"Well, I wasn't too bad yet suspicious, but Croce, that's my dog, he's a Shepherd mix, big old thing, I named him after that guy who sang about the junkyard dog, he was out here and a'sniffin' and barking at this Beemer, and I thought, well, I better go take a look, eh?" He walked over to the upturned car and knelt in the mud next to it. "He was a diggin' and snarling right here, and I had to admit it smelled kinda funny to me, too, but I don't have no dog's smell, ya know? Now, you gotta kinda lay down on your stomach almost to see, but if you look right in there where the trunk is sprung..." He pulled a flashlight off his belt and shined it in, "... you can see a hand."

Glory and Jake stepped to the BMW quickly. Glory exhaled and got onto all fours in the mud to look beneath the car. The odor down here did change somewhat. Could it be? She took the flashlight from Chuckie and ran it along the creased opening of the trunk. The sheet metal was puckered at the seams where the trunk lid met the body of the car, as if it had been pounded in the middle. Glory's eyes trailed the line to a wider bend in the crack that opened to maybe four inches. She shined the light inside. She stopped where the black turned putty gray. Sure enough, a hand. "I'll be," she said, standing up.

"Let me see," Jake said, getting down.

Sheriff Taggert then spoke. "Chuckie called me right away and I come up here and got the registration off the VIN, and, when I ran it I found you guys were looking for this car. So I called you."

"Oh, yeah," Jake said. He then stood up and began inspecting the tangle of curlicue pipes and connectors beneath the engine. His fingers probed the crevices and hidden places, occasionally emerging stained with dirt or grease or other black fluid that Jake raised to his nostrils and smelled. To Glory, the maze of metal filigree was meaningless, but from the look on Jake 's face she could tell that something was somehow emerging from the mess. She sidled up to him.

"Anything unusual?" she asked.

"I don't see where this car was actually in a wreck. Brake lines are secure. And along here, on the edges, no single significant point of impact. It's mashed up, sure, but probably from the weight of the other car on top of it. Just looks to me like it was stripped and dumped. Can't say for certain," he turned to the junkyard owner. "How long has it been here?"

"I don't know. Don't know how it got here, neither. Usually, we take inventory on everything. We're the biggest salvage operation in south central Wisconsin, though, and we buy pieces and parts from insurance companies. Even total wrecks with no resale value we can crush down and sell as scrap metal to the mills. I guess it's possible something could come in without being logged, but it ain't that likely."

"Can you turn it over?" Jake asked.

"Oh, yeah, sure," Chuckie said, pulling on a pair of gloves and grabbing a handle to pull himself up into the wrecker. "I would'a done it before you got here, but didn't want to mess up the crime scene, eh?"

"You did good, Chuckie," Taggert replied.

Chuckie turned the vehicle around and pulled a cable and hook from the winch. In a second he was back in the cab. The truck seemed to hunker down as the winch motor wailed and all the lights on the vehicle dimmed. The BMW stirred from its mud bed grudgingly, like a sleepy dog raising its head. Then it was on its side and bending carefully to its normal position. Jake and Glory stepped aside as the twisted heap was gently nestled down into a new position. The cable slackened and fell against the front end of the car. Then the operator shut down the motor and silence rushed in through the hole left by the motor's demise.

Everyone stood silently for several seconds, staring at the crumpled trunk. Jake finally spoke. "Well, it's Christmas," he said. "Let's open it up."

Chuckie came over with a crow bar, wedged it in place and popped the trunk. The lid opened, and this time the odor exploded outward, overtaking the previously dominant smells of oil and grease.

"Holy Christ!" Chuckie shouted, turning and burying his face in his jacket. "Jesus!"

Sheriff Taggert had backed away, invisible now in the darkness. Glory winced, removed a handkerchief she always kept in her coat pocket for just these situations, and moved closer. She had smelled worse, seen worse in terms of decay. Once went into a home and found a woman who had been dead for two weeks in the middle of summer. Her eyes had been replaced by balls of maggots. Cold weather had some advantages, Glory thought.

"Shine the light in here, Jake," she said. McKay moved closer, holding a handkerchief to his nose and ran the light across the crumpled form in the trunk.

The man was dressed in a suit. He had been wadded into a virtual ball to fit into the closed, confined space. The beam of amber light followed the contour of the body to the head. The back was a disfigured blob of dried blood. When the light moved to the face, there was a quick movement. Glory gasped and recoiled as a field mouse darted out of a round gape in the forehead that was ringed with brain tissue and bone.

"Shit!" she gasped, then caught herself and leaned in. "Rear entry. Look at that. Then out the front."

"Execution style," Jake replied. "Not in the trunk, though, no splatter."

Glory backed off. "What a mess," she whispered.

"Yeah, two weeks ago we had no bodies. Now we have more than we know what to do with."

"All except the one we're looking for," she replied.

27

It was a soft night, unusual for Chicago in March. At this time of year the city is usually inhabited by a cantankerous, carnivorous, bass drum-thumping wind that seethes around and through the natural vortexes formed by the proximity and arrangement of the buildings, accelerating at banshee speeds to cut through the souls, brave or stupid, or desperate enough to walk the streets.

But this night the wind rested, perhaps the season's first glimpse of winter's exhaustion, the first respite in its merciless assaults that become increasingly more sporadic until finally withering away by May. And this evening, in which Rich Baker found himself afoot on the sidewalk less than three blocks away from his apartment, was of such benign nature that he opted to walk outside with the huge pastrami sandwich he had just purchased at his favorite deli and eat it on the way home.

The absence of breeze allowed a certain radiance to emit from the walls and pavement. A huge crystal moon with a drunk happy face carved by clouds and craters dispersed a glow that hung like gossamer on the street lamps and neon and amber window lights. Even the familiar city sounds, as rhythmic and familiar as breathing, seemed muted. Horns were more distant. The rattle and clatter of the "el" were like the syncopation of a jazz backbeat. The squeal of brakes at traffic lights was somehow less urgent.

Baker unwrapped the sandwich, and the pastrami leapt out of the wedges between the slices of rye bread at uncontrollable angles, like puppies out of a box. He took a huge breath and the garlic aroma, hot, moist, making steam between his fingers, rushed him in a frenzy of delight. The first bite, hot, hot against his cool tongue, seemed to run through him and disperse to the far reaches of his body until he could almost taste it in his toes. He had virtually no memory of anything ever tasting or smelling so good. No, wait. Vague, murky memories of childhood, when every new experience had an exciting flavor, or an aroma, or a sound, whispered from the corners of his mind. Misty images converged. Christmas presents of miasmic red. The aroma of the season's first snow, like cold steel. Papa's new car, leathery, fresh. Granny's breath, milky, sour. First smells, new smells, new tastes and sounds.

Something strange had been happening to Rich Baker since the incident; something that pumped electricity into his blood. It was as though his senses had been scrubbed clean and polished, like old brass, to a new, shiny texture.

On this night he was acutely aware of everything surrounding him, and it made him wonder. He thought as he chewed, as he passed a row of narrow, quaint town homes, brownstone and brick with wrought iron gates and concrete stoops, perhaps it was the somehow exhilarating constant presence of fear and sorrow that gave a sturm und drang to his senses and sensibilities, much like, he imagined, a hunted animal must feel when the scents and sounds of its environment conspire to warn it of impending conflict. He was, after all, prey. Not only were the police poised in the thicket of his life waiting to pounce, but the apocalyptic demeanor of Miles Lundeen placed other assassins in the shadows of his psychic periphery. What's more, he could understand Lundeen's motives, could understand the need to kill someone who was an obstacle in his path.

But this evening, as the sandwich grew tepid faster than Rich could eat it, another revelation exploded in his mind. Perhaps this awareness of taste and smell and sounds was also the result of not having had a drink since that night, that night of blood and confusion. It sprang suddenly, this idea, ambushing him. When he drank, he'd never thought about it; he just did it. Like breathing. Not drinking happened just as easily, so easily he didn't even know it. Strange that the thought would come, just like that.

He found himself stopping to take another bite. As he did, he saw the man. A blur of dark gray trench coat zipping through the shadows across the street and somewhat behind him. A synapse of the survival instinct fired in Rich's brain. He had seen the coat first outside the deli, shrouded in a broken cascade of streetlight. A head, dark to almost invisibility, but round, perhaps held together by a stocking cap. No face. Just the transient orange glow of a cigarette being drawn upon, followed by a corresponding amoeba of smoke. Of all shapes on the street that night, some ancient gene in Rich's biology triggered the trench coat and placed it in the front of his mind for safekeeping, and now it was there, parallel to him, on the opposite side of the street. Rich folded the remainder of his sandwich back into its wrapping and tossed the wad into a waste basket. Attempting to be as inconspicuous as possible, he pulled his coat tight at his throat and walked a few steps faster.

The man's footsteps echoed his own. Even from there, across the street, they sounded like rifle shots, superseding all other sounds. It was like watching himself in a mirror. When Rich slowed down, so did the other man. When Rich stopped to feign tying his shoe, the other man suddenly became occupied with his fingernails.

Rich was now certain that he was being followed. He passed an alley that dissolved into darkness between two buildings less than a block from his apartment and considered, momentarily, jutting into it and circling around to approach his place from the opposite side of the block. But it was too perfectly dark and hidden and silent. If the trench coat wanted to hit him there, it could be done with relative ease. Rich decided to stay on the street and navigate the distances between shadow and light as quickly as possible. For an instant, the man seemed to lose ground, and Rich shook the paranoia temporarily from his mind. But less than a block later the man had made up the distance and more. Rich watched out of the corner of his eye. The guy flipped a cigarette butt into the gutter and coughed, as he stood at the curb waiting for a car to pass before casually strolling into the street.

Rich could see the lights of his lobby. He fumbled for the key in his pocket, noticing a slight tremble in his fingers as he extracted it. He only needed to get through the door and through the vestibule, closing the door behind him before the man could get in. The man would need a key to open the door. Or, Rich supposed, he could fire through the glass. Rich inhaled. The air was suddenly icy, and it made him shudder.

He took the steps by twos, extracting the key cleanly at the same instant. Through the corner of his eye he sensed faster movement. He heard staccato footsteps. The door swung

273

open and sucked air as it closed and clicked reassuringly. Rich sprinted quickly to the elevator and punched the button. The bell rang immediately, but the door seemed to float open as if in a dream. Rich knifed his way in and pushed the button for his floor.

He heard the opening of the main entrance door, footsteps on the quarry tile of the vestibule. His heart was an animal in a cage, banging against his bones to get out. The elevator doors exhaled as they slowly crawled together, and, for an instant, Rich glimpsed relief. A foot apart, now. A ratta-tat-tat of heel and toe against the hard floor. Six inches to silence and safety. Shadows falling through the crack. A few more inches. And then, a meaty, hairy hand jamming between the doors, causing them to bounce apart like the collision of two cars. A huge sheet of lobby light encircled the shape of the man in the trench coat, backlighting him, rendering him featureless, like a shadow. But as he came forward, Rich could see the face beneath the stocking cap, as puffy and soft as pudding, smashing together cheekbone and eyebrow until there was nothing but two blood black slits to squeeze the eyes.

The man paused in the threshold of the elevator doors, then pulled himself in. He was sparkplug short, square, straight down. He jammed his hands into his pocket.

"Sorry," Rich said .

The man made an indefinable noise, part breath, part word. He pushed a button without looking, or so it seemed to Rich, as if destination was secondary to destiny. The doors eased together with a gentle ring. The elevator lurched upward.

Rich stood in silence, head pointed forward, but eyes and instincts and interest aligned to any movement from the body next to his. The guy had his hands in his pocket. They seemed to roll, knuckles and fingers, against the shape of the trench coat. Rich's mouth emptied of moisture and breath as a million possible movements surged through his mind. He didn't know the man. Nothing was familiar, not the height nor the shape nor the tobacco smell on the coat.

The man turned slightly. Rich heard a click. The hammer of a gun? The snap of a switchblade? He opened his hand wide, stretching his fingers. He calculated the shape of the distance between his cocked arm and the man's chin. It was an old martial arts move he'd learned years before. Open palm, heel of the hand, rammed straight up using knees and elbow to the opponent's chin. It was virtually a finishing shot, snapping the neck back and the head upward as teeth disintegrated against teeth. And with Rich's height advantage and the leverage it afforded him, the results would be even more devastating. Rich pivoted slightly in perfect sync with the ever-so-slight move of the man. Adrenaline fired through his nervous system. There was another click; the man squared; Rich's arm recoiled; a bell rang.

And everything stopped as the elevators suddenly burst open. Rich heard the yip-yip of the fucking dog before the doors were clear, and the sudden intrusion froze his arm like a batter's checked swing. Smoky old Eleanor or Evie or Edie— the woman with the dog—seemed to snarl as she entered the elevator and waddled between the two men. The hairless zygote on a leash sniffed at the man's black square-toed shoe, and he grunted as he consciously pulled it back.

Rich's insides deflated like a gutted balloon. The goddamned woman, always in the wrong place at the wrong time, may have saved his life. He could see the man's eyes, glaring menacingly at him, as the elevator moved slowly up to the penthouse.

275

28

The jail gathering area emitted a pall of smoke, rising and settling like a sky, motionless over the people who had come to meet, to speak, to touch fingers. The corners had been taken up already by the first visitors in and the first prisoners out. They spoke softly to one another, women and men, children, not too close, though, the guards wouldn't allow it, even if it was only a jail and not a maximum security joint like downstate. The room was large with a low-hanging ceiling that seemed to press the bodies together, as if they were in a vise. Picnic tables with attached benches ran the entire length of the room. The white Formica tops were scarred by desperate knives and forks, and flecked with deep brown burns from cigarettes left to smolder. Everything was bolted down.

Look at this place, Tucker Hines thought as he glanced around, bullshitting the visitors with its chrome all shiny and the lemon smell of clean in the air. Facade. Hiding what's behind the walls, those walls over there. Cold concrete. Radiators that hiss and squeal in the winter, as they try to generate enough heat to get into the lungs of the prisoners in their tiny cells. Can't even warm up the bars enough so you could touch them for more than a second. No, shit no, doesn't look so bad in this

276

room. More like a school cafeteria. But if the visitors could only see into the guts of this place, into its soul, they wouldn't want to come back. No fucking way.

He had passed scrutiny at the gate and was now standing in the center of the chaos, carton of cigarettes under his arm, looking for a familiar face. Not so easy in this mob. The black guys and their families were on one side, the white guys on the other. Paco Rojas would fit somewhere in between. Which side? His eyes swept the room and whenever they came into contact with someone else's, those eyes would turn away, fascinated by his deformed shape, but ashamed to be staring. Everybody but the kids. The little ones especially. They stared at him, pulling on mom's coat, but mom was too busy talking to pay attention.

A feeling that something had rolled in from behind him caused Tucker to turn. Paco Rojas was threading his way through the crowd. The sight of him made Tuck recoil in pity. He knew that jail would not agree with the petite, almost feminine little guy, but what he was seeing now wrenched even his callous heart.

Rojas was coming at him with the swagger and attitude of a guy unfazed by his situation, but Tuck could see something else. Yellow dog eyes exploded from beneath the raven black eyebrows. Paco's cheeks were sunken, his eyes ringed with a stark darkness. His hands shook uncontrollably. Tuck reached out and took one of them, shaking it heartily, and guiding him towards a spot on the bench.

"Move the fuck over, pal," the hunchback said to a white guy who had sprawled out on the bench with both legs. The guy glared for a second then sat up straight and pulled closer to the man to whom he was speaking. Tuck and Paco sat down.

277

"Paco, you look like shit," Tuck said.

"Hell does that to you," the little man replied, his hand flitting to his face, picking sweat drops from the angled bones of his eye sockets. "What you got for me, man, a present?" Paco said, nodding at the carton of cigarettes under Tuck's arm.

"Yeah, merry Christmas," Tuck answered. "Marlboros, full strength, that's your brand, ain't it?"

"I don't smoke 'em no more. They're like money, man. Like gold," Rojas said, gathering the carton and pulling it into his chest where he rocked it like a baby.

"Things ain't going so well for you in here from the looks of things," Tuck said.

"It's okay, man, not so bad."

"Could'a fooled me."

"I got myself a new light, brother," Rojas said, pointing to the ceiling. "I got behind these walls, and guess who I found back there? Jesus! Yeah, like in Jesus Christ. He ain't too proud to come into a place like this and save my soul, no sir, brother, and that's exactly what he did."

"Good for you," Tuck said.

"Washed in the blood of the lamb. Righteous onto the last day. And it's something you oughta be thinking about, brother."

Tuck chuckled. Finding Jesus. It happened all the time. Happened in the dark. But back in the light of day, on the streets, when no one will hire you for a piss ant job and you don't know where you're going to sleep, it's awful hard to find Jesus out there. He may come to the jail, but he don't come to the ghetto. "Way I figure it, Jesus owes me one." He pointed to his hump. "Gave me this for no good reason or nothing I did."

"It's your cross to bear, brother. We all have them. Use it to glorify Jesus and you will be saved. Don't take my word for it, brother, it's in the book, the Bible, all you need to know."

"Yeah, thanks for the tip," Tucker said, smirking. So much bravado, so little veracity. It was the walk and talk of the jail punk.

"So, what brings you out my way, man, not like I'm choosy, but I ain't seen you for a long time, and, what the hell, you gotta want something from me, what to bring me cigarettes and all?"

"Well, with you being so happy in the country club here and with finding Jesus, it don't sound like I got anything you might need."

Rojas stared at him, obviously trying to figure it all out. Still clutching the cigarette carton, he slid closer to Tuck. "Man, I can't take it anymore," he whispered, and then the house of cards collapsed. The skin around his eyes had reddened. He began to shake. Then he wept, dropping the cigarette carton onto the table and burying his face in his hands.

"Goddamn, man, take it easy," Tuck said, soothing his friend with a gentle touch and looking around to see who all was staring. "Pull yourself together, for chrissakes."

"They're killing me in here, Tuck. From the first day, man, I became a bitch for a guy name of Darnell Clay, big albino nigger motherfucker," he looked imploringly into Tuck's eyes and grabbed his arm with two bony hands. "I gotta get outta here. I can't take it, not even for one more second."

"Settle down, Paco. For cryin' out loud, no wonder you're having such a hard time; you're like a hysterical old woman."

Rojas had regained a modicum of composure. "You gotta experience it to know what I'm talking about. You gotta have eyes on all four sides of your head," Rojas extended two fingers and pointed at his eyes, his temples, the back of his head, "to keep from getting your fudge packed or your guts opened for no reason known to man. Brother, I'm counting the days."

"What you got left?"

"One eighty six. It's a little more than six months. If they don't kill me first. Then I'm out and staying out."

"Well, maybe I can help," the hunchback said.

Paco grabbed Tuck's arm with both hands and twisted his sleeve. "Sonofabitch, brother, what's it gonna take?"

"What it always takes. Information."

"And if I get this whatever information you want, you can guarantee I'm out?"

"I've got some major connections."

"You guarantee I can get out?"

"I don't know. Give me something to take back to them, something good, something I can negotiate with."

Rojas shook his head deliberately, obviously mulling the scenario. "Man, you were bullshitting me. You can't do shit."

"I got to take something back, show them you're the man."

"Shit," he spat.

"You work for Bedrosian, yeah?" the hunchback said.

"Nicholai Bedrosian? The big man from Armenia or Lithuania or whatever it is?"

"No, Nicholai fucking Bedrosian the beauty queen."

Rojas paused, then nodded. "I work for the lord, brother."

"Well, you used to work for Bedrosian, yeah?"

"Indirectly, I guess, but if you want me to set up that bastard, well, it's safer and better in here."

"You hear what happened to Poteet and Benny the Razor?"

Hines could see the color drain from the man's face. Rojas diverted his eyes and shook his head. "Yeah, man, that's bad, real bad."

"You guys worked a job at The Pachyderm sometime back."

Rojas became visibly jittery, as if electricity suddenly and slowly was injected into his veins. He rolled his hands, looked out over the crowd, and closed his eyes. Then he came back to Hines. "Well, maybe," was all he said.

Tucker reached into his coat and removed an envelope. Unclasping it, he let a photo fall onto the table, a picture Glory Kane had given him. He then set it on the table. "You know these folks?"

Rojas pursed his lips and covered the picture with his long, slender fingers. He nervously glanced around the room. Then he shoved the photo back to Tuck and shook his head. "No, don't know 'em."

"Why don't you look at that a little closer? Then tell me what you know about these folks."

"Why? Am I supposed to know these people just 'cause I'm, like, the guy who shines Bedrosian's shoes?"

"The broad was supposed to have been there at the Pachyderm that night, the party, the one you and Poteet and Benny the Razor worked."

Rojas shook his head again. "What the heck? You think I was, like, partying with the big brass? Shit, man, I was just a factory worker, humping down on the shop floor. That means I kept my eyes and my mouth shut."

"This here broad and her pal were there."

Rojas lifted the picture again and studied it. "Yeah, maybe. But I can't for sure say I remember her being there. I mean, I was just walking around with a tray that night."

281

"And you're telling me that you didn't notice a chick that looks like this? What are you, some kind of noodle dick?"

"Yeah, well, maybe I noticed her."

"Maybe? You think Jesus wants you to lie?"

"Okay, okay, I seen her!"

"That night? At the party?"

"Yeah. What's this all about anyway? Never mind. Shit, the less I know, the better."

"Did you see her that night? What happened?"

"I don't know, brother," Rojas shook his head. "It doesn't sound like a task in the service of my Lord and Savior Jesus Christ."

"No? How about your savior Tucker Hines? How many times I bail you out of one predicament or another? Do I have to remind you of that little mix up with the bookies? The lost money and all?"

"Yeah, I owe you, man, but crossing the shadow of these guys is a one-way ticket to the graveyard."

"Well, then it looks like three more months at the County Hilton for you."

Rojas sat silent, obviously contemplating his words, his next move. His lips were moving and it became apparent to Tuck that he was praying. A full minute elapsed before he turned to the hunchback. "The Lord is my shepherd. Of whom should I be afraid?"

"How about your albino boyfriend?"

Rojas looked at his fingernails. "Shit," he spat.

Tuck leaned across the table again. "Look, it's a matter of credibility. Give me a crumb, one lousy fucking taste of what you know that I can take back to my friends and convince them that you, Mrs. Darnell Clay, deserves to get sprung from this joint."

Rojas put up his hands, "Okay, all right, point made. I'll give you something, maybe I shouldn't, but it will convince your pals in the badges of my credibility." He gathered his thoughts for several seconds. Rojas pushed the cigarette carton aside and leaned forward. His voice was a whisper. "I'm taking a case of champagne up to the penthouse in the elevator, and lo and behold, Bedrosian slides in. My first thought is to get the fuck out and let the big man stay, but then this here broad and her pal come in there with us. Bedrosian is looking fine, 'cause he's got the grandiose threads and the fine fuckin' tie and all, and he's carrying a briefcase that is loaded with horse or crack or maybe cash or whatever, but it's a real fuckin' fancy briefcase, gold clasps and shit. And big, thick. So the redhead says to him, 'Hey that's, like, a nice briefcase, what the fuck is it, alligator?' Only she probably don't say 'fuck.' Bedrosian says, like, 'No, it's actually crocodile from the fucking Nile River' or something like that, but he don't say 'fuck' neither. And it's all chit chat like they known each other for years, Bedrosian and the redhead. Then Bedrosian hands the briefcase over to this guy the woman is with. Says, 'It's his, anyway.' And the guy takes it and Bedrosian laughs then everybody else laughs, like on cue. This goes on all the way upstairs. Lots of chuckles."

"You're on the elevator with them?"

"Well, how the hell else do I know?"

"Yeah, okay, go on."

Rojas continued, "Everybody gets off the elevator, and this guy and the redhead take the briefcase and go into the other room that is, like I said, right off the main room of the suite owned by Bedrosian and his boys. They are, I presume, humping each other to death." He folded his hands and dropped them on the table. "Then the party goes on and everybody has a swell time until—until—that's it, that's all the further I'm going right now."

Tucker pondered the scene, his heart raced. "So, something happened after that. And you ain't saying what."

"Not until I get a key out of hell."

"You're three steps closer to the door. Let me ask you this: what was in the briefcase?"

"How the hell should I know? I ain't got x-ray eyes."

"Why'd Bedrosian give it to the guy?"

"Let me put it this way, guy was called 'Chink'."

"What kind of name is that?"

"It's a Chinaman's name, like spic or dago."

"What does it mean?"

"Yeah, ain't it the truth? Why is this guy called Chink on account of he don't look like no Chinaman to me or nothing." Rojas pulled even closer. "They call him Chink because he did the laundry for Bedrosian."

"The money. He laundered money for Bedrosian?"

"Yeah. Lot of cash. Can't spend it. Gotta hide it. That was Chink's job, I guess."

"What about the broad?" Tucker asked.

"Like I said, she was nothing. Just a girlfriend of the Chink."

Tuck shook his head. "Man, the broad is missing, maybe dead, the Chink is missing, maybe dead, and Poteet and Benny the Razor are dead. What the hell is going on?"

Rojas leaned across the table and grabbed Hines by the shirt, pulling him close. With his lips only inches from the hunchback's ear, he whispered, "That, as they say, is the rest of the story. But I ain't telling it unless I can get an ironclad guarantee of free passage out of this hell hole. Now, even if you tell me right now you can get me that ticket, I ain't gonna believe you, 'cause you're like I used to be, a liar and a cheat and a scum who will say anything to get what he wants. So, go back and bring me somebody who can get me out of here, and my lawyer to witness everything. Then maybe, just maybe, I'll talk." He let go and pushed the hunchback away.

Rojas stood up and clutched the carton to his chest. "Thanks for the CARE package." Then he leaned down and put his face a few inches from the hunchback's. "Don't you say nothing to nobody about what I told you. It don't take much to get killed in this crowd. That's all." He waved the carton of cigarettes at Tucker as he walked away. "Praise the Lord! And thanks for the smokes."

29

The stalker had made sure that Richard Baker was
sequestered safely in his apartment before leaving the apartment
building and moving on to other tasks in the cover of the night.
Things had escalated to a furious pace now, and he had two
stops to make. The challenge was getting to both of them
before the night was over. They were, after all, miles apart, and
the Robert Frost poem came to mind.

"Miles to go before I sleep."

A half block away he had parked his car with the fake paper
dealer plates taped in the window and the car insignias
removed. As if he needed these diversions. The streets of this
affluent suburb were empty at two in the morning, plus his
bosses grossly underestimated his intelligence and prowess. He
was, after all, the invisible man. And if anyone, by some absurd
chance, did see him, the policeman's uniform he wore would
certainly deflect suspicion.

He cut between two office buildings as silent as smoke.
Even the plastic tool kit he carried made not a single clink as he
slipped through a small opening in a hedge and gingerly took
the last few strides to the office building. He patted his coat
pocket to make sure that the envelope was there, knowing full

well that he never forgot anything, least of all the reason for being here, at a medical center in the darkest of nights, approaching a locked back door. His biggest hope was that the alarm system was one with which he was familiar, one he could easily circumvent. He was pleased to see that the back entrance was in a recessed alcove. Perfect, he thought: he could work beyond the purple hue of the dusk-to-dawn light. He entered the alcove and set down his tool kit. Opening it, he removed the light that was fastened to a Velcro band and quickly wrapped the band around his head, positioning the light in the center of his forehead. He flicked it on and a soft triangle of gold splashed onto the key lock next to the door.

Alleluia! It was a Titan system, probably a 1360, maybe 1380 if these docs had sprung for the upgrade. This would be a piece of cake. He figured he could be in, make the switch and be out in less than ten minutes.

Of course, then he had to make it all the way back to the south side of Chicago and slither his way into the evidence room at Area Two. Now that was a whole other kettle of fish.

As he worked, he recited the poem. "But I have promises to keep, and miles to go before I sleep, and miles to go before I sleep."

30

Tucker Hines lumbered, his feet slipping in the water on the pavement. His gait was clumsy, but rhythmic, step-drag-step-drag, pulling himself along like a wheel out of round. All because of the hump. The hump. The fucking hump. With him since day one. Still able to throw his equilibrium into a tizzy, especially when the footing wasn't so good, and tonight it wasn't, not at all. The rain had come from the dead sky, and it landed on the concrete and was now freezing there. He could feel it coming through the hole in his shoe. Worse, it was impossible to judge the slippery spots, the way the neon lights splashed across the dark pavement. Every little puddle skewed his feet akimbo, and the hump, with its extra weight, always wanted to go the way the feet did. So, every now and again, Tucker Hines would have to hold out his arm and steady himself against a building or streetlight or mailbox. He did it without thinking. It was the way it was, and that was all.

Now, all he wanted was to get out of the damn rain and into the warm and aromatic environment of the pub where he could get a hot supper and perhaps wait out the rain.

Ordinarily, he wouldn't have heard, wouldn't have paid attention to, footsteps behind him. But this time he did.

Noticed them, splash-splash-splash, staccato-like getting more frantic, closer to him. He picked up his own pace. Probably some punks, he thought. He would have turned to look, but that, of course, was impossible with the hump, impossible unless he stopped and turned the whole body, and his instincts said keep walking.

But he couldn't do it fast enough, couldn't get all the pieces and parts moving in the right direction at the right speed, not on this slippery terrain, and the steps were inches behind him now. His legs tried desperately to run, but the effort only threw him further off balance. His right foot hit a patch of ice and then the whole world went into a tailspin. Gravity grabbed him from the neck and feet and stretched him horizontal, throwing him onto the pavement. It was as though a spike had been driven into his back. He expunged all the air in his body and then rolled into the fetal position.

"Humpty Dumpty sat on a wall. Humpty Dumpty had a great fall," a voice intoned. Shadows came into Tucker's view. They pushed the milky white sky into the background. A face, a head, was now inches from his. Tucker tried to sweep himself back together, catch his breath, stop the pain. Suddenly, he recognized the voice and the triangular shape of the head, if not the shadow of a face.

Emo Nay.

"All the king's horses..."

Emo Nay was a massive stack of protoplasm with an unconnected brain stem.

"... and all the king's men..."

Not good.

"Couldn't put Humpty together again."

Emo Nay was a killer. What did he want?

"That you, Emo?" Tucker wheezed.

"No one less. And looks who's with me. My good pal Moxie Swain. You know Moxie, don't you?" Another shadow moved into the picture. Two heads now, both ugly as shit. Oh yeah, he knew Swain. Built like a pit bull, short, blocky, with drooping jowls and a vacant look in his eyes. Tuck had dealt with him more than ten years ago on a numbers fix. He hated the sonofabitch.

"You bastards help me up, please?" Tuck said, rising on one elbow.

Emo Nay put out his hand like a stop sign. "In a minute, Humpty Dumpty. In a minute. I want you to give me your undivided attention."

Christ, Tuck thought, what a moron.

Emo continued. "The story is you've been snooping around, asking a whole bunch of really dangerous questions. This true?"

"I don't know what you're talking about."

Emo pushed Tuck on the shoulder and the hunchback fell backwards. "You've been nosing around asking about your pal Poteet and Benny the Razor and that broad Maura Baker and her dick Aaron Clayton. Now what's the reason for that?"

"The reason is, it's none of your fucking business, that's what."

This time Emo stood up and pushed the heel of his foot onto Tucker's chest. "Make it my business," he said, jamming Tuck into the pavement.

The air was being systematically squeezed out of Tucker's lungs. What to say? He needed a story, and fast. He had one, but it was risky. At the same time, he was about to suffocate. Instinctively, he gasped, "Her husband..." Emo let up on the

290

pressure. Tuck continued, "... her husband hired me to, to find her." Fast thinking. *But where does he go from here?*

"Her husband?"

"Let me up, man. Get me up."

Emo Nay took Tuck's hand in his huge mitt and pulled the hunchback to his feet as effortlessly as picking up a rag doll. Tucker reached for a nearby newspaper box, steadying himself. He sucked in air rapidly. Then he began to brush the wet dirt off his clothes. "For chrissakes, I'm just trying to make a living here," he said.

Emo Nay grabbed Tuck's coat at the shoulders and adjusted it over his hump so that it hung more naturally. "There. There. Now you look almost human.

"Yeah, right," Hines growled. "Thanks a lot."

"So, you're working for the husband?"

"Yeah. Says he don't know what happened. Wants me to try to find his wife."

Emo looked at him for several seconds, pondering the explanation. Finally, he spoke. "Okay, that makes sense, but listen to me. Change of plans. You find anything out about this broad, alive or dead, you find any part of her, head, legs, little titties, in a garbage disposal, a sandwich, I don't care, you tell me. You tell me that minute. You don't call nobody until you tell me. You don't call the fucking husband, nobody except me. That clear, Humpty Dumpty?" He finished straightening the coat, then slapped Tuck's cheek gently.

"What's it to you, man?"

"It's everything to me, Humpty. So, don't fuck with me. I think you know me well enough to know when I'm serious. Don't fuck with me. See?"

"I won't fuck with you, Emo," Tuck said.

"And by the way, your pal Paco Rojas?" he made a twisting motion with his hand. "He's got a hole in him that even Jesus can't fix."

31

One of a hundred. Just one. The fifty-gallon oil drums were stacked helter-skelter in the storage yard, but one, this one, of all the others, was now lying on its side. It appeared as though it had fallen from an apparently precarious position on the stack. On impact, its lid had been sprung loose and spit across the still-frozen ground where it rolled on its edge for fifteen feet before spinning to a stop. Thus, the contents of the barrel were partially disgorged, and this was what occupied detectives Glory Kane and Jake McKay.

The area had been cordoned off with yellow tape. The patrol cars were parked and still barking several hundred feet away. The EMT vehicles sat further back, lights pulsing rhythmically but silently against the azure sky. The technicians leaned against the fenders and chatted. Their time had not yet come.

Dr. Henry "Bones" Jones knelt on the ground, gently probing with his gloved fingers. Before him, folded like some macabre Picasso sculpture were the remains of a woman, bones mostly, shreds of clothes. One arm, burned brown, stripped of flesh, laid outside the rim of the oil drum as casually as if she had been leaning on a table in conversation. The skull, a worn tapestry of exposed bone, skin and singed red hair, was tucked into the left shoulder blade. Her lower jaw hung loose, ransacked of the musculature required to hold it in place. The remnants of a violet satin blouse hung from the remains with no rhyme nor reason. First look, she had been doused with gasoline right there in the can and burned. Glory hoped that she was dead when it happened. Glory came closer, and knelt, looking into what remained of a face. Behind her, the flash from a photographer's camera lit up the corpse in a brief blue halo, revealing a hideous smile-like expression on the dead woman's face. But it was the stripping of flesh that bared the teeth, not a smile at all.

"Oh, my," Bones Jones sighed, gently tracing around the outline of the corpse with his index finger, glancing at the dirt accumulated there, then flicking it off.

"What?" Glory said.

"Oh, nothing, detective," Jones replied in almost a whisper. "I'm just making noises as I work." He stood up, turned away from the body, and clapped his hands, sending fragments of dirt spraying. Then he turned to the forensic team. "It's all yours, fellas. Take your time."

Glory nudged closer yet to the body, putting her own head nearly into contact with the skull as she glanced inside the drum. All the while she kept her hands behind her back, carefully touching nothing. Inside was as yet a bit too dark to reveal much, only a tangle of bones and clothes. There was a gold bracelet on one wrist, Glory noticed. No rings. She reached into her purse and withdrew a small note pad and wrote the words "gold bracelet, right arm."

Two members of the forensic team were measuring distances from various points on the oil drum to the remainder of the stack. "Looks like somebody threw it off," one of them said. "Unless it rolled." Glory glanced up at the men as she heard the words. They were right. Too far from the stack to have simply fallen. Then again, the ground was just now starting to thaw a bit. Maybe the container had rolled.

"I don't like it," Glory said, standing up and wiping invisible stuff from her hands even though she had touched nothing.

"Not a pretty sight," Jake McKay said. "But at least it, she, doesn't smell. If this was the middle of summer you'd be hard pressed to get that close."

"That's not what I mean," Glory said. She began to walk away from the corpse. McKay jogged two quick steps to come astride.

He said, "Oh, what now?" His voice did not disguise his exasperation.

"Look around, what do you see?"

"I see a dead body, burned beyond recognition in an oil drum, coincidentally similar to the former wife of a guy we found covered in blood whose wife, a redhead I might add," he jerked a thumb over his shoulder at the corpse, "is missing and ain't been found yet. Well, maybe not."

"No, stop," Glory said, taking his arm and turning him around. "Look at the whole scene. A storage yard full of oil drums. How many? A hundred? More or less. And one, one of all of them, one lying open with a corpse hanging out."

Jake put up both hands. "Yeah, yeah, yeah, I know, and we're here because of an anonymous phone call from a phone booth a mile or so from here."

"Nothing strange, nothing odd about that to you?"

"You look at the whole scene. Here, turn this way," McKay said motioning toward a blotchy field that adjoined the storage yard. Glory looked in that direction. He pointed. "Look across over there. Just on the other side of that clump of brown grass and cat tails, before you get to the lake. What is it? Quarter mile? That's where we found Rich Baker in his wife's car." He turned back to the corpse and made a motion with his hands. "You got here, you got there," he motioned back to the distant point. "And you can't make that simple connection?"

"Something isn't right."

"God help me," he cried.

"I'm not saying this isn't compelling…"

"I hope not."

"All I'm saying is that it just doesn't feel the way it looks."

"Feel? This ain't about feelings, lady. This is about what we see."

"It doesn't feel right."

Just then another unmarked police car pulled off the road and passed through the gate. It came to a stop between two others, and the door opened and out stepped Frank Rodriguez. "What do we have here, folks?" he asked, coming toward Glory and Jake.

Jake spoke quickly, "Janitor in a drum, burned to a crisp. Woman. Red hair." He glanced sarcastically at Glory. "But probably just a coincidence, at least according to Detective Kane."

"Call came in to June at dispatch at about six this morning, Chief," Glory said. "She called me at home after sending a car out here. I called Jake and we got here at six forty-one."

"Who made the call?" Rodriguez asked. "We know?"

Glory shook her head. "Nope. Anonymous. Wouldn't you know it? June said it sounded like a kid, sounded like a scared kid."

"Probably some teenage jagbag out here with his girlfriend, parking and getting down to business," Jake interjected. "Maybe some punks out vandalizing. Whatever, they find this stuff and get scared. One of 'em has a pang of conscience and calls the cops. Not too hard to believe, none of it."

"I'm glad you're so happy with the way things are working out, Jake," Glory said tersely. "Everything neat and clean."

"What is, is."

Glory glared at him, her eyes wide. "Yeah, and I'll tell you what is: there's too damned much about this case that is being done with anonymous phone calls. We get one call telling us there's a car out here. Won't identify himself. We get another leading us to a dead body in an oil drum that seems to have been thrown off the stack. Again, no ID. Look at the facts, Jake."

"Good lord, look at the facts, will you?" he responded, his voice rising. "This alcoholic scumbucket shoots or stabs or whatever his own wife, for chrissakes, then jams her into an oil barrel, maybe not even dead yet, maybe conscious, God only knows, and sets her on freakin' fire. Can you imagine what it's like to face that? To know you're going to die, that you're being killed?"

"What if it's not him?"

"Not him? Look at all this! What? You afraid to fry a perp? Your womanly, motherly instincts looking at a murderer as some abused, misused, accused victim with a deep dark secret in the past—maybe a daddy not home, or one who wailed his ass every day, a camp counselor with a plaything in his pants—that somehow forgives him for killing now? Forget about it."

"All right, knock it off, Jake," Rodriguez interrupted. "Both of you, get in my car where we can talk about this without the whole department hearing about it."

They both walked to his car like two chastened children. Glory took the passenger side of the front seat, Jake fell into the back. Rodriguez was last in, slamming the door. He turned first to McKay, hooking an arm over the back of the car seat and leaning over. "What the hell is the matter with you two? Starting right now you'll knock off the side comments and remarks, and you'll perform your duties to the best of your ability and with the right attitude. We have enough problems without letting whole damn world know you two can't get your shit together. Got it?"

"Yeah, yeah."

"Good." Rodriguez said, pulling his arm off the back of the seat and turned more toward Glory. "Detective Kane. I must remind you. You are a cop. You gather evidence. You're not a judge. You're not a jury. You're a collector. That's it. Whether you're scraping a minuscule, microscopic fiber from between the treads in a sneaker or disarming an ax murderer in the act, you do it, get it and give it to the state so that they can prosecute. You follow all protocols and chains of evidence. You don't speculate. Your opinions don't and can't overwhelm the evidence you piece together. Okay?"

He was correct, of course, Glory thought. She knew what Rodriguez wanted. Knew what Jake McKay wanted. Hell, it was what she wanted: a conviction in this case. Difference was, she also wanted the truth, and her instincts screamed that something about the whole thing was awry. Perhaps it had been the conversation with Lisette Darby, Maura Baker's mother. "Hunt down your own lie," she had said. "Take what you believe and seek not to prove it true, but to disprove it." Maybe Glory had taken that advice too far, until now what she had believed to be a lie was becoming, in fact, the truth.

"Okay?" Rodriguez repeated.

"Uh, yes, you're right, Frank," Glory answered, snapping out of her reverie.

"Okay, now, let's look at what we have," Rodriguez continued. "We have a body. Jake, it's what you've been looking for."

"Amen," McKay answered.

"Glory, it should be enough to get an arrest warrant."

"You're probably right about that, Chief. Even though there is still not a single witness to link Rich Baker with Maura that night, assuming the body is hers."

"Oh, it's her," McKay interjected.

"Forensics will determine that soon enough," Rodriguez said.

"Red hair. Silk blouse. Gold jewelry." McKay continued.

Rodriguez continued. "Devalane should be happy to hear this. What I'll need is for us to go back to headquarters and pull together all the files, all the evidence, wrap it up nice and neat. He'll get a warrant. You guys can make the arrest."

"It'll take forensics a few days to get a match on the dental work," McKay said.

"That's fine. Gives us time to pull everything together."

"This will take off the pressure," McKay replied.

"You don't know how true that is, brother," Rodriguez said. "What all do we have?"

Glory looked through the steam streaked windshield. The crime scene team was removing the remains from the oil drum. As they emerged, the bones stayed frozen in place, like a mummy Glory had once seen in a museum, arms and legs folded like the corners of a napkin. The fire had done its primary damage at the top of the remains, much less as it traveled downward. In fact, the slacks she was wearing were virtually intact, merely streaked with damage here and there. A charred shoe dangled from one foot. The gold bracelet Glory had seen earlier now caught the rays of the sun and duplicated them in miniature. The words of Rodriguez and McKay droned like music in the background, and Glory no longer listened to the litany of clues. For what the two crime scene guys were gently sliding through the opening of an oil drum was a human being, and the thought of it, plus the words of her blusterous partner, caused an ache inside her that was ferocious in its intensity. She opened the door and excused herself, much to the surprise and dismay of the two men in the car. The guys had laid the body on the frozen ground and were photographing it again. One of them carefully removed the gold bracelet and was placing it inside a plastic bag when Glory approached.

"Let me see that for a second," she said.

"Sure." He handed it to her gently with his thumb and forefinger. It squeaked slightly as it rubbed against the rubber of his glove.

Glory turned it over in her hands. It wasn't damaged at all. Not burnt or melted. Not cheap, either. A tennis bracelet, a design of woven gold, Celtic, Glory thought, punctuated with diamond baguettes flanking single stones of at least a half-carat each. Seven big ones altogether. Then she saw an engraving on each side of the clasp. A florid "M" on one side, a matching "B" on the other. Maura Baker, she thought as she handed it back to the investigator and he placed it in its bag.

The EMT's had come to the body now with a black bag and unfurled it alongside the remains. As they lifted the body gently, Glory stepped closer. The leather shoe, hardly touched by flames, dropped off the foot as they lifted her. Glory picked up a stick, inserted in the shoe and examined the footwear for several seconds. Then she took it off the stick with two fingers and gently replaced it on the corpse's foot. She didn't know why, not really. Maybe it was just that Maura Baker wouldn't want to go away like this, with only one shoe.

Two days later Rich Baker had awakened and was slipping into the new day. He followed his usual routine. Up at six. Some sit ups. Dressed now in casual clothes, chinos and a pullover, he was walking to the bagel shop for breakfast. Spring had poured over the city like sweet syrup, stirring things up, chasing people out of their boxes. Everyone on the Chicago streets seemed invigorated by the whisper of a season change. Rich found himself almost pulled into the same mood. Indeed, he had hoped, for a second or so upon coming into the day, that the new season would, somehow, signal an end to his nightmare. The sky was electric with puffy clouds. The gray of the slumbering winter grass was yielding to bright green. Lake Michigan sat calmly, cobalt blue, gently licking the shore like a cat cleaning its paws. Rich wished to succumb to the seductive lure of the weather, to lose himself in it, to grab a mitt and his bike and his friends and go play baseball, like the days long ago when sunlight was endless, and joy was a fly ball meandering downward into your glove.

Long ago.

But he couldn't fall into it, this false sense of well being. He knew that his was still a world of great horror, despite its clever disguise, despite its singing birds and gentle breeze. The turmoil in his own soul belied the tranquility outside. No peace within, if only for a second.

Part of it, the discomfort of it all, was, of course, the pall of fear that hung over him, regardless of the weather. But a big part of it was also the sheer boredom of routine, mindless time-killing activities. Meaningless things: television, movies (alone), dinner, books. He had gone a few times, even, to the symphony, had roamed the halls of the Art Institute to view the Renoir exhibit. There was no longer the adrenaline rush of negotiating a deal. The exhilaration was gone of turning a first shovelful of dirt on a barren patch of ground, then seeing something, a building, erupt from the nothingness like a miracle. The bone aching exhaustion of flying for twelve hours to Japan for a single signature, then turning around and flying back, the sheer glory of that agony, was a feeling he knew he would no longer experience. Memories, all. Replaced by this, these steps to nowhere, every morning.

But worst of it all was the gaping silence in the hole Maura left behind. It started like a whisper, but day after day grew to roar. She was not here. Her voice existed only in his head. She was his lover and simultaneously his combatant. She was his rock from which he had slipped many times. She had been the music in his life. He missed the fire in her eyes. Her obstinacy. Her independence. Her touch. Her voice. Her laugh. He missed her more than he would have ever imagined; because even when they were at their worst against each other, it was still "each other" in a private world that no one else could enter. No matter how far apart they drifted, there always seemed a way to navigate back through the gulf, regardless of the waves. Until now.

How could he have killed her? The question shot through him like lightning.

He bought his bagel from the woman who didn't know him, yet knew him from his almost daily visit. Blueberry. Toasted. And a cup of black coffee. This day, for some inexplicable reason, he folded a five dollar bill and set it in the tip jar on her counter, wedged it between the quarters and pennies in there. As if he somehow, somewhere knew what awaited him outside the door, that this very well could be a last visit.

Three cars arrived simultaneously at the scene, one plain wrapper and two marked squads from the Chicago Police. Rich had come out of the shop and was walking back to his apartment. He saw them immediately. Two of the cars slowed as they pulled next to him. One screeched ahead of the others, angling in at the corner as if to cut him off. His first instincts were to flee, but he hesitated. The middle car, the one parallel to him, stopped and the driver door swung open. Detective Kane leapt out. On the other side, the big guy, Mac something, rose above the roof line.

"Mr. Baker, I'm Detective Kane. I have a warrant for your arrest, sir, for the murder of your wife, Maura Baker." She said.

Rich froze in his tracks. A bite of bagel lay in his mouth. The scene blurred. All he could see was the glint of gold making electric stars in the middle of the day. His eyes had done that thing again, focused downward onto the finest detail. It took him a second to realize what they were, these star bursts.

Badges, picking up reflections and spinning them back. Two Chicago cops in front of him, coming forward. Several uniformed police officers moved forward. He looked down and saw red dots on his chest. Lasers. Detective Kane, too, from the side, pointing at him. Rich raised his hands. They were shouting at him. He knew he heard, could understand, because he was kneeling down now, putting his hands, one with a bagel in it, atop his head.

The big man came and knocked the bagel out of his hand. He forced Rich's arms behind his back. The cuffs slammed into his wrists, grabbing them, yanking them together. They chewed into his skin.

The big guy tugged him upward with a pull on his elbow. Pain singed his arm sockets. He could hear what the Mac guy was saying. "Rich, I forgot to ask you. Anybody ever call you Dick?"

They marched him to the unmarked car and bent him to fit him into it. From the back seat Rich stared at the bagel lying on the street as his captors took him into his future.

Across the street, nearly a block away, the stalker had watched the entire scene. He chuckled to himself and pulled a cell phone from his pocket. Two beeps, speed dial. A voice on the other end answering on first ring. "They got him," the stalker said.

Moments later, Evie was outside, walking her little Pasqualé. And, again, the dog pursued its own agenda, its own bushes and odors and secret places. But, like always, he came back to her, this time carrying something in his mouth larger than his own head. "What's that? What you got, Pasqualé?" Evie said. "Oh, my goodness, look at that, a bagel, and it's still warm."

32

Now this he understood. Richard Baker, case number XZ16496B, watched the interplay between lawyers and clients in the crowded corridors of the courthouse. He heard them, instinctually gravitating toward the sound of their voices, not just their words, but the tone, timbre, rhythm. Jesus God. It was business. Negotiations. Give me this, I'll give you that. Replete with all the bump and bluster of any deal. Two men in lawyer suits stood in a corner near a bulletin collaged with "Drug Therapy for Addicts" and "Help for Unwed Mothers" posters and variegated scraps of paper and business cards with lawyer names and other such stuff. The two men were arguing, feinting, jabbing around a settlement of some sort. "You don't want to take this into court," one warned sternly. "No, you don't want to take it to court," the other admonished. Even the law was negotiable, imagine that.

Rich had spent the morning in a cell that consisted of four walls less than an outstretched arm apart, a toilet, sink and cot with a dirty mattress, no more than four inches thick, but beaten by age and bodies to a lumpy pulp through which the springs beneath it had no trouble penetrating. The concrete walls and floor discharged moisture that made the whole place cold to the bones, eating to the soul. Rich sat on the edge of the bunk and shivered, partially from the cold, but mostly from the anxiety that satiated him. Within an hour after his single phone call, Nathan Timmins swept in with the cavalry—three lawyers including an old man and two young kids, man and woman, there, Baker surmised by the load of books and files, as beasts of burden. Nate carried a neatly pressed suit, shirt, tie, shoes. While Rich changed, Timmins explained the process. Initial hearing in front of the judge. The charges, statute and rights would be read. A plea would be entered on Rich's behalf. The prosecutor would likely move to deny bond, normal in these circumstances. Timmins was ready to argue.

They stood in the tumult of the corridors for more than forty-five minutes. Rich was much more comfortable now, clean, pressed, relishing the rigid, hard starch of his cuffs and collar. All that were out of place were the handcuffs. He hid them with a coat. Two uniformed policemen flanked him, walking him everywhere.

A dark-haired young man and an attractive woman rounded a corner and came towards them. Timmins leaned to Rich and whispered, "That guy coming here, Harold Devalane. I don't know the woman. He's the prosecutor."

"Any good?" Rich whispered back.

"Plenty," came the reply.

Timmins broke from his proximity to Baker and moved toward Devalane. The two men shook hands and then Timmins shook the woman's hand, as well. Rich couldn't hear their words, but the abject conviviality of the meeting bothered him. Then he remembered. It's business.

Nate was back in a few minutes. "Hang with me by the doorway over there," he said to Rich, motioning with his head.

"We want the best seats." They sidled over toward the closed door, nudging in front of Devalane and his companion. In a few minutes an elderly woman opened the door and beckoned them in. The two cops led Rich by the arm through a door.

The room was smaller than Rich had anticipated, with a dark wooden desk in front of tall windows. Two chairs sat in front of the desk, burgundy leather. A couch was pushed against one wall. The other wall and the entire back of the room were consumed with bookcases. Case books, red leather bindings, expunging sticky notes, lined the shelves. Timmins pulled Rich to one of the chairs. He took the other. The three other defense lawyers moved and stood shoulder-to-shoulder in the back of the room, as did the cops. Devalane audibly smirked as he and his companion took seats on the couch.

"What is this room? It's not a courtroom," Rich whispered.

"Judge's chambers," Timmins answered, then shrugged.

A side door opened and a man Rich presumed to be the judge entered, followed by a court reporter. Rich had expected a man in a black flowing robe, like on television, regal, even. Instead, what he got was a portly, short man in a dark blue suit. His shirt was long since white, turned two clicks off the dial to a faded yellow. His head was nearly bald, except for the ring of silver around his ears. How old? Fifty to seventy. He walked with a slight limp. In his hand was a sheaf of papers. "Good morning, well, I guess it's afternoon now, ladies and gentlemen," he said, glancing at a watch. "I am Judge Herman Wagner." He sat down and spread the papers out before him. Pulling a pair of reading glasses from his inside pocket he looked at the paperwork. "I see we have here docket number XZ16496B, the state versus Richard Charles Baker, in which is laid out the charges of, uh, murder. Mr. Baker," he looked above his glasses at Rich, "that's you, yes?"

Rich nodded. "Yes, your honor."

"Mr. Baker, bear with me while we read this charge aloud to you. It is required by law." Judge Wagner recited the words on the pages in monotone, barely pausing to take a breath. When he was finished, he dropped the last page on the desk. "It is now appropriate for you to enter a plea to these charges."

"Your honor, my client pleads not guilty," Timmins said.

"Very well, so noted," the judge replied. "You have a right, Mr. Baker, to a speedy trial. This court will abide by the wishes of your attorney and the prosecutors to ensure that this is accomplished with all due haste." He slapped his hands on the table. "Now, is there any other business to come before this court?"

"Yes, there is, your honor," Timmins immediately said, standing up.

"I am not surprised," Judge Wagner replied bemusedly.

"Your honor, we petition the court that fair and reasonable bond be set for the defendant so that he might be able to continue to live his life within reasonable limits pending his trial and its outcome."

"Your honor, on behalf of the people, we object to this request," Devalane immediately interjected.

"So far it's going according to form," the judge said. "Yes, Mr. Devalane?"

"We would remind the court that this is a capital murder offense, that we have accumulated a preponderance of evidence that clearly and concisely points to this man, and that no extenuating nor extraordinary circumstances exist that would warrant such consideration, and, as is precedent in capital murder cases in the state of Illinois, bond be denied on these grounds."

Wagner turned to Timmins. The judge simply raised an eyebrow. As if on cue, the young female attorney moved from the back of the room and handed Timmins a sheet of paper. The attorney turned and took it and addressed the judge. "Your honor, we respectfully request that you consider bond due to the following facts. First of all, our client is no threat to leave. He has been conspicuously under suspicion for this situation for nearly two months now and never once has he ever demonstrated the desire to abdicate his responsibility to face these charges and prove them false. He has not been more than twenty miles away from this jurisdiction since the commencement of this case, and, as I say, his likelihood of fleeing now is nil."

Devalane stood now. "Your honor, I don't think that this is merely a matter of whether or not this man will disappear. This is a capital murder case and it is our responsibility to..."

"Your honor, I was not finished," Timmins cut him off.

"Mr. Devalane, please be seated and let Mr. Timmins state his case."

"Thank you, your honor. Secondly, I would like to remind the state and this court that my client has been convicted of no crime as of this date, and, in fact, as we shall prove, the case against him is circumstantial at best and devoid of any and all merit at worst. In fact, in our opinion, there has been no proof as of yet that a murder has even taken place."

"Your honor, we have positively matched dental records to the corpse of a woman found not four hundred yards from where..."

"Your honor, please!" Timmins cried.

Judge Wagner rubbed his eyes. "I can see that this is going to be a real humdinger." He pointed a finger at Devalane. "Please, Mr. Devalane for the last time, allow Mr. Timmins to finish. You will have your chance to voice your argument."

Timmins reached back and took several more sheets of paper from his assistant. "Your honor, please allow me to share these notes with you." He handed a sheet to the judge, who picked his glasses off the desk and mounted them as he perused the text. "My client is a highly respected businessman in Chicago, one with no history of criminal activity of any nature, even to the point of never having a speeding or parking ticket. As you can also see by this document, Mr. Baker has won several citations for community contributions and volunteer activity, including one from the Mayor of Chicago and the Archdiocese of Chicago, the McCormick Foundation, Tribune Charities—the list goes on and on."

"Yes, yes, I see, quite impressive."

Timmins moved forward with two other sheets. "I also have here a copy of Mr. Baker's honorable discharge from the United States Army and other evidence of his military record including rank and decorations. As you can see, your honor, my client is a veteran of the First Gulf War, where he was awarded a Southwest Asia Bronze Star for the Liberation of Kuwait."

Wagner's eyebrows jutted upward. "You say? Operation Desert Storm? What division, Mr. Baker?"

"Eighty-second Airborne Division, your honor."

"Eighty-first Airborne for me," the judge answered, "Vietnam."

Rich and the judge locked eyes for a second. No words were spoken. None needed to be.

"Yes, sir, your honor," Timmins continued, his voice rising, taking on a new enthusiasm. "As you can see, Mr. Baker won several other commendations. Once was a time when these accomplishments would have generally been frowned upon by our society, as you well know, your honor."

"I remember it very well, son. Kids our own age, spitting at us." Judge Wagner said. "Not an easy time at all."

"We were just doing our jobs, sir, as were you. It's a shame some people did not recognize that," Rich inserted.

"Amen," the judge replied. "So, Mr. Baker, is it safe to say that you're not a runner?"

"A runner?"

"Someone who would run away from his responsibilities. Your record seems to indicate that you are, indeed, a man who faces his situations regardless of the consequences."

"Your honor!" Devalane jumped up and shouted. "Your simpatico with this defendant is hardly reason..."

"Sir, how old are you?" Wagner interrupted.

"Uh, thirty-eight, your honor."

"Do you remember the First Gulf War?"

"Of course, your honor. We studied it in grade school and high..."

"Mr. Devalane, I daresay that Mr. Baker and I are traversing an historical topography for which you possess not a scintilla of perspective, with all due respect to your schooling and, I'm sure, the fine teachers who instructed you there. So, perhaps these are the desultory ruminations of a man whose very brain was scrambled in the conflicts of which we speak; perhaps I am merely entertaining myself with the shared experiences of Mr. Baker and myself. So, please, indulge me in my frivolous side trip, for the sake of an old man."

311

"Your honor, I'm sure your record deserves much admiration. I just don't want you to rule based on..."

"Mr. Devalane," Wagner interrupted, "have I ruled on this request yet? No? Then I suggest you let me tend to the business at hand." He turned back to Timmins. "Anything else, Mr. Timmins?"

"In short, your honor, we believe that our client's many civic and charitable contributions, his conduct in this case thus far, plus his exemplary war record should be considered in your decision to grant us bond so that Mr. Baker can continue to live a relatively normal life until he is fully and completely exonerated of these charges."

"Or not? Yes?" Judge Wagner pursed his lips and turned to the prosecutor. "Mr. Devalane, the floor is yours."

Devalane looked defeated. Rich could see it in his eyes. There was a feeling in the room. "Your honor, with all due respect to Mr. Baker's war record, I must remind the bench that this is a capital offense for which only extenuating or extraordinary circumstances should be considered. Mr. Baker has no family to support. He currently is without a job due to this, ah, situation and, at the risk of trying the case here and now, his behavior has been somewhat less than exemplary in recent weeks."

"Explain, please," Wagner said.

"I have here a deposition from his business partner, well, ex-partner that is, where Mr. Miles Lundeen testifies that he was threatened by Mr. Baker on, let's see here..."

"Your honor! The defense has seen no such deposition, no record has been made of it, and we strenuously object to its introduction at this time," Timmins cried.

"Okay, okay, okay," Wagner said waving both sides to silence. He turned to Rich. "Sir, did you threaten your business partner?"

"I did not." *That sonofabitch!*

"Have you had any conversations with him recently?"

"Yes, sir. We had a disagreement on how my severance package should be structured, but it was hardly out of the realm of other discussions we have had in the past. At no time did I touch him or threaten him in any way."

"Judge Wagner!" Devalane interrupted.

"Please, sir. Mr. Baker, is it true you have no dependents, no children to support?"

"Your honor, if I may," Timmins interjected. "Mr. and Mrs. Baker had a son who was an innocent bystander tragically killed in a robbery of a convenience store."

The judge exhaled and slumped in his chair. He pondered for no more than five seconds. "Bond is hereby set at one million dollars. I trust you know how to handle the mechanics, Mr. Timmins?"

"Indeed I do, your honor. Indeed I do."

Outside now, Baker turned to Timmins as they walked to the attorney's car. "That thing about my war record, bringing it up. Did you know that the judge...?"

Timmins chuckled. "You're paying me six hundred and fifty dollars an hour. Now you know why."

33

Lisette Darby, Maura's mother, dressed in spring rose, not black, sat in the front pew of the church. She was positively translucent in the tender flicker of the candles. She glowed, angelically, stoic as she listened to the words of the priest with what appeared to be a bemused countenance. Glory had watched her and the ceremony from the rear of the church, a bit overwhelmed by the silent majesty of the old cathedral. How tiny she felt beneath the soaring arched ceiling. How many prayers still clung to the vaulted transoms? As the daughter of a Baptist preacher, Glory was not used to the mysterious, dark, reverent confluence of candles and statues and distant choirs, such sharp contrasts to the bright, electric, hand-clapping ministrations of her youth. But there was something comforting here, as well as a truth as pure and true as that found in her Daddy's church. A basic goodness. Yes, a goodness.

The coffin bearing the remains of Maura Darby Baker stood at the foot of the altar, draped in a white cloth. The beautiful harmonies of the choir wafted over the scene, belying the hideous twisted debris that occupied the casket, a sight Glory could not get out of her mind.

Lisette approached her after the mass. "Detective Kane, how nice of you to come," she said, extending a steady hand and shaking Glory's firmly. "I didn't think detectives did things like this."

"Mrs. Darby, you have my deepest sympathy," Glory replied, holding the woman's hand tenderly. "I'm very, very sorry things had to end like this."

Lisette's eyes widened and she smiled. "End? Well, now, that remains to be seen, doesn't it?"

"I don't understand," Glory said.

Lisette smiled again. "Whatsoever thou takest in hand, remember the end, and thou shalt never do amiss." And with those words, she turned to embrace another mourner, walking away.

34

Glory Kane sipped from a glass of ice water, spitting a cube back into the crystal clear liquid. She was in the tiny diner, waiting for Tucker Hines, and Tucker Hines wasn't showing. She glanced at her watch. Fifteen minutes late. Ordinarily, the hunchback would have been here for an hour, would have already eaten. Hell, maybe he lived here. Whatever, she didn't have time for this, the way the case was breaking. She leaned her temple against the rain-streaked window and angled a look down the street. People, plenty, but no sliding, lumbering hunchback.

The waitress came, bouncing on her hip, chewing gum. "You want something now, already or what?"

"No," Glory answered tersely.

"Whatever. But this ain't a bus stop, lady. Buy something or skeedaddle."

Glory reached into her pocket and pulled out her wallet, flipped it open to show her badge. "How much does another half hour cost? I'll pay with this."

"Whatever," the waitress said, turning on her heel and walking away, her ass bouncing from side to side.

316

Sleet ran down the windows like snakes. Would the weather ever change? Since that morning, that morning in the Mercedes, a pall had settled over Chicago. Glory wondered if Baker had caused it, he and his actions. Had he opened some forbidden box and unleashed the dismal, sunless sky on the world? Oh, Lord, what had he done?

Against the glass again now, cold seeping into her cheek, she saw the recognizable form, coming toward the bar, slower than usual. As Tucker passed, he looked into the window and, seeing Glory, beckoned her outside. Strange, she thought, standing up. The waitress quickly came over. "What? Now you're leaving? Without nothing?" she snapped.

Glory took a buck out of her pocket and dropped it on the table. "Live large," she said.

When she got outside, Tucker was already a hundred feet down the street, and she had to jog to catch up. She then noticed Tuck's head turning from side to side, as he wobbled from one side of the sidewalk to the other. His coat was flapping behind him and she saw that it was caked in mud. Something had happened, it was obvious. Tuck turned and disappeared. This time into a bar.

Darkness engulfed Glory immediately as she entered. Bar darkness. A black world with white windows and neon signs. It took a few seconds for her vision to adjust, and by then the hunchback was seated at the bar, ordering a shot of Jack Daniels. "And this lady is going to pay for it," he growled, thumbing at the detective.

"For you?" the bartender said to her.

"Uh, Diet Coke, Pepsi, whatever."

317

Glory sidled up to the bar and slid onto a stool. "So, what's this all about? Why are we here instead of at the usual place? What's wrong?" she said.

Tucker Hines lit a cigarette that throbbed between his lips. He exhaled in a cough of blue. "I'm done. I quit."

"What's that mean? You quit?"

"Quit. Finito. Done. Gone."

Glory swiveled to face the hunchback directly. "What's going on? Give me the story."

Hines exhaled again and shook his head. "You see this coat?" He held up the muddy stretch of cloth. Cinders were imbedded in the fabric. A slash, razor thin, ran from beneath the armpit. "Good coat. Nice coat. Ruined. It got ruined three days ago by a motherfucking assassin named Emo Nay. You ever hear of him?"

"No."

"Well, remember that name, 'cause if anything happens to me, he's the guy to look into. He's bad news. Bad fucking news. The guy is a paid killer. Give him money, kapowie, someone goes down. Well, he's the sonofabitch that ruined my coat. Knocked me on my ass and held me there and told me to get out. Then like a cherry on the ice cream, lets me know that my pal Paco Rojas took a shiv in jail, and that's what's waiting for me."

"My God," Glory whispered.

"And it's all 'cause I went in and saw Rojas in jail."

"What's Rojas got to do with our case?"

"You ever hear of a guy named Nicholai Bedrosian?"

Glory paused. "I don't think so. Why?"

"He's the guy behind the curtain. A real piece of work, that one."

"What's he got to do with Rojas?" Glory asked.

Tucker lit another cigarette off the end of the one he was smoking and then spit as he inhaled. "Well, Rojas was with our friend Maura Baker the night of the party. And that ain't all." With those words, Tucker Hines laid out the entire story for Glory Kane, and every word made her heart beat faster. When he was done, he stubbed out his cigarette and waved at the bartender for another drink.

Glory took a deep breath and collected herself. Aaron Clayton a money launderer for an Armenian syndicate! He certainly had the opportunities, the connections and the skills. It changed the entire complexion of the case, but instead of clarifying it, this news just made the whole thing more confusing. She leaned to Tuck and patted him on the arm. She understood his need to extricate himself from the case, and she certainly didn't want to see another death as a result of this mystery. "Tuck, you did good. I appreciate your help," she said.

"Yeah, well, thanks. But now it's time to reconcile our account, so to speak. Gimme that little notebook of yours and a pen."

Glory handed the items to him. He began writing on the open page. Then he handed it back to her. "That's where you can find me. I'll be hiding there. Now that the broad has been found and buried, I don't know if Emo Nay is going to back off or not, but I ain't taking any chances. You paid me a partial, now I want the rest and my passport, and I got to have it quick because if I don't, it might could be..." he made a slashing motion across his throat. "... and that's on your conscience."

"Give me a couple of days," Glory replied, not knowing if she could pull it off that fast. "Lay low. You want us to find you a safe place to stay?"

"Naw, I'll keep my head down and my eyes open. Just fast it up for me, please." Then he stubbed out his cigarette, threw down the last swallow of whiskey, put another cigarette in his mouth and proffered his hand to her. "It's been interesting doing business with you."

As he walked away, Glory looked at the information Hines had written in her notebook. The handwriting on it was perfect—almost calligraphic, as if it had been written by a monk.

35

The faces had begun to run together, the voices, the words pureed into a slurry of gibberish. The notes on her pad dribbled off the edges in virtually illegible squiggles, like blue worms escaping a box. Glory Kane had been consumed by the case. She could feel that it had eaten away her soul like some kind of psychic cancer, leaving her numb, disconnected, devoid of feelings one way or the other. She was still perplexed by the inconsistencies in Rich Baker's case, and she was—what, fearful? No, maybe apprehensive was a better word—that the prosecution would not prevail. Not with high paid criminal lawyers like Nate Timmins and his minions. So, she tried to develop a contingency plan—call it a trump card that she could pull out at the last minute. After all, it would do her career good to get a conviction, too.

The body in the trunk of the BMW had been positively identified as Aaron Clayton, to no one's surprise. Perhaps she could pull Baker into that scenario. So, she tried in her mind to pull together a strain of logic to connect his death to Richard Baker. Jealous rage? Perhaps. After all, the two deaths were likely only days apart at the most, judging by circumstances and forensics. But the MO on the two was completely different, and the pattern of activity was as frantically desultory as the runnings of a church mouse. So disjointed and confusing, in fact, that the prosecution had decided not to introduce Clayton's death into the Baker case at all. But maybe that was not the best approach.

She was sitting in Harold Devalane's office, a modest, governmental-official cube surrounded by smoked glass, but she was miles and miles away in her thoughts.

Devalane was sitting at his desk, feet up, breaking open pistachios and flipping them into his mouth. Frank Rodriguez and Jake McKay were there, as well, seated next to Glory on mismatched chairs.

"So, just thought I'd bring you up to speed on the state's case and congratulate you for your fine work," Devalane said. "The trial will begin sometime within the next six months."

"How long you think it's gonna take? Ain't gonna be one of these twelve-part television mini-series or nothing, is it?" Jake McKay asked.

Devalane caught a pistachio on his tongue and crunched it. "Oh, no way. It's really pretty simple. The vehicle, and the suspect, yielded a veritable cornucopia of evidence, blood, as you know, tons of blood. Hair, threads of clothing, fingerprints, candy wrappers. We've got Baker in the bedroom and the car. We've got a body, thank God, found nearby where Baker stopped the car. We have a DNA match to the blood in both places, and the hair matches, too. Should only take us two days or so to present our case, but we'll probably draw it out a bit longer than that, for dramatic effect. Couple of days, maybe a week, for the defense and—badda-bing—Rich Baker is in pajamas and heading to an eight by eight for the rest of his life."

Frank Rodriguez beamed and rubbed his hands together. "Well, sir, we appreciate your compliments and thank you for keeping us up to speed."

Glory conspicuously cleared her throat. "I don't think he's guilty," she said, somewhat quietly.

Devalane stopped, a pistachio deftly held between his thumb and forefinger. "You what?"

"I think you need to check some other angles before starting this trial, and, most importantly, I don't think Baker has any more to do with this murder than with the assassination of Lincoln," Glory said emphatically.

Jake McKay burst out of his chair like the Space Shuttle launching. "What the...! Don't listen to this person sitting right here!" he bellowed, pointing down at Glory.

Devalane took his feet off his desk, leaned forward and looked her in the eye. "I know you took this case very personally and worked very, very hard on it, and the state appreciates your commitment and dedication. But at this stage of the situation, it's our turn. We know what we're doing."

"But we don't know the whole story," she replied.

"Glory, we talked about this," Rodriguez cautioned.

"I know, Chief, but I have to say what I have to say, to go on record with my perceptions of the case. Tucker Hines..."

"A piece of shit washout who didn't give us dick," McKay interrupted.

"The guy with the..." Rodriguez bent over, raised one of his shoulders and motioned over it with his other hand, "...you know, the...hump."

"Yes," Glory continued, "he was getting close to learning what happened at the party at The Pachyderm that night. Talked to an eyewitness name of Paco Rojas..."

323

"He's a punk, Glory, we had him in a dozen times," Rodriguez interjected.

"...who took a shiv while standing in the grub line, but not before giving us some real interesting stuff." Glory went on to provide the details.

When she was finished, the room was silent for a few seconds. "His story don't mean shit, Kane," McKay argued. "Like Devalane says here, we got blood and guts all over Baker, and we can put him in her house that night. We're done here, let's go home."

"What about the truth?" Glory asked. "Does the truth matter?"

Jake lurched forward again. "No, no, it doesn't matter. How many scum bags are walking the streets, that you know and I know are guilty as hell, but they got off because the law let them off?"

Devalane waved his hands. "Let's not get into that right now, folks. The philosophy of law isn't the topic at hand." He turned to Glory. "I think Detective Kane, due to her diligence on this case, deserves a response to her concerns." He cleared his throat and took a sip of water. "I hear what you're saying, Glory, and I know that there are a lot of very odd coincidences at play here. But here's my problem with your premise. The death of Maura Baker is entirely outside the MO of all the other murders you mentioned. Clayton and these other guys, they went down in the dark, were dumped with nothing left showing. Hanging Maura Baker out for all the world to see, well, it just doesn't fit. It's a piece from a different puzzle. Yeah, maybe she saw something that night, maybe she was on Bedrosian's list. But from what we've been able to put together, her ex saved Bedrosian's assassins some bullets."

324

Glory shook her head and started to speak, but knew that the argument was over.

Devalane relaxed again in his chair and wiped the salt off one hand with the other. "Detective Kane, your concerns are duly noted and I appreciate your perspective, but we are going to try this case with what we have and pray that your good work, up to this time, pays off in a conviction that would make us all very, very happy." He clapped his hands together and stood up. "Gentlemen, and lady, wish us luck in court."

Jake McKay rode in the back seat as Rodriguez drove them back to headquarters. His mind also raced through the disjointed and disconcerting facts about this case, but he had done his job, hadn't he? He had helped bring this Baker guy in. That's what he's paid to do, after all. He's not the judge, not the jury. If the case crumbles now, it isn't his fault, is it?

If the case crumbles now. A jolt of paranoia tingled through his veins momentarily. If anyone else finds out what he already knew, the case wouldn't just crumble, it would explode.

36

Tucker Hines stood at the window smoking. The street below was nearly devoid of traffic, and a boiling, seductive fog ambled the avenues in a milky froth just three or four feet off the ground, giving the night an eerie, surreal attitude. He imagined a similar silent turmoil in his own lungs; the smoke from the sizzling crack percolating there, making him as serene and untouchable as the night. The illuminated sign that hung just below his apartment window crackled and hummed with frantic electricity that continually attempted to light the gas tube sections of the "c" in "currency" and the "ex" in "exchange." The noise only added to the rhythm of the night. Tucker was used to it. It had been that way for three years. It buzzed him to sleep that first night, and every night thereafter.

Now the fog of the night and the fog that was descending upon his mind were stoking his euphoria. To a man born twisted and slow, there were few moments of absolute perfection, and way too few to ever balance the relentless, perpetual agony of living as a freak; from the cradle where he still could conjure visions of his mother weeping; to the school kids who spat at him and chased him to the farthest corner of the playground; to the class of retards they finally sent him to, where spastics drooled and mongoloids shit their pants; to the whores who refused his perfectly good money because they couldn't, just couldn't, do it with him at any price. But if they just could see him now, even if he was in a sleeveless undershirt that revealed the apex of his hump peak in craggy flesh through the back straps. If they could feel the power he held in his hands. He squeezed his fist and held it up to the window. The feeble gasps of the currency exchange light streaked his bones and veins in blue, like ice. He took another long, hot pull on the dovetail end of the joint in his hand and let the smoke settle in his lungs. Sweet.

Even to someone as wretched as he, came occasional moments as sweet as chocolate, and he gobbled them down. This was one. This was his chance to get out of the sewer once and for all. All he had to do was lay low for another day or two when Glory Kane, a nice enough broad and not a bad cop at all, would get him his passport, and he would be on a plane and gone from this godforsaken place forever.

Tucker Hines went to his closet, moved back the coats and clothes, slid some boxes aside and carefully pried the baseboard off the back wall while peeling back the carpet. Slowly, carefully he removed the satchel. He unzipped it and saw the faces of his friends smiling at him. Dead presidents. Framed in green. Money. Neatly stacked in bundles, some thin and comprised of hundreds, some thick, mostly twenties and fifties. Fifteen thousand dollars, put to rest here instead of into a nicer home or better clothes. He ran his fingers through it. Five more would make it just over twenty grand. A magic number he'd been working on for seven years. It would take him, once and for all, out of this place.

He rummaged through the cash to reach the bottom of the bag. From there he removed the travel brochure. Australia. Sprawling, empty, open. He would buy a farm there for next to nothing. Live as far from here and these people as he could get. Alone, where no one would bother him, where only he would know about the wretched body he carried. A place to live out his life in solitude. And now it was within reach. All he had to do was get the passport and the rest of his cash from Kane and move, move, move on.

But that was for tomorrow. Tonight was for enjoyment, that's what it was for. So, he smiled as he replaced the cache and re-hid the satchel. Tonight was a night not to pummel the brain, but to seduce it with smoke, with ecstasy, with the wondrous sea of foam rolling below, with the humming of the sign. He turned the sound into a song, and began to dance as he improvised lyrics. "All around the fucking world, folks are dancing to a brand new beat. 'Cause summer's here and the time is right for dancing in the fuckin' streets. They're dancing in Chicago, oh yeah, down in New fucking Orleans," he sang as the electric sign hummed. He twirled around his living room, stepping on the plates and wrappers strewn on the floor and mashing half-eaten pizza between his toes. He stumbled like a running back into the mottled gray couch with stuffing splotches that dotted it like cauliflower. He knocked over a plastic plant he'd stolen from a restaurant dumpster. "All we need is music, sweet music, there'll be music everywhere."

He fell into the television and it teetered precariously on its pedestal. He snatched it as it swayed downward. Jay Leno on the screen didn't even flinch as the box turned parallel to the floor, and this made Tuck laugh all the more. Nothing could dim his euphoric dementia, and he tumbled over the back of his couch, landing in a clump on a pile of greasy pillows. Leno droned on in the background. The sign hummed. A horn honked somewhere far away. Darkness clogged his consciousness, and all was still.

He bolted upright. He saw the room first, realized he'd been sleeping, didn't know for how long. The television was cooking white snow. The noise came again, an insistent thumping on his door. He was standing. He didn't remember standing. His legs just decided to do it and did it, propelled him erect like some immutable force of nature. Thump, thump, thump came the door. Who the fuck is it? He wondered. The landlord? "Who the fuck is it?" he shouted.

A muffled voice. "Open the fucking door and hurry up." The voice was familiar.

Tuck fumbled with the deadbolt and turned the doorknob. The door imploded upon him as four men rushed in. One grabbed a fistful of Tuck's undershirt and virtually strangled him with it as he shoved him to the couch. "What's this all about?" Tuck said incredulously. He looked up. Emo Nay. The man mountain was carrying a canvas gym bag, black, its sides a mass of hard, heavy angles. One of the guys closed the door and stood in front of it.

The other three men moved like choreographed dancers through the apartment. He recognized one other of them. Moxie Swain. He remembered the sonofabitch from the confrontation on the street.

Swain acted as if he'd never laid eyes on Tucker as he moved directly to the window and pulled down the shade, then stood there with his arms folded. Another man, taller, with yellow-green skin like olive oil, began groping and poking and tossing

329

the desultory debris of the apartment. The third man positioned himself in front of Tuck and lit a cigarette. He was average in every way. Maybe five ten. With thin greasy hair through which his scalp grinned mockingly. He took a short puff and then removed it from his mouth. He squatted down, sitting on the coffee table next to the couch and offered the smoke to the hunchback. Tuck took it and immediately placed it in his mouth, trying to suck some equilibrium through the filter.

Olive Oil was in the kitchen. A crash and shatter of dishes made Tuck jump. Greasy moved in front of Tuck, smiled and lit an ultra thin cigar. "So, you're the famous hunchback I heard so much about?"

Tuck just eyed him warily. "Who's this asswipe?" he said, turning to Emo Nay.

"Better cooperate with him," Nay replied, his triangular head turning red.

The man looked into Tuck's eyes with a cold, sinister glare. "Name is Peter Bedrosian. You know me?"

"No."

"Brother is Nicky Bedrosian? You know him, yeah?"

Tuck had already made the connection, but he wasn't going to say shit. "Don't know him, neither."

Bedrosian continued, "Been sticking your hump into places you got no business sticking it," he said, taking a long, angular finger and poking it into Tuck's collar bone hard enough to drive him backwards into the couch. "What do you know?"

Olive Oil moved like a cat out of the kitchen and disappeared into Tucker's bedroom. A soft amber light came on, throwing itself against the hallway wall. Tuck could see the shadows of furious activity fluttering within the frame of the light. Swain walked over and slapped him, a fiery jolt that ripped his bobbing head back into the line of vision. "I asked you a fuckin' question, Quasimodo," Bedrosian said. The hunchback lurched forward to defend himself, but thought better of it and sagged back into the couch.

"I said, humpback, what do you know?" Bedrosian repeated.

Tucker Hines took a drag on his cigarette. He held it deftly between his thumb and forefinger and calculated quickly. If he could plunge it into Bedrosian's eye, then drive Moxie Swain through the fucking glass—but there were still two more. He looked up at his tormentor. "Know about what?"

Swain, saying nothing, struck like lightning again. A flash erupted in Tucker's cheek and his head vibrated on his neck. Bedrosian spoke softly, "You know, I hate dumb fuckers and I hate freaky fuckin' hunchback assholes, and if you don't start talking, hump boy, we're gonna tear you to fuckin' pieces."

Tucker shook the pain from his cheekbone. "Look, I don't want no fuckin' trouble. Just tell me what it is you wanna know."

Emo Nay circled around to the back of Tuck. Now they had him surrounded. "You lied to me for one thing, and that just ain't kosher in my world," Nay growled. "I saw you coming out of a bar and who the fuck comes out five minutes later but the woman cop who's been on the television about this situation. So, I may be an ignorant motherfucker Slav, but I can add up two and two, and that adds up to you dealing with the cops on this issue, and that is a definite no-no."

Oh, Jesus, Tuck said to himself.

"But I'm going to give you a chance to redeem yourself here. Just tell me everything you told the cops. That's all."

331

Tucker Hines didn't know what to do. Betraying the cops could blow everything. He just needed to hold these guys off, convince them that he couldn't add anything. "I don't know shit," Tuck replied. "Besides, the dead broad is in a box and the old man is going down for it. Who gives a shit?"

Wham, another bolt of electricity erupted in Tucker's head, this one knocking him sideways and launching his lit cigarette into the sky. Swain had literally left his feet to leverage the blow with all his weight, and now Bedrosian was standing over the suddenly supine hunchback screaming. "Don't you fuckin' talk to me like that, you freaking reptile. Who gives a shit? How about you? How about that, asshole?" Spit was flying from his mouth, dotting the throbbing face of Tucker Hines.

Fear and fury commingled in the hunchback's bowels. What the fuck do you want to know, he wanted to say, but the room was spinning wildly in his head. He felt himself falling away from the scene, felt himself scurrying for the safety of unconsciousness. Bedrosian's voice grew more wane, more distant, and only bits and pieces of his words came through intelligibly. He screamed names at him, asking him what he knew about these people. Tucker looked up and through Bedrosian. Moxie Swain had backed off now, standing at the window passively. Then he and the wall suddenly accelerated, as if being spun on a merry-go-round, and the room went dark.

Wet. Wet in his face. Wet slithering down his cheek like a cool snake. The room was still vibrating, and Tucker was coming back to it. He was back on the couch. He could feel the pillow under his head. He looked up into the stream of water cascading upon his face. Olive Oil was pouring it from a bowl. Tuck jerked away from the stream, and it stopped. He looked up. Bedrosian was once again sitting on the coffee table.

"Sorry about that, Tuck," Bedrosian said in a conciliatory tone, "I just, you know, lost it there for a second. It's been a long week. It's late. I'm tired. Getting a bit edgy." He leaned forward and proffered a plastic tumbler that smelled of whiskey. The hunchback took a sip and the booze shook him like hot oil. Bedrosian continued, "Sometimes Moxie over there don't even know his own strength." Swain glanced at the open palm of his hand. It was still pink from abrupt contact with Tuck's face.

"Fuck you, greaseball," Tucker said, spitting onto the floor a clot of blood he'd coughed up from his throat.

Bedrosian shook his head. "You're one stubborn sonofabitch, I'll grant you that," he said. "Ordinarily, that's a very fucking admirable trait in a guy, very admirable, indeed. You know, there's a future for you with us, if you'll just give up what the fuck you know about the deal. It's so simple." He opened his palms and shrugged.

Tucker had made up his mind. His hatred for these assholes superseded any other emotion or logic that may have had residence in his fiber. His voice was suddenly calm and controlled, "Like I said, fuck a whole bunch of you. I don't know nothing." He braced himself for another blow, but Bedrosian just smiled benignly.

Then Bedrosian folded his hands and leaned forward. "You know, Tuck, I apologize for coming in here with my boys and trashing your fine home like this. I admit, we got off on the wrong foot, and I'd like to try a little different tack if you don't mind." He nodded toward Emo Nay, who was, once again, behind the hunchback.

Tucker could hear the sound of long zippers being moved. Must be the gym bag that Emo Nay carried in, he thought.

Bedrosian continued, "I'm thinking, maybe I can do a favor for you."

Tuck heard a rustling in the gym bag. A rifle. Was he about to suffer the same fate as his good friend Taters Poteet?

"Sort of make up for being so rude at first." Bedrosian leaned forward and took the cup of whiskey from Tucker. He set it behind him on the table. He looked into the hunchback's eyes. "Now, I know that being, what shall I say, deformed all your life must be a fucking drag; kids makin' fun of you; the broads being repulsed by your ugly hump; shit like that. I'm right, ain't I?" He reached over and gently pulled Tuck upright by twisting his fingers in the undershirt in an almost seductive way. "Now, here's my strain of thought. What if I could, like, make you like other men, then you'd be so grateful to me you'd tell me what I want to know."

There was a sudden explosion of sound from behind Tucker, the rip and pull of a motor starting and the unmistakable whine of chain spinning invisibly against a blade. A shock of blue smoke darted over Tuck's shoulder, leaving a wake of oily aroma behind it.

Bedrosian continued, "And you would owe me one because, presto fuckin' chango, your hump would be..." he hesitated and disappeared from sight, "... gone!"

"No!" Tuck screamed.

"On the other hand, maybe you like the way you look and don't want to change, and the price for that is exactly the same. Tell me what you know. Shit, it's a small price to pay, either way."

334

"Look, okay, okay, okay," Tuck cried, screaming to be heard above the chain saw. "I know that something happened upstairs that night and that Nicky Bedrosian was there, but I don't know what the fuck it was and that's the God's truth. Rojas wasn't going to tell me until I guaranteed that I could get him out of there." He looked up, his head spinning. Drool ran uncontrollably down his chin.

Peter Bedrosian took Tuck's cheeks in his hands and shook his head playfully. "Now, Tuck, that's very interesting, and I think I believe you, and maybe we should just leave it like that. But I don't know if my friends here buy your story." He turned to the guys. "What do you guys think?"

Emo Nay came over Tuck's shoulder, the chain saw screaming and spewing smoke and fear into his eyes. What now? Tuck's head throbbed with pain, blood curdled in his mouth. He knew the type of pricks these guys were, knew that no matter what he said he'd be killed, that he'd crossed that line the minute he opened the door. He only had one chance, slim as it was. Fight.

Adrenaline shot through Tuck's veins and he leapt forward instinctively, burying his head in the stomach of Peter Bedrosian and driving the man upwards off his seat on the end table and onto the floor. Bedrosian let out a loud huumph of air as his back imploded on impact. Tucker pulled back his hand to strike and his arm suddenly froze in mid flight as someone grabbed him from behind. The room rolled over again in his vision and he literally flew back onto the couch. Moxie Swain snatched Tuck's wrists like a bear trap and wrenched one arm backwards, sending frantic pain through his shoulder sockets. The hunchback writhed as he tried to free himself from the man's grip. Then, there were two more hands on him, as Swain rolled him over on his stomach and pinned him to the couch with a knee. Tucker gasped for breath as his head was driven into the pillows. He turned. Bedrosian's face was only inches away from his own. He was combing his hair and smirking.

The hunchback inhaled, marshaling every molecule of strength in his sinew and erupted upwards, screaming as he did. But the weight of men upon him caused spittle to pour from his mouth and his lungs to burn.

Bedrosian's breath was like cat shit in his face. "You are an obstinate fucker, and a stupid one. I've tried to reason with you. I give up."

The chain saw whined like a banshee past Tuck's ear. At first all he felt was pressure as it chewed through the meat and gristle and bone of his affliction, spewing wet particles into the air to mingle with the gas exhaust. For a millisecond it was just noise and putrid stench to Tucker, but then the pain bored into him, white, hot, excruciating, and he felt bile erupting from his stomach. His right arm flopped spastically against the pressure, popping out of the shoulder socket in yet another eruption of fire. In the compressed and distorted perception of time and space he could hear someone screaming in the distance. He didn't realize it was himself until just before he blacked out.

Time. Lost. Lights. He saw two feet standing in the sticky puddle of blood on his carpet, the pool that also held his cheek. His right arm hung akimbo behind him like a broken branch, no feeling, dead. A hand grabbed his hair and yanked his head upward. "There it is, your hump, see it?" There was something lying on the rug a few feet away, looking like a ghastly slab of beef. Bedrosian's face came into focus, again inches away.

"You hit me, Tuck. That was a stupid fucking thing to do. Now, if you would simply apologize to me, I will make all this pain go away."

Tucker Hines could see the blue steel spirals of the silencer at the end of the pistol. Yes, yes, make it go away, he thought, the blinding pain. He tried to speak, but his mouth was full of vomit and blood. He coughed a wad of debris into the carpet, nodding his head.

"That's a good boy, Tuck. Is there anything you want to tell me?"

Tuck felt the life force detaching itself from his own body, as if it were struggling out of a tight suit of clothes that had to be pulled over shoes and wet skin. A sweeping feeling of calm came over him. The fear was gone. An explosion of lights erupted from behind his eyes. He was standing on a beach, and he knew in his heart that it was in Australia. Strange that he knew. Most miraculously, he stood straight and tall, light, floating almost. His head he could tilt up to see the hot white sky, something he had never been able to do before. He felt no pain, no fear, and he knew instinctively that they couldn't hurt him anymore.

So, he was goddamned if he was going to apologize to this scumbag. He formed the words in his mind and then mumbled them from behind the liquid and mush of his mouth.

"What did you say, Tuck?" Bedrosian asked.

Tucker Hines whispered the words again and Bedrosian leaned down to hear them, his ear only inches away from the hunchback's mouth. "One more time, please," the man said. "I still didn't get it."

Tucker amassed his last scintilla of strength. "I said, 'fuck you, asshole.'"

337

Bedrosian dropped the head back onto the carpet. "No, you goddamn lizard, fuck you," he said, firing a single devastating shot into the temple of the hunchback Tucker Hines.

37

For a change, Jake McKay was driving as they cruised the street, scanning the boarded up and burned out buildings of a neighborhood bathed in unmitigated gloom. The place exuded a grime that was palpable, that seeped into the skin. Papers and crushed boxes pushed against the curb in the wind until eventually, inevitably losing grip and taking to the skies. The car rolled slowly past a currency exchange with windows zigzag barricaded by fold-out metal bars.

"I think that's it, right there, that doorway between the currency exchange and the barber shop," Glory said suddenly, pointing diagonally across the dashboard.

"Where?" Jake asked, snapping his head this way and that.

"Pull over there on the left, turn in that alley."

"Yeah, okay, is this going to take a week and a half?" McKay groused.

"I just want to give him his passport and the money we owe him, ask a couple more questions and be on my way. Shouldn't take but a few minutes."

As the car moved slowly into the alley, Glory saw two mongrels snapping and snarling as they fought over a large piece of raw meat. Jake saw it, too, and honked at them. But the dogs would not abandon their treasure. They merely skittered away, both growling and shaking the meat.

Glory stepped out of the car and watched as the two dogs grew more furious in their fight. She glanced upward and noticed an open window on the second floor. Odd. An open window in this weather.

Glory Kane and Jake McKay had to jimmy the paintless, crumbling wooden door. Getting it unlocked took about two seconds, and they entered a dark stairwell only two steps from the threshold. Three rusty mailboxes hung on the wall, the one on the right end catawampus from a missing screw, yawing toward the ground, spilling its contents. Each box contained a handwritten piece of paper wedged in a tiny frame. "T. Hines," the paper on the broken box read, in a flourishing Edwardian script.

"Yeah, this is it," Glory replied, waiting for her eyes to adjust completely to the darkness. "He's in apartment three." The stairs were rubbed raw of varnish and color. The end of one hand rail lay on the floor.

"Hey, he lives in the penthouse," McKay said. Then he reached inside his coat and removed his service revolver.

"You're taking out your gun?" Glory asked, surprised.

"This place don't feel right. You want to go up there unarmed, be my guest."

"Yeah, maybe you're right," Glory said, unsnapping the strap on her shoulder holster and removing her weapon. Jake was right this time. Something didn't feel right.

From outside, the fight of the two dogs grew more furious, exploding in a rage of unrestrained barking and snarling. Glory stopped at the foot of the stairs. "You want to go out there and shoot those two fucking dogs first?" she asked.

"Whoa! Listen to you. The preacher's daughter."

"Yeah, fuck you too," Glory said.

The stairs moaned under the weight of their steps. Other than those rhythmic yearnings, the place, the building, reeked of ominous silence, and it was not a tranquil sound. It whistled like an approaching storm to Glory, some frantic calling from another dimension where words were impossible to understand, save for their tone. Most tangible was a cold wind that seemed to rush into their faces the higher they ascended on the stairs.

They passed the first landing, then the second, finally stopping on the third. The cold ran at them, and they could see that it came from the partially opened door to Tucker Hines' apartment. Glory surmised that it was a knife of wind slicing through the open window she had seen from the alley. Without speaking, they moved forward. Jake, gun drawn and held against his chest barrel up, gently placed a hand on the door and pushed it open.

Outside, the dogs continued to snarl and howl.

Glory saw it immediately, a spray of blood on the wall, and she sensed the presence of death encircling her. Moving into the room, it became obvious that no one living was there. "Good God almighty," Jake whispered. "What the hell happened here?"

"Go check the kitchen; I'll go down the hall," Glory said.

She moved more quickly now, gun drawn, past an empty bedroom strewn with clothes, toward a door she assumed led to a bathroom. She took a deep breath and opened it. Empty. There was only one more place to look. Probably a closet. She put her hand on the doorknob and pulled.

She caught her scream before it escaped, as she stood face-to-face with Tucker Hines.

He was dangling from the clothes rod, a belt wrapped under his arms and looped over the support. His right temple bore a small bullet hole caked in blood. His left eye had been blown out as the bullet exited. But what repulsed her most was the man's back, a bloody swamp of gristle and meat.

My god, she thought, the dogs!

"Jake! The dogs!" she cried, turning out of the bathroom and towards the kitchen. "They're fighting over him!"

"What the hell are you talking about?" McKay said, coming toward her in long strides. Without a word he looked into the bathroom. "Holy lord!" He snapped backward toward the kitchen, darting to the open window, and looked down into the alley. The two mongrels had obviously reached a truce. Each was now gingerly gnawing on the opposite end of the meat.

Glory Kane sat on the bottom step at the entrance to Tucker Hines' apartment. Her head rested upon her up drawn knees as her back leaned against the wall. She needed a few minutes, that's all, a little time to catch her breath. Upstairs, in the room, the police went about their work, work with which she was entirely too familiar. Jake McKay stood at the other side of the vestibule smoking, the effluent circling blue and escaping through the crack he had considerately opened in the door.

"Thought you quit that," she said, nodding at the cigarette in his hand.

"Yeah, well, give me a break. It's not often you come across something like this."

Glory could use a smoke about now. Maybe a drink. Maybe both. What in the world had happened here? What madness had rendered Tucker Hines into pudding? And who was behind it? How many people were now dead who had been

tangentially connected to that Mercedes in the abandoned lot?
Five? But this one, what did Tucker Hines know that would get
him killed? Tortured, for crying out loud.

"Hines told me if anything happened to him to look for a
guy named Emo Nay."

"What the hell kind of name is that?"

"This whole case is full of weird names. Nobody is who he
says he is."

She exhaled vigorously and pushed herself back to her feet.
"Tell you what, let's see if anybody here saw anything. I'll go
outside. You wanna take the other tenants?"

Jake flipped his cigarette out the door and into the streets.
"Yeah, sounds okay to me. Dime'll get you ten nobody saw
anything."

Glory shrugged. "Well, I need the air, anyway."

The presence of police cars, blue lights whirring, always drew
a crowd, and this event was no exception. Glory saw several
dozen people rimming the crime scene barricades that had been
set up. She moved toward them. "Anybody here see
anything?" she asked.

There was a general murmur of denials that rustled from the
group, but then she noticed a man ambling through the group
towards her. Homeless, she thought, as she surveyed him. He
was puffed up in a mélange of ragged, filthy clothes. His head
was almost obscured by the wool navy blue cap that covered his
ears. A scraggly home-trimmed beard framed the bottom of his
face that was composed of gray skin as thick as a turtle shell.
As he approached, the stench of his life leapt off his clothes and
body. He stopped at the yellow tape. "Can I come through?"
he said.

"You got something for me?"

He nodded almost imperceptibly. "Yeah, maybe."

Glory lifted the tape and he bent to get under it. He walked past Glory, motioning with his head. She followed him to the corner of the building near the alley. Then he nodded at the bodies of the two dead dogs lying in streaks of blood. Jake had killed them both when they wouldn't give up their booty, the severed hump of the hunchback. He tried to scare them away, shooing them with his hands, shouting, but they wouldn't let go. Even when he shot the first one, the second didn't flinch.

"I knew them two dogs. Mean dogs, them were," the man said. "Had to fight 'em for food. Never won."

"What's your name, sir?" Glory asked, leaning a weary shoulder against the brick wall.

"Name of Ed Rager." He kneaded his hands anxiously as he spoke, the ends of his fingers protruding from his ragged, unmatched gloves.

"You got something for me, Ed?"

"You're a real pretty cop."

Oh, brother. "Ed, I'm real busy here. You got anything?"

He tangled his fingers nervously. "Can I get some money?"

"Look, if you have anything that proves useful, then monetary remuneration is certainly possible."

"That means yes?" he said, eyes glowing.

"Yeah, sure."

"Okay, okay. Well, I sleep around here, different times. And last night I was back over there," he pointed down the alley. "There it's not so cold. So, I hear all the noise upstairs up there. And then the window opens and they throw something out, and I think maybe I can have it cause it's...it looks like a pillow or what-have-you. But when I see it, it's an animal, a dead animal or something, and I don't want that."

"What time was this?" Glory asked.

"Well, I don't know too much about time or nothing. It was dark. Probably after midnight, at least." He rubbed his hands together and then blew into them, momentarily warming them with fetid steam from his lungs. "So, anyway, I still heard all kinds of noise, so I stood back here in the corner. A while later after the noise stopped, four men came out of the door right there."

Maybe there was something to this guy, Glory thought. The number of people coincided with the evidence they had found in the room. The blood on the floor revealed at least four different shoe imprints. "Did you get a good look at any of them?"

"Oh, yeah, yeah. I was only standing right here," he said, backing against the wall less than ten feet from the sidewalk. "They stopped under the lights up there on the sign and lit cigarettes. I saw them pretty good, but they didn't see me."

"Mr. Rager, any chance you might recognize them? Could you pick them out of a photo book, say?"

"Oh, yeah, sure. Especially the big one. His head was square, like a concrete block."

Thirty minutes later Ed Rager sat at a scarred wooden table encircled by cops, carefully turning the pages of a huge photo book. Glory and Jake stood to one side. Two of the local headquarters detectives flanked Rager. The third, the headquarters captain, sat on a sill by a window. Finally, the homeless man stopped on a page. His eyes froze in place. Then he looked up. "You said that you might have some money for me?" he asked.

The detective on the sill answered. "You help us, we got money."

"Okay. Okay, then. This here guy..." he pointed with a dirty finger, "...this is the guy I told you about, the one with the square head, like Frankenstein. He was there."

Glory stepped forward and glanced at the picture. "You know this guy?" she said to the detective seated next to Rager.

"Oh, yeah, we know him all right. Name is Colissemo Nyatrovocich. He's a Serb or Croatian or Bohunk, something like that."

Yep, that was him. She looked up from the book. "Does he go by the name 'Emo Nay'?"

"Yeah, sure does. How'd you know?"

The cop from the sill stood up and came forward. "Guy's an animal. Hired gun for the mob, drug lords, whoever. Can't just do it clean and neat, though. Likes to make a statement when he offs somebody. He hit a guy once—somebody who'd screwed up a drug deal, stole the cash or whatnot—so Emo Nay whips the guy to within an inch of his life with a sock full of coins. Then he staples the guy's eyes open so that the poor bastard can see what's happening to him, and cuts open his stomach and pulls out the guy's intestines. Wraps the guts around the guy's neck."

"Sounds like our man," Glory replied. "Do we know where to find him?"

Suddenly Rager piped in, "Hey! Here's another one. This guy, too, I think." He was frantically tapping at another photograph.

The chief detective leaned over and looked. "Yep. Benjamin Swain. They call him 'Moxie' cause I guess he ain't scared of nothing. Hangs with Nay. Makes sense."

"I think Mr. Rager has been very helpful," Glory said.

"Yeah, now can I have some money?" the homeless man said eagerly.

Glory turned to the Chief. "Do you know where we can locate these guys?"

"Yeah, but you ain't going there by yourselves." The captain turned to the other detectives. "We need to move fast. These guys will be covering their tracks, probably disappearing for a while. Get a SWAT team assembled. Thirty minutes." The detectives nodded and departed.

"That rough?" Glory said.

"You can only imagine," the Chief replied.

38

This was what copping was all about. All the fantasies of Glory Kane's childhood, the reshaping and refitting of television programs and movies into her own world, contained scenes precisely parallel to the one in which she was now immersed. She had trained for it, expected it, lusted for it, and, today, after five years on the force, it was finally materializing. For half a decade, being a cop consisted of a numbing litany of routine crimes: burglaries, robberies, small-time drug busts, corpses with no names. But there had been nothing like this, this moment of sublime anxiety, of lungs bursting with dry anticipation, of the stoic, crushing silence of tension. This was real, and Glory sucked it in long and hard.

They were two blocks away from Emo Nay's apartment, the two detectives from the headquarters whose names were Casey Mueller and Kenny Mankiewicz, five guys in SWAT gear, and Jake and herself. She was standing at the open trunk of their own car. McKay was handing her a bullet-proof vest.

"Put it on," he said.

"Where's yours?"

Jake tapped his chest. "Never leave home without it."

Glory fingered the accoutrement for several seconds, and the reality came rushing home again. She removed her coat and the cool breeze raked her skin as Casey Mueller approached them. "Good. Hopefully you won't need that," he said, nodding at Glory. "Okay, here's the drill. We want to do this as clean and neat and safely as possible. But you gotta understand that this guy is capable of anything. Chances are he throws up his hands and just comes along quietly. He's been there before, and he's always walked, so the whole thing could be a piece of cake. Just as likely, he goes nuts. That's what we plan for."

"Is it likely he's alone in there?" Glory asked.

"Good question, and the answer is no. He's the ringleader of a group of sycophants and leeches who stick to him like hair. Expect two or three of them to be in there with him. That's why it's not as simple as walking up and knocking on the door."

"What's the plan?" Jake asked.

"You saw the apartment complex as we drove by the first time. It's a horseshoe-shaped building, two stories, exterior balconies, almost like an old motel. We're going up from the west, or left side, because we don't want to pass his windows. Kane, button up your coat and you go to the door, twenty-four, and knock. Tell him you're with the gas company and that there's a reported leak and you need to come in and check each apartment. Now, meantime, we'll be against the wall next to the door, 'cause he'll peep through the hole. The fact you're a woman makes him drop his guard, if only for a few seconds. Okay, so far?"

Glory nodded. "I'll have my gun in hand and in my pocket, just in case."

"That's fine. We don't want him to know you're a cop," Mueller said. "Now, the SWAT team will blow the door open,

349

and me and Kenny and the big guy here, we're going to bust in front of you as soon as that happens." He turned to McKay and Mankiewicz. "Guns out, boys. Quick. I'll go first and take whoever opens the door. Kenny, you're number two and you take whoever shows up next. Jake, you got the third one if there is a third. Subdue as rapidly as possible. Don't shoot unless you have to. We want zero carnage if possible. The one we want is Nay, but the others are going in, too. Kane, you pull the cuffs for Nay. Everybody got it?"

Everyone agreed, using nods and grunts. Mueller continued, "Now the corporal here, he'll follow us and stay outside in the squad car. He's our backup. He's our radio. Everything copasetic?" He paused, scanned the faces. "Okay. We'll leave the cars on the other side of the street. Let's go."

The instant the door blew open, the whole world changed. For Glory, it was like diving into a pool of water: a furious flight of blinding speed that blurred the surroundings, followed by a sudden impact that rattled through every fiber in her body, then a series of breath-crushing, languorous motions in a swirl of eerie silence.

The door exploded inward, banging against the wall as Mueller led the crash team into the apartment. Glory was in the hall, behind the others, but in that dreamlike moment, she saw the bullet riveting through its own cloud of silver smoke, saw it spinning through the air, despite its ferocious velocity, she thought, like an angry bee. It zipped through Mueller's throat like a needle, veering downward before bursting through his scapula, carrying bone and fabric past Glory's ear before coming to a flattening stop in the wall behind her.

In the same instant of fury, as Mueller pitched first back and then down, Mankiewicz somersaulted to his right, springing to a crouch, his gun blazing. Four bullets ran like a parade into various parts of the shooter's anatomy. One took his right cheek, chopping the jaw bone at the joint, and three splattered into his torso, pinning him against the wall where he hung momentarily before sliding down, leaving three streaks of muddy blood on the wallpaper.

Simultaneously, a huge hulk of motion, at first just a dark mass, erupted from the opposite side of the room. The man leapt over the back of a couch and immediately came up firing. By now, Jake McKay was barreling through the door. In a move of surprising speed and agility, he rolled to his right and bounced up, pumping heat through the couch as bullets pinged into the wall behind him. The effluent from his own gun caused the couch back to implode in puffs of cotton. One shot, at least, got through, instantaneously lifting the shooter above the rim of the piece of furniture, and Jake aimed quickly and fired. The bullet painted a spider of dark crimson on the blocky, square face of the man. His eyes flared wide and white, a look of disbelief in them. The mouth opened, words struggling for formation, and Emo Nay tumbled backwards, his days of torture and murder finally complete.

Approximately ten seconds had transpired.

Now Glory was in the room, gun drawn, arm steady. She scanned the still electric environment. Mankiewicz was on one knee, screaming into a walkie-talkie as he held a blood-soaked handkerchief to the throat of his partner. SWAT members spread into the kitchen and backroom. McKay was rising after checking out the rapidly cooling corpse he had created behind the couch. Glory saw a movement in the hallway, seemingly at

351

the same instant as Jake because they both moved toward it at the same time.

"Careful," she said to Jake as he disappeared into the semi-darkness. In an instant, she was behind him. They were sliding against the wall. Less than eight feet away, on the opposite side was a door, partially opened. Ten feet farther was another, completely opened. Jake drove his back into the wallpaper, as he cautiously approached the slightly open door. He motioned with his head to Glory to move to the opposite side of the corridor, on the same side as the door. For what seemed an eternity, the two detectives crept. Jake was now nearly square with the threshold. Glory could see a single bead of sweat burst and trickle down his cheek. She knew he was ready to move.

Suddenly, a flash, a brief specter of light appeared over Jake's shoulder. Glory saw it instantly. Movement! Where? Then the scene jelled. Only a foot or so from Jake's head, a mirror! Angled to reveal a portion of the bathroom! Someone there!

"Jake!" she whispered loudly, "watch out!" And with those words she leapt forward, jamming him in the back with her left hand, trying to throw him away from the door at the same exact instant that the gun from the bathroom went off. But McKay, too large to move, tumbled forward, emitting a huge oomph of air as he hit the floor. Glory instinctively dove for the same place, her gun drawn and firing as she kicked the door open with her flailing foot.

For several seconds she was lost, lost in a cacophony of explosions. Glass was spraying over her like powder. Chunks of the floor were erupting. She couldn't distinguish between her shots and the ones coming from behind the shower curtain, but she kept firing, screaming inside. The plastic shower curtain, festooned with seashells and seahorses, bright blue and green, melted around the holes that she had created. Then, in a crash and tumult, the plastic rings holding it in place scattered in staccato fashion. The curtain came down, hugging the falling body of a man. Bent like a folding chair, he spilled out and over the edge of the tub, coming to rest motionlessly on the tile floor. Glory lay on the floor of the hallway, gun still pointed. She took in a mouthful of air and waited. Then she pulled herself to her feet.

Jake!

He was lying on the floor, face down. She crouched to him and turned him over. The front of his shirt appeared almost alive as a bright red amoeba ran outward against the stark white background. "Jake! My God!" she said, turning him completely face up.

His eyes fluttered open. "I'm okay, I'm okay," he whispered.

She ripped his shirt to survey the damage. A huge bullet hole coughed out blood almost dead center in his chest. "Where in the hell is your flak jacket?" she said, angrily. "You said you never leave home without it."

"Too fat," he grunted.

"All right. Lay still. Take it easy. Help is on the way. You're going to be okay."

He closed his eyes for a second, then opened them again. "What did that sonofabitch hit me with, an elephant gun?"

Glory glanced at the corpse. A .44 magnum lay in a pool of blood. "Forty-four," she said. "Not nearly enough to kill you."

McKay reached up and grabbed her sleeve. "I walked right into it. You tried to save me, but I'm too... too…"

"Just lay there, Jake. Help's coming."

"You did it, Kane. You did good." His eyes slowly began to close. "For a broad," he whispered, a wistful smile on his face.

"Stay here, Jake," Glory screamed, shaking him. He was, by now, floating in a pond of his own blood. "Keep your eyes open! Damn it, Jake, open your fucking eyes!" she cried, shaking and pounding him. But she knew he was gone.

Within minutes, the paramedics had arrived. They quickly assessed the situation and turned their attention to the living. Glory stood in the center of the room, her gun still in her hand, hanging unconsciously at her side. An abrupt, eerie calm had descended on the apartment. The EMTs were carefully preparing Mueller to move him out the door. Kenny Mankiewicz stepped over the supine body of the first shooter and moved to the hallway, glancing down at Jake McKay and then at the corpse in the john. In a minute he came back to the big room and came up to Glory. Gently he removed the gun from her hand and placed it in her holster. "You all right?" he whispered.

"How's Mueller?" she said woodenly.

Mankiewicz nodded. "He's gonna be all right."

Glory glanced over at the corpse behind the couch. "Did we get the right guys?"

Mankiewicz smiled. "Oh, yeah. That big blockhead there is Emo Nay. McKay took him out. The other guy over there is Swain. I get his scalp. But the big winner, lady, is you."

"What do you mean?"

"The guy in the shower you smoked? His name is Peter Bedrosian. He's one of the heads of an Armenian mob that makes a lot of its money from drugs. You just saved about a million kids."

PART THREE:
TRIAL AND ERROR

39

Dr. Henry Jones straightened his tie and sat up in the witness box as the razor thin attorney for Richard Baker slid from behind his table and approached the bench. Immediately, Jones didn't like the guy. Something about his demeanor, the fake smile plastered on his boney countenance, the walk, a strut almost. No, he didn't like him at all.

"Dr. Jones, let me first say this, I am honored to have this opportunity to cross-examine you," Nathan Timmins said. "I am actually quite a fan of your work, so to speak. I have both of your books and use them, occasionally, in my work."

"Thank you," Jones replied rigidly.

"And I am very impressed with your presentation today of the forensic evidence regarding this case, and won't attempt to dispute this testimony," Timmins continued, turning now toward the jury.

Maybe this guy wasn't so bad after all, Jones thought.

"First of all, I just want to clearly understand how you were able to positively identify the body found in the oil drum as that of Maura Baker."

"Well, as a matter of fact, we used a method as accurate as DNA, but not nearly as high tech. We compared the teeth of the corpse with Mrs. Baker's dental charts."

"And this is quite accurate?"

"Quite."

Timmins turned back to him. "Now, to reiterate, you then compared DNA from the corpse with the hair samples and blood found in the car and the bedroom of Maura Baker?"

"That is correct. Including hair samples from her brush and saliva from her toothbrush."

"And you're certain they matched?"

"Yes, indeed, I am."

"Were there, Dr. Jones, any samples that didn't match up?"

Jones fidgeted in his seat. "Of course, there are always renegade artifacts, sir. We live in a dynamic world. People come and go and leave evidence of their visits behind in many, many microscopic ways. For example, if you were to hand me that pen you're fidgeting with, my DNA would be on that pen. In an instant. So, of course, there were hairs and whatnot that didn't match either Mrs. Baker or her ex-husband."

"I see," Timmins said, making a fist and bringing it up to his mouth. He coughed into it gently before continuing. "Were you able to determine anything else from the corpse, such as manner of death."

"Well, no, as a matter of fact," Jones said, repositioning himself, once again, in his seat. Damn, these seats were uncomfortable. "The body had been burned—well, at least partially, there was not enough oxygen in the bottom of the barrel to sustain fire—and it was severely decomposed. In addition, a caustic had been used to speed up the decay. By the time we found her, there was very little to go on."

"A caustic, you say? You mean, like an acid or something?"

"Yes. Common muriatic acid, in fact."

"In what form?"

"Well, a dry powder form, most likely, mixed with water, it appeared. There were crystals on what skin remained."

Timmins paced in front of the bench for several seconds, his hand on his chin as if he were pondering what to say next. He then turned to the jury. "You also examined Mr. Baker, did you not?"

"Yes, I did."

"That's where you got his DNA samples."

"Correct."

"And your examination of him, would you say it was thorough?"

"Very. I am always very thorough," Jones answered tersely.

Timmins turned back to Dr. Jones and put up both hands. "Oh, Dr. Jones, please do not misinterpret my questions as being disrespectful of your work in any way. I mean, I know you once identified a body with mere fragments of remains and, if I am not mistaken, this breakthrough advanced the use of DNA evidence to a new level."

Jones straightened up a bit and fidgeted again with his tie. "Yes, quite correct."

"In your examination of Mr. Baker, did you detect any residue of this, this caustic, any crystals on him?"

"Well, as a matter of fact, no."

"How about any remnants of an accelerant—something used to aid in burning.

"No."

"Isn't it a bit strange that he could apply this concoction of dry acid and water and even an accelerant onto this body and then somehow wrestle it into a fifty gallon oil drum and not get even one flake of residue on him? Anywhere?"

"Perhaps he put the body in the oil drum first and then applied the material."

Timmins turned away from him as if pondering the answer. With his back still to the witness, he continued. "And he could do this without getting *any* residue on him? On his hands? His clothes? Somewhere? Is that even possible?"

Oh, shit. "I, uh, don't...I suppose it is," he stammered.

"How about impossible?" Timmins shot back, still perfectly in control.

"Objection!" Harold Devalane said, leaping from his seat. "He's putting words in the witness' mouth."

"Sustained," came the terse reply from Judge Herman Wagner.

Timmins paused, then continued. "Now, about the DNA—did Maura Baker have any kind of DNA profile in any database?"

"No, she did not."

"Then what did you use as your baseline? Do they call it a baseline? I'm not sure."

Jones fidgeted. "I understand what you mean. As I mentioned, we used several different samples, including blood from Maura's bedroom and the blood from the car. They matched."

"So, you presumed they were from Maura?"

"Well, if you trust science, that would be an educated conclusion."

"And, of course, they matched the evidence from the corpse?"

"Indeed."

Timmins rubbed his chin and ruminated for several seconds, as much for dramatic effect as actual concentration. "Would there be any other way to possibly verify that the blood found in the home and in the car was indeed Maura's."

"Well, we could have, I suppose, tested it against that of a close living relative," Jones replied.

"Like, perhaps her mother? Who is here in this courtroom today?"

Jones squirmed. "Yes, I suppose so."

"But you did not compare the crime samples to Mrs. Darby, is that correct?"

"That is correct."

"May I ask why?"

"Well, we had blood matches. Hair matches. As well as dental records. At some point in time, enough is enough, you know? I mean, what are the chances that the DNA from Maura's apartment and from the car would match a completely anonymous corpse? "

"Oh, I suppose it's a bit farfetched, but not impossible. Am I correct?"

Jones chuckled. "I guess in certain bizarre circumstances almost anything is possible, sir."

"I see," Timmins continued. "But it would certainly change the tone of this case if those samples did not match, would it not?"

Devalane jumped from his seat again, "Objection!"

"Sustained," Wagner said tersely, staring at Timmins.

"I withdraw the question," Timmins replied, turning to the jury once more. "I have no further questions of this witness, your honor."

Later that night Rich Baker was lost in the caramel-hued whiskey in his tumbler as he watched it lazily grab fractions of light and dance them across the ice cubes and water in a pageant of abstract shapes. Monsters. Beautiful women. Faces calling out at him. It was to these visions that he was attached, not to the giddy revelry that surrounded him at the table. It was the first time he had held hard liquor in his hand since...

He moved it slowly, wondering if he would drink it.

Nathan Conrad Timmins, Esq. was holding court this night, the end of the fourth day of Rich's trial. Cigar smoke piled above the entourage like a mountain in the mist. Here were the old lawyer whose name was, humorously enough, Johnny Carson, and the two younger assistants, Lydia Knight and Ben Glover. But in the center of it all was Timmins, his chair leaning against the wall, its front legs rising like those of a rearing horse. The Lone Ranger and Silver, Rich mused, coming to the rescue. Timmins was punching out his words with his huge Cuban cigar and inhaling the praise and adulation of the colleagues who had helped him frame the defense. The chatter was convivial, euphoric even, but Baker was a distant observer.

The team had spent the first few days systematically eviscerating the prosecution's case with scathing cross-examination of witnesses that was textbook big city defense. And the tactics were taking their toll as Harold Devalane and his assistants attempted to blunt the obfuscation and doubt that the defense lawyers churned out at an alarming pace.

"Did you see the face on that woman cop when you set up that map on the easel?" Lydia exclaimed, pointing at Nate with her cigar. She was young, two, three years out of law school, Rich surmised. She was short, frumpy, with hair pulled tightly against her scalp and thick black glasses. Probably a lesbian, he thought. "I think you got her flustered, even though she was pretty cool, but the map, you killed her with it!"

Everyone laughed at the remark, but Rich's eyes were on a white bird floating gracefully across an autumn field, right there in his glass. The relief he should have been feeling at the tone and tempo of the trial was, oddly, not there at all. Instead, his mind was being pricked and prodded by another event: the upcoming presentation of the plan for the world's tallest building that Miles Lundeen would orchestrate this weekend, a plan with its genesis in Richard Baker's own soul, a plan stolen from his very being by the business partner he had so trusted.

What a cruel coincidence that his trial and the big show would happen virtually simultaneously. Somewhere some devil was laughing.

"You start out with a huge map of the area, okay, innocuous enough, saying that you simply want Detective Kane to help you recreate Rich's pattern that night. And then you take a marker and begin to trace the prosecution's version of the events. I almost started laughing," Lydia said.

Carson chimed in. "Yeah, okay, Ms. Kane, let's see if I got this straight. Baker is at a party here in downtown Chicago from approximately seven until midnight, one, whatever? So then he takes a cab up to his wife's home in Lake Forest, what, thirty miles away. Gotta be a cab, 'cause he ends up in her car. But first he stops by his own apartment nearby and gets a pair of boots to wear. So, up there he assaults, maybe kills, his wife in her bedroom and then puts her in her car and drives, like, forty miles south where he disposes of his wife's body in an oil drum and sets it on fire. Then he drives back to his apartment

362

to take off his muddy boots, then back to where he left his wife burning where he passes out. Right?"

"Of course, by now the map is all zigzagged to pieces with this frantic running back and forth," Ben added. "Yeah, right."

"And Nate is going so fast with that marker, like Zorro, the cop can hardly keep up," Carson added.

Lydia interjected, "And what does the cop have to say? 'Well maybe he dropped the boots off on the way to the site, not on the way back.' Yeah, that helped clear things up."

"I thought Devalane was going to shit his pants right there, and then the jury, holy moley, their eyes glassed over," Carson remarked.

"The old adage is if you can't convince, then confuse," Timmins said. The entire group erupted in laughter. Timmins put his hand on Rich's shoulder and shook him. "Hey, buddy, you're not having nearly as much fun as we are."

Baker looked at him. "Well, yeah, you're doing great. I'm just tired."

But Timmins had already turned away and was addressing the troops. "Look, we began with a simple premise, and so far it's holding up. No one, not one of dozens of witnesses who saw Richard that night can place him with Maura. In fact, they all saw him without her for a large portion of the evening."

"And if you can't put them together, then you can't have him murdering her," Carson replied, setting his drink emphatically on the table.

Richard had gone back to his drink and its reflections. What was it he was seeing in there? Some cosmic symbolism of his own life? Perhaps it was the booze working on him even if he wasn't drinking it—first gently, giving him refuge, then stirring up emotions, anger, rage, lust. He felt at that moment like he was not a very good man, not a good man at all. What he wanted, more than anything in the world, was to talk to Maura about what he was feeling. She would know. She would understand. She would make him feel better.

"I wouldn't be surprised if the judge dismisses the whole thing, the way it's going," Ben Glover said. "He can do that, you know."

"Well, I wouldn't go that far," Timmins replied. "Besides, next week we begin our case. If Wagner dismisses it, then we miss out on all that fun."

"It wasn't that bad," Samantha Townshend said to Harold Devalane. The office was dark except for the triangle of light discarded onto Devalane's desk by the brass lamp with the green translucent shade. The prosecutor was behind the desk, back dropped by the dark blue scene in the window behind him, a surrealistic tapestry of lights and surging plumes of burning gas from the towers of the refinery in the distance. Townshend was seated in front of him, a stack of files on her lap.

In answer to her question, Devalane slammed a sheath of papers onto his desk, sending others skittering. "No, no it was worse. They don't have to prove jack shit. All they have to do is confuse one juror and we're screwed. What are you? Two weeks out of law school?"

Townshend stared at his outrage for a second, obviously collecting her thoughts. "Maybe we took it to court too fast, Harold, before we had an airtight case. That is possible."

Devalane leaned back in his chair. "Tell that to the mayor and the city council. They're the ones who wanted it done now."

"It's all politics, then?" she asked.

"These days, everything's politics, kid. The media all believe he did it. The people out there from the Loop to the hinterlands all believe he did it. Shit, I believe he did it. We're just not doing a very good job of proving it."

"Well, then, we're going to have to ratchet up the prosecution a few notches," she replied.

"A few? Shit, the wheels are coming off!" Devalane screamed, turning his back on his assistant. Then he calmed down. "Christ, did you see poor Detective Kane on the stand? Timmins ate her up. And if I wasn't so fucking obstinate, she would never have had to go through that. She told me—she fucking told me—we didn't have a case."

Devalane knew he was dead. Hell, Nate Timmins had more money tied up in the suits he wore to trial every day than the state had budgeted for the case. Timmins could hire the best. Devalane, on the other hand, was sitting in a dark room on a stormy night with an assistant with a total of two years' experience, earning less money per year than Timmins and his ilk spend on a typical Christmas vacation. Devalane turned back to her. "In case you can't recognize one, today was an unmitigated disaster for us."

"How could we know Timmins would turn that cop, Gearhardt, from a witness for the prosecution to one for the defense?" Samantha asked, shaking her head.

"Who the hell do you think we're dealing with here? The law firm of Larry, Moe and Curly? You know, you could have found out about that restraining order Rich Baker took out against Maura. You could have freaking told me that she stabbed him!"

"I told you about the restraining order."

365

Michael J. Griffin

"Bullshit."

Townshend's nostrils flared and her eyes widened. "No, bullshit you. It's right here in this report." She began rifling through the folders on her lap. "Those two cops, Kane and McKay, they told us about it. They also sent over a copy of the hospital report on Maura stabbing Baker with the scissors. It's all right... here." She handed him several sheets of paper.

Devalane scanned them briefly and tossed them back to her. "All right, all right, I apologize," he said, rubbing his temples. A fine rain began to pepper the window, and he turned in his chair and stared at it, not really thinking, merely trying to regain his equilibrium in the rhythmic impact of drops against the glass. Then he swung around. "Before we kill each other, let's try to get this thing back on track. Tomorrow the defense begins its case. It's Friday, so Wagner is likely to go short, shut down after lunch. That means we have the entire weekend to reconnoiter, really get tight on the DNA evidence with Dr. Jones. That's the key." He paused, letting out a cloud of air. "And our only chance."

"Who's Timmins' first witness?" Townshend asked.

"Cavanaugh. Dr. Cavanaugh. It's Maura's dentist," Devalane answered.

"God, I hate dentists," she said.

40

The sketches on the yellow legal pad took several random shapes: geometric three-dimensional studies of converging lines and angles disappearing over imaginary horizons, a subconscious paean to Richard Baker's frustrated architectural instincts. These intriguing spurts of pen and mind elbowed for space on the page with not-half-bad portraits of people in the courtroom. The best was an accurate portrait of a specific juror, a willow thin black man in a white shirt with a collar hanging inches below his Adam's apple. But probably the most significant of doodles was the hastily invented calligraphy that spooled out in stacks and lines, spelling a single word over and over again.

Maura.

Glory Kane, in the courtroom for the first time since she had testified, sat in the front row directly behind Baker and felt somewhat guilty watching him doodle. But to her, it wasn't strange that he had scribbled his ex-wife's name over and over again on the page. Not strange at all.

Lisette Darby entered the room. To Glory she looked even smaller, as she gracefully threaded her way through the gallery and to her seat in the first row behind the prosecutor's table.

But make no mistake about it, she carried with her, like the scent of perfume—invisible but in the air, nonetheless— nobility, a regal aura that transformed this petite lady into an imposing presence that dominated the room. Holding her chin high, dressed in a dark burgundy dress and clutching a small leather purse, she floated to her seat, glanced at Glory, smiled and sat down.

In front of Baker, Nathan Timmins preened and strutted, so full of himself and his impending triumph that the color of his face had actually brightened from its usual sallow ochre to an almost healthy pinkish hue. And why not? He was on a roll. And at this precise moment, straightening his tweed coat, as he nestled into the witness chair, was Dr. James Cavanaugh, DDS.

"Dr. Cavanaugh," Timmins began, "Thank you for joining us this morning. We sincerely appreciate your cooperation."

"It's not like I had much of a choice," Cavanaugh replied with a droll tone to his voice, a comment that elicited audible snickers from throughout the room. Judge Herman Wagner, bemused himself, allowed the buzz to die a natural death rather than raising his gavel.

"Yes, I suppose that's true," Timmins continued. "Nonetheless, thanks." He walked across the courtroom, thrusting his hands in his pockets. "Dr. Cavanaugh, how long have you been a dentist?"

"Nearly forty years."

"That's a lot of teeth."

"Millions, I suspect."

"Do you know your patients well, sir?"

Cavanaugh fidgeted in his chair, though not in an uncomfortably conspicuous way. "Well, dentistry is a relationship business; it builds over time, and, yes, I do become very familiar with my patients as this time goes on."

"Could it be said, sir, that you might even be able to identify a patient by his..." dramatic pause for effect, "...or her, teeth?"

Cavanaugh nodded. "Perhaps, particularly if there was some, say, unusual feature about the mouth. Bridgework, things like that."

"Dr. Cavanaugh, did you know Maura Baker?"

"Yes."

"She was a patient of yours?"

"Yes."

"For how long, sir?"

"Oh my, at least fifteen years. I could have looked it up if I had known you were going to ask. But about fifteen years or so."

"No problem. The bottom line is that you have known her for a significant amount of time."

"Correct."

Nathan Timmins walked over to an easel that had been erected directly across from the jury. He reached beneath it and lifted a large poster board onto the holding tray. To the untrained eye, at first glance, the black and white and gray shapes and forms had little or no meaning. Glory put two and two together and quickly recognized the images as blow-up reproductions of x-rays. Dental x-rays. She wondered where Timmins was going with this one.

The attorney steadied the poster with the tips of his fingers, slowly backing away. Dr. James Cavanaugh leaned forward in the witness box for a better look. Timmins turned to him. "Doctor, can you see these all right?"

"I can see them, but if you want me to study them, I'd have to come closer."

Timmins walked to the witness box and gently pulled open the hinged door at its side. He glanced at Judge Wagner. "May I, your honor?"

"Please, continue."

Cavanaugh stood up and moved closer to the posters. Timmins asked him, "Dr. Cavanaugh, do you recognize these images, I mean, what they are?"

"Of course, they are typical dental x-rays of a full set of teeth."

"Have you ever seen these before?"

Cavanaugh squinted through the bottom of his bifocals and scanned the boards with his mouth open. "No, well, I don't really remember them. But, like I said, I've worked on millions of teeth."

"You said you could identify a person by their dental work."

"I said, perhaps, I could."

"Can you tell me whose teeth these may be?"

"No, sir, I cannot."

"Then you can't really identify someone by their teeth. Is that right?"

"What I meant was I could tell you if these teeth belonged to someone if you gave me the name of the person. In other words, perhaps—and I stress, perhaps—I could match teeth and name to my memory. But expecting me to remember a set of x-rays out of thousands of patients, over several decades, well, I'd like to see the dentist who could do that!"

"Please, sir, I'm not trying to question your capacity for memorization of clients'… er, patients'… x-rays," Timmins replied kindly. "I'm just merely trying to establish whether or not you may, perhaps, remember enough about a specific patient to make a determination."

"I understand. I will try to do as best I can," the dentist replied, stepping away from the board.

"Dr. Cavanaugh, these exhibits were made off the x-rays that the prosecutor used to identify the remains of a dead woman, found badly decayed in an oil drum. These x-rays were received from your office."

"Yes, I remember the subpoena for them. But I must tell you that these could not be the x-rays from my office."

Timmins turned to the jury and raised an eyebrow and, with his back turned to the witness, continued his questioning. "Dr. Cavanaugh, please examine these again closely, because, according to the prosecutor, they match the teeth of the corpse found that day in the oil drum."

Cavanaugh took a cursory look at the exhibit and then turned back to Timmins. "I understand what you're saying, but these cannot be the x-rays from my office."

Rich Baker leaned forward. Where was this going? Timmins inhaled and held the breath, his chest sticking out. "Now, why is that, sir?"

Cavanaugh didn't hesitate. "Because, according to what I've heard, these x-rays were used to identify the corpse as that of Maura Baker."

"And why is that a problem?" Timmins asked, an evil gleam in his eye.

"Because these are not x-rays from Maura Baker," Cavanaugh replied confidently.

A sound erupted in the room, born as a tremor, escalating in an instant to a blanket of sound that rattled the courtroom. Judge Wagner rapped his gavel three, four times, demanding order. Rich Baker couldn't believe what he was hearing. He glanced up at Timmins, who was now hovering in front of him. The attorney briefly released a tiny smile and winked at him. Glory looked across the floor at Harold Devalane, who seemed to have shrunk in his chair, the color in his face pouring out and leaving behind an ashen, empty vessel.

It took four more raps of Judge Herman Wagner's gavel to completely still the courtroom. Nate Timmins strutted over and stood shoulder-to-shoulder with his witness, who was still standing by the exhibit.

"Dr. Cavanaugh, how can these not be the x-rays of Maura Baker? I mean, the prosecution has based a huge portion of their identification of the corpse on these identifying marks."

"I don't know how or why they would say these are Maura's, because they're not. I knew her for fifteen years."

"And how do you know that, simply by examining these photos?"

"Well, Maura had a bridge, right there, over her number four molar on the right side. She'd had a serious infection beneath the tooth several years ago. We did a root canal for her, but then the tooth eventually broke, so we replaced it with a bridge. There is no evidence of this on these photos."

"You're certain? Perhaps your memory is not serving you well. I mean, a root canal from several years ago."

"Well, the root canal was several years ago, and the replacement procedure hmmmm… perhaps a year or so after that."

Timmins shook his head emphatically and escorted Cavanaugh back to the witness box. "I'm afraid I don't understand, doctor. These x-rays, you say, cannot be Maura's, yet it was your office that sent them to the prosecution, and I'm afraid they matched perfectly the teeth of the corpse. How can that be?"

"I do not know."

"Did you not check the x-rays before sending them to the prosecution?"

"I had no need to. My assistant went into the file and pulled the x-rays."

"Is there any way this could be a mistake, Dr. Cavanaugh? I mean, could your assistant have sent the wrong x-rays?" Timmins said, steering Cavanaugh back to the stand.

Cavanaugh settled into his seat. "Of course, anything is possible, but it is highly unlikely. Do you have the folder these x-rays came in? And the actual x-rays themselves?"

"Of course, they're right here," Timmins said, producing an envelope. He handed it to Cavanaugh, who turned it over and over again, examining it for several seconds.

"It looks to be the correct folder. Properly labeled. But I'm telling you, these are not the correct x-rays."

Timmins folded his arms and pensively stroked his chin. "Okay, let's assume that you are correct for the moment, that your assistant pulled these specific x-rays out of these files that are clearly identified as belonging to Maura Baker. Is there any chance, any chance at all, that these x-rays could have been misfiled?"

"Certainly. But there is one more point that I was trying to make earlier. These pictures were not taken with our machine."

Again, there was a gasp from the audience that Wagner quickly banished to oblivion with a single rap of his gavel.

"How can you tell?" Timmins said.

373

"Our camera is a Dentu-Ray 2000. It takes almost square shots. These, as you can see, are more horizontal. Definitely not taken with our camera."

Harold Devalane jumped to his feet. "Objection, your honor! This witness is by no means a technical expert in the art of x-ray technology."

"Overruled," Wagner said quickly.

Cavanaugh continued. "More significantly, these are obviously digital x-rays. I hate to say it, but it took us a while to go from traditional film to digital technology. Couldn't afford it. But we converted about two or three years ago, I believe. Regardless, it was well after we had done this procedure for Maura. Her x-rays from that would have been film."

Timmins paced the room. "Doctor, let's speculate for a second. Is it possible that these x-rays could have been slipped into Maura Baker's file by unknown persons motivated to setup my client for murder?"

"Objection, leading the witness," Devalane said.

"Sustained," Wagner replied. "Please rephrase your question, counselor."

"Certainly, your honor. Dr. Cavanaugh, how could these pictures have gotten into Maura's file?"

"Objection, your honor, he's asking the witness to speculate," Devalane bellowed, losing control.

"Sustained," Wagner said, turning to Timmins. "You know better than that, counselor."

"Your honor, I'm merely asking this witness..." Timmins suddenly stopped mid-sentence. He took a breath and then continued, facing Cavanaugh. "In your expert opinion, Dr. Cavanaugh, if these teeth match the teeth of the corpse, as the prosecution claims, then what does that tell you about the corpse?"

"Well, quite simply, that it cannot be Maura Baker."

The courtroom erupted again as Judge Wagner smacked the gavel repeatedly.

Nathan Timmins turned to face the jury, raised his chin and began to walk back to his seat. "No more questions, your honor."

By now the air had gone out of the room, replaced by electricity. What next? Glory wondered where the prosecution was going with this.

Harold Devalane shuffled papers nervously on his table and conferred with his assistants as Dr. Cavanaugh fidgeted nervously in his seat. Finally, Devalane stood up. "Your honor, the prosecution… it has been a long week, your honor, and we would anticipate a lengthy cross examination of this witness that we would prefer not be interrupted by a weekend. Thus, we would request a recess until Monday morning. If it so pleases the court."

Judge Herman Wagner raised an eyebrow suspiciously, sending a very clear signal to Devalane that he knew exactly what was going on: that the prosecution had been caught with its pants down and needed time to figure out how to pull them up. He pondered the situation for several seconds, finally saying, "It has, indeed, been a long week. Motion to adjourn is granted. Court will resume Monday morning at nine a.m. Have a nice weekend, ladies and gentlemen."

41

Miles Lundeen tried to dial down the anxiety that vibrated through his fibers, but he couldn't. He was a human bumblebee in a field of newly blossomed flowers. The hotel's conference room had been transformed into a virtual studio for the big event. This was his day, the day he would reveal his vision to the world. The mayor would be seated on the dais on the stage. All the major television news teams would have camera crews there. The media kits were complete, crammed with color photos, flash drives and data, stacked neatly on a table at the back of the room for distribution as the guests entered. A congratulatory message from the President of the United States would be transmitted via the web to the huge screen on stage. And everything would be perfect, even if Lundeen had to squeeze it into perfection himself.

He flitted between the podium, where he repeatedly tapped and tested the microphones, to the refreshment table at the back of the room. "Don't put the ice out so soon," he shouted to a waiter in a white coat, "The event isn't for thirty minutes, and it will melt!"

Dark blue curtains framed the projection screen, and behind it a video projector purred in readiness. The video operator and sound technician sat in the muted lights of their control devices. Lundeen's voice knifed through the curtains. "Let me see it again, just once more."

The technician immediately activated the computer, and sound and images slowly filled the room like air being blown into a balloon. A violet star field faded up on the screen. To the ominous underscore of eerie synthesized new age music, the stars on the screen began to shoot outward, trailing streaks of light like electric eels. From a point-of-view perspective, like a video amusement park ride, the screen virtually reached out and grabbed Miles Lundeen and pulled him inside its electronic environment.

The deep azure edge of the earth appeared, floating in a feathery bed of clouds. Then the globe swallowed the entire screen, as the animation gave the sensation of ripping through a cloud bank on a perilously rapid descent toward the unmistakable shape of the North American continent. The music swelled, building, building as layer upon layer of instrumentation was added. Miles Lundeen's heart raced in perfect syncopation with the thumping of the bass drum. A dip through another cloud and the animation was soaring over Lake Michigan toward a jagged, undulating three-dimensional horizon. The horizon assumed a shape; the famously familiar skyline of Chicago with the Willis Tower to the left, the Hancock Center to the right, and between them, erupting majestically from the very epicenter of the city was Miles Lundeen's Novïa Center, the world's tallest man-made structure, an architectural wonder of design and imagination.

Tears glistened in Lundeen's eyes, as the video zoomed into the computer-generated three-dimensional graphics model of the skyscraper. The model looked strikingly real, as the visualization swooped in 360 degree arcs around its distinctive peak that was a sublime combination of neo-classical design and high-tech embellishments. Once, then twice, the image was circled, showing in detail the glistening steel accents that seemed to erupt from the observation deck like sprays of water. Suddenly the animation was diving down the side of the building, past fluttering windows and onto the street where it then darted under the ornate facade and into the Center. The visualization roared past elaborate lobbies, plush office layouts, a shopping center, like a frenzied rat in a maze, until it burst out through a window. The music was now at full throttle. Strings swelled, trumpets blared.

Lundeen had seen this video a dozen times from its story board conception, through wire diagrams of the animation, through the completed piece; but each time this climactic moment came, he involuntarily held his breath.

The animation banked out and away from the building, soaring seemingly to yet another part of the city, but then suddenly pivoting in the sky back to the Novïa Center, as if catching one last glimpse over a shoulder. And there it stopped, this frenetic tour of the structure, framing the Novïa Center in the exact center of the screen. A halo erupted around the building as the music reached a crescendo, and in an explosion of sound and video, the peripheral skyline disappeared, leaving only the outline of Miles Lundeen's dream on the screen. Letters of type seared into the base of the structure to complete what was now the logo of the Novïa Center, and the music faded in pulsating waves.

"Perfect!" Lundeen said, as if somehow the video presentation might have changed since the last time he'd seen it, which was less than an hour before. "Cue it up."

He ascended the riser and moved behind the lectern. He looked out at the nearly empty room. Rows of chairs fanned out before him. A waiter brought a huge spray of flowers and placed it on the dais to Lundeen's left. Almost ready, he thought to himself, looking at his watch.

Indeed, the room was empty now, but soon it would be full of stockholders, dignitaries, politicians, architects, big shots and the media, and every person in that room would be focused on him. Triumph, he thought. The flames of power made his skin burn. And then, for a second, he thought of something else, and a slight eruption took place in his stomach, a start, a pang. He thought of Rich Baker and how much that man had done to make this happen, and for a fleeting, guilty millisecond, Miles Lundeen wondered where his old friend was.

Rich Baker wasn't far away, not, at least, in the geographical sense. He sat in an overstuffed chair in the piano lounge of a hotel across the street. Through the fronds of a potted plant, and, whenever the traffic cleared, he could see the corner of the building across the street where Miles Lundeen orchestrated his day of glory.

The trial had recessed for the weekend right after lunch. Timmins had completely eviscerated the prosecution's case, tearing their evidence to shreds, and now it seemed almost a certainty that Richard Baker would walk. Incredible, he thought. Yet, there was scant triumph in it, not with what was going on across the street, and it was this impending event to which Baker had been inexorably drawn, as if fate had willed his presence.

Lundeen. The thought of the man boiled the bile in Baker's guts. If it hadn't been for Rich, that bony-assed, cadaverous

379

motherfucker would still be scrambling to find enough investors to open a car wash. Baker had carried the bags. Baker had put his dick out on the chopping block by daring to offer bribes to the environmental jack-offs and zoning bastards and local citizen fucknickels that could deep six the project quickly. Any one of these turds could have turned against him. So he had to manipulate, cajole, wine and dine them, all in the very complex, carefully designed guise of legitimate business. He had to make a bribe look like something else, a donation, a fee, an entitlement. He had to assuage the guilty feelings of people before they could float to the surface by creating an illusion so thick it could barely be penetrated.

And this was his reward. This was the moment for which he had worked most of his adult life. This was the culmination of all the eruptive anxiety he'd experienced in closed offices under mounds of elaborate paperwork and documentation designed to funnel money secretly around the world and then back into the pockets of the politicians he needed. This moment would be his reward for blowing holes in his stomach as investors backed out, threatening to collapse this delicate house of cards he had built. This moment. Alone in a hotel lobby while Miles Lundeen, Miles fucking Lundeen, paraded and preened in front of the spotlight.

Thoughts tangled around themselves like the roots of weeds, choking off the fruitful plants. Lundeen had turned him away, discarded him out of—what?—fear, paranoia, or, perhaps, convenience? Was all of this carefully orchestrated by Lundeen and his cohorts to get Baker out of the picture, so gluttonous was Miles of the triumph that awaited him? And what now would be the appropriate revenge? Something sinister inside his guts had brought him here, across the street from the event. He

380

had come with a singular thought in mind, to thrust himself into the program, like a knife into flesh. But something anchored him to the chair.

"Sir, can I get you something?" a voice delicately shook Baker from his reverie. He looked up to see a waitress, tray in hand, standing before him.

"Jack Daniels, a double, on the rocks," he answered.

She was back with the drink in a few minutes. Rich Baker held it in his hand and swirled the caramel-colored liquid over the crystal clear ice. He contemplated it, allowing its smoky-sweet aroma to waft gently to his nostrils, where it conjured up such a thirst, not just for the booze itself, but for the promises it made to him as it beckoned. He could have it again, the peace that had eluded him these several weeks. Here was the cover. Pull it up over your head, it said to him.

Rich Baker closed his eyes and swallowed almost half the drink. The fire of contentment rushed through him, tingling his fingertips, warming his forehead. He opened his eyes as the last few drops settled into his stomach. The lights in the room seemed to dance. He chuckled and tipped the glass to his lips again, draining the remainder of the Jack Daniels. Then he signaled to the waitress for yet another.

"Good afternoon, ladies and gentlemen, and welcome to this most momentous of occasions," Miles Lundeen said. More than a hundred faces, muted by the dim lights of the room, stared back at him. But they were mere swirls in the twilight, undefined, a mass of dim colors, individualized or separated only by an occasional cough. In the back of the room, behind the neatly arranged chair, the red lights on no less than seven television cameras blinked rhythmically. Lundeen paused for effect, gazing out to them as if he could actually see them. Then he continued, "In 'Julius Caesar' Shakespeare tells us, 'There is a tide in the affairs of men which, taken at the flood, leads on to fortune; omitted, all the voyage of their life is bound in shallows and miseries. On such a sea are we now afloat, and we must take the current when it serves, or lose our ventures.'" He paused again, then moved on, "Today, I most graciously and humbly thank those many people here who sail together on a voyage into a new and exciting future."

The crowd politely, but enthusiastically, applauded. Lundeen waited for the last ripples and continued. "I would first like to introduce our guest of honor, the mayor of the city of Chicago."

"You look like a puppy that's lost his way," the soft, purring voice said, and Rich Baker again bounded out of the layers of thought that insulated him from reality. He found himself staring into the eyes of a ravishing woman dressed in a business jacket and skirt, holding an amber colored drink with both hands. Crystal blue eyes smiled at him from a motif of ink black hair and porcelain white skin.

Baker's mind rang with the four drinks he had quickly ingested, but his senses were not dulled enough to not notice the spectacularly long legs that flowed like silk from beneath her skirt. "Well, good afternoon," he said, allowing his eyes to travel upward past her minuscule waist to the two perfectly formed breasts that jutted seductively from her blouse, producing a sliver of cleavage accented by the hint of nipple.

"Mind if I join you?" she asked, sliding onto the couch that abutted his chair without awaiting an answer.

"Be my guest," Baker said, rising slightly.

The Mayor of Chicago bent the goose neck microphone arm downward to compensate for his being a full six inches shorter than Miles Lundeen who had just acceded the podium to him. The man who was arguably the most powerful political force in the state of Illinois glanced at the audience and spoke. "This is a big day for this city. Most everybody who has worked together on this has really done a good job." It was obvious his remarks were off-the-cuff and unrehearsed. "Chicago is one of the great cities of the world, and now, with the building of the Novïa Center, we can say that we will regain our stature as home to the tallest building in the world. That is good for this city and for the citizens to be proud of. I would like to congratulate all of the folks up here who have put this deal together. It was no small undertaking."

"By the way," the striking brunette was saying, extending a hand, "my name is Nina. Nina Colina."

Rich Baker set down his drink and gently took the hand in his own. "Nina Colina, is it?" he replied. "That kinda rhymes. I'm Rich."

"It was cute when I was little; now, not so much, but it is what it is," she shrugged. "Are you visiting Chicago, Rich?"

"No, I'm from here."

"I'm here on business. Well, actually, was supposed to be closing a deal this evening, but, unfortunately, everything fell through, and now I'm stuck here all night with nothing to do."

"That's too bad," Baker replied, sipping slowly from his fifth Jack Daniels of the hour—his fifth in almost a year. "I mean, that the business deal fell through, not that you're, as you say, 'stuck' here. That, in fact, could prove to be most fortuitous." He gently clinked his glass against hers.

She smiled. "Perhaps."

"Listen, Nina, you can't let blown business deals get you down. Happens all the time. For every one you make, five get blown. It's like craps. Shit happens over which you have no control. But if you keep doing the right thing, it pays off, eventually."

"Well, I know that, I mean my head knows that, but it's still pretty depressing."

Rich Baker sized her up and decided to take a chance. What the fuck, he had nothing to lose. He placed his hand on her knee and leaned forward. So far, so good, she didn't flinch. He looked into her eyes. "I happen to have a complete library of techniques proven to cure depression."

"I can only imagine," she said, leaning into him now, so close he could feel the warmth of her breath.

His instincts had kicked in. He was inches away from a kill. "And some you can't imagine."

She threw her head back and laughed, a soft, birdlike trill. Then she locked him in her eyes and placed her hand over his, which was now slowly massaging her knee. "Now you've piqued my curiosity. Do I need an appointment, doctor?"

Rich chuckled and glanced at his watch. "Well, now, would you look at that. It seems my four thirty appointment has canceled. I think I might be able to squeeze you in."

"Do you make house calls?"

"Absolutely. They're my specialty."

"I'm staying at the Hyatt on Wacker."

Rich stood up, a sense of giddiness rippling through him as he unfurled. "That's a long walk. I'll get us a cab."

A wispy, colorless, but visible mirth washed over Nina's face. "I have a car," she whispered.

Miles Lundeen was milking the moment for all of its dramatic impact. The crowd had gone quiet. Even the television cameras seemed hypnotized by the palpable eagerness in the room. He came back to the podium. "Sixty-four months. More than five years. That is how long we have pursued this dream," he said. "And there were many times, many times, in the past sixty-four months when it all seemed impossible, when this day seemed impossible. There were people, many of whom are on the dais with me this afternoon, who never quit, who held onto the dream, despite the storms. People who would not be swayed by those disbelievers who churned out lists of reasons why it couldn't be done, why the costs were too high to build buildings like this today. Throughout it all I was driven by the desire to prove them wrong. And today, that proof is here." He turned to the video screen. "Ladies and gentlemen, I proudly present to you the world's tallest, the world's most magnificent building. The new crown jewel of the Chicago skyline. Novïa Center!"

The lights in the room faded to total darkness. The low, ominous music started. The screen twinkled with a vibrating star field. And Miles Lundeen's heart raced.

"My God," Rich Baker said, stumbling a bit on the slick pavement, "This is a strange place to park a car." The drinks had definitely gone to his legs, rendering them rubbery and unstable, and he struggled to keep up with Nina Colina, as she led him down a somewhat darkened dead end street.

"There, see, there it is," she said, pointing to the Cadillac parked half way down the block. "My business partner owns this old warehouse. He lets me park in front of it for free."

"I thought you said you weren't from here." Rich slurred. Nina Colina smiled at him. "No, I didn't say that."

Seconds later they were a few strides from the shining new car. Nina paused and rummaged through her purse, finally extracting the keys. She pushed a remote button and the door locks popped up. "Go ahead and get in," she said, motioning toward the passenger side door.

Ordinarily, Rich would have preferred driving, but he was struggling to focus his bleary eyes, mentally trying to wrestle with the buildings and objects that vibrated through his skull. He could have sworn she said she was in town on business. Yet, her business partner owned this warehouse. His instincts pounded on the walls of his consciousness, but he could barely hear their screams.

He slid into the seat. The smell of new leather wafted into him. He watched through the front windshield as Nina Colina's long, perfect legs carried her past the hood of the car, and he uncontrollably yipped as he imagined those long appendages wrapped around him like tendrils.

Nina was standing at the driver's side door now, again rummaging through her purse. What could she be looking for, he wondered, she just had the keys? Her back turned toward him and shielded her actions. Her arms were moving quite deliberately, it seemed. She turned and, oddly, her left hand reached for the door handle; her right was bent slightly behind her, hidden in the folds of her coat. The door began to open.

"Oh, Christ," Rich said, drunkenly fumbling for the inside latch as his instincts suddenly kicked in. How could he be so stupid? He rattled the door handle, but nothing happened. His hands climbed the interior of the door like water bugs frantically searching for the lock pin.

She turned toward him, her eyes afire, an electric smile on her face. Suddenly, there was a flurry of action behind Nina, two blurs of black sweeping by. Rich heard a distinctive pop, pop. Nina Colina seemed to jump slightly, then fell violently into the door, and it thumped shut, making Rich recoil in terror. He watched, frozen, as she slid down the side of the door, smearing the window with streaks of crimson and jellylike pink and gray ooze like paint from a brush.

Then his door flew open. One of the black blurs, a man in a dark overcoat, reached in. Rich recoiled into a fetal position on the seat. For a terrifying second he could do nothing but pray as he awaited the sound, the pain, the darkness.

"Hurry up, get the fuck up," the man was saying, grabbing Baker by the sleeve of the coat and jerking him upright. "Get up, goddamn it, Rich."

Baker sat upright, one leg protruding from the car door. "What? Who?" he stammered.

"Come on, come on, come on," the man said nervously, helping Rich to his feet. Another car roared up, nose to nose with the Caddy. The second man, who had been standing over the body of Nina Colina, ran towards the car and wrenched open a back door. The first man forcefully shoved Rich towards it. "Get in, get in," he said.

Baker, out of control, confused, blurred by booze and adrenaline, stumbled towards the open door. Glancing back, he could see the frozen open eyes of Nina Colina who sat, legs akimbo, back resting against the door of the Lexus, as if she were merely resting. A small dot of deep scarlet marked the center of her forehead.

And just before Rich Baker was swallowed up by the dark interior of the sedan, he noticed one other thing about the beautiful woman. In her motionless hand, setting in a pool of blood, was a nine millimeter semi-automatic pistol, topped off by a silencer.

42

Midnight hung on the city like a black shawl, and Glory
Kane felt, for the first time in a long time, alone. She also felt
safe in the darkness, safe in the silence. She feared it not. And
this was a clear night, a starlit night. Despite the milky haze that
the city expunged into the sky, she could still see pin dots of
long-ago planets in ancient galaxies where time was more clearly
understood, more accurately balanced. It always amazed her
how small she was compared to those distant lights. And, yet,
she had something in common with them. She, like the planets
and the galaxies, was also alone, millions of miles away, just as
one star was millions of miles from another, burning their own
lights, living off their own gasses, regardless of how close they
appeared. She understood their solitude, and, perhaps in some
cosmic way, they understood her. Extraterrestrial kindred
spirits.

As many stars as she could see, that's how many thoughts
flickered in her brain. Scattered, like the holes in the sky, but no
more random than the gravity and physics that kept the planets
in their orbits. Everything had its place. This night she was
simply wandering, going nowhere in particular, and the next
thing she knew she was less than a block away from Richard
Baker's apartment. Something from out there, out in the sky,

perhaps, had drawn her here without telling her where it was taking her. But that must be what happens when one goes through what she had been through. She had killed a man. She had lost a colleague. You don't simply do those things and sleep at night like a baby, do you? Even if the man was a despicable murderer. Even if the colleague was, well...

The death of Jake McKay was her fault wasn't it? Her fault because she had pursued a possible useless angle. Yeah, maybe it was Baker after all, simple as that, and, because she couldn't let it go at that, Jake McKay, a blowhard to be sure but still a cohort, was dead.

But what if it wasn't a wild goose chase? What if there was something there that could save Baker's life, prove his innocence? Her job wasn't just to clear the case, but to make sure the real killer was convicted. Or maybe not. Maybe that was the prosecutor's job, making sure the right guy was found guilty. Maybe, like McKay believed, her job was to turn over the person and the evidence and let the chips fall where they may. It was too much to ponder.

She came out of the galaxies and back into herself. She looked at her watch. Twelve eighteen, the old-fashioned dial blared in white. Time to turn back and go home.

She heard a sound, strange in the night, nothing familiar about it at all. Not a traffic sound, or a screaming sound, or the whooshing sounds of Lake Michigan in turmoil, slapping at the beach only a block away. No, it was a squeaky, nippy sound. *Yip-yip-yip*. Out of the bushes to her left, barking frantically, skittered a dog, a tiny, blonde dog. It ran to Glory, hysterical in its ministrations. Dogs. She wasn't afraid of dogs, especially not small ones. Even the monstrous ones with drooling jowls and black eyes didn't frighten her.

The tiny dog came towards her, still frantic, sniffed her shoe, backed off. Glory bent down to address it eye to eye. She reached into her pocket. Something left over from dinner. A few bits of meat in a waxy bag. She took out a piece and held it out to the animal. The dog sniffed from a yard or so away, then shot forward, snatched the meat and ricocheted backward as he worked it between his tiny jaws.

"Pretty rough stuff, eh, buddy?" Glory said. "I could hardly chew it either." The dog swallowed and then came for more. Glory held the meat up and the dog pirouetted, yipping happily.

Suddenly, there was a voice from the darkness. "Pasqualé, Pasqualé, come back here, boy, come back here." And Glory realized that this sound had come immediately with the first yips of the dog. She put out her hands and the dog jumped into them, wagging his tail in a blur.

"Pasqualé!" the voice was behind her now. Glory turned to face an old lady, hair silver blue, dressed in a housecoat and furry slippers. Inexplicably, a ratty knit purse dangled from her arm. "Get your hands... give me my baby, you... you!" she cried.

"No problem, ma'am. Here, here he is," Glory said, handing Pasqualé back to her.

She took him in her arms and wrapped him beneath her housecoat. "Are you okay, my baby, my little baby?" Then she looked up at Glory. She was bathed in a soft sheet of light coming from the apartment building, and her eyes immediately traveled up and down the torso of the detective.

"You were going to take him," the old lady cried.

Glory consciously pulled her coat tighter. "No, no, don't worry, ma'am. I'm a police detective. I just saw him running at me and I didn't want him to dart into the street."

"Pasqualé doesn't run to other people. He's afraid of other people," she said, backing away and holding the dog closer.

"Oh, no, he's not afraid of me. Not at all." Glory gently reached out and the dog licked her. "Dogs aren't afraid of me. Strays used to follow me home. Drove my daddy crazy."

"He's not this way with strangers. Usually he protects me from them."

"You should trust the instincts of your little Pasqualé here. See, he knows I'm harmless."

"He was running into the street?"

"I didn't want to take the chance," Glory replied. "Cars come around the corner too fast, too fast, and there's so many, you know, drunks on the road this time of night."

"Oh, yes, yes, yes there are."

"Which raises a question, should you be out here this late? Even here the streets can be dangerous."

"Oh my, my, I know. But Pasqualé is fourteen years old now, and doesn't have the, uh, control he once had. Once he barks to go out, I take him out, and fast."

Glory gently petted the dog's head. Pasqualé closed his eyes and leaned into the detective's gentle caress. "Well, you still have to be careful."

She patted her purse. "That's why I bring this. I've got mace."

"I'm very glad to hear that."

"You're a very nice person. My name is Evie, and this is, as you know, Pasqualé." Then she put out her hand. "Are you really a policeman?"

"Glory," she said, gently shaking her hand. "And, yes, I am."

"Thank you for keeping him out of the street."

"That's okay."

Evie hesitated, as if there was more to say, then nodded to her. "Goodnight."

"Goodnight, Evie. Goodnight Pasqualé," Glory bowed slightly and began to walk away. Suddenly, some instinct stopped her and she turned back to the woman. "Excuse me, Evie, one second."

She was at the door of the apartment building, illuminated in the lobby's glow. "Yes?"

"You walk Pasqualé frequently this time of night or thereabouts?"

"Frankly, almost every night at this time. Pasqualé is not only frequent, he's regular."

Glory reached into her pocket and removed an envelope. Strangely enough, she still carried it with her. Because, as far as she was concerned, there were still questions to be answered. She pulled out a penlight and illuminated the papers. "Take a look at these photographs. Do you know these people?"

Evie took the two photographs and turned them to catch the light. Immediately, she answered. "Oh, goodness, yes, I know them. This woman here, she was nice enough, but her husband I didn't like, didn't like at all. But this guy isn't her husband. They both were like that, you know."

"Like what?"

Evie leaned closer and whispered. "She was a slut, if you ask me, and he wasn't worth a fiddle, either. But I told all this to that other policeman," she raised a hand above her head, "the big guy, when he came to my apartment and talked to me about if I had seen anything the night before, I mean the night she was, uh, she disappeared."

Big cop? Jake. Then, through all of the time and smoke and fire and death, it came back to her. She had sent McKay to talk to Evie that day they came to search Baker's apartment. She was the little old lady peeking through the door crack. McKay said she had nothing, that she was looney. "What exactly did you tell him?" she asked.

"Well, I told him that that night I saw her. She was in her car right out here. I was back, back there a ways with Pasqualé. Are you sure you're a policeman or something?"

"Yes, yes, I am. Go on."

"There was a commotion of sorts out here. Her car, and she got out. And then the other car..."

"There were two cars?"

"Yes. Well, first there was only hers. I saw it when I first came out. She was waiting, it seemed, and I thought that was strange, because, I mean, she lives here, but then again, maybe she didn't want to leave the car double-parked, even though people do it all the time here. I'm so glad I don't have to drive; it would make me crazy, all these cars here..."

Glory, her heart racing, interrupted. "There was another car then? It showed up later?"

"Yes. Are you sure you don't have a badge or something?"

Glory opened her coat and flipped out her badge. Evie looked at it quickly and then continued. "Anyway, the other car came up and a guy got out of the front. Then another guy. They both got out. Then they opened the back door and in there, dead drunk, I presume, because he was always three sheets to the wind, was her husband, and he was laying like a corpse, passed out, and they, the two men, lifted him up and carried him to her car. Then one of the guys got in her car, and she got in the other car. Then they left."

My god, Glory thought. "You're sure it was them? I mean the woman and her husband?"

"Oh, yeah, yeah. I see them all the time," she handed the photo back to Glory. "The other two guys I don't know."

"And you told this to the other policeman, the big guy?"

"Oh, yes, yes, yes. In fact..." she fumbled with her purse, but couldn't quite work the zipper with the dog in her arms, so she handed Pasqualé to Glory. In a few seconds she pulled out a haphazardly folded piece of paper. "... here."

Glory put the pictures back into the envelope and took the paper. "What's this?"

"Oh, that's the license plate numbers on the two cars."

"You wrote them down?"

"Yes."

"Why?"

"Because I thought I might need this if something went wrong or somebody got hurt that night, but I told him, the other policeman..."

Glory Kane reeled. McKay. What had he done?

"And I gave him the license plate numbers, but I kept a copy, just in case." Evie leaned closer to the dumbstruck Kane and looked in her eyes. "I did okay, didn't I? I'm not in trouble, am I?"

Glory came back. "No, Evie, you're not in trouble."

Three hours later, her head buzzing from lack of sleep, night still furiously assaulting the windows of headquarters with its silence, she got the identifications on the license plate numbers that Evie had given her, and the knowledge they revealed made her shudder. With a kinetic hand fueled by exhaustion and caffeine, she took the report and carefully slid it into a manila folder.

Now, she thought, she knew what had happened during Richard Baker's last stop before dawn. The question now was: could she get the information to Harold Devalane before he hangs himself?

43

Glory threaded her way through the crowds in the corridors of the courthouse. Her badge, which flapped from her lapel pocket, moved her to the front of lines, got her inside faster and, like a skeleton key, opened doors that were closed to the civilians amassing in the hallway. The trial of Richard Charles Baker of Chicago, Illinois had become, over the course of a single weekend, a media event. The deft turn in the trial manipulated by Nathan Timmins had sucked the public into its vortex, and now the newspaper and television folks were clogging the arteries of the courthouse with their television cameras, sun guns and microphones. Glory had come in through a back door and hung close to the wall as she made her way to the courtroom. The idea was to stay behind the crowds, lest she be recognized and converged upon by these hungry vultures like the carcass of a wounded beast. But she was coming close to a moment of truth, when she would have to weave through the mass of people to actually enter the room.

Since the commencement of the proceedings, the story had thrummed twenty-four hours a day, it seemed, on the internet and on cable courtroom shows, including a continual blow-by-blow broadcast of the action. But today, Monday, the trial had somehow, suddenly and exponentially increased its hold on worldwide media. Glory assumed, as she twisted through the clump of people, that this, too, had somehow been orchestrated by Baker's high-powered attorney, floating on a cloud of impending triumph.

The entire tone and timbre of the case had now changed with the apparent evidence that the body found in the oil drum was not, and could not have been, the body of Maura Baker. So, who was she? "The sad woman of mystery," one television reporter called her. What relationship did she have to Richard Baker? Most critically, did he have anything to do with her death? And where, then, was Maura? The whole story unfolded like a mystery play with things unknown, things untold.

Glory stood at the periphery of the crowd, partially hidden behind a pillar. She, of course, hadn't slept all night, not after the meeting with Evie, but she was fueled with a renewed rush of adrenaline. She stood on her tiptoes and scanned the crowd, looking for Devalane. As much as she wanted just to keep the information to herself, her integrity wouldn't allow her to do so, even though she had no idea what Devalane could possibly do with this knowledge at this late date. She had called him all morning, but, of course, he wouldn't take, nor return, her calls. Too busy. That was understandable, particularly in light of the fact that she, Glory, had been his chief antagonist since the beginning. But the crowds were so thick, and she simply didn't want to be swallowed up by the media. And the way things were going now, she wasn't going to get to him in time. Maybe at the first recess she could corner him, just for a second.

To get to the courtroom door she would have to part the sea of bodies, and she waited to make a break at just the right time to avoid them. And then, in an instant, it became so much easier. The crowd, en masse as if on cue, seemed to swell upwards in a cacophony of sounds and agitated motions, and then move away from the courtroom doors like a huge amoeba to converge upon the men ascending the stairs. Glory, now suddenly nearly alone, emerged from behind the pillar and watched the bizarre scene unfold. Rich Baker, with Nathan Timmins at his side, his hand on Baker's shoulder, knifed into the center of the crowd.

Baker. How much he had changed since that first day, that early, cold November morning months and seasons ago when Glory Kane first confronted him. Then, he was muddied in blood, his skin a pallid yellow, his eyes burnt red, his shoulders rounded as if under a great weight. Today he was taller, somehow, certainly impeccable in his black suit and blinding white shirt, hair perfectly coiffed. He could have been any businessman walking into that courtroom. And yet, there was still something wrong with him, some distracted, distant, detached, almost frightened look in, not his face exactly, just his eyes. Yes, in his eyes. They seemed to be saying something, even though he spoke not a word as he pushed through the crowd. The questions of the media came at him like bullets, but they seemed to bounce off as if he were Superman in a cartoon. He curled his lower lip and shook his head, using his hands to move through the bodies.

Nathan Timmins, on the other hand, seemed more synchronized with the moment. His gaunt pale face beamed. His thin hair was shining, plastered in place. He briefly stopped to answer a few questions that Glory could not hear, and as he spoke, friendly, open, smiling, he kept hold of Rich Baker's arm as if keeping him from breaking free. Baker, at the same time,

399

seemed miles from his attorney, despite the hand on his arm, and this is what intrigued Glory Kane the most. The tumblers on her instincts clicked rapidly in place, opening a door of speculation that left her uneasy.

While Timmins was obviously relishing the moment, full of confidence, bravado, even, Baker appeared as though he hadn't gotten the message that his ordeal may very well be drawing to a successful closure. His face was furrowed with worry lines. Or, were they crevices caused by deep thought? There was a fear there, coming off him, like some kind of evil aura. He made eye contact with no one. Glory wondered what was going on inside his mind. Something told her she would soon find out.

With the crowd safely away from her now, she jogged across the hall and was let into the courtroom by the guard. There she made her way to the still empty front row and took a seat directly behind the defense table. Ten minutes later Baker and Timmins and their entourage entered, followed moments after by Devalane and his assistant, and soon the courtroom had filled to capacity. Among the spectators, Glory noticed, sitting directly in line with her in the opposite bank of benches, was Lisette Darby, who stared straight ahead woodenly.

Next came the jury, seven men, five women, each staring intently at the task at hand, not looking at the defendant, nor his attorneys, nor the prosecutor and his staff, nor the audience. Outside, the day had come alive with a vengeance, bright, sunny, pouring in through the windows on the west wall, casting splatters of light and shadow onto the floor. Glory found it ironic that a single, pure, uninterrupted sheath of sun lay gently on the table in front of Rich Baker, turning the dark wood white. She could smell his, or, perhaps, it was Timmins', cologne. Had she reason or desire to, she could have reached out and tapped either man on the shoulder simply by standing up and leaning forward.

The room seemed to tremble slightly from the whispers and shuffling of its inhabitants, and, yet, there was still a silence that overwhelmed the atmosphere, a silence of monumental proportions like the breathing of a huge beast. Timmins leaned over and whispered something to Rich, who did not react at all. Then, as Glory watched the second hand sweep past the number twelve on the industrial clock behind the judge's bench, Herman Wagner entered the room, sweeping in like a raven as everyone stood.

"Please be seated," he said, fluffing his robe as he sat. "Today, we continue with the people versus Richard Baker. We are at this time hearing from the defense, so..."

Suddenly Baker stood up, "Your honor, may I address the court, please?"

Nathan Timmins launched himself out of his chair and grabbed Rich's arm. Glory leaned forward to hear the attorney whisper frantically, "Rich, what the hell are you doing?" Then Timmins looked up at the judge. "One moment, please, your honor."

"What's going on here, counselor?" Wagner growled impatiently.

"I'm going to find out... just one... one moment... please bear with me," Timmins stammered, pulling Baker downward. Glory strained to hear the words tumbling out in front of her. They came like the sound of a badly tuned radio station. "What—doing? You—can't—let—let me—fatal—mistake—tell—me—why?" Timmins ranted.

Devalane had nudged forward himself, looking as though he was about to stand, but, at the same time, mesmerized by the theater being played out before him.

Baker shook himself loose and stood again. "Your honor, I'd like to simply make a statement."

Wagner looked at Baker warily and shook his head. "Mr. Baker, it is obvious that whatever you wish to say to this court is against the better judgment of your attorney, and I must warn you that there is a potential here to severely compromise your situation."

"Your honor," Baker said, emphatically pushing Timmins downward and into his seat. "I have a very simple statement to make."

By now the audience had leapt into the sudden turmoil, murmuring, whispering, and Judge Wagner rapped his gavel. "Order, please." Then he turned to Rich. "Mr. Baker, I'm afraid I cannot allow you..."

"I killed her," Baker said, insistent, just a few decibels below a shout.

The room erupted in a deafening clamor. Reporters stood, women shrieked, some people applauded. Judge Wagner pounded his gavel. Glory's eyes swept the turmoil. Even the jury had fallen back, heads swiveling as they mouthed their disbelief.

"Mr. Baker, I cannot allow..." Wagner shouted over the noise as his gavel rattled against the block. But, of course, the genie was out of the bottle, and the judge looked perplexed.

Glory found herself standing, the air drained from her lungs. This, this she had not expected. My God, what was going on? Timmins was back on his feet, standing in front of Baker now, holding him back as if trying to prevent him from attacking the

bench. "Your honor, please disregard... I must speak with my
client," he turned to Rich and semi-whispered, "What the fuck
are you doing here? Are you out of your fucking mind? Sit
down and let me..."

"Your honor," Rich said, leaning over his attorney's
shoulder, "I'd like to change my plea to guilty, sir."

Now the room had gone totally out of control. Wagner and
Baker locked eyes, and Glory watched. Wagner's countenance
could not disguise his distress. A sheet of red had swelled from
his cheeks to the crown of his bald pate. Timmins dropped into
his chair like a man through the door of a gallows. Devalane
was standing at this table, leaning on both hands, his head
bowed and shaking from side to side in incredulity. And
Baker—Baker stood in the eye of the maelstrom, suddenly
serene, a glimmer in his eye.

Wagner hammered his gavel three quick times and shouted,
"This court is in recess until further notice. I need to see Mr.
Baker and all counsel in my chambers immediately. Bailiff,
please return the jury to its quarters." And with that he
disappeared through the open door behind his bench.

The people who remained in the courtroom stirred up a
mélange of stunned pandemonium, and Glory found herself
bombarded by the same thoughts. How long do I stay? Are
they coming out? Is the trial over? What's happening next?
Cell phones were beeping rhythmically in the background, as
reporters and spectators pressed the dial pads. News crews
surged in and taped the turmoil. And Glory Kane, who had
been with the case since its genesis, felt strangely unique and
utterly out of place until she turned her eyes toward a single
image in the morass. Lisette Darby, across the room, was
standing now, snapping shut her purse. Her face glowed in the

pouring sun. A subtle smile creased across its ancient lines. Glory muscled through and around people, finally catching her from behind and gently taking her arm. "Lisette," she said.

The woman turned. "Glory," she replied, smiling broadly. She almost sang Glory's name, and there was great and wondrous warmth in the familiarity it showed.

"Lisette," Glory stammered. "I don't know quite what to say."

Lisette Darby smiled warmly again. "Don't worry, dear," she said, patting Glory on the hand. "Isn't it amazing what true love will do?" And with those words she leaned up and kissed the detective on the cheek, then turned and disappeared into the crowd.

"Yes, it is," Glory whispered, believing that she understood all too well what the woman meant.

Judge Wagner swept into his chambers like a tornado, robes swirling, sucking papers from the desk like rooftops. His head, burning red with fury, seemed to burrow into the fabric of his garment, and he growled as he flew toward the chair behind his desk. "I'll not... I will not... " he repeated, pursing his lips, "... allow my courtroom to be decimated in the manner that I just witnessed."

Rich Baker was directly behind him, followed by Nathan Timmins, who was grabbing at his client's arm, "What the fuck is going on, Rich?" he said in a voice louder than a whisper.

Judge Wagner stopped in his tracks and turned on them, his eyes flaring. "Mr. Timmins, I remind you that we are still in a court of law, and such language is inappropriate and inexcusable and in contempt. In fact, I am this far..." he held his thumb and forefinger an inch apart, "... from issuing contempt citations to

404

each and every one of you, your families and your pets. The absurdity that I just witnessed..." He waved his hand disgustedly at the group and dropped into his chair. Again, his eyes ignited as he scanned the room.

In addition to defendant and attorney, Devalane was there with Samantha Townshend, and Timmins' team, Lydia Knight, Ben Glover and Johnny Carson, crowded in amongst them. The court reporter followed, moving her machine to a desk next to the judge's. Wagner looked them all over. "Okay, I want Mr. Devalane, Mr. Timmins and Mr. Baker. The rest of you, out, out, get out," he said, angrily gesturing with both arms.

When the room had cleared, the remaining three men sat down. Baker took the chair at Wagner's right hand, and for the first time in Rich's long ordeal, he felt oddly, strangely, comfortingly tranquil and unafraid. The invisible psychic fetters that had wrapped and strangled his soul had been magically removed, cut away by the events of the weekend, and his spirit was soaring, free, giddy, riding the jet stream of a new wind on a new vista. And there was nothing—nothing—that Wagner could say or do to him now for which he was not prepared, nor about which he harbored even a scintilla of fear.

"Okay, Mr. Devalane, perhaps I'll start with you," Wagner said, calming down, the color gradually fading from his head. "Do you have anything to tell me about what is going on?"

Rich noticed Devalane's eyes, lost, vacant, like a deer's in headlights, yet revealing a hint of glee. "Your honor, I am as surprised at the turn of events as..."

"That's a no," Wagner interrupted. He turned to Timmins. "Mr. Timmins?" he said, raising an eyebrow.

"Your honor, I request a recess of these proceedings so that I may speak in confidentiality with my..."

"That's a no, too, I presume? And motion denied," Wagner said, dismissing Timmins with a perfunctory flip of his hand and turning to Rich. "Mr. Baker, in light of the fact that you have obviously ambushed your attorney, the prosecutor and me with your outrageous and, might I add, extraordinarily dangerous and foolish behavior, perhaps you can enlighten all of us as to what's happening here."

Rich took a deep breath and looked at his watch. They had been in the room less than three minutes. But now, as he contemplated what to say, he knew that every second of silence seemed like an hour.

Where were they?

As if on cue, there was a quick knock on the door at the rear of the chamber, and, before Wagner could shout his denial of entry, it swung open. A county policeman started to enter the room, but was swept aside as two men entered. The first one, a huge, dark man in a navy suit, pulled identification from his pocket. "My name is Kenneth Phillips from the attorney general's office in Washington, D.C. With me is agent Sheldon Ramsey of the Federal Bureau of Investigation."

The sheriff's deputy nudged in behind them. "Your, honor, they just came..."

Wagner, who had arisen from his seat at the sudden intrusion, froze momentarily, then settled back down. "What in the hell is going on here, gentlemen?"

"Your honor, we're extremely sorry for the sudden and unexpected appearance of Agent Ramsey and myself," Phillips said, moving in front of the judge's desk. "And we apologize for what has transpired here this morning. But when we explain the situation, we're certain that you, Mr. Devalane and Mr. Timmins will understand."

"May I remind you, sir, that despite your impressive credentials from the Department of Justice, and those of your FBI friend here, that this is a court in the sovereign state of Illinois, and that I am its steward," Wagner said.

Phillips held him for a second with his eyes. "What we say here, stays here, gentlemen," he said, looking intently at the two attorneys as he spoke. "We expect you to cooperate fully."

Glory Kane had stood in the courtroom for fifteen minutes, staring at the door into which Wagner had led Baker, the prosecution and the defense teams. The place was still in a state of eruption, with flashbulbs exploding and a swell of noise and confusion that washed over the room like a tsunami. The hallways were also clogged with bodies. People from other cases in other rooms had emerged and stayed to witness the excitement.

My goodness, Glory thought, if they only knew what she knew. And even that was still not fully formed in her mind. The puzzle pieces had almost been fitted together, creating a scene, a picture of incredible complexity in its composition, but of simplicity in its concept. But there were still some minuscule jagged parts that left tiny holes in the panorama, and she knew that it might be months, or years, before she would ever truly know the truth.

After nearly one hour, the frenzy began to tire and the crowd began to thin. Reporters and camera people lounged on the benches and railings; newspaper people leaned against the pillars. Finally, a side door at the end of the hall swung open and Nathan Timmins emerged, followed by Harold Devalane. Immediately, the mass of media re-jelled and swept towards them. Microphones on booms and flesh-and-blood hands were thrust into Timmins' face. His color was, once again, sallow, exaggerating his Ichabod Crane features. He swallowed, and his protruding Adam's apple bobbed nervously. He looked up at the crowd. "In concert with the prosecutor's office, we have agreed upon a plea bargain for a reduced charge of reckless homicide on behalf of my client Richard Baker of Chicago, Illinois. Sentencing will be determined by Judge Wagner, and my client has been taken into custody." He paused. "I have nothing else to say," he replied, plowing into the crowd and wincing as the barrage of questions rained down upon him like hail.

The absence of Richard Baker in this frenzy told Glory Kane that the real story was no longer out here in front of the media, but likely taking place in the private entryway behind and beneath the courthouse. She pulled her coat back and ran inside to the stairwell, catching herself on the banister as she plunged down the steps, her shoes clattering on the marble surface. In a few seconds she was there, in the dark garage where prisoner transports could safely and securely deposit and pick up their passengers. The door was open, throwing a triangle of light into the dark corridor, and she ran toward it, arriving just in time to see a black Lincoln pulling away and turning onto the street, in a direction opposite the media feeding frenzy. She could clearly see the license number, and then it all came together. Of course, this car—this FBI car—was just like, perhaps, the same one that Evie had seen outside the apartment that night. The same one Jake McKay had known about and not told her, because it would have ended the case right there. And she knew something else at that moment.

Rich Baker was in that car. And she wasn't ever going to see him again.

44

Thus did it end, as quickly and simply as that. Within days, it disappeared from the news broadcasts and newspapers—except for periodic sightings of Baker and rants from the conspiracy bloggers. But, in truth, after all, hadn't the case been wrapped up neatly, as well as spectacularly? Richard Baker confessed. It was the way such things should end.

The most lasting effect of the situation was, of course, felt by Glory Kane. She had become somewhat of a hero—to her fellow detectives and to women's groups who lauded her for her work in bringing Richard Baker to justice. She went along with it, not because it beguiled her or she craved the attention, but because not doing so would jeopardize things of much greater importance. Now she understood: some things simply superseded others. It was the nature of things, after all, wasn't it?

But the concept of it gave her no sense of satisfaction. In a strange way, she found herself becoming more like Jake McKay than she would have preferred. Cynical, distrusting the system, realizing that there exist in the ether of the world people, organizations, missions and influences over which cops like her—the bottom of the jurisprudence food chain—had no control.

So, she did her job, nonetheless, as best she could, always awaiting a specific event that would fill in the few holes remaining in the case of Richard Baker. She surfed the internet, devoured newspapers, scanned memos looking for it, waiting for it. When it finally came a couple of months later, she almost missed it.

The warmth, the inner glow of her home washed over Glory as she entered, and she felt, at last, as if she could release the tension and realities of the day and deflate and sag like a melted candle. Without removing her coat, she fell onto the soft sofa, dropping the stack of folders onto the coffee table in front of her. She hadn't seen the house in daylight for more than three weeks, and it seemed to assimilate an artificial ocher aura cast by the incandescent lights. Dust sprouted like rye grass on the furniture. The cushions were askew, the sink engorged with dishes, and the trapped furnace heat gave the place a vaguely sour smell. But it was home, and everything about it was reassuring and secure to Glory Kane. She immersed herself in it, lolling her head on the back of the couch as she almost unconsciously reached for the remote control and flipped on the television.

The Eyewitness newscaster on Channel 7 was sober-faced as he retold the story of yet another teenage girl caught in the crossfire of a gang shootout. The images cut to a street corner, steel gray with an almost invisible, mystical covering of snow. A large woman, red-black against the pallid background, was rapidly firing words at the reporter about crime and guns and kids and police and gangs and drugs and jackets and shoes and..."

Glory tried to hold on, but couldn't. Everything seemed to swirl away in a dark iris. It was as if exhaustion had reached out with a huge hand and yanked her off that street and away from those people and into the forgiving darkness of sleep.

It could not have been more shrill, more deafening, more jarring if it had been an alarm clock cutting through the darkness like a knife. Even in the muffled comforts of sleep a few loyal strains of her consciousness stood sentry, watching, listening for anything important, anything foreign to the environment, anything dangerous or meaningful. In her line of work the senses become super-charged down to the tips of the fingers, so that within the context of myriad sounds and images, the mind can pick out those she needed at any given time. It was, Glory remembered, when she was very young, school-aged, that she learned to pick her name out of a page of text instantly without reading any of the other words. She could almost see it the moment the page was placed before her. Now, on this night of exhaustion, she had done it again. Something rang through Glory's subconscious and rattled her awake. The first prick came from a string of disconnected words: district court, drug cartel, and the two that slapped her awake as certainly as any alarm could do.

Nicholai Bedrosian.

She bolted upright and leaned toward the television set, shaking the last drops of unconsciousness off her mind. How long had she been down? Perhaps only a few minutes. The news was still filling the room with little flickers of light that turned blue as they emerged from the set. The story had already switched to the birth of a white buffalo in Wisconsin.

Thank God for digital video recorders, she thought, as she scanned backward. She fired quickly through the scenes, the commercials. She realized suddenly that she was still in her coat. She extracted herself from it and tossed it across the coffee table and onto a chair that failed to grasp it and it fell to the floor.

"Come on, come on," she cried as the TV screen scurried backward. Then a flicker. She stopped the DVR. A picture came into view of a suave, handsome man in an expensive suit. His hands, joined in a pair of silver cuffs, were raised defiantly above his head as if he had just won some sort of prize. He smiled, and preened, it seemed, at the cameras. "You will never keep me!" the headline screamed

"Well, well, well, Mr. Bedrosian," Glory said. "They got you a lot faster than I thought they would."

45

Maria Jula Taylor heard the car pull into the driveway next to her house and her heart stopped for an instant, as did her hands which were wrapped like a mummy's in the bread dough that she had been kneading. Bread. Baking. Cooking. They had become familiar activities in the litany of outlets for her nervous energy since the disappearance of her father months before. At first she was paralyzed by it. She had stopped eating, couldn't sleep. Every sound at night, every phone call, every passing car stuck her like a needle. How many of those cold nights had she stood out on her porch, watching every set of sweeping headlights, knowing that the next one, or the next one after that, would bring back her father, Roy, who had disappeared as totally and as certainly as night disappears at dawn, without warning, without a sound.

She had completely wallpapered every bedroom in her home, had gone almost daily to dad's to clean and get his mail, to make it right, just right for when he finally returned. But as the days and weeks evolved into months, the prospects faded like a dying rose. She had, at the urging of her husband, gone to therapy, and, while it helped clarify her anxiety, it explained, even amplified that which she already knew. And she and her

413

husband and her children had all finally agreed that Dad—Grandpa—had probably stumbled into the cold, dark, deep, unforgiving, ruthless lake on which he fished every morning, and had been swept under forever.

So now, on this otherwise glorious autumn morning, with the window over the sink behind her open to receive the gentle singing of birds, she heard the unmistakable sound of tire against asphalt, the purr of an engine, its abrupt cessation and the opening of a door. Nervously, she shook her hands free of her bread dough and wiped the white flour off her hands on her apron as she moved gingerly toward the front door. She was running now, through the living room, pushing open the front screen and descending the porch in total disregard for the steps. She came to the side of the house and could see the black car, an expensive car, sitting there. A man in a dark suit had emerged from the front passenger side.

"Yes, yes, what is it?" Maria said, still unconsciously kneading her hands.

The man did not reply. He merely moved to the back door of the car and opened it. First a leg emerged, followed by a shadowed shape, and Maria knew, the moment the frail bundle began to unfold, who it was. "Papa!" she cried, running.

Roy Jula pulled himself to his feet with the help of the door armrest, just as his daughter dove into him, kissing him, running her hands over his face and through his hair. "Papa, papa, I have prayed... where have you been?"

"Been fishing," Roy Jula said. "In Florida, on a big boat! You won't believe it."

414

46

It was nearly a year later. The heat clung to Glory Kane like cellophane. She could never quite get used to this kind of weather, heavy and wet so that walking through it was like slogging through water. This was how it got, now and then, in Chicago in the summertime, when the cool lake breezes turned their attention elsewhere and kids on street corners opened fire hydrants and laughed and splashed until the police chased them away, so the water company could shut things down.

The trial had been going on for more than a week, in a crowded courtroom where the windows poured with condensation as the air conditioners groaned to cope with the heat. Finally, today, her eighth, was what she had come for, and her heart fluttered in anticipation as she ascended the long stairs to the courthouse. For this was the day that the final answers would at last be given to her, nearly ten months after she had walked up to the car bearing Richard Charles Baker on a cold morning, the attributes of which had, by now, faded from her memory.

Glory had stood outside as she had every morning. Her badge might have opened doors for her, but it couldn't guarantee her a seat near the front where she could study the

415

face of the defendant and virtually feel the emanations of hatred coming from his skin. At the same time, the sessions themselves were seldom terribly crowded. In August, in Chicago, there seemed to be better things to do than to witness the trial of a yet another gangster drug dealer and murderer, even if he was one of the most ruthless and powerful in the world. Perhaps this was why the feds had moved so fast. Perhaps the strategy was to use the heat to keep people away.

Security was fierce, nonetheless. All spectators passed through two metal detectors and were swept with an electronic baton before entering the courtroom.

Certainly the heat seemed to be the least of Nicholai Bedrosian's worries. Every day he entered the courtroom, hands and legs shackled by chains, dressed impeccably in cream suits that betrayed not a drop of his concern. "You will never keep me," he had proclaimed triumphantly upon his capture. Testimony in his trial also had him telling his friends, "I will kill them all." But today, this day, the day of the missing pieces, Glory was almost certain that Bedrosian would find that his boast had been too pompous, too self-filled, too arrogant. Indeed, if Glory's hunch was right, Nicholai Bedrosian, drug runner, gangster and murderer, would soon discover that he had, indeed, not killed them all.

Glory moved to her seat near the back of the court, fanning herself with an old-fashioned fan that she had purchased years before at EPCOT Center. Even with the air conditioning, a full courtroom generated heat. Then the judge came. She closed her fan and stared intently at the drama before her. The prosecuting attorney stood up and called his first witness, and, at the sound of the name, Glory's entire being shuddered. Tears welled up in her eyes, and she saw the face of Lisette

Darby in her mind, a soft smile there, smoothing out the ancient wrinkles, a twinkle of untold wisdom and understanding in her eyes. The doors to the courtroom opened behind Glory and she turned.

Of course, she knew her immediately, despite the raven black, page boy haircut. The incredible, piercing green eyes gave her away. This exquisite lady, her hands tenuously folded around a small clutch purse, moved regally up the center aisle and stood before the witness stand to take the oath.

For Glory Kane, everything she had believed herself to be, everything she had dreamed of becoming, all of the myriad reasons she had chosen this profession, had come to the content of this tiny, almost unnoticed moment in time. This moment of epiphany. This moment of revelation. This moment when what emerged from the mystery and darkness and vagaries of two years was all and everything that had ever mattered:

The truth.

The prosecuting attorney stood before the woman and asked her to state her name. When the words came, they took Glory's breath away.

"I am Maura Baker," she said.

"Do you know the defendant?" the attorney said, pointing to Nicholai Bedrosian, who glared at her with electric hatred in his eyes that seemed to shoot across the room as a silent warning.

Maura did not flinch. "I met him several times. But even with that, and the things I see in the news, it would still be an exaggeration to say that I know him."

"When was the last time you saw him?"

"Two Novembers ago, at a party in Chicago."

417

"Ms. Baker, would you please tell us why you were at this party."

"I went with a friend."

"And this friend, what was his relationship with the defendant?"

A ceiling fan spun noiselessly above her, running streaks of shadow across her torso. She cleared her throat. "He worked for Mr. Bedrosian. He laundered money, presumably from drug trafficking."

"Objection!" the defense attorney shouted. "Even the witness admits to speculating."

"Sustained," the judge replied.

The prosecutor came in front of Maura and leaned on the enclosure. "Your friend's name was..."

"Aaron Clayton," came the reply.

"Were you aware of the details of the business relationship between your friend and Mr. Bedrosian?"

"I understood them to be associates of some kind, but no, sir, I had no idea of the nature of that relationship—until later, of course. I'm not particularly inclined toward business dealings, personally, and my instincts about such things are, thus, not well developed."

"Did something, shall we say, unusual happen at the party that night?"

Maura straightened herself and, in an act of defiance, stared at Nicholai Bedrosian as she began her story. "We ate in the restaurant Mr. Bedrosian had rented for our group. After dinner we were invited upstairs. On the elevator ride to the penthouse, Mr. Bedrosian gave Aaron Clayton a briefcase that I learned later was filled with money. Aaron took the briefcase to a bedroom and placed it in a safe where it would be, well, safe during the party. I was extremely curious—no, concerned is a better word—that Aaron was so, so comfortable and, uh, familiar with everything, I mean, he knew where the safe was and the combination and all."

She reached beneath the counter in front of her and lifted a glass of water to her lips. "Is this for me?"

The judge nodded.

She took a sip. "Thank you," she whispered, then continued. "So, we stayed at the party for a couple of hours and I kept asking Aaron to take me home. I simply didn't like the atmosphere there. There were drugs, cocaine and marijuana, plenty to drink and people were becoming louder. In the main room, Bedrosian was having an argument with another man."

The prosecutor leaned forward. "Could you tell what this argument was about?"

"No, there was just so much noise I couldn't make out the words, but they were obviously angry, shouting at one another."

"Do you know who this man was?"

"I didn't then, but I know now he was Aldo Nurmi."

"And what did you see Mr. Bedrosian do to Mr. Nurmi?"

"Well, first, Bedrosian stopped the party. Threw everybody out. Herded us to the elevator."

"You and Mr. Clayton, as well?"

"Yes," Maura said, nodding.

"So, you left with everyone else, then?"

Maura cleared her throat and seemed to be choosing her words carefully. "Not exactly. We got to the lobby and Aaron realized he had left the briefcase upstairs in the safe, and that he had to have it for some sort of transaction that had to take place the next day. So, we got back on the elevator and he had a key for the penthouse button and we went back up."

"Did he also have a key to the suite?"

"The elevator opens directly into the living room, but, yes, a key was needed to access that floor, and Aaron had one."

The prosecutor moved across the floor to the defense table and asked her a question with his back turned. "Please describe what you saw when those doors opened."

Maura Baker steeled herself for the next words. Certainly she had rehearsed them, but they still came out haltingly and filled with much emotion, for she had seen something for which people like her were never prepared. She straightened her skirt on her lap. "Mr. Bedrosian was beating Mr. Nurmi with a baseball bat." She lifted her hands and moved them to the back of her head. "All over this area."

The prosecutor let her catch her breath before asking: "Was Mr. Nurmi still standing?"

Maura Baker's eyes had turned moist. Her voice trembled. "No, he was on the floor, motionless. His skull was split in half. Blood and, and stuff was all over the place."

Glory Kane felt the breath go out of her body.

Two days later, Nicholai Bedrosian was convicted of murder and sentenced to life in prison. Glory wondered, as they took Bedrosian away, if he would ever die in prison, of if he would continue to conduct his hideous gang orchestra from an eight by eight cell.

And now and then Glory would see again in her mind the black Lincoln pulling away from the courthouse the day Rich Baker confessed and hear once more the words of Lisette

Darby, "Isn't it amazing what true love will do?" And she would think to herself that, yes, it was truly amazing. At the same time, she would never have believed Rich Baker capable of making such a sacrifice. He had given up his life so that Maura could live. Go figure.

And Glory wondered where he had gone.

PART FOUR:
HOW SUCH THINGS END

47

It was a sky to get lost in, an azure so dominating that it even swallowed up the mountains it framed, and that was exactly what Scott Sullivan hoped it would do, enfold him like a warm blanket, hide him, keep him safe and far away from the night. The Jeep Cherokee with the upholstery that still emitted an aroma of new leather was leaping up the winding path like a young mountain goat, sure of foot, frisky in the utter glory of the day. Sullivan gazed out the window at the breathtaking alpine meadow that swept like spilled honey across the landscape, the tops of huge ancient firs peaking over the curb, swaying at eye level as the vehicle ascended. If you had told him a year before that he would be here today—that he would be "Scott Sullivan," an Irish name chosen by his wife—climbing a mountain along a firmly packed dirt road, jutting into the wilderness like a knife, he would have looked at you as mad. But he was here, cool, clean mountain air filling his lungs, so close to the sun that he could taste its nectar.

And all the time, every slow mile of mountain lane, every invisible, vaporous mile of airplane flight over patchwork farm fields, every interminable minute of their shared experience—all of these times and distances carried with them a rhythm that pulsated through his heart, a promise, an anticipation that now, at this moment, was rising from the ashes of the past years.

Finally, the Jeep veered to its left, traversing a terrain that, if there had ever been a road or trail there, was almost impossible to discover. And then the vehicle, once again, dove downward, plunging into the alpine forest until it was completely wrapped in green-black trees. Then a few more turns and he could see it, an airstrip somehow carved onto the one flat area in these mountains that would hold it. As usual, his timing was almost perfect. A Lear, its engines whining to a halt, was rolling to a stop on the paved tarmac.

Scott Sullivan stepped out of the Jeep and took a huge mouthful of air into his lungs. Then he moved as quickly as he could to the plane. Perfect timing, he thought to himself. But what did you expect? Timing was always one of his strong suits.

The door opened and his gaze narrowed to a single vision, the woman stepping out, elegant and beautiful, her hair short, raven black. She watched her step as she descended and then, in a motion as graceful as a bird taking flight, her head moved upward, and, like the first time he had ever seen her, he was seized by the green fire in her eyes, an eruption of color that even the dark, short hair could not hide.

"Hello, dickhead," she said.

"Hello, Irish," he replied, breathlessly.

He moved in front of her and she walked more briskly toward him. For several seconds their visions entangled and then, together, pulled by instinct and familiarity and a lifetime of shared memories, they fell into each other's arms.

He held her in a way he had never held a woman before, tight, like he would never let go, yet as gentle as embracing a baby. Her breath softly brushed his cheek. Her breath. A breath he thought had stopped. Life. He kissed her tenderly on the cheek and she leaned into him. Then she pulled back and took his face in both her hands and kissed him passionately, her breath mingling with his, such a sweet, familiar, wonderful thing.

As they pulled apart, a voice from behind her caused them both to turn. FBI Agent Gary Lucas smiled broadly from behind his sunglasses as he clambered down the stairway of the jet. "Well, looks like you two are on your own now." He held two large envelopes out to them. "Here's the paperwork, passports, birth certificates, drivers' licenses, bank transfer statements, a complete new history. Scott and Margaret Sullivan, welcome to the world."

Scott Sullivan took the envelopes and an awkward silence hung over them for a few seconds. "I'm not sure if we're supposed to thank you or what," he said.

"Well, I'm not too sure, either, considering the circumstances," Lucas replied. "On behalf of the Bureau, I want to express my gratitude and wish you the very best." He extended his open hand. Scott took it firmly in his.

"I need to ask one question," Scott said. "The woman in the oil drum. Who was she?"

Lucas pursed his lips and shook his head slightly. "Don't really know for sure. We needed a body to move the whole plan forward. The Bureau works with forensic labs, mortuaries, hospitals, whatnot. We had an APB out to all of them. Usually, we get derelicts, homeless people, but we needed a little higher caliber this time. Took us quite a while to get one that was the right age, height, weight, hair color, with good teeth. Finally got one; from what I understand she died of AIDs and her family wanted nothing to do with her. So, we had to make it look like she had died several months before, let the body decompose so that it was not recognizable, obfuscate the cause of death, then pull hair, blood types and other samples. We x-rayed her teeth, ran DNA and traded everything out for the evidence that had already been collected. That was the tough part."

"How did you do it?" Scott asked.

"I thought you said 'one question'," Lucas chuckled. Then he continued. "Guy named Wally Mattox, you remember him. He saved you from that speeding car and from the woman with the gun. Well, he can walk through walls, they say. He got into the dentist's office, the pathologist's, even the birdcage in the police headquarters where the evidence was kept."

"All to make it look like I did it," Scott whispered.

"Or at least confuse them enough so that they wouldn't hunt Maura—uh, Margaret—down. As long as they thought she was dead, she was off their radar. Especially after they killed Aaron Clayton. She was all we had left who was there the night of the party, who saw the cash and, most importantly, the murder. We needed to protect her, or three years of investigation was going down the crapper."

"Three years!" Scott exclaimed.

"Yeah, and we almost blew it because an insomniac fisherman saw the ruckus in the factory lot," Lucas said, shaking his head in disbelief. "We had to kidnap him and take him to Florida on the longest fishing trip he'd ever been on."

Scott thought for several seconds. "Did you know Clayton was in on it?"

"We found out almost a year ago that Aaron Clayton was laundering money for Nicholai Bedrosian. That didn't surprise us, what with his international connections, his Vegas contacts and so forth. Bedrosian's got thousands of fingers on his hands, and they reach into every prison, every state senate, every mayor's office that can do him good, even the federal government."

"It's amazing what you can do with millions of dollars," Scott replied, and he knew what he was talking about.

"Billions," Lucas corrected him. "Bedrosian's got it stashed in offshore banks, Switzerland, the Cayman Islands, and even in banks in the boondocks of Kentucky. All under perfectly legal names, businesses, accounts."

"It's not as hard to do as you think," Scott replied offhandedly.

Lucas stared at him for an instant. "I know you know about that sort of thing," he said cryptically.

"That's over now," Scott replied.

"Goddamn right it is," Margaret interjected. She punched him lightly in the stomach. "You're in freaking prison, bubba."

Scott turned to her. "Did you know Clayton was involved in this?"

"Not at first. At least, I wasn't paying much attention to it. Frankly, I think deep down inside I was just using him to get to you. I mean, he was, had been, an associate, even a friend of yours. I thought it would really piss you off."

"It did."

"The more we were together, though, the more I began to think something was up. We were going to these parties and everyone was getting all coked up in one room, drunk in another. Then I met Bedrosian."

"A real prick," Lucas said.

"On the contrary. He was charming, gentle, kind. Always kissed my hand when he saw me. And funny. God, what a

sense of humor! Dirty jokes! He rattled them off like a
machine gun. I thought he was very dashing and
cosmopolitan."

"Until you saw him brain a guy with a baseball bat," Lucas
replied.

"That did change my perception," she said.

"And set into motion the biggest nightmare of my life,"
Scott interjected.

"Sorry," Lucas shrugged.

"Hey, think how hard it was on us. We had to get your
lanky ass into my car. It wasn't easy, pal," Margaret said.
"Even after they had whacked you with the tranquilizer."

"Christ, no wonder I felt like shit when I woke up, not to
mention scared."

"But we didn't want you to go down for the crime, so we
created evidence that was purposely vague and inconsistent.
Hell, a horseshit lawyer could have gotten you off. All we
wanted was to confuse the issue, at first." Lucas continued,
"Then, to protect you from Bedrosian's hordes, we had you
covered, virtually day and night. Came damn close to losing
you a couple of times."

"But why would Bedrosian want Rich, uh, Scott, I mean?"
Margaret asked, suddenly gripping him tighter through the
crook of his arm.

Lucas shook his head and laughed. "My God, I feel like I'm
being debriefed by my boss." He took a breath and continued.
"Anybody who was still around after the party that night was in
jeopardy, and everybody and anybody they came into contact
with. You gotta understand, Bedrosian didn't care if the guys
he whacked saw anything or not. Bang, bang, bang, knock
them out. For all he knew, Margaret—well, I guess it was

Maura at the time—ran home and told you everything. Bingo! You're it. Until, of course, it appeared you did his dirty work for him." Lucas opened the palms of his hands, hesitated, looking at Scott and Margaret Sullivan of Utah and then clapped. "So, anything else?" he said.

"Just goodbye," Margaret answered.

Agent Gary Lucas nodded, turned and disappeared into the Learjet. Within a minute, the plane was hurtling through the sky. Scott and Margaret watched it disappear.

Silence settled upon them. So that was it. Scott glanced over his wife's shoulder and watched the sun explode across the sky as it descended, throwing pink and orange hues onto the mountains in the distance. He reached over and stroked her neck. She closed her eyes and leaned into his gentle touch. "You ready to go home, Mrs. Sullivan?" he whispered.

"Yeah, finally," she replied.

"I kinda like this black hair," he said, twirling a finger in the short, straight mane. "It sure is different."

"Yeah," she said nuzzling his neck. "Maybe if I'd have dyed my hair every week or so—given you a little variety—we wouldn't be in this mess today."

"A mess?" he said, turning and walking towards the Jeep. "Look at this place, Mrs. Sullivan. It's hardly a mess. What do you say we stay?"

"For how long?" she asked, her green eyes taking him, wrapping him up, holding him.

"Maybe forever," he whispered. "This time."

The End